I0613753

Eden's Sins

by

Jaclyn Tracey

This is a work of fiction. Names, characters, places, and incidents are either the product of the author's imagination or are used fictitiously, and any resemblance to actual persons living or dead, business establishments, events, or locales, is entirely coincidental.

Eden's Sins

COPYRIGHT © 2021 by Jaclyn Tracey

All rights reserved. No part of this book may be used or reproduced in any manner whatsoever without written permission of the author or The Wild Rose Press, Inc. except in the case of brief quotations embodied in critical articles or reviews.
Contact Information: info@thewildrosepress.com

Cover Art by *Debbie Taylor*

The Wild Rose Press, Inc.
PO Box 708
Adams Basin, NY 14410-0708
Visit us at www.thewildrosepress.com

Publishing History
First Line Rose Edition, 2021
Trade Paperback ISBN 978-1-5092-3530-8
Digital ISBN 978-1-5092-3531-5

Published in the United States of America

Dedication

Callie Lynn Wolfe, Madam Editor, my friend, mentor, sister from another mother, without you I wouldn't be here. Thank you for your dedication to making good stories better and not giving up on a day dreamer who can't spell or knows anything about punctuation. To my husband, I haven't forgotten the Porsche. It is better to want than need!

Jovan never dreamed she would stoop so low as to recite a love charm, but desperation combined with impulsiveness could be such a burden. She didn't want to be alone. She loved her brother Julian dearly, but life had so much to offer and she wanted, nay needed, to experience it all. Julian might have given up on wedded bliss and raising a family, but she held no desire to be called a spinster or the old biddy who lived with her crotchety older brother.

Her newfound elation quickly dwindled wondering what would happen if she met the wrong man? What if she trapped some poor bloke by accident? What if she met her Prince? Would she ever really know if it were true love? Would she be able to trust it, the love, or him? Would there always be a huge cloud of doubt he was only beside her because of this desperate act to divine love? Would she ever find Eden with this sin? Well, it was too late to take back the words. The spell loomed, like a lost gold coin on the ground waiting for anyone to grasp.

"Goddess help me, I am now that gold coin. What have I done?"

Part One: 1892, Lore Cove, England

Chapter One

The distant chime of the church bells clamored loud enough to rattle Jovan Hause's mood whilst she lazed away her morning, comfy in a nice warm featherbed. Her usual cheerfulness shifted to disquietude. The clanking bells could only mean one thing: Today some fool's happily ever after would ring true. Jovan wondered if a love spell or potion had been conjured. Seemed like everyone but her lately was doing the two-step to the alter. She toyed with the idea of casting a spell. Maybe a little charm wouldn't be the end of the world as Jovan knew it, or, maybe it would. Jovan didn't know which frightened her more, being a sad old spinster or a sassy spouse, but she so loved a challenge. Getting a vision of the church Jovan held on for whatever her sightings brought forth.

The little bride would wear fine silk and lace as the tart trot down the aisle, her dear papa in tow to deliver her to her heart's desire. The vestal virgin would, of course, be nervous. Was she about to embark on a lifelong journey of wedded bliss or worse, end up legally bound, in misery, wishing for the "Until death they do part," finale to end the charade. She would glance forward to her groom in search of his smile, a special glint in his eye. Or perhaps a nonchalant rise beneath his trousers conveying he was as anxious for the honeymoon to begin as she. Did she meet his expectations? Was she everything and more to him? His world?

She better be.

Her vision slowed, the images somewhat clearer, giving her the sense this was personal.

The enchanted prince would stand upon the alter dapper in the midnight's glow with his gaze devouring her, his black curls wispy in the night's autumn air with a kiss on his pouty lips waiting, wearing only what he entered the world in. He'd wink and then graze his bottom lip with his teeth as she neared. Waiting for Jovan to taste him. Waiting for her to offer herself, to show the full contours of her breasts, the hourglass shape of her tummy, her dainty *derriere* and what lay between her thighs, the unsullied woman every male desired.

The temperature in Jovan's bedchamber spiked. Mist covered her face. Tiny droplets of sweat trickled between her bosom headed lower yet, where a little itch in need of a good rub summoned trouble.

The blasted church bells struck an unharmonious chord again. She grit her teeth. "Under the moon's beams? A naked groom? An unsullied woman? Seriously? Well, truth be known, I do fit that. Please allow me yet another glimpse? Please? This is my dream wedding, not the tart in the church."

Well, it wasn't her wedding. Not today and if she were being realistic not tomorrow… Two reasons popped into her head. Relationships didn't last. Or at least her mother's three failed attempts hadn't. Her mother often warned, "Men will leave you, Jovan. They will run. Give them one opportunity and you will find yourself standing in a cloud of smoke without so much as a second glance from them with a baby glued to your breast sucking you dry."

Her mother's little inspirational chats never ended in fairytale bliss.

Regardless, buried deep in her heart, Jovan had a simple fantasy that included some devilish rogue to share her secret desires with, to grow old beside and have a small brood of children to cherish. And most importantly, to tangle their nude bodies into every naughty position attainable.

Yes, her body still yearned for the ministrations her day-dreamy prince could lavish upon her.

And more to the point, it seemed men didn't realize Jovan existed. With trepidation Jovan reached over and grabbed her hand mirror from her nightstand. The scowl reflected back to her solidified why she lay in bed alone while the crone in the church pussyfooted her way down the aisle. Puffy, red eyes, hair askew and a rosy red nose portrayed a lovely image of Jovan. She snorted at the ridiculousness of what her life had become. She set the object back on her nightstand and threw back her covers.

"Julian would taunt me to no end if he knew I lay here brooding. Well, he'll taunt me regardless. Nature calls. Time to move me dainty arse." She bent over the edge of the bed and dragged her slippers out from under it. Tootsies covered and robe now donned, she flitted down the creaky stairs and came to a staunch halt at the back door.

Lips pursed, she eyed the trail to the outhouse through a frosty windowpane. Icy tentacles adhered to the glass better than an octopus to its prey.

Book in hand, she opened the door and brought the edges of her robe tighter against her, not that it helped stave away the chill. Ice chips crunched beneath her feet as she crossed the yard to the proverbial potty. Cool air nipped her nostrils and her eyes watered as they adjusted to the bitter temperature. The entire experience equaled a hard slap in the face. Spring in England could only be described as fickle. Fantastic one day. The rest of the month? More fickle.

Held captive in what felt more like an icebox instead of an outhouse, Jovan fingered through the blank pages of her Grimoire until she found the page with the edge folded over along with a raspberry colored fingerprint smudged in the center of the page. On a splintered shard of wood Jovan picked her finger until a small mound of blood formed. Going against everything she believed in, everything she'd ever been taught, and that relentless little voice in her head trying to tell her casting spells had consequences, especially if used for personal gain, she smeared the fluid over the page.

Her pulse quickened watching as words mysteriously bled from the cream-colored paper; her favorite part of casting the spell. The scripture had to be invoked by recitation.

"To find one's soul. To make mine whole.

To match the beating of one's heart, so ours are no longer apart.

Two lives together to spend, side by side 'til time doth end.

Help me find my true love's desire. Let him be someone to admire.

Along my quest, do not send me through hell's fire,

or lead me to any bleeding vampire.

Allow us a love to cherish, until we do perish."

Jovan never dreamed she would stoop so low as to recite a love charm, but desperation combined with impulsiveness could be such a burden. She didn't want to be alone. She loved her brother Julian dearly, but life had so much to offer and she wanted, nay needed, to experience it all. Julian might have given up on wedded bliss and raising a family, but she held no desire to be called a spinster or the old biddy who lived with her crotchety older brother.

Her newfound elation quickly dwindled wondering what would happen if she met the wrong man? What if she trapped some poor bloke by accident? What if she met her Prince? Would she ever really know if it were true love? Would she be able to trust it, the love, or him or would there always be a huge cloud of doubt he was only beside her because of this desperate act to divine love? Would she ever find Eden with this sin? Well, it was too late to take back the words. The spell loomed, like a lost gold coin on the ground waiting for anyone to grasp.

"Goddess help me, I am now that gold coin. What have I done?" Her head swam of every possible scenario that could go utterly wrong. Then another vision began to flicker in and out as if she were looking through a pair of spectacles of someone one blink away from being blind.

Most of the time her aura trickled in to allow her sightings time to adjust and other times they flashed before her the way a shooting star careens through the sky. This one left her gasping, hands hard-pressed against the rough pine walls for balance. And no longer chilled. Her book tumbled to the ground.

Caught in a dreamlike euphoria her tongue slowly traced the outline of her mouth where his lush, full lips pressed hard against hers. He threaded his fingers through her long, blonde locks, and gave a slight tug. When he had her angled just so he licked the length of her neck, with a nibble here and a kiss there. Passion warmed her to her very core. With a sinful grin on his full lips he covered her mouth again in one scorching hard-pressed kiss. Their tongues dueled, each hungry to taste what the other coveted. And as quickly as the vision came it vanished. "Umm! I fancied that." She clamped her legs together hoping—nay praying, the sweet arousal would linger.

A face or name would've been splendid to call out her enchanter, yet she had neither. Where was her mysterious, tall, dark and handsome prince?

Probably back at the castle being lavished by courtesans. She huffed a curl from her eyes.

Was this a direct result of the charm she cast?

Puzzles. She despised them. They were for small children placed in a corner to keep them from further mischief. It had never stopped her in the past. She gave up a grin.

"Breathing has returned to semi-normal and daydream's done you little vixen. Time to stir up the pot, the flowerpot this time." Out of the pine box, with a breath of fresh air in her lungs she headed to a large oak barrel beside the barn. Floating inside the cask brewed a slushy green concoction mid-fermentation. The frothy bubbles reminded her of pond scum. Wasn't the most pleasant recipe, but it worked like magic. As it should. Around the container seepage of the liquid produced dainty blooms in all colors of the spectrum. Her handy work left even her in awe from time to time.

Light green moss covered the pail's handle. This morning the usual velvety-soft growth crunched under her grasp due to the night's crisp air. No matter how careful, when she dipped the pail into the mixture her fingers always ended up the shade of grass for days to come. She scanned the area thoroughly to make certain there were no nosey Nellie's vying to catch a glimpse of her. Would truly be the last thing she needed and probably the last thing she did.

Witch hunts.

Not today. Tomorrow?

After she spread the alloy she stood back, anxious to see her efforts spring to life. How apropos, she decided.

****

"Blossom!" Julian Hause yawned as he meandered his way to the kitchen. The room empty, he eyed the stove hoping for coffee or tea. The burners were bare. Ah, but Jovan had been very busy in other matters. Eggs, painted in green and red decorated the table nestled in a black wrought iron basket beside a steaming loaf of honey bread. Along the fireplace's mantle a fresh bouquet of daffodils mixed with wild purple crocus lay draped across the mahogany as an offering to the Goddess. His heart picked up its pace. "Those flowers weren't here yesterday." A fire roared in the hearth and stole the chill from the air. Dragon's blood incense had him sneezing. Jovan adored the fragrance, not him. Julian knew all too well what today meant for his sister. Spring, her favorite season. And someone's impulsiveness had gotten the best of her.

"Blossom?" He whined, a pout firm on his dry lips. Room by room he searched for the impetuous blonde. Opening the front door, he spotted her on her knees, elbows deep in the earth.

"Dare I ask?" He walked outside and looked around at her version of the Garden of Eden. Yesterday the yard had been an unpleasant combination of mud, manure and slush. Today, blooms of wildflowers, roses, petunias and a thick, lush blanket of new light green grass covered the ground, blades sprouting right between his toes while his level of anxiety grew with it.

Fist clenched, he feared someone would notice. Incredibly hard not to detect the only house on the way blanketed with vivid blooms while other homes waited patiently for a bleeding weed.

Up to her elbows in soil, Jovan rolled her eyes upward. "I see the tall statuesque heathen before me has awoken. Good morning."

"Is it, Blossom? A tad overkill, don't you agree?"

"Truly, Jules, you act as if you've never seen a flower. Spring shall never come if we do not help the goddess of fertility, Eostre. If you'd slept much longer, I believe you'd have missed it all together."

"Actually, wished I had."

"Me too. You sleeping that is." Jovan stood, brushed off a few clumps of dirt clung to her leggings and tapped his nose in passing.

"Blossom, one flower is one thing, but our yard now resembles Holland late spring. Notice I said late spring." He slapped the spec of dirt left behind from his face, annoyance most obvious. "You now know why I call you blossom!" With an added ounce of sarcasm, he tossed in, "It's your bloomin' personality."

Jovan ignored him. "I am going to town this morning for a new gown I noticed in the ladies' boutique."

"What? Why? We don't need any hounds sniffing about. What occasion is there that you need to adorn yourself to make something all ready ravishing more so?"

A man to take note of me? Jovan sent Julian that little message through the mental path they shared since birth.

Julian stepped back noting his sister's mounting frustration. The scrunched lips, furrowed brows may have been a sign of things to come.

Jovan pointed to her tattered, baggy clothes and cringed. "Look at me, Julian. Look! My hair hangs like a dirty mop, limp, as lifeless as my existence. 'Tis been so bleeding long since I've had an occasion to pamper myself, I can't recall the last time I've combed my hair, let alone washed it. There is no gallant man in wait—no occasion to. I've worn your begrimed trousers so often you no longer recognize they are yours."

Curious, Julian studied her for a split second. "What? Wait! I've been looking all over for those."

"Buggar off." She turned to him. "Out of everything I said all you care is about are these? Never mind! Bigger question. Jules, did you forget?"

He scratched his chin, his silence thicker than the hair on his bare feet. "What? I still can't get over you swiped my knickers."

Frustrated, she blurted, "Jules, the train comes today."

Arms tossed to his sides Julian conceded, "Just tell me, sister. You're going to anyway."

"My future arrives this day, brother. I don't know who or what it is, but I know at noon it shall roll into the station and I'll be there waiting for whatever may come."

"The circus arrives as well! It best not be any of those Carney's. Damned gypsies are connivers. Sell ya their mum if they needed a pot to piss in. Nothing but fast-talking, drunken, Irish leprechauns they are. The last thing I need is you traipsing off with one of those twinkle-eyed elves." Julian sucked in a huge breath and cupped her cheek gently. "Were you scrying, or did you read anything you'd promised not to?"

"Guilty… and guilty." Jovan remained poised.

Julian straightened his stance, pulled his shoulders back and puffed out his chest.

About to say something Jovan cut him to the quick. "Tis the lamest attempt at intimidation I've seen you produce yet. And trust thee me, I have witnessed some extremely lame attempts on your behalf, brother."

Julian watched her turn her head, biting back laughter. How could she be so cavalier using her powers? "I don't know, I thought I transcribed my purpose with utter aptitude."

Eyes crossed, Jovan went on to point out, "Scrying? Why don't you just yell it a little louder, brother? I believe the people a few homes down didn't quite catch that! This will happen. You know I have foresight. I saw this as I sat in the outhouse this morning and…"—she hesitated, shifting a culpable gaze toward the floor before dropping her voice to give her miniscule confession—"a little poetic embellishment might have been involved."

"You mean invoked! This is so much clearer now.

What really happened, dear sister, and this is my story and I'm sticking with it even as I am locked in the stocks being sodden with manure and rotted veggies, is you were consumed by noxious fumes in that shite hole and became delirious."

"You're vulgar, you are." Jovan spun and disappeared inside. The front door rattled as it slammed shut.

The hollow click of the latch forced Julian's attention. "Blimey!" His voice rose as he begged, "Blossom, my apologies. Please allow me entrance."

Julian waited, watching her peek between the curtains, arms crossed under her bosom with that same blasted scowl he knew all too well meant he had pushed her too far. His nose against the frosty pane, Julian gave her his best you-can't-resist-me-pout. She shook her head no.

"Truly?" He bat his ridiculously long lashes at her.

Jovan shook her head no again.

Defeat weighed his words. "Jovan, it was said in poor jest."

"Most your words are, brother." With a shrug of her shoulders, Jovan did an about-face and marched up the stairs.

"G'day, Vicar."

Julian turned to see who caught his attention. "Is it, Mr. Fee?"

"I see your beautiful sister's green thumb has been very busy." Nygal Fee, an emaciated gent, at least twenty years their senior pointed to all the flowers as he trudged past Julian, stood at the front door half-dressed shivering. "As gorgeous as she."

"My sister has been very busy planting, and she's

not all that pretty." Under his breath he mumbled, "Lord forgive me yet again. My sister's sins have become mine." He turned and took out his frustrations on the door.

****

Half asleep with his face jammed against the window, André St. James's head bounced off the glass when the train made a sharp, grinding turn around the bend as it slowed down for the approach to cross the trestle. The view from the window displayed a raging river, mucky brown with white caps and spray as the water bashed anything in its way. Fifty-foot or better craggy embankments made of sheer mud and shale held the water in its place. The sheering noise of the wheels against the tracks left him a banger. Or it might have been the scotch he and his cousins shared the previous night. With a slight shift in his seat he noticed his other head throbbed as well. The material of his trousers remained taut, constricting the sudden rush of blood to his groin. The dream he'd been lost in just before the sudden jolt of the train had been delightful all for the abrupt ending. His eyelids fell shut again in hopes of returning to the fair maiden he pleasured. He wanted his turn. She'd tasted of the sweetest nectar. Oh, if only he'd seen her face. Long sun-kissed blonde tresses of spun silk masked her beauty. Even longer, slender legs rested upon his shoulders as he dipped his head between her thighs. Her moans and soft pleas had his control on the edge of abandonment. And his control was the one thing he prided himself in.

His eyes fell shut once more yet his mind remained engaged. Exhaustion didn't begin to explain his current disposition. Chasing a monster that fed off women? The scourge of the earth had violated his dear cousin, Raven St. James and left her for dead. And the worst bloody part, the monster still roamed free despite all efforts to destroy him.

Here and now, André sat on the train wide open for any attempt on his life. He glanced backward, having the eerie sensation eyes were scorching a hole in his thick skull. He didn't see anyone he recognized, but there was one woman wearing a black veil, weeping to the high heavens. Obviously mourning. Unable to escape the woman's pitiful wailing, André was certain everyone around him was as uncomfortable as he. And then there were the children. There seemed to be no end to their energy as they charged up and down the aisle screaming and exercising their rights to be loud and boisterous. He rubbed the side of his temples. What would it take to silence them?

"Two more stops, Ands. You can do it. Then you can board the ferry back to Paris where you can spend your days surrounded by horse's arses and your evenings acting like one," he mumbled a tad too loud.

"Mister? You do not resemble the behind of a horse in the least." A woman with reddish-orange hair and wide lavender-colored eyes giggled from behind a gloved hand.

André watched her gaze drop to the bulge in his pants. Her reaction, eyes wide, cheeks flushed made him even more uncomfortable. There he sat, still hung in there like a stallion. Damn his dreamy girl.

André looked her over. Disheveled to the next day she was, regardless of her beauty. She held one baby tucked under an arm with another beside her in a basket covered in mushy peas, soggy from the waist down.

"Could you—please?" The woman wiggled the tot in his face. "Hold her, please? Only till I straighten this wee one out?"

His heart stammered. Before he opened his mouth in protest, a baby no more than ten or eleven months old occupied his lap. With the little doll in his grasp he noticed all the women's attentive gazes aboard the train focus on him, eyeing him differently. Affectionately? Wanting? He bit back a grin. Is this all it took to get a woman's consideration? He decided to ham it up. He glanced down to the little girl whose giant, green eyes seemed to grow wider when she realized her mother no longer held her. He smiled and cooed at her. Made funny faces until…

The infant screamed and proceeded to vomit down the front of his shirt. "Oh *shite*." He jumped to his feet. With outstretched arms he held the baby as far from him as his arms allowed until another passenger snatched the petrified child from his grasp. The infant's mother shot him a seething glare.

"What?" He couldn't keep the obvious annoyance in check. For Pete's sake, his shirt had some sort of congealed goop down it and his leg seemed much warmer than he remembered. He glanced at his leather chaps and realized the child had done more than spill her milk. He decided, right then and there, he would get the hell off this train one stop earlier and never—ever have children.

André swiped a clean nappy from the woman's satchel and blotted his clothes dry.

When the conductor called, Lore Cove, André couldn't gather his belongings fast enough. With haste, he made his way to the door and waited for freedom.

Behind him, a wily mob of youngsters flattened him against the wall, in attempts to beat him from the train. With a menaced glance, André faced the little spitfires. His tall, muscular stature towered over them.

"Children," he said wearing a grin as evil as he felt, "the nice conductor at the opposite end of this carriage has treats for each of you. Taffy, I believe." Not a moment later he stood alone and the poor unsuspecting attendant at the other exit had sugar-starved beggars cornering him with their greedy, outstretched paws.

André jumped down from the train, looked left, then right trying to see past the pungent cloud of steam as it rolled into his view while the locomotive pulled away from the station. The whistle blared in his ear. He noticed a few men stagger out onto the road, holding one another up as they laughed and swayed through the cobbled street topped with whopping dollops of manure.

"The pub!" He picked up his bags and his pace.

Chapter Two

When his sister entered the room, Julian's jaw dropped. "Jovan, you look regal, like you're going to have tea with the queen."

She picked up the hem of the dress and spun in a circle to show off the gown. "Just as soon as Prince Charming sweeps me off me big feet."

"They are rather large. Don't believe they make glass slippers in ogre sizes, Blossom."

Jovan punched his arm. "Jules, I'll be back by supper, unless I meet my match."

"Nonsense!" He grabbed her shoulders and spun her to face him. "You will be home well before this or I'll come looking for you. Jovan, these streets are not safe, especially for a woman without an escort. You know this in your heart. Look what happened to our brother and his wife."

Jovan wasn't about to recall that dreadful day. Not now. It was time to look forward, not digress into a state of depression. Damn Julian. Her mind filled with images of her oldest brother and her best friend, her pregnant sister-in-law savagely murdered. No, Jovan closed her eyes and shook her head in hopes of erasing the dreadful impression. Unfortunately, it never worked. Some memories traveled from nightmares to daydreams.

Today was all about hope. A chance for a love of her own and damn all the consequences of her spell. She'd done the deed and would have to live with the cost. "Wish me well, brother." With a quick peck on his cheek she whirled in a half circle, picked up her book, tucked it inside her satchel, and scooted out the door. She heard him holler, "No later than four or I'm coming after you."

If she knew nothing else of her brother, he would keep his word. Julian was her rock, whether he knocked her over the head with it or protected her. Someone had to.

With a slight lilt in her step, Jovan made her way down the cobbled street. The clink of her new shoes delighted her until one heel sunk between two bricks and jolted her sideways. She fought for balance. "No falling on your face today." She prayed while she regained her posture. "First impressions are key because once I open me mouth the illusion of me being anything other than a commoner with no schooling will be public knowledge."

The train's whistle startled Jovan. "Bollocks!" She hiked up her skirt and sprinted down the street regardless of almost toppling over seconds past. She couldn't help but laugh. Looking lady-like was one thing. Acting like it, well, there was a first time for everything. Just not today.

****

Before André could blink, he'd been run down and left on his rump, his bags scattered. A blur of soft pink and magenta trampled him and continued past, oblivious without so much as an apology. Her intoxicating scent lingered in the air the same way a fresh baked custard pie did. His nostrils flared. His hungers awoke, but food wasn't what he craved.

"Madam, slow down. You run as if the devil chases you. Although," He took a pleasurable moment to view her backside dashing away, "if it is the devil chasing you, the demon's bloody brilliant." André stood, brushed off his trousers, picked up his belongings and finished his trek to the pub.

"A pint, please." André plunked his bum on a wooden stool, one leg shorter than the others. He rocked the stool back and forth to find out just how off kilter the seat was then spread his feet to each side of the chair for balance. The barmaid had a glass of hearty ale in front of him before he finished his sentence.

"You'll be looking all hot and bothered, Sir. Is there anything, anything at all I can do for you to make your stay more cozy?" The barmaid leaned in close, too close, and made certain to press her breasts against his shoulder. Her words were laden with spittle, his cheeks the unwanted target. She leaned back and batted her puny lashes at him as she pushed her arms under her breasts, nudging an overabundance of flesh upward.

André backed up and regardless of squaring off with the stool prior he had to fight to remain seated and not upon the floor. With a quick hand and squelching the urge to gag, he brushed the woman's saliva from his face and onto his shirt. At this point he cared not what the shirt looked like. It was ruined; the wee baby made certain of that on the train. André's eyes were drawn to the barmaid's bosom. A natural progression no matter what woman stood before him. Her blouse appeared...lumpy.

André's jaw dropped. He'd never been good at

turning down women, especially ones that might have been born from siblings or first relatives. Had to tread lightly around them. Crazy as a loon in most cases. Some of his family members were living proof. Bloody royals had no idea how to keep their knickers on when they saw someone of the opposite sex, sister, brother, aunt or cousin they fancied. The blooming lot was more promiscuous than the strumpets working the tunnels in White Chapel. They were most likely related too.

He eyed the maiden with dread. Her wall-eyed gaze made the hair on his neck prickle. Her top lip appeared to be tacked up inside her nose, showing off a set of yellow horse-sized buckteeth in need of a good scrub. Her eyebrows looked more like a welcoming matt to brush the dirt from your shoes. She was not a sight for sore eyes by any means, ah, but indeed an eye sore.

Trying hard not to stare, he turned his attention to the chap seated beside him and grinned before he chugged his first pint without a word. The gent winked at him and chuckled. "Another please?" André held his hand out for the mug. When the barmaid slid the beer to him, her hand lingered upon his fingers. He snatched his arm away alarmed. "I thank thee for the generous offer, but I am only in town till the next train departs."

"Comes three days from now, Sir." The lady licked her bottom lip.

André couldn't pull his gaze from her mouth. He gave it his all-out effort to not gawk. She, simply put, had to be the oddest female he'd ever laid eyes upon. Her tongue had black hair growing on it. "What is—?" André grabbed his right hand with his left as he went to point and bit his tongue before he said or did anything truly offensive. "Christ, if I'd known that I'd never have gotten off the bloody thing in the first place. Is there a hotel in this town?"

The woman crooked her index finger to him. "Aye, Sir, indeed. I'll walk you to it meself."

"No!" He shot out impulsively. "I'm a big boy. I'll be fine."

"Aye, indeed, you are." The woman puckered up.

André placed a hand between them. "No! Thank you." His voice came across brash, but he didn't care. He wanted this woman nowhere near him and in a hotel even less. "This could end up being the longest three days of my life. I'll have a shot to go with that ale now."

The gent on the opposite side of André stood, pat his back and whispered, "Fresh blood!" He snickered all the way out the door. The fine hairs on André's neck stabbed at him this time.

****

"I missed the train?" Jovan flopped on the bench outside of the now vacant station, multiple layers of her dress and all its lace billowing around her in an itchy, uncomfortable cocoon. "Bloody thing is never early. Well, I just set me pockets back a month of Sundays, and I've missed whomever rode in today. See what scrying does, Blossom? See what that pathetic book of blasphemy does? Do you never learn?" She pounded her fists into her thighs. Her eyes burned from humiliation. How could she go home to face her brother? After their conversation earlier he would of course taunt the daylights from her. She pulled her feet up on the bench and hugged her knees to her chest, lost in disappointment.

"Mith?"

This was it. The moment of truth. The moment she'd been waiting for all day. The man of her dreams and the same poor bloke she'd cast a spell over to make love her through eternity just beckoned her name with a distinct lisp. Well it was do or die so she poured on the best chattering teeth grin she owned and allowed her gaze to drift upward. Her breath caught in her throat as she took in the unsightliness of her future.

Oh Julian wouldn't taunt her. He'd kill her. If he didn't die laughing first.

Before her stood an impecunious man, his clothing caked with goddess only knew what, his beard gnarly, crumbs dispersed throughout the whiskers. His nails, longer than hers, embedded with grime. With a quick glance at her own hands, her nails were a lovely shade of green. There would be no stone casting today.

"Do you need anything?" he asked. He jiggled a small bottle of some sort of alcohol in front of her.

Jovan wiped her eyes and silently prayed. *Dear Goddess, I do realize I brought this on myself and I know beggars can't be choosy, yet I beg of thee, please do not let this man be the chosen one whom my spell encased.* "No, thank you."

"Good, well then get off me seat ya little snitch. I sleep here each night unless ya want to lay with me then we'll have a grand frolic. I may not have all me teeth, but you can bet your britches all me other parts work just dandy. Come to think of it, I'd love naught more than have us a little cuddle." He reached for her.

"No-no-no-no-no!" She sputtered and made haste to get away from his grasp. Before he could try again, she spun on one heel and upped her stride putting as much distance from the vagrant as she could. With a quick shot over her shoulder she found he was not in pursuit of her, and she stopped to one, catch her breath and two, smooth the wrinkles from her worthless gown. With her head hung lower than a scolded dogs', she headed home.

Before she knew it, her feet were in the air and her head met the ground with a pain-filled thud. "What in the blue moon?" Jovan went to stand, but a meteorite of angry stars exploded. She lay back down before gravity best her.

"Madame, my deepest apologies. Are you well?" André sat up and reached over to the woman to check on her. Running blindly from the pub might not have been his best made plan, but when the bar wench revealed a third nipple for him to suckle upon, well, the fat lady had sung her last opus, and he'd never acquired a taste for the opera. He knew the shirt appeared lumpy. He'd protested his way through the first two breasts, begging the woman to redress her unsightly self, but she persisted through all three breasts. *Three!* Logic told him he needed sleep until he gazed into this beauty's wild blue eyes. Sleep was a luxury the dead deserved, and he was far from departed. "I'm so sorry."

"You bloody well should be, you giant horse's arse." Despite an upset woman at his feet, André couldn't help but laugh. "Not even home yet, and I've been found out."

"Is there no chivalry left in this world? Are you going to help me or just ogle over me?"

"Mademoiselle!" Seeing all the pink and magenta sprawled out upon the walkway, he recognized the lady before his feet. Ogling didn't seem like such a bad idea.

Her delicate pink, silk camisole veiled her shapely bosom. Her magenta skirt bunched beneath her hips flashed a set of long, slender gams André wanted wrapped around his waist hugging her to him. Her ears were decorated better than a Christmas tree with pink sapphires.

I can think of three things I can decorate her in. Me. Myself. And I.

It was when her eyes met his, his heart stammered. They were the purist, light blue, and they drew him to her better than a starving babe to an overflowing tit. Pretty much how he felt at the moment.

And with that his focus lowered to her chest. Index finger working left to right he counted two soft mounds beneath her dress. There was a grin to be found after all.

****

"'Ello? What are you bloody well pointing at?" Impatience obvious, she snapped her fingers to lift his wandering gaze to her face.

He held his hand to her.

Jovan's anger spiked. She ranted, "First you plow me down. Then you insult me and then you offer your assistance? Me thinks not!" She slapped his hand away, stood on her own, straightened her rags for a second time, and squared off to face the ruffian. She started with his feet and worked her way up every scrumptious inch of the man. Big—no make that huge, black leather boots peeked out beneath black leather chaps that left her needing no imagination as to which side of his trousers he tucked away his sword. She took a deep breath when she noticed the large swell beneath the material. Not polite to stare. Impossible not to.

"Now who's being nosey?" The man held a sinful grin followed by a cocky head nod.

She bit her tongue and forced her gaze north. A wild mane of jet-black curls spilled down his back. Goddess help her she wanted those curls all over her, tickling her with his every move. When Jovan's eyes met André's deep blue—almost black ones, she swooned like the love-struck virgin she was. Bastard wore a sinful smirk on his rugged face. Those lips, full, with a slight kissable pout, she needed to see how they worked. His nose? Perfect. Not too big. Not bulbous. Not a brilliant red most the English gents wore as a beacon to find their way home after a long day at the pub. He was almost too beautiful to be male. Almost. She quickly shot a second look back to his trousers. One hundred percent full-blooded male filled out those pants. She then wondered if his naughty bits came anywhere to matching his hubris? That was when the twitch in her left eye kicked in. To her it seemed as noticeable as a two-headed person arguing over which direction they were going. This man had to be blind to miss the jig her eyelid did. His hand stretching toward hers was the last thing she recalled.

****

André floated on air as he admired the spirited woman standing in front of him—no make that lying in the dirt at his feet. "Now what? My fortune with women today has been lost. One babe vomits on me and the second passes out before I even had a chance to steal away her breath. Or," He chuckled, "—maybe I did." André crouched over the woman to assess her again. No blood, no bumps, well—other than the two soft creamy mounds of flesh rising and falling before his eager eyes. Against every ounce of his being, he pulled her skirt down to dress her legs. Covering up such bounty was the hardest thing he'd done today. Come to think of it, ever, but a woman's legs were to be coveted, only seen by a lover or spouse. He'd work on this. A white leather journal lay beside her in the roadway. He grabbed the book, dusted it off and tucked the diary inside his trunk for safekeeping. After lifting her limp body from the ground, he reneged that, her voluptuously relaxed body, he headed for the hotel.

He laughed aloud when the clerk gave him an evil eye. Couldn't blame the bloke. Here he was with an unresponsive woman draped in his arms and asking for a room for three days. What would the man think? More importantly, did he care?

No.

"Could I have your and the sleeping beauty's name, Sir?" the clerk asked.

André shifted his new friend in his arms and pulled up his knee to balance her so he could write. He picked up the feather-tipped pen, dipped the end inside a small jar of blue ink, then scribed his name on the parchment.

With a slight gasp, the clerk bowed behind the desk then peeked up wearing a nervous grin.

"Dear man, you needn't bow before me. Please stand."

"Of course, my Lord. I see you two have been to Lenny's. A fine establishment, aye? Did your little woman have one too many ales?"

André ticked his head to the side. "Possibly!" He sized up the gent, although there wasn't much to him. A bald, pasty-white midget, no taller than his aunt with enormous brown eyes gazed at him in awe. André had never seen flesh so pale, ah but then England wasn't the tropical isle people came in droves to each summer, was it?

No, they instead came to try and catch a glimpse of his family. He didn't understand it. He put his pants on like everyone else did. One foot at a time, unless of course someone's father came in unexpectedly and there was need to make a hasty exodus to the door. Not him of course. He bit back laughter.

André glanced down at the woman draped in his arms. He'd captured an angel. He believed it whole-heartedly. There would be no fast departures from this one. Ever. He knew just by looking at her. This strange realization left him a little short of breath, or possibly it was her weight. Carrying a woman conscious versus out cold were two different scenarios. A conscious woman could wrap her legs around your waist and hang on for the ride. An unconscious one, well you could drop her, and she'd be none the wiser. He shifted his position.

My beloved, André, are you well? I seem to be picking up strange vibrations from you today.

Able to communicate since birth telepathically with his cousins Raven and Lucian, André welcomed the conversation. *Ah, Raven. How you fairing, beauty? Are they going to release you from the loony bin, I mean infirmary?*

Funny. Lucian sprung me hours past. He made our Duncan dress in a woman's gown, pull his hair into a twist, shave and then act as though he was my nursemaid. Don't ever repeat this but Duncan makes a beautiful woman. Even found him leggings and shoes that fit. Ands, oh my goodness, Duncan can move his hips better than I can. Even had one of the orderlies chasing after him.

André's body jerked with laughter as he spoke to his cousin. He tried to picture Duncan, one of his closest mates, someone he considered an older brother, stood six-foot-tall, one green eye, one brown eye, a handsome gent, dressed as a dame. It made him smile. *Ray*, his nickname for Raven, *allow Lucian and Duncan the opportunity to care for you. Promise?*

You mean kiss my derriere, don't you? The fools gave me a little bell to ring if I want or need anything. Of course, I'm going to drive them insane till I'm up on me own accord.

Ray, you always have even without the little bell. You can jest all you want with me, but I know how—

Don't, André. I'm putting the horrid ordeal in the past, where it belongs. This shall never be spoken of again. Promise me.

André could feel the terror of her ordeal as if he were trapped inside a spiked casket being aerated. She tried to appear as tough as her aunt, the queen, but the woman was the kindest, gentlest creature he'd ever encountered. To have her life nearly snuffed in such a horrific manner made his blood roil. *I promise, beauty. Please have someone get a photo of Duncan? Blackmail works wonders.*

Already did.

Raven sounded like herself, but there was still something missing. André so wanted to restore her equilibrium. Give her back normalcy and see that brilliant smile in her eyes light up a room once more but it would take more than funny words to achieve the unachievable. A tapping of a pen on the counter dragged André back to his present situation.

"My lord? You look as if you're a million miles away and your little woman has not stirred."

Words filtered in. "His—little—woman?" Had a nice ring to it. He looked down at her cherub face and wanted to kiss her and damn all the consequences. "The key please?" Curiosity getting the better of him he asked, "You don't recognize her?"

"Should I, Sir? No, trust me. There is no woman in these parts with such elegance. Even slumped over your arm with her jaw hung open and tongue flopped to the side. She's a treasure. Must have come in on the train. The fifth floor is where you'll be staying. Sorry the lift isn't in order. We had a slight incident this past week."

"No worries."

"You say that now," the clerk added absent of any humor.

André went to ask about the *incident*, but decided he had more important things to explore, the woman he held close to his heart for starters. "Please send the bags up?" André nodded toward the middle of the road where his luggage lay sprawled. The concierge sighed as he donned a wide-brimmed hat then headed out into the street.

After four flights of steep steps, André's thighs burned. This one wasn't a featherweight. And the gown didn't help. Probably doubled the load. One step further he feared, he and his fair maiden might topple backward down the mountain he just scaled.

"I've gone soft, Cherié," he told the unconscious woman as he pulled up a step to rest and sat down with her flaccid body draped over his lap. "Allow me to rephrase that, I'm not used to carrying women up five flights of stairs. Where you are concerned, I doubt I'll ever go soft again. Or at least I pray naught." As he caught his breath, he wondered exactly what his intentions were once he got to their room. A flurry of thoughts, none gentlemanly in the least, came to view.

"Do you think you could wake up, Cherié? I've got some ideas that require two consenting adults, and I don't think you'd much appreciate me starting without you. You'd miss out on so much fun." André dipped his head to hers, his nose buried in the crook of her neck. He inhaled a musky-rose scent. Without a doubt he understood why kittens acted like they did with catnip. By the Gods, the woman intoxicated him without lifting a finger. Watching the way her blonde lashes blanketed her fair skin, he prayed she'd wake up sooner rather than later.

Instinct kicking in, he searched her fingers for a telltale bauble of belonging. So taken aback by her, he ran his fingers through the length of her silky-blonde tresses and then moved to trace the lush contour of her lips. He pulled back. His dream on the train. Could this be the woman? Was this fate? Coincidence? Was he this exhausted he now made things up? He didn't care... until all blood flow on him took a direct route to his groin. Conscious decisions no longer existed. He wanted his mouth covering hers, nothing else would do.

"Well, this is how it's done in all those silly tales I was forced to listen to growing up. God forgive me, I know it's lame, but I cannot help myself. My Mum always said a kiss makes everything better. Wake for me, my wild English rose." André bent to her, his eyes closed, his lips slightly parted when he covered her mouth in a soft kiss. After a few awkward moments, he fast realized he was the one doing all the work. He pulled away a little disappointed. "Sleeping Beauty woke up like this. So much for love's true kiss." He snorted. Attempt two he added a little more oomph.

****

A fuzzy sensation of being smothered stirred Jovan. Her head pounded. Never had she had such a headache. Something pressed against her lips, tugged at her hair and had her wrapped up so she couldn't move. Hot, sweet smelling breaths slapped her cheeks. Panic awakened with the strength of a hungry bear. Her eyes sprang open, and she bit down on something wet, probing her mouth, her scream for the time being muffled. Realizing the assailant tried to flee, Jovan chomped harder. Nausea hit once she found out what was in her mouth. His bloody tongue. Revulsion trumped Jovan's notion to finish the thing off. Jovan gagged while her assailant reeled back yelping.

Next dilemma—the royal question of the day: to swallow or spit? She couldn't spit, no matter how vulgar the bitter fluid in her mouth tasted. Spitting disrespected women. The fluids pooled in her mouth and with a giant gulp it lodged in her throat. More gagging followed. *Lady-like my arse.* She rolled her eyes.

His hand over his mouth, André mumbled, "What in hell did you do that for?"

"I felt ill."

"Not that, the bite? Are you rabid?"

Jovan watched as he leaned forward and spit out a glob of blood. Men! "I could ask the same of you. Who and what right do you have to touch me?" Unaware she sat on the top landing of the stairs, Jovan went to stand when he released her. She slipped on the step. "Holy shite!" Arms flailing, her body started going backward.

André reached out and caught her wrists. "My apologies, Cherié. I found your beauty impossible to resist."

She shot him a reprimanding glare. "You do realize that explanation wouldn't exonerate you even if you were the king. Do you always take before asking?" Jovan snapped her arms down out from his grasp. "You're the brute who trampled me."

"We're even, Cherié. You knocked me on me arse in the first place."

"I'll do so again if you so much as come near me." Seeing two heads instead of one, Jovan teetered backward again. A second later, she found herself back in her assailant's arms being cradled.

"I'll behave, I promise. You didn't want to fall did you?"

André winked at her, and it took all her will to fight off his charm. Those eyes, God help her, they twinkled as though the stars lived within them and his lips... well she's already decided where he could plant them. An elfish grin hogged his face. Mad as a hatter but she knew a handsome rogue when she saw one. "Your name?" she demanded.

"André St. James at your service."

At a glance Jovan noticed they had company headed toward them. "What about the bloke behind you with the blackest eyes I've ever seen? Will he behave as well?"

"Huh?" André tapped a finger to his eye turning his head ever so slightly so she could get a better look. "Take note, Mademoiselle. My eyes are the blackest you've ever seen." André gave a playful shift of his brows.

Jovan shoved him. Might as well have been a boulder. He didn't flinch. "All right, Mister Full Of Yourself, your eyes are deep stormy blue, close to black, rather striking, but the thing behind you with the ax aimed at your thick skull are black with a malicious glint to them."

"What?"

"Ax! I said. Duck!" André went to turn back, but Jovan yelled, "Duck," again as a hunk of metal came fast. André followed her advice, the rusted blade swooshed past sinking into the banister, wood chips splintering. After a short struggle the intruder yanked the ax out of the wood and wound up for a second attempt.

Fragments of an elderly man with sunken, coal eyes filtered into view. With no time to think, Jovan was shoved behind her new friend.

"Make your way to the reception hall. Go."

Barbarian. "Like bloody hell. Close your eyes," Jovan snapped. Quick to realize he was of course one hundred percent male and not used to following directions from a living being, Jovan covered his eyes from one of her favorite powers, her flash of light, as she named it. He grabbed her hands and tried to pull them from his face. "Stop bleedin' fighting me. Close them. Now!" She whistled and called, "You-who, Mister ax-murderer," to catch the beast's gaze, then focused and produced a mind-altering state of amnesia through a stream of blinding-white light, the intensity inconceivable. This gave them a few extra seconds to figure out how to get out this mess. "Now do your thing, Mister St. John."

"St. James, Mademoiselle. The name's St. James," André repeated as he reached down into his boot and yanked out a silver blade.

"Nit-picker." Jovan grabbed his head and twisted it back to their assailant.

"I hate nits," André confessed in a low tone. Before the ghoul moved, André had the blade to his chest pressing it through his flesh. When the tip scraped something hard he'd hit bone, and with that André gave one final thrust.

Pungent sludge splattered the walls. As if he could ignore the deathblow, the uninvited stranger lunged for André, his jaw snapping faster than a shark caught on a hook. Fangs descended and the overpowering scent of death filled the air to replace Jovan's musky-rose scent. Talons sliced their way through a leathery hide in place of fingernails. The ghoul spit out, "You royal piece of shite, die all ready," as the decayed corpse collapsed at their feet.

André turned to Jovan and they both took a second to look down at the creature. After an awkward moment of silence between them André finally spoke. "Please, you don't want to see this. Make your way to the third floor. I'll meet you there."

A lower level would have suited her just fine, but Jovan couldn't move. "Ma—ma—Mister St. John?"

André nudged the tip of his boot into the limp body. Nothing. When the man didn't move, he corrected her. "St. James, Cherié. You all right?"

After taking a deep breath, she whispered, "No. Are you? What is that?"

"Zombie?" He shrugged his shoulders. "Never seen

anything like it. And hope to never again. I have to finish him off in case he rejuvenates. Please—go downstairs?" André bent over, picked up the ax and waited.

"Oh dear!" Understanding his intentions, Jovan left on unsteady legs. Unfortunately, the sounds of bones breaking chased one step behind her.

Curled up in the corner of the landing, waiting for what felt like eternity, Jovan's eyes widened at his bloody appearance when he rounded the corner.

"This is insanity!" With the head in one hand, André yelled as he chased the headless body down the stairs. The mouth still snapped at him, regardless it was no longer connected to the rest of the torso. With outstretched arms the bloodied torso lunged toward Jovan, whose jaw hung open yet not one syllable came out. Not one seething remark. Not one cuss word André had already grown to expect from her.

The disembodied head produced a series of long drawn out gurgles. Unable to fathom this thing could still communicate André pulled the talking head into his view. When it hissed at him, his fingers splayed. Reflexes! Sometimes they saved your ass. Sometimes they handed said ass over to someone else on a silver platter. The head dropped and rolled to a dead stop at Jovan's feet. "Oops!"

Jovan passed out when the body landed atop of her. Fingers groped at her flesh and left behind deep scrapes and lines of blood. Laughter spilled from the head's lips. Oddest macabre vision he'd ever witnessed. Enough was enough. One swift kick and the head got launched over the banister and down the stairwell. The ax still clutched in his other hand, André hoisted the trunk from Jovan and hacked off all protruding body parts.

Approaching the front desk, the deskman stepped back, his face losing what scant color he had in the first place. André couldn't blame him—his lady draped across his arms looking as if death knocked down her door, and André now covered in what resembled blood pudding. "There's been a slight incident on the third floor," he told the startled man. "We need a room on one of the lower levels and a doctor as soon as possible."

Without question, the keys to a suite on the first floor lay in André's palm and the clerk left. Whether the gent went to retrieve a doctor or ran for his life, André couldn't begrudge the gent if were the second option.

Chapter Three

In their room, André placed his newfound lady on the bed, and then went to the washroom for cool cloths for her head. When he returned, he removed her boots and proceeded to roll her leggings down to her ankles. He quelled the sexual urges she instigated without even being aware. She needed medical attention. Time to get acquainted. Her health and happiness would forever take front stage.

In disbelief at the direction his morning had taken, André shook his head. Derailed was more like it. He had to get out of this town, but looking at this innocent woman, the very idea of leaving her stopped him in his tracks. What if some other creature loomed in the darkness waiting to steal her from him? Or him from her? How did that thing he'd just executed know his whereabouts or that he was a royal? Or speak after the head had been severed? Or the king of all questions, how did it live in the first place? What had this earth become? Someone or thing had erased the fine line between fantasy and fact. Nightmarish creatures no longer cowered in dark alcoves. Now they moved among those basking in the sun. The rules to the game of life changed. Damn shame André had no idea what game he played. With the knock at the door he retrieved his blade, the blood of this last assailant still adhered to it, the hilt sticky.

"Who is it?"

"Doctor Tobias."

André gripped his blade tighter with his left hand. His eye jammed against the peephole, he saw a giant green orb staring back. He jerked away from the door not expecting to see someone looking in. "Back up," he shouted through the thick wood. He heard a loud thump-thump. Second attempt he viewed a bald gent with what appeared to be an insatiable appetite take up most of the window. Extremely short statured though. Made him wonder how the man reached the peephole. A large square black bag sat on the floor beside him. And there in lay his answer as to how the man peeped in. From a front pocket on his coat a silver syringe poked its way free. André's toes curled. He despised needles. He'd been attacked by so many as a young lad by some mid-wife claiming it was all in good health. He still had marks on his arms. She came weekly and got Raven, Lucian, Duncan, and their parents as well.

A stethoscope hung tight around the doctor's double chin and reached his knees. "Open the satchel please? I need to know we are safe." Even saying it, he knew the syringe could do more damage if filled with toxins. The queen always made her physician give himself a shot before she allowed any injections in her body. No one was going to oust her by a lethal injection.

"Squire, I beg your pardon?" André thought the doctor sounded curt. Looked it, as well, with his nose all scrunched up. He jammed his spectacles back into place with a thumb giving his nose a little wiggle at the end.

André let out a heavy sigh.

"Hello? I received a call of an ill woman?"

"I believe my lady has a head injury. We had a minor incident." André opened the door to the gentleman and stepped aside.

"Minor?" The physician's voice reached octaves excited young pubescent boys couldn't achieve. "Is that what you call beheading a shape shifter a few floors up? Minor?"

"Oh, that wasn't what I made reference to. No, indeed, that wasn't minor. I'm not certain what to call that."

"An attempt on your life for starts," Dr. Tobias answered. "How long has she been like this?" Dragging his black box to the bed, he jumped up on it and went to Jovan's side.

"Since we ran into one another outside. She's lost consciousness twice now."

The doctor assessed Jovan beginning at her head. He pulled gently on her eyelids and noted her left pupil reacted normally to light change. The black dot shrank to a pinpoint. Her right eye had a sluggish response. He undid some of the hook and eye closures on Jovan's camisole and slid the stethoscope under the material over her left chest, plugged in the earpieces and listened.

"Is she—"

"Shush!" The doctor slapped André's arm. About one minute passed before he spoke again. "I can't hear well when young men's lips flap. Her heart is strong. She is lovely. No one in this village with such angelic features. What is her name? If I weren't happily married, I'd relieve her of your charge."

Discretion at this juncture couldn't hurt. Couldn't tell the man he had no clue what this gorgeous creature's name was, that when they were just getting acquainted they were rudely interrupted by the clump of decayed flesh upstairs. "Cherié."

"Well, Lord St. James, your lass has been concussed. Took a good bump on the noggin. Check out this lump on the back of her head."

André reached over her and slid his hand under her head. The man didn't mince words. A soft, warm bump grew from her.

"She needs bed-rest. Keep her awake as long as possible, comfortable, and feed her lightly. Nothing strenuous if you understand me. I've heard how you royals work." The doctor nudged André and gave a quick wink, then switched modes and went back to being medical. "She may or may not have amnesia, nausea, slurred speech or imbalance, but it shall pass in a few days' time. If it worsens, come see me. I am hearing many similar accounts of these creatures as they consume not only the countryside, but also innocent bystanders. I cannot care for these people. I have no magic pill to make them better, but I do have a gun loaded with silver." The man opened his waistcoat and flashed a Colt 45 with a clip loaded with shiny silver bullets. He ran his fingers across the weapon and sighed. "I signed up to save people, not slay them. Live your life to the fullest, young St. James. You never know what's around the corner and especially in your world. Power begets greed."

After repacking his bag, the good doctor's hand shot out waggling his fingers. "Darkness draws near. God speed on her recovery and keeping yourselves safe."

Frustrated, André shoved his wallet back into his pocket after handing the gent a hefty chunk of bills. "Bleeding berk forgot to tell me to ice the lump." With the rustle of sheets, he turned toward the bed. Jovan shifted. "How you fairing?" He removed the now warm cloth, went to the sink and ran it under cool water. After ringing out the excess fluid he sauntered back and placed it to her forehead, sitting on the edge of the bed at the same time.

Jovan reached up and held her head. "You again," she whispered. "What happened? What's that smell?" Her nose twitched and a soured face followed. She inched her head back gingerly. "You're covered in demon shite. Please make the room stop feeling like a carousel."

"You don't recall?"

"Sadly, yes. Well, most of it. Right up till that meat scrap landed on me. Why am I lying down?" Jovan attempted to sit up, but dry heaved with the change in position. "Oh no!" came one belch too late.

"Again? Truly?" André stood in haste as he undid his buttons to the shirt.

More bile projected in a solid stream onto his leather chaps. She wiped her mouth with the cloth he'd given her then pulled her body up against the headboard and held her knees to her chest. André began to undress in an exaggerated fashion before her wide eager eyes.

"Mr. St. John—I'm—"

Hand out in front of her face, he cut her off. "For the last time, Mademoiselle, the name is St. James." Three times now he'd told her his name. Most women heard it once and never forgot it. Not this one!

"No need to get huffy, St. James. I was about to apologize, but no, you have to go act like you're a member of the royal court due to your last name."

Mid button André stopped hopping around with one leg out of his trousers and glanced at her, his eyebrows raised in an amused fashion.

Eyes and mouth wide, Jovan squirmed. "Oh. Dear. Lord. You're pulling me leg. Tell me you're not." Hands flying in all directions, she leaned over and finished with a jab to his chest. "St. James is a rather common name, right?"

André bit his cheeks. "Tell you I'm not what? Related to my aunt, Queen Mattie? Shall I lie to make you feel better?" He resumed undressing.

"Please, Sire?" Shyly, she peeked up to him from under thick blonde lashes. "I truly am sorry, my Lord. I'd wash your clothing if I could get up off me arse."

"You'll do no such thing and never call me that. The name is André. I still don't know your name." He brushed a few golden tendrils from her face and allowed his fingers to linger on her petal-soft skin.

He watched as she tried to answer him. She even went as far as to open her mouth, yet no name formed. She scrunched her lips, nose and brows, confusion and frustration obvious.

"What did you call me earlier? Isn't that me name?"

"You can't remember your name? No wonder you can't recall mine."

She shook her head no. "Apparently it was not worth remembering, mine that is." Tears leaked from the corners of her eyes.

Absentminded of his lack of dress, André sat

beside her in only his skivvies. "Well, the doctor said you might have amnesia." He reached across her and handed her his handkerchief from the bedside table, his thigh hard against hers, even through the blanket. That was when he realized what he wasn't wearing. He acted indifferent, hoping if he didn't behave strangely it wouldn't make her anxious. He blotted a few tears before she grabbed the cloth from him.

Jovan inspected the hankie closely.

"It's mostly clean." He gave her a cheeky grin.

"At least you think you're funny." She dabbed at her cheeks. "There was a doctor here to see me? Did he recognize me?"

He leaned in closer to her and tapped her nose. "Yes and no in that order."

Jovan jerked back. "Are you going to get dressed? Do you have spare clothes?"

"No and yes in that order," he teased.

Jovan tapped her finger to her lips before she spoke. "The fact is I may not remember who I am, but I'll never forget you as long as I live."

"Aye, my beauty, that's quite the compliment."

"I weren't finished." She poked her finger into his thigh hard. "Your ego is unrivaled. First you try to kiss me as I am unconscious, then bring me to a hotel room, undress me, and now you lay beside me as if we are lovers. I don't care how handsome you are or rich or blue-blooded."

Feisty little woman. Finally, someone to spar with him, engage in conversation and not be afraid to step on his toes. All his life André had been, "Yes, Sir'd," until his balls were blue, and his eyeballs rolled into the back of his head. This lady was different. He could feel it.

Being brought up breathing nobility all the women he'd met had a certain savoir-fair about them. They were all certainly pretty enough and each one adorned with the finest silks, laces and dowries offered, but their personalities matched the dress code of the guards, all identical in thought and mannerisms. Not a single one of them caught his attention and kept it like this fair maiden. Looks change, but intelligence, personality, spunk and honesty remained the standards he lived by.

She poked again. "Hey!"

André did not budge.

"I'm sorry. This day has been full of surprises, you being a most pleasant one despite your temper, your tummy, and your use of the English language. Cherié, you expelled your stomach contents on me two times. This is why I shed my belongings. I promise to redress and my word to you, I will remain a gentleman until you ask otherwise of me." Her smirk, he'd already come to cherish it.

"You are arrogant yet entertaining."

"You should meet my cousin. He's ten times worse. His nickname is imbecile."

"Truly befits you. Maybe you've a long-lost twin. Find it hard to believe there could be anyone else out there with your spirited sense of self." She gave him a wide toothy grin.

Her smile warmed his broken heart. "I've a question for you. What in God's name did you do to that zombie? You blinked at him or something and stunned him. I caught a glimpse of a brilliant flash. The area resembled a shooting star. It crashed into him and knocked him senseless."

"It must have gotten you as well then. I closed me

eyes looking upon that vile being. I've no special powers to stun a ghoul. Can you believe we sit here speaking of such things?"

"In all honesty, I cannot." *I cannot believe I waste my breath with words when I could put it to such good use on you.* The more she spoke, the more André fell head over heels in love with her. Love at first sight. He'd always scoffed the very notion, labeled all those doting morons hopeless romantics—until now. His inner voice, the one that usually steered him into rather than away from trouble, had this quality of never shutting up when it wanted something or in this case, someone. The voice told him in unequivocal terms his Cherié was his match in every way, from her attitude to her beauty to the way she handled herself in the midst of danger watching over him, even though she had no recollection of trying to save him. He'd seen what she'd done.

The woman had talents that others like her were being burned upon the stake for still to this day. André decided right then and there this woman would never burn upon a stake, but she would most certainly heat up his bed. He'd spent too much time alone. Living on the outside looking in. Never allowing a relationship to bloom for fear of being cast away—again. It happened when he turned sixteen. His aunt Lorelei sent him to Paris a few years after his mother turned up missing. Separated him from Raven and Lucian and all he had known in a once loving home. His secure world turned upside down a second time, and a third, when Lorelei and his uncle Christian were murdered. Through it all he'd become an independent man; capable of doing whatever he set his mind to. He no longer needed anyone, but desire? This woman in front of him would be his undoing. He had to protect her. The way of the times had changed. Vampires roamed the earth in search their next meal. Zombies sloughed through the dark alleyways and witches, like the one in front of him, had come out to play with the rest of the mere mortals. And play with her he would.

Until she left him.

He watched her eyes roam... from his face to his chest and further south. Her gaze fixated on his groin. She licked her lips. Under the covers he ducked when her hand hit her chest right where only moments before the stethoscope rested. He didn't want to scare the daylights out of her when those sultry eyes of hers saw what equaled his variation of the crown jewels. Some jewels were meant to be locked up and taken out and played with only on special occasions. Others were there to unleash pleasure whenever the situation arose. André felt the situation rising. Head injury or not, Jovan impressed André when she sprung up from the mattress.

"Look," she accused, "just because you've been a gentleman and saved your damsel in distress for the day, oh, and just because you're related to her Majesty, don't you for one bleedin' minute think I'm going to slip under the covers with you and lay flat on me back to show you me gratitude, so you can collect your royalties!"

He watched Jovan backpedal to the powder room where once in, he heard the lock on the door click behind her. "That was not my intention. I did not want to give you a fright."

"Right," came out laced with derision. "There's

that larger than life sense of self again."

"Well in all earnest, my lady, it is larger than life."

"Please shush." Up against the powder room door after a quick yet embarrassing get away, Jovan slid to the floor and practiced breathing. How did she finagle her way out of this dilemma? Men! This man in particular. What was it about him? Everything. His humor. His looks. His devilish grin. His body. His carefree charismatic attitude. The way he'd cared for her and protected her from the beast. Could he be the one? With every ounce of her being she wanted to join him between the sheets and lay beneath him, or atop of him as he wished. Him in his skimpy loincloth! God help them both. She stood, made her way to the sink, and dowsed cold water across her face. In the mirror, a woman she no longer recognized stared back. No name, no memory, no past, but a future? He could make her dreams come true. She leaned into the mirror, rested her head against the cool glass and prayed for guidance. Once composed, she opened the door and eyed the room.

Vacant.

"Damn! St. James, where are you? Come on. I even got your name correct." Jovan searched the room. His clothes and bags? Gone. Even the soiled linens. "This cannot be happening." In a huff, Jovan threw her boots back on. Her quick change of position reminded her of the tumultuous headache on top her shoulders. Why in hell didn't he have any residual effects of their ram-like encounter? A thick-headed male indeed. The corner of her lip curled.

She steadied her gate by holding the wall on her way to the main desk. On a mission, she reached the counter and slammed her fist down hard on the tiny silver bell in search of anyone with a pulse. Her impatience alone might have scared people off. When no one approached, she chucked the tiny ding-a-ling-thing through a window and stomped out into the walkway, blocking other pedestrians as they tried to pass. She looked to her left and then to her right for her missing companion.

What would she do? She had no idea of her name, had no money for the food her stomach now demanded, and the pounding head would soon pummel her into the ground, but despite all that had gone wrong Jovan found the silver lining in her misery. She looked good. It might buy her dinner if she played her cards right. And if not? She couldn't think so far ahead. Her nose led her in the direction of the aromas of beef over a fire-pit. Lenny's.

Chapter Four

Hearing footsteps and bickering, Jovan turned around. She had a small troop of strange men arguing with their wives and then following her, each with a giant asinine gleam in their eye. Morons, all of them. One hopeful man approached. "Miss, I had a bouquet of flowers all set for my wife until I saw you."

Jovan gasp. "Have you gone insane? Shoo." She tried to push him back to his wife who stood in the middle of the walkway red-faced, her fists knotted. Oh goddess! "Go back to your wife. Please. Right this bleedin' second before I am bleeding." Jovan peeked around the man and repeated it to the other four men shuffling toward her. "Do I know any of you? If not please leave me be. I'm so sorry," she said to the women. The first gent still tried to give her the flowers. Jovan grabbed the roses from him and swatted him with the bouquet until all that was left were stems then turned on her heels and sprinted toward the pub.

Not inside the establishment one minute a gentleman greeted her. All this attention from the opposite sex unnerved her. Jovan had no idea why every man seemed to migrate to her. With a quick peek she checked to make certain her bosoms were where she left them, tucked away and that the back of her skirt hadn't gotten caught in her underskirt, showing off her dainty little *derriere*.

The gent escorted her to his table, pulled her chair out for her, seated her, offered her dinner, drink and conversation that didn't revolve around killing monsters. And a marriage proposal out of the blue for which she instantly yet graciously answered, "Are you daft? I don't even know your name." Never mind not knowing hers. She almost got up to leave until she eyed her new roommate at the bar with a shot glass in his hand and three women pining for his attention.

"No, no, no!" Jovan grasp her head, frustrated. "I think I might die." Weren't her head, but her heart that ached. She'd known the man less than one day and seeing him surrounded by strange women made her want to what? It was right on the tip of her tongue. What was it? Seemed something important to her. Crucial to her wellbeing. Out of the corner of her eye she noticed the gent she sat beside wiggle something.

"Drink this, buttercup, and you'll feel better. And if that doesn't work, I'll lick you better myself. My name is Allister." He gave her a giant grin. "Alley cat for short."

His smile lacked something. Teeth! Every, last dent. Jovan backed up in her chair. There was just no comparison between André and this gummy bloke. It was like being offered a bowl of sweet cream or a glass of milk loaded with soured curds.

"I do not want nor need your clots—ah-kisses, Mister. And, I don't believe I drink. I shan't be dining with you either. I've lost me appetite." In a huff, she stood to leave, but her dress caught under something. The gent's foot as he stamped down on it.

"I offered you a free meal and marriage," he

shouted. His angry tone caused heads to turn their way.

"And I do believe I answered no." Jovan stepped backward and tripped.

"No, you asked if I were daft?" he sniveled.

"Point proven." Jovan tugged to get the hem of the dress freed.

Hearing a commotion, André turned around. He had to fight the smirk on his face but lost when he saw his Cherie in a slight pickle. Had she followed him here? What was this crazy woman up to now? And more importantly, why were all the men hovering around her? A sliver of panic needled its way into his heart. What if one of these men was her spouse? Was he about to lose the one woman he'd dreamed of his entire life? He counted to ten quickly to see if any man came forward to help her. A sigh of relief slid out when no one claimed her. He downed his shot and walked over.

When the slight edge of a boot tapped her backside, Jovan turned her head and found herself knee high to André.

André held his hand out. Flustered, Jovan looked up and came close to melting right then and there. He had the most mouth-watering to-die-for grin on his lips. "Lose the smirk, imbecile," she bit out.

"You always seem to be on your backside when we meet. I rather fancy that, Cherié. Up you go, my little queen. Abstinence is supposed to make the heart grow fonder, not wander!" André hoisted Jovan over his shoulder.

"Insane man, put me down." She punched at his buttocks.

"Harder, sweetheart."

She obliged, and he laughed. He turned to the toothless gent, now headed toward them with malice in his eyes and a steak knife in his hand. "This is my bride, mate. She lost her memory after we bumped heads, whilst bumpin' other body parts if ya get my drift. Sorry for any inconvenience." André threw a few quid on the table and headed toward the exit before the miscreant could argue. Or inflict bodily harm.

"Aye, you're back again, me strappin' brute. Come back for me, did ya? Drop that trollop back on the floor with the rest of the rubbish and come take what's rightfully yours." The three-breasted barmaid yelled from the kitchen doorway. "You ran out on me so fast the first time I never got your name."

André glanced over his shoulder. "Oh no!"

Jovan pinched his bum. "Who in 'ell is she?"

"Jealous?" André laughed and slapped Jovan's bottom. He answered the barmaid, "This one here, she's my wife, love. Apologies."

From her upside-down view of the world Jovan was seeing things. The woman had three breasts. To get André to quicken the pace, Jovan bit his butt.

"I like a girl who plays rough."

"It'll be the front I sink me teeth into the next time."

"Promises, promises."

Then the room spun or was it her *husband*? Wasn't he the court jester? With an abrupt jolt, Jovan's head bounced off one of the oak chairs when André turned again. Oh, did she have a mouthful for him. "Ouch!" It was getting a wee bit claustrophobic for her likings. The men in the pub began to form a semicircle around them. Jovan tapped his thigh. "The door. Now!"

With a firm hand he secured his grip on Jovan's dainty derriere André nudged and shoved his way past the patrons to get out. He made his way to the side of the road and plopped her down, dust mushrooming around her.

When yelling filtered out into the street they both glanced back at the pub. Glass shattered onto the walkway when the three-breasted woman careened through the window. Cut up and bleeding, she stood, lost her balance, wobbled a few feet, slipped from the sidewalk and landed dead in the path of a moving horse-drawn carriage. Jovan buried her face in André's shoulder and muffled a scream.

"Stay here," André stressed. "I'll go check on her."

Jovan sat in shock as to what the mangled woman resembled once André and a few others were able to get the body untangled from the undercarriage. The dead woman was in no better shape than the beast they'd been attacked by earlier, and Jovan quickly found out neither was she. Silvery sparkles hindered her vision. Was there a fairy in the proximity dusting her? Putting her head between her legs was the last thing she recalled.

Arms circled her waist and brought her to her feet. A warm body embraced her from behind and held her close. Sheltered. Jovan felt his lips atop her head and her heart slowed. "St. John!"

"Close enough." He held her until her equilibrium returned.

"You two again. I'm beginning to believe you both have a death wish." Dr. Tobias strut across the road and came to a standstill beside them.

He reached up to pat Jovan's shoulder, teetering on

his toes to do so. "Didn't I tell you nothing strenuous? You're looking fit, Lass. Even lovelier conscious. Good to see I was of some help. Death calls. Pay attention to my orders or you'll be next." The doctor waddled off toward the wagon.

"Did you recognize the doctor?"

She gave a ginger shake of her head no. Jovan's moue couldn't have made her look any sadder. "Why do men keep giving me the feeling they're attracted to me?"

André threw his arm over her shoulder and drew her near him. "I have no idea." That statement was followed by a jab to his abdomen. André laughed off the pain.

Out of nowhere she turned and buried her face in André's chest. He crushed her to him and rubbed her back. He gave her the sense the man would be there for her, make her feel safe throughout eternity. "I feel as if I'm stuck in a nightmare and can't wake up."

"I'm your dream catcher, Cherié. I got you." André tilted her face to his and wiped the dirty tears from her cheeks. "Are you hurt?"

"Just me noggin from you rearranging the barroom furniture with my head."

André rubbed her head. "I thought I felt something."

He had the audacity to laugh, in the midst of life and death.

"The moon is full, Cherié. We need to get to safety if all this nonsense is true of mystical creatures."

"André, you believe in werewolves?"

He nodded yes. "Let's not forget zombies and vampires."

"Who were the women surrounding you at the bar? They seemed eager to please you." Jovan noticed a smile work its way to André's lips, the exact opposite of her current disposition.

"Do I detect a hint of envy? I'm touched."

"That you are." Jovan kept walking, her grin now large.

"The one with the three breasts, the dead lass, claimed to be your stepmum and the others your stepsisters. All bitches. Said you best earn your keep and to take care of me. Whatever I desire. And ooh, Cherié, I think you'll keep me rather tied up."

"I'm not seeing any glass slippers in me future, Lord St. James."

André bent and lifted her skirt up past her ankles. "They don't make them in ogre sizes."

Jovan planted a well-placed kick into his shin with that ogre-sized boot.

"Not nice."

"That, what you said, sounds so familiar. I wish I could remember who said it."

"Probably anyone who's ever seen your feet." "Imbecile."

"No, my cousin Lucian is the imbecile. You'd be wise to remember that."

Did I hear my name used in vain? Ands, what in the name of everyone short and sassy is going on? Been plagued with vibrations from you today that run the gamut.

Women, cousin. Plain and simple. They can't keep their paws off me. André laughed heartily, because if he didn't he was pretty certain he'd go insane. The look he received from his new lady solidified it might already be a moot point.

Although cozy in his grip, Jovan wiggled free. "Oh and what did you say to the man in the pub? Your bride? Whilst we were bumping?" Jovan didn't know whether to laugh or clobber the man. "I thought you left me, St. James. I wasn't in the washroom that long."

"Oh, Cherié, to leave you would be a fatal mistake on my behalf. My amour for you grows by the minute."

Jovan bit her lip. Her gut tightened. Her mouth went bone dry. Did he nonchalantly just tell her he loved her? They'd only just met. "Truly you must be a glutton for punishment."

"So it seems."

André brought her hand to his mouth and kissed each knuckle. Jovan's cheeks flushed and that wasn't the only place on her turning into an inferno. With each delicate caress, Jovan craved more. She wanted to get to know this man, his likes, dislikes, pesky habits, endearing qualities, what made him laugh, cry, what his dreams were and if she could be a part of them. After that, or during, she wanted him stripped of all clothes. Hers alone to admire. To have her way with. To love, cherish, honor through eternity. That rung a bell…wedding bells? Before she could recall why wedding bells meant anything to her the thought faded.

"So, you promise you won't leave me until I find out who I am? My past?" Goddess, what if he said he had to go? What if she had already begun to have feelings for this egotistical, overzealous, teddy bear and he left her? What if? Jovan had no tolerance for conundrums.

"Cherié, I'm not leaving you. Period. Come, let us get away from this insanity and grab supper."

"Supper? Despite this blood bath, I'm famished."

"What's your favorite meal?" Hoping to spark her memory, he suggested, "Say the first thing you think of."

Jovan glanced over her shoulder as they walked past a few men placing the body of the deceased barmaid onto a long wagon. "Well it's not steak and kidney pie."

"Touché."

"Pancakes with strawberries and sweet cream," She felt as if she'd remembered something important. A little piece of herself perhaps. A satisfied sigh escaped.

André ruffled her hair. "Sounds delightful for breakfast."

"Breakfast?" A demure grin graced her lips. Jovan's curiosity piqued. What would happen between supper and sunrise? Oh, she'd work up an appetite all right. His too! She added a little sultriness to her sway, tripping on a pebble. He caught her around the waist and steadied her.

As if reading her mind, he answered, "Usually comes after a good night's sleep! Doctor's orders. Not mine. Trust me. What's your second try?" Close to the fish market, André inclined his head toward the store making his lips form and reform circles trying to imitate a fish out of water.

Laughter filled the air. "That's the worst imitation of a fish I've ever seen."

"Oh, my Cherié, how do you know that with no memory?"

Her smile faded and just like that a few stray tears slid down her cheek.

"What did I do this time?"

"It isn't you. You're rather funny until you open your mouth."

André's rebuttal was short lived. Jovan covered his lips with her fingers which he wasted no time kissing. "Would you please help me find my way home? Find me?"

"I've already found you. Come, my absented-minded beauty, we'll go have our supper and then take a nice constitutional about this little village in the morning once it's safe and see if you remember anything or anyone recognizes you. I placed an advertisement in the daily chronicle's lost and found before I stopped at the pub. It will run on the morrow." André tugged his sleeve down over his palm and dabbed the remaining tiny beads of water from her cheeks. "Fair enough?"

"St. James," Jovan stood on her tippy toes and placed a soft kiss on André's cheek, and finished with "thank you."

Enjoying every moment with this gentle giant, she didn't allow her disappointment to show. They sat at a white wrought iron table under a bower of fragrant lilacs. Dinner as promised included fish, fried to perfection smothered in malt vinegar with golden chips. Both devoured their meals without a word in edgewise.

Lifting her finger, Jovan pointed. "There." The sunset cast an orange haze over the treetops to lend a little extra warmth to the area. In the far distance the moon's iridescent contour outlined the horizon. "I should paint this sometime soon."

André brought her hand into view. "Such delicate fingers. Do you paint or draw? Your fingers seem to be tainted light green."

Jovan shrugged her shoulder. "Possibly." There it was once again. That nagging sensation she knew she should know something important yet couldn't quite reach out to put her stained, grassy colored finger on it. Vexing, it was.

"Well then, the night's not been a complete waste. Your memory shall return, bit by bit." He held his hand to her and once up they started back to the hotel. "Tomorrow, we'll continue our search and get you some new gowns."

Between her index finger and thumb she grasp her dress tugging the once gorgeous gown out in front of her to inspect. "Ruined."

"I have people who can restore it."

Jovan glanced at André with her head cocked, her long blonde tresses falling in soft curls over her shoulder. "You would do that for me?"

There isn't a thing I would not do for you. He kept that thought locked away. These feelings mounting for this woman were the most intense, insane, desires to ever ravish his heart and mind. "There isn't a thing I wouldn't do for you." So much for holding a few things back. He gave a playful wink to her.

"Careful, my lord, I may hold you to that."

He dipped his head to hers and kissed her cheek. "The night is young, my dear, and you're not." An elbow to his ribcage stole his breath for a moment. Laughing didn't help either. "Geez, let me finish. Allowed to sleep. Not allowed to sleep. I would not taunt a woman of her age. Other things perhaps, shoe size maybe, but never age." André lifted his brows a few times. "Whatever shall we do till the wee dawn hour?"

She slugged his arm taking his mind off the same thoughts she held. "Would you read to me?"

Astounded he asked, "Can you not read?"

"Yes, but my eyes are weary, and I find it is relaxing to lay back and have someone else do all the work." She clasped her hands in front of him while she reciprocated the same eyebrow wag he loved to bestow upon her.

"Cheeky woman! What else do you have in mind?"

"I saw a posted note of the circus. We could visit the sideshows. Possibly some of your family is participating."

"You have a sense of humor."

"I weren't joking." She didn't even crack a smile.

"I have no desire to share you with any carneys."

Another *déjà vu*. Eyes squinted shut, she tried to remember, but decided the more she tried the more stress played into it only to frustrate her. "This is infuriating, André."

"What is? Stop making that face. You'll get crinkles."

"Not having a bleedin' clue who in hell I am. I give up. Seems I am unworthy of anyone's affections or love since no one seeks me. If this is true, you'd best say fare-thee-well to me. I must be a wretched woman."

"Nonsense, my lady. You are kind and caring of this I am certain. You could have slapped me silly when we first met on the steps—"

"Someone beat me to it," Jovan mumbled, not daring to look up at him for fear of uncontrolled laughter.

André bumped his shoulder into hers. "Instead you saved me. So, from here on out no more putting yourself in the dredges. What's our agenda this evening?"

"Poetry perhaps?" Jovan scrunched her nose to him. "The front desk held a book of poems."

"Which circus show did you want to see?" He asked all too fast. Poetry? He'd rather have scrubbed down the tunnels after a fortnight of fornication from every strumpet doing triple time. "The amazing Isaac VanAmbugh has his portrait in me auntie's castle. Lion trainer extraordinaire he'd been dubbed. He's passed on now, but his show remains."

"Animals belong in the wilderness. No constraints."

"How about you? I have a few ideas of tying you up. Come, my blushing bride, allow me to serenade you." Before Jovan knew what hit her, André held her in his arms, entered the hotel and crossed the threshold to their room. He set her down and suggested, "Freshen up and crawl in bed. I'm going to get linens for my bed, some brandy and your poetry." He reached to her, placed his fingers under her chin and tilted her face to his. "Are you comfortable with this? I can get the adjoining room." When she gave him a quick nod yes, he wasted no time and placed a soft kiss on her head. "Be right back."

Chapter Five

Anxious, Jovan paced, uncertain what her night held. Would this be her first night with a man? She hoped yes. In the washroom she found it stocked with every toiletry she could desire. And it was indoors! It just didn't get any better than this. A quick flash of an outhouse with a dirt floor engulfed in a bitter atmosphere of cobwebs and exoskeletons trapped in them filled her vision. She said a quick prayer hoping the outhouse wasn't hers because if it was, she knew why she didn't want to remember it. This bathroom even came with a white, lacy bath gown and slippers, however sized for a woman with a healthy appetite and a slow metabolism. Jovan undressed, bathed and put it on. She swam in it, but it was only one night and Goddess willing, maybe he'd help her out of it. Back in the main room, she lit the candles and watched shadows dance across the walls in soft sways as clouds slipped past the full moon. Jovan crawled under the sheets and waited for André to return.

Once washed up and settled, André sat atop the bedding, leaned against the headboard with her head resting on his shoulder. He opened the pages of an Edgar Allen Poe book only to have a stray slip of paper fall out. He picked it up and read it:

"When things look bad and you're all confused,

look again… it's only the blues. So take a long walk in the bright sunshine, and think to yourself, is this all mine? As you grasp the beauty along the way, pray to your God, please let it stay. And if by chance you look again, to see a stranger with an outstretched hand, never see that tear in his eye, never ask or wonder why. Just always remember to clasp his hand with a good firm grip so he'll understand. There are good friends along life's roads. So when things look bad and you're all confused, look again it's only the blues!"

André wet his lips. "Definitely not Poe's work. Nothing dark or spooky here."

"Except you."

His lips curled on one side and a small burble escaped. He tucked the paper back inside the book and closed it. "This poem defines you and I don't you agree? Two strangers in the night caring for one another?"

"Yes, it does. St. James, this is the most romantic night of my life."

"You say that now. What happens on the morrow if some crazy man reads the post and comes to claim you?"

"You seem to be the only berk who foots the bill. I would think I would know if I were married. Wouldn't there be a ring on me green finger?" Jovan waggled her left hand in his face.

André grabbed her hand. "Hold on, you're fingers truly are the color of a blade of grass. How is this?"

"Maybe I'm a garden fairy." Jovan giggled out of nerves. The idea didn't seem so farfetched at this point. The notion of being some sort of freak had crept into her conscience with as much surreptitiousness as this man did her heart.

"Well, as far as a husband goes, I'd have a chastity belt on you."

"How do you know there's not one securely fixed to me already saving me from the likes of you?"

Playfully he tried to lift the covers, but Jovan pressed down on top of the coverlet and stopped his attempt to peek.

"My fair lady, if this is your first night with a man, then by all means, we must make it an evening for you to cherish. I'll walk you through Eden's primrose garden."

"Been more like a path filled by picker bushes. Nothing has turned up rosy since we met."

"That's all about to change."

Jovan watched with enthusiasm as he grasped his brandy, gave the glass a slight jiggle and followed the deep amber fluid as it swirled in a circle and coated the glass. The strong scent brought tears to her eyes. After he took a long swig, he offered her the glass. "Care to try it?"

Jovan shook her head no. "But I'd like to taste it upon your lips." His full grin warmed her like nothing ever had.

"As my lady wishes," he answered, his voice whimsical. He set the glass down on the night table and turned to face her. He weaved his fingers through her hair and with soft strokes caressed her cheek with his thumb. With his free hand, he traced her plump lips. He confessed, "I've dreamt of this from the moment you knocked me down," as he met her lips with his in one slow intimate kiss. His lips moved with hers, his tongue tasted, then probed. Together they mated, their lips hard pressed, both eager, both hungry. André tightened his grip, pulled her closer and continued to kiss her with everything he had. There were other things he wanted to probe her with, mate with. His groin heavy, ached with need. His heart oddly never felt more sated.

Jovan couldn't help it, she giggled through their kiss. Nerves. Pretty certain she'd never been kissed before, with the exception of the stairwell disaster, she pulled away and smacked her lips together. "I fancied that." He tasted sweet, yet the liquor left a bold aftertaste. Pretty much summed him up.

"So, what's the verdict?"

André's gaze looked more like he was searching for approval: a young schoolboy uncertain of his skills. Jovan found it odd that a man of such stature and wealth needed endorsement, but not everything came at face value. Maybe not everything that glittered in the palace was truly gilded. Look at her. All dolled up with nowhere to go or call home. She ran her fingers through all those jet-black curls of his and answered, "I am not sure."

His hand slapped his chest feigning disbelief. André leaned into her and whispered, "Second time is the charm." Lips puckered, he went in and planted a second one covering her mouth in nothing short of ecstasy. His teeth grazed her lower lip and he sucked, drew her in and didn't let go. The things the man did to her lips—she wanted to find out what it felt like to have him explore her body, every last nook and cranny with his mouth, or tongue alone. Deep in her groin a sassy little tingle flirted with her and traveled to the areas that made her legs clamp shut.

Or was that spread?

"May I lick some of this from your sweet lips?" André leaned back and grabbed the glass, ticking it to the left and then right, swooshing the amber fluid.

You can lick wherever you desire. Staunch in her decision, Jovan took the glass. "Cheers!" Two eye-watering, fire-breathing shots of brandy later, Jovan lay curled around the most beautiful man she'd ever lain eyes on, singing, "Show me the path to go home," her voice although usually angelic, held a slight slur to it. "I'm tired, and I want my bed, but this crazy man... by my side, won't let me, because he fears I'll wind up dead!" With a slipped smile and glassy eyes Jovan shrugged her shoulders. "I'm here all night!"

André burst out laughing. He reeled her in closer to him and sang, "She chugged a little sip 'bout an hour ago and 'tis gone straight to her head." André finished, "Oh, I'd love to get you in my bed, da-da-da-dah... but I'm following what the doctor said... Would be a true mishap—if you slipped and fell upon your pretty little head... again!" André ruffled her hair from her face. "I believe we're onto a great song, Cherié. Maybe someday it'll become famous."

"I have no doubt some shark will come along and claim it. Shall you claim me, my Lord?"

****

Lost in the reflection of her glimmering eyes, he knew exactly what he had to do. There would be no mishaps, no regrets on the dawn's horizon. Tonight, he would sleep with her wrapped safely in his arms. On the morrow, if she still desired him, then he'd watch the sun rise over her soft curves, and he'd warm her where the golden rays couldn't reach.

"Cherié, allow me to read to you for now. I can see

into your heart what you want from this night, but I must decline. Please believe me when I tell you it is not for lack of desire, but quite the contrary. I want everything perfect when I make love to you. I will not steal your virtue. Or place your reputation in danger if you are indeed another man's desire. I have never experienced such emotion or need just from being in the same room with a woman. You look at me as a woman who loves a man with deep passion and yet even though we have only met I feel the same."

"Then do not deny us this time together. I am not so far gone that I would question my motives in the morn."

"But I am. You intoxicate me." He held her chin and looked deep into her eyes. "Do you trust me?"

"With me life. But now you must trust me. It's this ridiculous nightgown, right?" Jovan wiggled her way from him and stood. She bent to her toes and grabbed the edge of the hem and with one swift, fluid move, the material slid up and over her head. Beneath, she wore only the suit in which she'd entered this world.

Awestruck, André memorized every rapturous inch of the woman before him. By the God, she held curves that would mold to his every move. Her breasts were firm, her nipples rosy pink, piqued by the cooler air or perhaps her desire for him. What was that she'd said earlier? Nothing had turned up rosy since they'd met? The little woman lied. Those two little twin peaks taunted him. Begged for attention. He sat on his hands to keep them contained, because the wanderers wanted to travel the length of her graceful body to tickle her into submission until she screamed his name repeatedly and got it right and begged for whatever lavish ministrations he bestowed upon her. And there would be an entire evening of different positions, kisses from every angle, tongue lashings, foreplay to bring her to the edge, to make certain her night held only pleasure.

Her flat tummy, he decided, would look beautiful swollen with his child. *Oh cripes! 'Twas only this morning I'd sworn off babes.*

He peered into Jovan's wishful eyes. André saw a need so deeply seeded it left him speechless. He'd never been more torn between doing the noble thing and honoring her or doing what he wanted to, grabbing her, throwing her on the bed, spreading her legs and dipping his head between her thighs to run his tongue across her little nub of flesh and taste her sex. His pants just weren't loose enough when she was around. He glanced toward her nightgown.

The dress held possibilities.

He sat there stiff as a nail as Jovan spun around and flashed her firm little backside in his face. She peeked back over her shoulder and winked as she bit her bottom lip. His cock begged for freedom. "Can I interest you in anything at all this night, Milord?" She wiggled her bum at him once more.

"Who's taunting whom?" He could barely think. "It appears you are in need of one good spanking, Mademoiselle."

"As you wish." Jovan turned to the bed, stretched her arms high over her head and then in a slow seductive move, bent over the mattress, leaving her little derriere wide open to his desires. "Do unto me as you would enjoy done to you, St. James. When you're done, I'll return the favor." Elbows sunk into the mattress she rested her chin in her hands with only a sinful grin upon her lush lips, then she blew him a kiss.

Chapter Six

A soft, almost nondescript thud drew André's attention to the outer balcony of their room. Abrupt in his actions, André jumped to his feet whispering, "Get dressed now," as he grabbed the gown from the floor and threw it at his mystified goddess. Instinct kicking in, he cleared the bed, and had his gun drawn on the curtains. "Get behind me, Cherié." He knelt down on the floor behind the bed so he had a clear shot of the window.

His urgency stymied Jovan. She clutched the gown to cover her nakedness. However, it would not cover the shame of her lame attempt at seduction. Gowns did not come large enough.

"What was I thinking? You must think me a child." Angry, she threw the nightdress in his face before she stomped to the closet. "I'm sorry I've wasted your—"

André bent as far as he could, reached out and latched onto her arm startling her. He yanked hard, tripping her and landing her naked little butt beside him. Before she opened her mouth to ramble on, he bent down and covered it with his hand as he waved the gun under her nose, mouthing the words, "Shut up, my beauty." Foolishly, he removed his hand.

"I'll just bet you'd like me to shut up! And disappear too?" Jovan reached for the tent-of-a-gown to cover herself again. She scrambled, twisted the material inside out, getting nowhere.

Naked, she stayed. Her temper flared faster than a bull with his penis strapped in a sadistic knot to his groin. "Damn! What is it? Am I not the correct pedigree? Or not buxom enough?" She cupped her breasts offering herself to him one last time.

Frustrated? André rolled his eyes and let out one long growl. If he hadn't heard something outside their window he'd have taken her right then and there on the floor and latched his lips to her bosom and suckled until she surrendered beneath him. He pointed to the window with the safety on his gun now removed.

Jovan's eyes grew wide as her gaze followed the waving gun back and forth. "Please don't shoot me," she begged. She got up on all fours and attempted to crawl away.

Getting a bird's eye view of her heart-shaped bottom moving across the room, André swore, "Damn you, woman." He grabbed her leg and dragged her to his side, yanked her on his lap, wound her hair around his fingers which landed her face inches from his. Breathless, he whispered, "Cherié, please shut your luscious lips before I never get the chance to kiss them again. Dear God, woman, you are stubborn, thick in the head and a raving beauty. Your breasts are beautiful and if you don't allow me to take care of a few things, I'll never get to finish what I started."

Jovan's glare: He'd seen that angry mask in other women. Never went well after that.

Not a second passed before André found his cheek on the receiving end of five scorned fingers. "What the bloody hell?" He rubbed at the stinging flesh.

"You bloody well had your chance, St. James.

You, Sir, are no saint! You tried to take advantage of an inebriated, concussed woman! You're royal all right—a royal pain in me bum."

"You've no clue what you want!" André grumbled while he turned fast and searched the room for intruders, praying no one slipped through the window while he dealt with this hotheaded beauty. "We have company outside," he whispered, his tone bitter.

"Is it me husband?" she asked, her tenor a little less hostile.

His jaw tensed causing every vein and artery in his neck to explode. "You're married? Now you remember him?" André couldn't help the disappointment in his words.

Temper rising to match his, she bit out, "I 'ave no clue if I am. And I'm at a loss for words as to your outburst. You just turned me down so my marital status should be of no concern to you." Jovan unwound the gown and as she dressed, added, "What is with you? Who wants you dead?"

"For the record, I didn't turn you away. I placed your impatient little self on hold. 'Tis two entirely different things. How do you know it is not your scrumptious behind they're after?"

Jovan's eye flinched once, twice, then turned into a rapid blinking-eye-watering-free-for-all she couldn't stop. "Damn." He had a point. Maybe someone did want her dead. "Do you have a spare gun, any stakes, a cross or holy water?" She lifted an ireful brow. "I'm not about to stay here like a bleedin' sitting duck."

"Of that, I have no doubts." He'd never met another woman like her. Reaching around his neck, he tugged off his cross and handed it to her. "Put this on and never remove it. I've more weapons in my bag under the bed."

"Really?" She swung the metal in his face. "A cross? Rather intimidating weapon of choice. I will be the most daunting woman in town. 'Ooh, run away, the amnesiac has a cross!'"

"Just put it on. Please?"

"You can have it back after we get this thing." Jovan reached beneath the bed and pulled the heavy black leather trunk to her. Once she unlatched the thick leather buckle and had it open, she glanced at her companion in an entirely new light. An arsenal of armament cluttered the bag. Inside the case hung more crucifixes, two vials of water, each with a crucifix label, holy water perhaps? Two more vials labeled salt, a flask of some liquor, a flint, a bible, guns, silver bullets, wooden stakes, pliers and the worst thing she could've imagined, the pear of anguish, rusted, dinged with teeth marks and caked with dried blood.

"Do I need to know why you carry this much enforcement with you?"

"No," he answered, at a loss. How could he tell her he'd spent the past months searching for a monster that fed from women after raping them? He choked on his anger. He'd tar and feather the bastard that assaulted his Raven. "Never remove the cross. My promise before God, I'll allow no harm to come to you." *It is also my promise I'll marry you someday soon.* First things first, live through the night.

"If you tend to take that vow serious, I'd turn with much ado and pull the trigger."

Did she just read my mind? André swung around and there *it* hid behind the curtains. Only the soft ripple from the breeze outside gave it up.

"Shoot it," Jovan yelled.

André aimed the barrel between two empty eye sockets surrounded by a fortitude of leathery wrinkles. "Cover your ears."

That suggestion came one second too late. Jovan stood on shaky legs; her entire body pulsed with fear. The deafening boom vibrated her very core. Sulfur titrated the room and filled her lungs. Coughing and sneezing followed. The zombie went face first into the floor without one muscle moving to break its fall.

"Insanity!" André set his gun on the mattress and tugged his fingers through his hair. "In the name of all things petite and mouthy!"

With a questioning glance Jovan asked, "Excuse me?"

"My aunt. We make up all sorts of things to call her related to her size instead of saying, 'In the name of the queen'. That gets old." A moment later, he noticed a second *it* with a ridiculously long dagger coming straight toward him. Most people, he mused, in this situation see their life flash before their eyes.

Not him.

André became upset because *it* number two had a bigger blade. His self-esteem hit an all-time low.

"The book. Give me the book." A clawed bloodied hand reached toward Jovan.

André glanced at Jovan. "I didn't know they could read. Did you?" He waited for Jovan to answer.

She shook her head no. "It wants poetry? You've got to be kidding. This is a circus act."

It, for lack of proper euphemisms on André's behalf, slashed the knife at him.

"Duck!" Jovan shouted.

Swift thuds soared past him. André arched his back and snapped his neck and head back to get out of the range. He watched in awe as Jovan maneuvered a silver-tipped wooden stake launcher with as good as accuracy as he had. "How the hell did you learn to shoot like that?"

Jovan shrugged her shoulders wearing a coy smirk. "Amnesia. We'll be needing another room, won't we?"

"Go tell the concierge we've had another incident, and I'll pack these two up. Wait for me in the lobby."

Once Jovan had the nighty on, André crossed to her as she opened the door. He pushed the door closed, placing her against the hard wood, one hand on each side of her head while he lost himself in her husky-blue eyes. "You did good just then," he told her. "You, in all likelihood, saved my sorry life. Thank you."

This close to her he could no longer deny himself the pleasures this woman repeatedly offered. He bent to kiss her cheek, but she turned into his mouth.

"Your aim is so far off." She giggled before she kissed him again.

With the lightest brush of her lips against his, liquid fire ignited his veins and poured through his mouth into hers. His kiss devoured her. Passion, primal and fierce ignited in his groin and spread. Her lips quivered beneath his. Little guttural pleas of, "Please don't stop," came through chattering teeth. For a moment there, those might have been his words. No longer sure, so consumed by this woman, he didn't care just as long her lips were attached to some part of his body for the rest of his life. He squashed her against the door, his hips hugging her, ready to knock her up in more ways than one.

****

Pinned between a rock and a hard place and oh-so happy to be there, Jovan couldn't decide which was harder, the door or the mammoth bulge beneath his trousers jammed hot and solid against her tummy. The door she could have cared less about. As he pressed that solid shaft into her, Jovan heard groans and fast realized she was the one making the noise. She couldn't control it, and she didn't want to. Past or no past, her future stood in front of her. And what a beautiful picture he presented. She knew it deep in her heart. This crazy man that attracted creatures nightmares were born of mingled with her soul. A little soberer now, she realized the man had truly been a gentleman, saving her, trying so very hard not to sully her reputation while she on the other hand came off as the randiest tart in town. She cracked up laughing beneath his kiss.

André broke away from her, a puzzled look across his mug. "Must you always laugh when I kiss you?"

"Um-hum." Jovan crooked her finger back to her mouth. Just as André bent to kiss her, the door rattled and shoved inward knocking Jovan's head. She saw stars. "Damn."

"My sentiments exactly, Cherié." André caught the limp woman and brought her back to the bed. "I dare you to come in."

Seeing a pretty lady unconscious, and two clumps of putrefied flesh on the floor, the bellhop bolted for fresh air in the hall. With his back to André he asked, "We heard shots and screaming. She's not dead too, is she? Are either of you injured?"

Did André need to point out the obvious? "Could

you get these out of here?"

The boy tossed André an iron key. "Room six. It's the honeymoon suite."

With an altered state of despair with regards to his nonexistent erection, he muttered, "Thanks for naught."

Chapter Seven

Musical melodies of timed snorts and grunts filtered into Jovan's dreams transitioning her from a sultry slumber to a real-life daydream. She stretched. Wiggled her fingers and latched onto something with a weighty substance. With a subtle pat down, Jovan found two sacs with wiry hairs harden beneath her grip. One eye popped open.

Further inspection seemed imminent. Her fingers crept back up to the solid shaft, and she gave a little squeeze. A slight jerk and moan followed. Someone shared her bed. The only odd thing about her predicament seemed she had no idea how she ended up at this juncture. Being pinned against the door and having a tongue probe her tonsils had been her last delightful memory. These blackouts had to stop. Albeit, each time she came to she found herself in a bed, a different one, but always beside the same man, no make that a dashing, devilishly, beautiful naked man.

Naked? I better not have missed anything!

André rolled over on his side away from her in his hard as rocks muscular birthday suit. Without moving another muscle, she tried to peek at the rest of his scrumptious body. Her breath picked up. Her heart raced, and between her thighs smoldered a fiery inferno in need of a good hosing to dowse the flames. It was only natural she decided. Someone would have to be dead to not react to this much sinew and his bum? By the goddess she wanted to run her hands over his smooth, firm skin and possibly slip her fingers between his thighs and fondle those little-ah-not so little balls of his again. Right here and now Jovan prayed she didn't have a husband because she could get used to waking beside this one, or atop of him—or better yet flattened beneath him! The position didn't matter… eventually they'd try them all out.

She glanced to his angelic face. He slept like the dead. She envied him. She woke to a feather falling on moss. Moss. Her gaze shot to her green thumb. *What in 'ell's wrong with me?*

****

Sound asleep until someone's delicate fingers choked his cock, André woke up with a single thought. *Torture.* This, simply put, was a divine intervention gone awry. Every single time he and this beautiful woman even thought about consummating their relationship someone or something dropped in uninvited and put the royal kibosh on it. Not today.

André lay very amused by the antics of his woman. When she went to touch him a second time, he jerked. "Good morning, Cherié. I see someone's awakened with a wee bit of inquisitiveness. Don't start anything with that you don't intend to finish." With a slight roll he shifted her way and lifted his arms in the air. He stretched then brushed a tangle of unruly curls from his face.

"Pardon, dear man? Finishing you off is something I look forward to."

"I know you meant something completely different

when you said that, but it came out cynical."

Her face quizzical she said, "Pardon," again. Louder.

"You didn't mean what you said you did, did you? Off me?"

"You want me off you?" Jovan gave a fake pout. "I've not had the opportunity to get on you."

"Yet." André winked at her.

With her head crooked to the side and her fingers precariously close to his groin, she asked, "What's that?"

With much enthusiasm, André watched as she climbed to an upright position and rested her bum on her calves with her hands folded precisely in front of her blonde cresson coveting her world. Damn! So much beauty to take in and all he could focus on was the impish smirk her luscious lips held. Maybe her next move would be atop him? This morning couldn't get much better from his vantage. Her golden locks tussled in morning disarray, her cheeks rosy red, either from her disconcert or just waking he didn't know, but he did know there wasn't another woman in his lifetime he'd ever desire to wake beside. Or on top of or under. Just as long as they were together.

"Cherié?" André waited for her to show a sign she only jested about his manhood. None came. "Please tell me you are aware of the differences between kings and queens." He gave his penis a little jiggle. "Looks like someone's waking up."

Jovan backed up laughing. "You could poke an eye out with that. Milord, I am most aware of the differences between said kings and queens. You've more than proven your point! For your information I was referring to that!" Jovan marched her fingers across his hip purposefully missing his erection to trace a crescent mark with a little splat of a colored blue mole that resembled a star just to tip of the crest. "Quite the brand."

"Birthmark. Each of my cousins and I have an identical mark. Our royal lineage shows through."

"Something else is showing your lineage up." With his erection gaining in length, Jovan inched back and lost the mattress beneath her.

André sat up and got to his knees then peered over the edge of the bed. He shot his hand out. "Come on, Gracie." Long slender, fingers popped up from the floor. He grabbed her and with a slight tug helped her back on the bed beside him.

"I have to tell you something before you and I— before we—ah—good—goddess—do what I think we're about to do."

"Relax." André whiffed his hand in a circular momentum under nose gesturing for her to breathe. "My dear lady, we won't do anything you aren't ready for. I am more than willing to wait for you."

"No!" Jovan blurted it then immediately covered her mouth. She sounded beyond desperate.

"No, you don't want to go ahead with this?" A sharp jab of disappointment pierced his heart.

"No, not no!" Jovan shook her head and waved her hands frantic. "I don't want to wait another second." She gave up the biggest grin he'd ever seen. Innocence and confidence combined; there was no greater aphrodisiac. His smile matched hers. "Well then, if by the grace of your goddess, you're not married, this would be your first time, and I will make this the most pleasant morning of your life."

"Not hard to do since I only have two days to draw from."

He shook his head and gave her a side view smirk. "Thank you for that. The pressure's been relieved."

"From the looks of that, I'd say the exact opposite." Jovan pointed to a tall, thick pulsing muscle. Their eyes met and neither one said anything for a moment.

Icebreaker time. With his index finger, André poked Jovan in the chest and tipped her backward. "It's now or never. Last chance to exit with my heart."

"I believe I already have your heart. I'm moving on to other body parts now."

"You don't play fair. You go straight after the two most important parts on a male." He straddled her then slid his finger purposefully up the inside of her thigh. He stopped just shy of her mons. The look of surprise on her face mixed with anticipation made him realize how much fun this was going to be. Then he traced the delicate outline of her abdomen and skimmed further to land under her chin. Breath held with her eyes wide open, he tickled her in hopes to elicit a smile instead of listening to the chatter of her teeth. She covered her face. "You have naught to be ashamed of, Cherié. Our relationship is in its infantile stages. We have much exploring and learning of one another to accomplish and what better way with nothing between us to hide behind?"

"I don't want to disappoint you," came out a whisper.

"Impossible."

****

"You say that now." Jovan went to sit up, but somebody had her pinned beneath him. She grunted. He crawled from atop her, and she propped herself up on an elbow facing him. "Our relationship? What do we have other than two people obviously attracted to one another, held up in some random hotel as we attempt to save one another from eerie creatures of the night?" Unable to control the urge to grab his penis again, she threw the sheet over his groin. His manhood distracted her like nothing else ever could. She noticed his delicious smile grow. "You think you're funny? You think I'm embarrassed by your flagrance?" She challenged him.

"Mademoiselle, if I know nothing else of you, I know you are incredibly strong willed and intelligent. You are bold beyond reason and the more time I spend beside you, I realize eternity would not be enough to sate this need I have to see you, to be with you, to lay with you for the remainder of my days."

With only her intuition to go on she closed the gap between them and kissed the tip of his strong, straight nose. Without realizing it, she cupped his cheek, her fingers did a gentle sweep across the welts she imprinted him with the night before. "I'm so sorry. It must have been the...."

André brought her hand to his lips grazing her fingers with a slight kiss. Something low in her gut tightened in a delicious swirl.

"Never apologize. I deserved that. A true gentleman would not have offered his lady liquor. But, in my own defense, I didn't turn you away last night. I would never. Had we not been interrupted, we'd be having an entirely different conversation right now. It's not too late." His grin widened.

Those eyes glimmered. The lips were an invitation to paradise. The corded muscles protecting his masculine frame begged her fingers to knead, relieve the tension and explore. Simply put, he was beautiful. A loud gurgle rose from her stomach, which they both looked at. "Breakfast before dessert?" For as much as she wanted to find out what it felt like to have this man ravish her dreams, the more rational part of her brain sent a message she wasn't quite as ready as she thought. "I appear to be famished. I thought I wasn't supposed to sleep last night."

André began to climb off her. "Come. We'll dress, go to the boutique, have tea, and go for a ride. You snored like the devil all night. How are you now?"

Insulted, Jovan scoffed, "I did no such thing."

"Trust me, you did. Do you see bags under me eyes?" He pointed to his lower eyelids.

Her belly roared again. "I did not do that," she emphasized one more time. "And those bags were there when we met."

Chest puffed out, one shoulder back, André defended, "They were not."

Chin jut out and head bobbing, she finished with, "Where too," in a snooty tone.

****

Inside the boutique, the extravagant gowns André picked out showed his taste in women's fashion eloquent, but then she almost forgot his heritage. He grew up accustomed to wealth and beauty surrounding him. Jovan loved each dress and eagerly tried them on. The reflections in the looking glass suited her. For a moment, she felt like a princess.

When Jovan stepped out of the changing room in a light blue linen gown gathered at the waist with a low-cut scooped neckline showing off a hint of her bosom, André shifted uncomfortably in his chair. Oh, the things this woman did to his body from afar! With her by his side, his life would be completely uncomfortable in a tantalizing way. Ready to pay the storeowner, toss the ravishing enchantress over his shoulder and high-tail it back to the bogyman-infested hotel, André did a double take at the woman working. "We meet again. Yesterday on the train, you had the two babies."

"Aye, Sir. My apologies for my daughter's untimely toiletries." The woman glanced to Jovan. "I can see why you were in such a hurry to get off the train, Sir. She's a beaut, she is."

André smiled. "That she is. Where are your little ones?"

"This is my sister's shop. I'm filling her shoes til she returns. My two are with me niece. Me sister, she's turned up missing. I can't believe she'd just up and leave. She's a family, a husband, maybe not the best, but he provides a roof over her head. I'm sorry for haranguing you with me personal problems yet again. You sit tight a little while longer, Sir. I'll go do your lady's hair for her and then you can be on your way. She's one more dress to try on."

The woman scooted out from behind the counter and disappeared into Jovan's changing room.

With time to kill, André snooped through the racks of clothing, sniffed a few bottles of perfume, sneezed, and found one intricate bottle that intrigued him. Eden's Black Rose. Had a soft musky rose scent that delighted his senses. The ornate bottle looked like something the queen would own. Ruby colored stones and crystals embellished the pink, crackled glass. He set the bottle on the counter with his other items to purchase. Then he placed a tiara with sparkling gemstones atop his head. "You're a royal loon, Ands," he told the berk looking back at him from the mirror with a stupid grin.

Outside the shop, a man's distraught cries drew him to the door, jeweled headpiece and all. In the middle of the street, a man begged, one step short of harassing people if anyone had seen a woman, a blonde woman who'd been missing. André glanced over his shoulder for the Grimm Reaper, certain his time had come. This strange man couldn't want Cherié. It had to be another woman, possibly the owner of this shop?

What to do? Ethics! Moral dilemmas were a pain in the bum. About to do the right thing and go out into the street and shoot the man dead, André stopped. Maybe that wasn't the best choice, but dammit, it worked to his vantage. His lady couldn't love this ruffian. Of course, André understood he'd probably been out all night searching for her and this was why his current appearance begged for attention. André would have. He'd never let her out of his sights. Pondering his choices, kill the man now or later, angelic notes of her voice floated through the shop and tried to lure him from the door. He wouldn't give her up. He turned and glanced out into the road, torn. The stranger, now on his hands and knees sobbed mercilessly. He latched onto another sod's ankle only to be dragged down the street with the man trying to shake him off as if he were a mangy mutt humping him. It became more than obvious the gent's mental capacities were compromised. It would be in his best interest to save his Cherié from this madman. He turned the knob on the handle.

"Milord?"

"Cherié, I will be back in one moment's time." The door opened and closed with André now on the opposite side, guilt and fear sparring. He followed the gent down the roadway. When he got close enough, he noticed the man's shirt stained reddish-brown. His beard too dripped with congealed fluids. He reeked of bowel and blood. The man's appearance as he looked up at André, shocked him. Glazed red eyes, lost, begged for resolve.

"Have you seen her? My wife?" His voice sounded raw, scratchy.

André jumped from the sidewalk and met the man. "Sir, you don't look well. Allow us to help you."

"Get him off me," the other man yelled while he tried to pry the crazed man's hands from his leg. André extended his hand, but the man shooed him away and yelled, "I want my wife, Joanne. Have you seen her? Please somebody help me find her!" The man crawled further down the road screaming her name, "Joanne!"

Words tumbled from his lips. "I know of a woman who has amnesia." André's heart couldn't take any more. The anguish he felt for this poor slob trumped his fear that his Cherié belonged with this insane being. He couldn't take finding out the past two days had been naught more than a cruel hoax on his heart, but he wouldn't live an ignorant life either. And then it happened. Jovan opened the door and stepped out. "André? Is he all right?"

A lifetime of silence passed as the man looked her

over. André blurted, "Is she your wife? Answer me man!"

"Uh no." The man stood and stumbled down the road.

"Is he going to be all right," Jovan asked again.

"I don't think so. I have a really bad feeling he did something he's going to live to regret. Come, my lady. I want you off this street."

Jovan watched André settle back into his skin so to speak. His nerves were razzed. She touched his chin and brought his gaze to hers. "You thought he was my husband."

Too wound up to say a word, André nodded.

Jovan did the same hand gestures André used on her earlier whiffing air under his nose. She winked. "Breathe, foolish man. Nothing about him sparked recognition. Now you, on the other hand keep sending scorching flames along me flesh. What do you think, my dark knight?" Jovan spun around in a charcoal grey silk dress with a navy-blue sash. "I shall need help getting out of it."

Insane man on the loose? André forgot all about him. The front of the dress had ruffles going down one side of the skirt with a giant navy rosebud gathering the material mid-thigh. He'd ruffle her backside when they returned to their room. The front of the dress had a deep V cutout with an ivory lace yoke sewn in giving him a slight glimpse of Jovan's décolletage. This would be the dress he brought her to meet his aunt in.

"Dinner tonight in that one. You are stunning! Now find something appropriate for brunch. I'm famished as well. Shopping is tedious." André directed her back toward the changing room. Four outfits later, he handed the woman a small fortune for Jovan's purchases.

"I'll be back in a dash," the clerk added as she disappeared to the changing room again.

"Ah—"Jovan pointed to his hair"—are you purchasing that as well? What was that whole spiel you gave me on kings and queens this morn?" She waltzed him to a mirror and whispered, "Your head is much too large for that," as she pointed at the little jeweled headpiece. In a playful tone she asked, "Do you have secret fetish, Milord?"

In a blur, André crushed Jovan against him, his arms tight around her waist and without sensor he leaned in and kissed her neck. This close he whispered, "Many secrets and fetishes, Mademoiselle. Many. All for your ears alone."

The store clerk returned and tapped Jovan's shoulder. "Miss?"

Jovan knew her cheeks flushed. How could they not being so close to the man of her dreams? She gave up a shy grin.

The woman handed her a spool of thread and a few darning needles. "In case you need any mending. The thread's a hard color to match on the grey silk dress. Tough as nails too."

André offered, "Your sister's name wasn't Joanne was it?" The woman shook her head no. "God speed on your sister's return and thank you," as he closed the door behind him.

Chapter Eight

As they stood in the hotel's restaurant waiting to be seated, André noticed every patron lift an envious eye to his lady. And how could they not? She carried herself with more grace than anyone in his aunt's court.

The two-piece outfit she'd finally decided on did her justice. Her black silk and satin blouse had a scooped neck with silvery-black beaded ruffles that bounced ever so lightly as her breasts stay tucked into her lace corset and pushed up and peeked out, and for that reason alone André always admired the uplifting device. The garment gathered at her waist in an accordion fashion and closed with hooks and eyes. The three-quarter sleeves also held intricate beadwork and ruffles. Her dusty-rose, silk skirt cinched her tiny waist with a black satin sash and hugged her the way André wanted to, up close and personal. He actually envied the material as it slid across her every curve. Once seated he watched her as she swung her feet out from the chair, eyeing her boots with a smile each time she glanced down.

"Foot fetish, Cherié?" André did the most inappropriate thing he'd done since he'd met her. He knelt on one knee and lifted her skirt revealing her calf in public! He demanded her attention as his fingers inched their way up her leg and tickled the back of her knee. His lady turned flaming red. Truth be known, he worried whether it was due to embarrassment or anger. Behind him all sorts of snorts, murmurs and gasps filled the room. He continued, uncaring of anyone other than the lady in front of him. "I too have the same one. Only 'tis your feet I fancy and other parts of your heavenly body as well." With a subtle whisk of his hand he brushed a delicate caress where the other women watching could only imagine what it felt like to have the attentions of one of the most sought after eligible royals lavishing pure desire over one spitfire of a goddess.

Handheld fans from women seated at other tables went into full motion.

Jovan wiggled to smooth her skirt back over her toes. A nonchalant glance showed men with their heads cocked at different angles to get a better glimpse of her.

"Dear lord man, have you lost your wits? What are you up too?" She gave him the full weight of her stare. "Don't answer that."

"Cherié, marry me." André rested his lips across her free hand.

The delicate little teacup Jovan held in her opposite hand slipped from her grasp and shattered across the floor. She jumped. "But—"

"I know—I know it's ridiculously fast, but I've never felt this way in my life. Destiny has united us. We are meant to be together. There are so many things clogging my mind when I look at you, I can't think straight."

Jovan's face contorted, lips twisted, and nose scrunched, she bent to him and whispered, "Then how do you know you should ask me such an important question?"

"That beautiful face."

Jovan's brow arched. She quipped, "I'm not buying it."

"Fine then. Because of this." André pounded on his chest. "It hurts when I look at you."

Jovan threw her hands in the air. "I give you heart ache?"

André nodded. "And then some! To this day my life is so on the straight and narrow that I could recite to you verbatim my schedule of teas, bowel movements, polo matches, horse races—oh, I race horses just in case you wondered. I have nothing in my life. No one to share my tea or afternoon naps with or a long walk around my manor in the evenings…" His voice trailed off. "Or my bed!" He leaned across her lap, only inches from her face. "You want personal? I'm a virgin too."

Jovan burst out laughing. "Liar."

"I swear. I've never consummated a relationship in the biblical sense. There has been—"

****

"Enough!" Jovan cut him off. "Please excuse me? Powder room calls." She tamped her tone down a bit. Truth be known she had no desire to hear of other conquests or romps between the sheets with any other women. Once in the ladies room, she inhaled and released slowly, in hopes to calm her nerves. By the Goddess, he told the truth again. It gnawed at her that she knew this yet she didn't know how she came to this conclusion. And there it was again, that annoying little fly in her drawers she couldn't quite swat away. What would it take to relieve her of the unknown she'd left behind. And for the love of god, why hadn't anyone come searching for her? Was she a scoundrel? A woman no man wanted, well with the one exception of the beautiful gentleman that only moments ago proposed marriage to her?

After a few minutes of staring blankly into the mirror and getting caught by one of the wait staff, Jovan made her way back to the table and before she even realized what she'd done, she flashed her ring finger to him. "Where is my bauble that promises you to me?" *Oh dear lord! I just answered him!*

André scratched his head. "Hadn't quite thought this whole scenario through." He lifted a finger to her. "One moment." In a flash he dashed to the front desk.

Of all the things he could have come back carrying, a cigar was not what Jovan would've guessed. He was busy peeling the band from the outside of the dark, oily, Sumatra wrapper. Jovan opened her mouth to launch a major objection, "No—"

He stopped her in her tracks by popping the bulky tube into her mouth. He leaned into the crook of her neck and whispered, "Suck on this for practice," and grabbed her left hand. He slid the flexible metal band around her finger and squashed the edges together to hold it in place. Back down on his knee he asked, "Marry me, Cherié?"

Jovan spit the fetid stogy back at him, with a shocked dropped jaw. "You know where you can stick this? You are loony. If it's true that you're related to the queen, then how is it I only rate a cigar wrapper for a promissory ring?"

"Temporary, dearest."

Jovan looked at the clump of flimsy metal hugging her finger and then she looked at André. She loved it.

She'd never seen anything more romantic.

Jovan flashed the cigar band under his nose. "This is the finest bauble a woman could ever own."

"Nothing but the best for my lady." André's heart thudded when Jovan smiled. This woman was going to turn his life inside out. "So, is that a yes?"

"Let me sleep on it. I don't want to give you false hope. I'm not saying no, but I'd love one more day to see if my memory returns. I do not want to break your heart."

You just did. He stood, straightened his pants, and gulped his disappointed pride down. He needed her to throw herself on him, to confess her dying love for him and forsake the rest of the world as he had. It didn't happen. She kept her innermost thoughts coveted. He'd never said, *I love you*, to another woman. Never. This did not go well at all. He'd never proposed before. He'd been proposed to just recently and said a flat out, "Hell no!" This marriage proposal went about as well as the one he turned down. That union would have spawned evil. "I can wait one more day," came out as enthusiastically as a child dragging his feet to the dentist once he saw the doctor a little too eager with pliers in one hand, and a gigantic needle in the other hand. "Would you care to go for a ride after we eat? Look at the countryside? Possibly you'll see something that rings a bell." He sat and feigned a smile.

"Rings a bell?" For a second time the words rolled from her lips. "I live close to a church. I recall hearing bells and oddly enough fantasizing they rang for my wedding." She glanced at her new ring and smiled. "Hmm…" With the waiter's approach Jovan scooped up her utensils ready to dig in. Once her steaming plate of pancakes dripping in butter, strawberries, and cream were in front of her, she did just that.

"Is there anything else I can get you, Miss?" The waiter asked, his cheeks pink, his gaze melting over her better than the toppings on her pancakes. "Anything at all? You name it. I'm yours. I mean it's yours," he quickly corrected.

Embarrassed Jovan answered, "No, truly, thank you. We're all set."

"Anything. Don't hesitate to wave that delicate green thumb, and I'll be right over."

Ready to stand and toss the man outside, instead André controlled his emotions and tapped the waiter's back. His voice carrying, he said, "My lady said she's all set. Thank you. Run off now."

The man didn't acknowledge André, instead he whispered, "Anything!"

Jovan cocked her head to one side and with a shrug of her shoulders smiled innocently. "I do not understand all the attention I receive."

"If you saw yourself through my eyes you would. You make a man dare to dream." André blew her a kiss then dug into his breakfast of a mixed grill of sausages, kippers, eggs, and crumpets. If he couldn't fill the hole in his heart, he'd fill his belly.

"I have a sweet tooth, it seems." She stabbed at her last piece of cake and popped it in her mouth. "My favorite."

"Until you try something new tomorrow. Then that'll be your favorite."

"True." Jovan giggled. "So, what do we do now?" Jovan set her fork down, dabbed at the corners of her lips with her napkin, dropped it beside the plate, and then held her hand to him.

"We find your previous existence so we may begin ours as soon as possible." André wrapped his fingers around her hand and escorted her out of the restaurant. "I saw a stable nearby were we can get some horses. Shall we? I had the hotel pack us some wine and cheese just in case we work up an appetite."

Jovan wiggled out from under the wall of muscles. Her fingers marched their way up his chest only to linger on a button. "Yes," she answered in a slow drawl, "I do suppose riding a horse could work up hunger." Her eyes were drawn to his mouth. Those lips of his were as wicked as chocolate was decadent.

André squared his shoulders and puffed out his chest. "Not just a horse, Cherié, a stallion. The Queen's finest." His one eyebrow went up as a devilish glint to his eye lit up.

Jovan pat her mouth through a wide drawn out yawn. "Are all royals as full of themselves as you?"

She watched him putter with his five o'clock shadow before he spoke. There were other things on him she would like to putter with as well. Stripped of his clothing, she was beyond certain she'd find at least one or two things on his person she could amuse herself with.

"Lucian is worse by far."

Jovan tried to hide her interest. "Doubt it—highly."

André reached down to her backside and with a little oomph behind it, pat her bottom. "Never doubt me, woman."

Together, hand in hand they strolled to the stables and both saddled the horses lent them. André studied her ability to work with horses and mentioned, "You have done this many times before. You handle horses as if it is second nature."

"You're right. Maybe we should visit some farms. Especially since I seem to be one with nature." She threw up that green thumb the waiter had made mention of.

"Do you need a hand—" André stopped mid question when he witnessed Jovan reach up and grab the horn to the saddle in one hand, bunch that eloquent dress up around her thighs, swing her leg over the animal and mount the horse.

"It appears not." Jovan smirked. "Let's ride. If I can't have you beneath me then this stud will have to do."

André's jaw dropped. "I love you."

Jovan burst into laughter. "All it takes is a little innuendo of naughty thoughts spoken aloud to bring men to their knees?"

"Let's not forget an insane blonde with no inhibitions."

Straight-faced Jovan declared, "I'm probably a Vicar's daughter."

André choked. "I'm not feeling it."

"No, but I am." Jovan slid her hips back and forth in the saddle and gave him a look of smoldering passion. She tossed her head back and shook out her curls. "Oh, this feels naughty."

"Stop," He begged. "You shall be the death of me."

"Well if I can't have you…"

"Patience my lady. I'm worth the frustration." He reached over and grabbed her hand placing a kiss in the center of her palm.

The first farm they approached had a yard full of

screaming children in muddy clothing chasing a peacock, its tail feathers brilliant shades of blues and purples and adding not an ounce of camouflage to save the bird as it ran for its life. The bird's cry made her cringe. She and André never even dismounted. Rode right on by. The second home André made the distinct mistake of asking a young lad, "Do you recognize her? Do you know her name?"

The boy laughed. "Don't you? Foolish imbecile. She's with you." He slammed the door in their faces. André lifted a defiant chin. "Oh, like I've never been called that before."

"That went well," Jovan muttered. "I've this next home." Jovan slid off her horse, rubbed under her eyes, gave her cheeks a slight pinch and approached the small thatched cottage. A man roughly the same age as she and André answered the door. She smiled. The man reciprocated. He was handsome. Shorter than her, but then she was tall for a woman. Blonde hair and inquisitive dark brown eyes waited for her to speak. "I'm new to the area," she explained, "I had a slight accident and lost my memory. Just wondering if you know me?"

"No but I'd love to get too. Ta!" The guy waved to André and snagged Jovan by the waist. "You're a gem mate," he yelled as the door slammed shut.

One second Jovan stood outside, the next inside some lunatic's home, with André breaking down the door to get her.

"That went even better." A little ruffled, Jovan got back on her horse and didn't know whether to laugh or cry. They'd spent the day in the outlying area of the village within an earshot of the church's bells. Nothing.

No one knew her although there was that one offer to get acquainted…

Headed back to the hotel there was one last home on the lane. It was pretty enough. Flowers abounding even though spring had only just arrived. André went to the door and knocked while Jovan gathered some hay and fed her horse. With his nose to the window, André saw a broken clock on the floor. No one answered the door. The clock disturbed him. Someone left in a huff. The hairs on the back of his neck prickled. Uncomfortable in their current surroundings André yelled, "Sorry love. No one's home. Let's scoot. This was fun. We should do it again tomorrow."

From the corner of her eye Jovan smirked. "We'll hit all the same homes and use you as bait."

"I think the one bloke with his pig in his parlor fancied me as it were."

"I think he fancied his poor pig more… Can we head back to the hotel? I'm knackered."

"Whatever my lady wants."

"You say that now."

The horses safely back at the stables, André swept Jovan from her feet as they crossed into their room. Beside the bed he tossed her onto the mattress and had to laugh at the look she shot him back. "What?" he sheepishly asked. Hearing footsteps coming down the hallway André stuck his head out and flagged the bellhop.

"Lord St. James, good evening. What can we do for you at this late hour?"

"A bottle of your finest champagne, a steak—rare, and some chips for two? Oh, and chocolates and fresh flowers? Is all well?"

"Just dandy, Sire. Your meal will be a bit. There seems to be a ruckus in the street. We're just making certain it doesn't creep in here."

One glance at his lady and he forgot all about the troubles of the world. "Ta!" He shut the door.

Jovan snapped her fingers in his direction. "Is this your plan? Just throw me on this bed, strip me of my cover and have your way with me?"

"Unless you have a better idea, yes." With the slow prowess of a cat, he slinked his way up the bed and draped his body over hers. Debating on where to begin, he plotted his map to cover every delectable destination her feminine form offered. From the center of her cleavage to her chin he ran a finger in a playful zigzag pattern then tilted her head to meet his gaze. "May I?"

"Oh, so now you ask!" Jovan rose to meet him. She was met with an instant palm to her forehead with a slight shove back on the pillow to halter her advance.

Goose bumps rose to the occasion where his fingers skimmed her collarbone and trailed down her arm.

With a slow deliberate shift, he hovered above her breasts. Hot breaths steamed her dress and gave rise to two delectable points of interest that needed further investigation. He never released her gaze as he lowered his lips and nibbled through the material. Her little whimpers excited him to yet another level. Anticipation. His pants suddenly felt two sizes too small. When done, lip imprints rested upon the material of her top. "You doing all right, Misses?"

"Yup, but, André, I can't breathe."

"Want me to slow down? Am I going to fast?"

"No, you're perfect, but I can't get a breath in. It's

this corset. I'm lightheaded."

"You certain that's not my doing?"

Jovan tapped him on the side of his head. "Get me out of this?"

"As you wish." André got down on one knee. Never did he lose sight of Jovan's curious gaze. "Sit, Bebé." Jovan sat at the edge of the mattress. Hands on the hem of her skirt he tossed the layers of material up in her lap, unlaced her magenta boots, and removed them. Then his fingers took a small uphill excursion to her thigh until he reached the top of her stockings. He unraveled the red velvet ties that kept them in place. "We can use these later." A playful brow shifted in her direction.

Jovan fanned her face with her hand. "Getting a wee toasty in here."

Thumbs and forefingers busy, he rolled the silk hose down and slid each one from her feet.

"André?"

"Working as fast as possible." André stood and held his hands to her. "Stand and face the bed. I'll undo all the thingamajigs on this dress. It is rather warm in here."

Jovan added, "I know the feeling," under her breath.

"What's that you say? You feel like squealing? We can accomplish that." Hearing Jovan's laughter brought a smile to his lips.

"I'll be blue by the time you get this off me." She faked a gasp.

"Makes two of us." With a wiggle here and a tug or two there, the dress fell to her ankles. He raised an arm in the air in triumph until he noticed the corset held a little monkey's knot. "The woman at the boutique has a morose sense of humor. I can't undo this."

"Cut it off," came out in desperation.

With a nod of agreement, André reached for his knife. A few little sawing motions later, the corset's binding parted, and Jovan sucked in large gulps of air.

Once free of the bony device, he ran his hands over the curve of her back and hips. He hooked his thumbs under the edges of her lacey drawers and slid them down to the floor. Her bottom. Her skin held no dimples or stretch marks. Her cheeks were small. Firm. Her legs were just as his dream revealed. Long, slender.

His.

Jovan turned around. "You done ogling?"

"No." Not a hint of guilt on his face.

"Join me." Jovan grabbed his hand and whisked him toward the bed. "Lay down."

"Thank you, God," he whispered.

"That's goddess to you, if you've not noticed."

"Trust me, I noticed."

Jovan straightened her stance, brushed her hair back to allow him full view of her offering.

Gaze devouring, André followed every ravenous, curvaceous inch of her beauty. A long neckline made for kissing. Shoulders—strong enough to carry the weight of the world, not that she would ever have to. He would do it for her.

Her breasts piqued his interests. Round, rosy and ready for his ministrations. Her flat tummy showed no markings of ever having carried a child. Those gams of hers most definitely belonged draped over each of his shoulders so he could explore the patch of soft blonde curls, which coveted her world. What would she think if he were to dip his head between her thighs to taste her?

He fought the urges. Didn't want to give the woman a fright. Didn't want to come off as some dastardly rogue whose only interest was in pleasuring himself. When she squat in front of him the world as he knew it vanished. He caught a glimpse of her womanhood and went from a man teetering on the edge of abandonment to watching the end of the rope fray before his bulging eyes or was that something else? His manhood couldn't get any harder. Had never been this solid. Engorged. Fully. Worried even him.

She unlaced one of his boots. With a bit of a tug her body fell backwards, but his boot came off. Balance regained she discarded the second boot. "Up and at 'em." She motioned for him to stand.

"Pretty certain this has been accomplished." With both index fingers he circled in and pointed to his pants with a huge wolfish grin.

Jovan stepped back. Her lips formed a small 'O'. Went to speak, but instead bit her bottom lip. "I think you need to cool off more than I do. You're so—so…" Her voice trailed off.

"Hot?" With a little off beat dance, André drew his shirt over his head. He danced around her, his arms spread in front of him, his shoulders shifting back and forth, his fingers making jesters for her to come hither. He spun in a few circles, shook his butt, flaunted it in her face, and flexed his muscles while his eyes were closed. Yes, he was laughing and so was Jovan.

She'd never seen anything like it. The way the fool moved. He had a unique way of expressing himself. Not anticipating an abrupt halt, she bumped into him when he stopped. Arms automatically wrapped around his waist to steady herself and what the heck she decided—as long as she had him, she held him close to her. Without thinking twice, she leaned in and placed a soft kiss on his chest. Her fingers explored, wiggled through the black silky curls across his chest and landed on hard nipples.

This close to him she inhaled. He reminded her of a fall day walking through the woods, musky, invigorating. Jovan rested her hands on his trousers and with painstaking precision unbuttoned them. She slid her hands under the band and worked her way under and around to the back. She went further down and allowed her fingers to knead his muscles. How something could be so firm and supple at the same time left her puzzled, but she loved the way he felt and when she tugged him closer, she felt something else both firm and soft. A growing need, tantalizing and annoying at the same time, tugged her inner core. She wanted him inside her, deep, awakening her proper. From a sultry glance she tilted her head and puckered up.

André closed the distance. He met her lips hard and fast, kissed her as if it would have to last her a lifetime. With a slight shove, down the pants dropped into a heap around his ankles. He kicked them aside.

He mirrored her actions. Hands tight on her cheeks, André grabbed her derriere and pressed his solid mass into her.

If she ever got her lips near his shaft she'd be happier than the Queen's jester. In all likelihood though, she might not be able to articulate her words as well as the cynical little clown. She'd be busy with a magic trick or two of her own keeping the robust heir to the throne entertained, making his juicy erection disappear, swallowing it with more skill than one of those nincompoops who choked down flaming swords for attention. Although, this one appeared ready for battle.

Jovan released him and did her own little dance for his gleaming blackish-blue eyes. She clasped her hands in front of him and raised her arms and swayed her hips side to side. She waltzed around him, getting a bird's eye view of pure perfection. With a deliberate approach she pressed her body into his back and wrapped her arms around his waist. She lowered her hand to feel his bottom, but he turned at precisely the wrong moment, or… possibly his timing couldn't have been better, Jovan ended up with a shaft in the palm of her hand. Hot. Thick. Long. Solid. "Whoa!"

"Hello, Bebé." André gave her the weight of his full-blown grin. "I am but putty in your hands."

"I'd say right now you're more like solid clay."

"Play with it. See what you can mold." That damned smirk on his face melted her. He leaned in. She closed her eyes, parted her mouth slightly awaiting those plump lips to meet hers. He kissed her nose. Yes, she felt a wee bit foolish.

"All in due time. If I were to engage in one on one right now, this would end here on the floor."

"Thought that's what we were doing? One on one."

"Soon enough there shall be one entangled mass of orgasmic fun."

Jovan knew without a doubt her cheeks went three different shades red. It was one thing to act out and engage in the art of lovemaking. It was another thing to speak of it.

She fanned her throat with her free hand because she'd be damned before she let go of his penis.

Her fingers tightened. His shaft pulsed with life. His eyelids fluttered, and his body jerked once. Was it a silent sneeze or a hiccup? She had to be certain. She gripped a little harder. His chest heaved and fell. The top teeth crushed the bottom lip. Tossed his head back and shook his curls. Grunted some primitive guttural plea.

Interesting. What would he sound like as he made love to her?

Before she could further instigate, her body had been whisked from the floor, flipped upside down and draped over his shoulder, headed back to the bed.

"Bottom's up!" André tightened his arms around her and placed one hand firmly across her bum. Gave it a little pat.

"Do that again?"

André laughed, but who was he to deny her any wishes?

In the meantime, she grabbed his backside. For balance of course. If that wasn't the lamest line she'd ever conjured up. If she had her blasted memory back, she was positive she could've topped it.

"Need I remind you, I've been upside down quite enough lately?"

Lost in a whirlwind, she found her body being hurled through the air like a cricket ball, tossed on the bed. Bounced once. The momentum and inertia kicked in, and she flew off the opposite side of the bed. Landed flat on her back beside the armoire.

Arms, legs and a supple heart-shaped buttock flashed before his eyes and then disappeared.

Cautiously, he leaned on the mattress and looked over. Two very surprised blue eyes glared in his direction. "I'm so sorry. That went in a different direction from what I envisioned."

"Well, I went in a few. Pick one." Her hand shot up like a white flag for help. He jumped over the bed and squat beside her only to find Jovan hysterical, tears streaming down her cheeks. "I promise no more mishaps. I'm beginning to think you and I are destined to live a life of chastity."

Jovan swat his arm. "Bite your tongue. All right, me bum is starting to throb."

"Say no more. Allow me the pleasure to kiss your…" André hesitated.

"Arse. Yes, you are one and yes, you will kiss mine. Daily." Jovan pointed to her aching bum.

"Did you just read my mind?"

Jovan nodded. "Of course."

"Holy shite."

"Not!" Laughing she answered, "Read minds? Ya daft twit, I can't read minds any more than you can hit a target but humor me some more and try to figure out what's going on in me head now." Blunt and to the point Jovan tapped her finger to her sore, slightly red bottom again. Puckered her lips up and made little kiss-kiss sounds. When the only reaction she received came as a blank stare, she made a sad pouty face.

André chuckled. "I pray you don't partake in the arts or theatre." He stood and dragged her with him. "Bebé, if you please." With a gentle sweep of his hand he gestured for her to lie on the bed.

Jovan wasted no time, no more playing hard to get, not that she ever did. On her side, propped up on an elbow, her hair back, she, hoped she resembled Lady Godiva.

"You are as sinful in appearance as chocolate is to the tongue. Yes, I too, have a sweet tooth. For you." He flipped her onto her tummy and began a massage at her feet. He went up one leg stopping just below her bottom. To be there exposed and open to whatever the man wanted excited her in ways she'd never knew possible. Pulsing low in her belly intensified as he repeated his motions with her opposite leg, massaging her toes, her calf muscles, and the back of her thighs.

With the lightest stroke, his fingers brushed her bottom. She took a deep breath and held it. *Here it comes,* she prayed, *he's going to relieve the itch I've had since I first slammed into him at the train depot.* If only he was inside her! What then would he tickle? All the queen's money and all the queen's horses couldn't answer that. But her nephew could!

Tussled black curls outlined the contours of one strong face. He hid a dimple. The little divot only came to light when he smiled. Those full lips. It would always begin and end there for her. For as gorgeous as his eyes were his lips rivaled their splendor. His shoulders were broad. Strong. Covered with a fine mist. The man truly glistened. Muscles played hide and seek in his arms and chest as he moved over her. With each divine stroke he gave one would show itself and another would disappear only to reappear with a change in his position. There was one other muscle she could play hide and seek with. Her glance shifted back to his groin. She licked her lips.

"Stop focusing on me and enjoy this. Turn your head back around. Relax. You're tensing up on me."

"As are you." Jovan snickered as she pulled one leg back and slid her foot between his thighs.

"The term football has new meaning."

Fingers slid under her leg and with a slight tug he spread her legs wider. His hands caressed her outer thighs, her hips and moved to the lower portion of her back. Just a wee lower, she prayed. He skipped her bum. How could he miss it? Truly! It wasn't that small.

"André?" With a shift André straddled Jovan. This was it. The moment she'd been waiting for. He plunked his butt right atop of hers and she could make out exactly where his naughty bits landed on her. This had to be the most erotic position she'd ever been in. If she wiggled a little... If she arched her back and pushed her butt upward a bit... Jovan imploded with laughter. She'd look like some feline in the alleyway in heat begging to end her torture. At this precise time, she understood why the pussies acted out as they did.

Chapter Nine

"Position change. Up!"

"But I liked this position." Regardless, André slid off her and got comfy on his side. Jovan pushed her body up to rest on her elbows and turned his way.

André tucked a stray lock of her hair behind her ear. "Cherié." He whispered her name. "You are a vision."

"Then make certain of your wants and desires, as I am of mine."

"What is it you desire, my lady?"

"Passion that withstands the test of time. Love that holds no boundaries. For you to have that exact look in your eye every time you look at me."

"Deal."

"That's it? Deal?" Jovan shoved at his chest. "What do you desire of me?"

André grinned as he looked at her from beneath heavy lids. "To get you back on your belly. I liked that spot."

Jovan gasped. "And—to board the train tomorrow with you beside me. Did you know you have the eyes of my old husky and her spirit as well, sincere, loving, a wet nose. How is it I found you?"

Jovan punched his arm. "That's what happens when you're not watching where you walk. Some

ravishing bitch walks by and knocks you on your arse."
Jovan snuck in a sheepish wink as she went in search of
the hard object that poked her backside moments past.
She skimmed over the silkiness of his plump head, now
slightly damp. "This is indeed fit for a king."

"And only my queen shall reap its benefits."

Jovan smirked. "Lay back. I owe you a massage."

"How is it that you turned the tables on me? I was
ready to make love to you and now you take the lead."
André braced himself against the headboard.

"Is that what I did? I'm sorry."

Somewhat skeptical he added, "You don't appear
sorry. In the least."

"Nor you, Sire." She swirled her thumb in circles
around the tip of his penis.

He dug his fingers into the covers and held on. She
turned away, ecstatic she could produce such cravings
in him. Even with no memory, she knew she'd never
done this before, yet she knew what he desired without
words.

About to perfect the act of fellacio, she noticed his
anticipation too, came forth. "You seem to have sprung
a leak, Milord."

"Nay, ma beauté, 'tis just me bubbling over with
joy."

"You're more like a volcano, ready to erupt. Now
relax and allow me the pleasure of pleasuring you."

"Didn't I say that earlier? Thieve of words, you
are."

"Shoosh!" Hearing his pleas, "Whoa! What are you
doing? Dear God don't stop." She did as asked.

Another guttural sound hit the air. "Dear lord
woman, you have a gift. Thank you for sharing it with

me."

Jovan let his heated cock slowly slip from her mouth. "Do I?" Jovan couldn't help but smile. "What gift shall you share with me?"

André twisted his fingers into her blonde tresses and gave a gentle tug. "You'll ruin my gift if you keep that up. Trade places with me."

"A gift such as that would last a lifetime."

****

"Cherié, a lifetime with you is not enough. I want eternity." In one bold, hard pressed kiss, André blanketed her body with his. He broke away and kissed her cheek, her eyelids, her nose, her neck—so many places to explore—so little time.

His fingers wandered her satin flesh, took in the few freckles she owned and memorized each and whispered promises with each beauty mark. The soft supple curves of her breasts were a blatant invitation. Unable to hold out he lowered his mouth to her. Her nipple bloomed in his mouth. She groaned just as he had. He continued teasing her as his fingers delved lower. He parted the cresson of curls protecting her private lips. She arched her back and pressed harder into his hand. "You are anxious as well, Cherié." André gripped his shaft, and ran the tip of his cock between her private lips back and forth. Her breath caught in her throat as his rushed out.

"Oh, no more teasing. Do this, André. End this torture. There is an insatiable itch deep inside me."

"Shush, Cherié!" He whispered in her ear, "Trust me, I will end this itch and give you a reoccurring one."

"Nothing contagious."

A light slap on her bum left her in hysterics. With a

gentleness he had to fight to acquire he inched his finger inside her delicate skin and immediately stopped when he hit a barrier. "Ma beauté, I have to tell you something." He explained, "You are indeed new to this. And the next move I make may cause some discomfort."

"How do you know?" Jovan strained to lift her head.

"Trust me, your maidenhead is intact." *No husband!* André fought the urge to get up and shout it to the world. "I'll be as gentle as I can. Forgive me for any discomfort."

"Nothing you could do to me would cause me suffering." In an impatient move, Jovan thrust her hip into André's hand. She hiccupped once, her hips frozen in midair. "I may have spoken with haste." She flopped back down on the bed, his arm clamped more securely than someone in the stocks, between her thighs.

"Silly woman." André kissed her knee as he searched for the one little spot inside her to replace pain with pleasure.

After a short time she confessed, "Oh, this is sinful. I love it!" After another minute passed, she was grasping at air. She caught his chin. "André, please," she begged, "now?"

"You're one hundred percent positive?" He prayed she didn't change her mind because right now, if she said no, his heart might fragment. The rest of his body would survive, but not his heart. With a nudge to the left and then the right, he settled between her thighs. Her twinkling desperate eyes gave him his answer. His heart burned as he nudged his shaft into her one slow, tight inch at a time. He'd never experienced anything like it. "How we doing?"

A bit breathlessly she added, "Don't stop."

Once fully inside her, he felt her succumb. Her body relaxed beneath him, trusting him. "Oh, Cherié, I've never felt such exquisite torture in all my life. I want this to end and yet I want to pump into you until my balls turn blue."

"Blue happens to be one of my favorite colors."

She surprised him, meeting his demands with as much enthusiasm. The little zingers he incurred ricocheted from his groin and slammed his heart with better precision than Mister Tell's arrow. André reached underneath Jovan and cupped her ass and pressed her against his groin, then primitively grinded into her over and over again. "Surrender to me, your heart, your soul. Allow me the pleasure of our joining. I want to experience your body with mine." With a slipped smile he planted his lips over hers and slid his tongue in her mouth, probing her from both ends.

Pleasure, like nothing Jovan had even experienced deluged her core. There was absolutely nothing gentle about her orgasm. It rolled hard and fast throughout her body, beginning between her thighs, then flowing all the way to her throat and leaving her with a grin that reeked satisfaction.

She never took her gaze from his face. Expressions went from strained and serious to giddy and finally relief when he thrust once more into her. One contraction after another left her squirming beneath him. He collapsed atop of her, his chest heaving. He tucked one arm under her and pulled her close to snuggle in.

Barely able to whisper he teased, "I am inclined to

believe my lady did have a jolly good romp."

"When can we do this again?"

"You truly are the devil's advocate. What spell have you cast upon me? You're going to kill me with death by sex, aren't you?"

"And never get to do this again? I would never cast such a spell upon you." Then his words taunted her, 'What spell have you cast upon me?' Her mind still remained foggier than the moors on a warm damp night.

André gave her a peck on the nose. "With a little help I should be up and at 'em in no time." A small grunt escaped when he rolled to his side and grabbed a silk scarf Jovan had for her hair and a handkerchief from the nightstand. "Close your eyes for a second."

Jovan faced him, her brow shifted upward. He'd already come to understand this look.

Intrigued. Suspicious. "Why?"

"Please, no questions?"

"Are we playing peek-a-boo? Hide and go seek?"

André shook his head laughing. "What part of no questions did you misunderstand? Close those baby blues."

Jaw jut out and nose scrunched up she did as asked. André placed the silk scarf over her eyes and tied it loosely in the back of her head.

"What are you doing, Milord?"

"Possibly I should have covered your mouth as well." He leaned in and placed his lips hard over her mouth. Her heated responses to him would have his sanity questioned with every dawn, because right here and now he questioned it. He knew he'd never leave her side unless... He couldn't dare to think if something ever happening to her. It would kill him. How he felt so completely connected to her soul baffled him.

Before Jovan could protest, he had her secured to the headboard.

"You're insane," she muttered as she struggled to break free. "I cannot fathom how awkward I appear at this moment."

"Awkward, no. Tantalizing, yes. I promise not to hurt you but lavish your senses in a whole new light."

"You mean dark."

"Lay back and enjoy." With a slight shift he hopped off the bed and squat beside it.

"Are you leaving me?"

"Just for a bit."

"André!" Jovan yelled, panic infused into each syllable of his name.

He let out a small chuckle as he tugged the trunk to his vampire staking kit from under the bed. Inside, he grabbed a bottle of anointing oil which was derived from Vetivert, used to remove charms and hexes of all denominations, Dragon's Blood, used for love, protection and exorcisms, Sage, for cleansing, and finally Clover, used for restoring memories—why he didn't think of this earlier? Well this just went to show how befuddled this woman left him. When he hunted vampires, he used the oil as a send-off for the departed. Tonight, he would use it to send his lover to the heavens.

Stuffed in the side of the trunk, he noticed the white binder he'd found the first day they'd met. The journal lay open beside her in the road when she'd collapsed at his feet, the pages blank. He'd return it later so someday she could fill the pages with all the intimate, sensual details of their first encounter. Then he prayed the book would be a novel of their life together, not one page of mystical encounters.

"André?"

If he lived that long. After uncorking the bottle, he dribbled the oil between her thighs.

An immediate shriek of, "Cold," followed.

"Just making sure you're awake, sweetheart." Hands together, with a brisk momentum he rubbed them to produce heat and slid one hand up the inside of her thigh then parted her legs. He tipped the bottle upside down to allow more oil to trickle out. With his free hand his fingers went to work in a feverish fashion of circles, pressing into her.

"Seeing you like this, tied up for my eyes only, is one of many guilty pleasures. Oh my sweet beauty, the things you do to me. After I finish you off shall we spruce up and chow down? You have worked up an appetite on me."

Jovan barely lifted her head. "You sound like a cowboy. Do not forget over here we wear crowns not ten-gallon hats."

"I'll crown you all right, my lady."

"With what? These?" Jovan lift her leg and with her toes prodded between his thighs. "Mere trinkets!"

"Aye, and they're worth their weight in gold." André laughed.

She teased him further, "Let's pray we never have to cash them in."

"You have enchanted my heart. Now it's time for me to steal yours."

"Me first? I so love a beating heart—once it has been ripped from a royal chest." A brusque voice from the far side of the room carried over.

Both André and Jovan froze. He dropped his voice down to the point it was barely audible. "Don't be afraid."

"Too late. Untie me."

A man dressed in a waiter's uniform stepped into the room. "Please, don't stop on my account. You two put on an outstanding royal romp. Your aunt would be proud."

"André!" Jovan's hysteria erupted. "Untie me."

André sprang to his feet and reached for his gun. Hearing a swooshing sound behind him, he turned into an oncoming bottle of bubbly.

Jovan heard the smash and her gut tightened. Then she was blanketed by dead weight. "Who's there? What in 'ell is going on? Help!" Jovan screamed.

Chapter Ten

The stranger stomped over to the side of the bed. When he ripped the silk scarf from her eyes, Jovan took in the room and the intruder. Once again André had her pinned and unable to move, only this time his face held chunks of glass. Blood and champagne soaked into the bed covers.

"The book. Just give me the book." The man picked up André's gun and cocked the trigger.

"What book? This one?" Jovan nodded to the side table since she remained tied to the headboard. He leaned over and grabbed the book of poems André had read to her.

"Rubbish!" He yelled throwing the book to the floor.

"I have no clue what bleedin' book you seek."

The man nudged her with the gun. "Lady, don't test me."

Defiant until the very end, Jovan snapped, "I do not believe you are smart enough to pass any tests."

He bent and got right in her face. "Give me the real book." He jabbed the tip of the gun into her forehead.

This was getting old fast. "Please take that out of me face. I can't think."

"I have an itchy finger, little trollop. Speak now or else."

"You did not just call me that! Who sent you?"

"Ask your lover." An evil sneer spread across the man's face.

He inclined his head toward André. "His dear mama. Did you truly believe you met per chance? How well do you really know him? Two days? Give a girl a hotel room and a prince to ride, and she thinks she's the next bloomin' queen."

"You scoundrel. André would never lie to me."

"No, he'll just ride you into submission. Are you so naive you think this is really all coincidence? You truly think a member of the royal court would want the likes of you to bring home? Grow up, foolish girl. Give me the bleedin' book and maybe I'll let you live to grow out of your ignorance."

"Point the weapon at your own face. Trust me, no one will be wearing black lace, or shed a tear over your vile face. Say good-bye to the world as your life is hurled into an abyss, where you shan't be missed."

"You truly are a witch! Stop the rhyming!"

She wiggled and kicked for freedom and in the process was certain her foot connected with one, or possibly two of André's royal jewels. He would be rethinking his blue balls wish later.

Jovan stuck her toe out from beneath André's dead weight and pointed it at the gunslinger. "Bang, bang!" She watched the man turn the gun on himself and bring his index finger back once. A blast shook the room.

Not a second passed and a bellhop charged in the room, eyes wide with revulsion. He gagged when he one, saw Jovan tied to the bed in her birthday suit covered with God only knew what, and a member of the royal family either dead, or almost dead and two, when he took in an actual dead man missing half his face. He looked back at Jovan and took a step back.

"Please don't leave? Please set me free." Tears spilled down Jovan's cheeks.

"I heard him, lady. Right before you killed him. He said you are a hag."

"Clean your ears out. He said witch! Do I look like a hag? Seriously, there is a difference." Madder than a bee that just had her hive knocked down, Jovan screamed, "How could I kill him? I'm tied to the bleedin' bed for Goddess' sake. I haven't touched him. Please undo my restraints, or at least have the decency to cover me. Please?"

"Nay, witch. Did you kill him as well?" He pointed to André's listless body. "Look at you. You are an evil siren calling men for your pleasure and one of the Queen's own no less."

With precise steps he scooted around most of the mess and tossed the covers across Jovan's chest. He took a spare blanket and draped the dead man. "Don't go anywhere." The boy fled the room.

"Call the Commissioner," she heard the fool yell. *Fabulous!* She had only minutes to free herself, get the fiancé put back together and run for the hills before the commissioner or the Sorcerer's Squad were next to come calling. In all likelihood, shock got the better of her. "Did I make him do that? Did I kill him? Is there really something wrong with me?"

She looked at André and wanted to cry for more than one reason. The first being his beautiful face needed sutures. Possibly even more if he really was behind all this nonsense about a book and all the attempts on their lives. The second, he lay butt naked across her bed with one leg bent showing one of his testicles a ripe shade of blue from where she kicked him earlier. Well, if she truly held witch blood there was only one way to find out.

"Goddess release the restraints which bind me here, so I can help mend someone dear. The longer I lay the more I fear, my beloved André will be taken far from here, and I shall swing from the gallows all to near."

The handkerchiefs disintegrated to ash giving Jovan her freedom. Much later, when she had time to have a breakdown, she'd touch on these little nuances she powered. She admitted it; she was a witch. Deal with it later. The two men were spot on, but she still knew nothing of her past. Instead of dwelling over something she had no control of she focused on the unconscious man before her.

Freedom came with a struggle. Dead men, she reneged that thought immediately. André wasn't quite dead. Men that had lost a courageous battle with a champagne bottle to the face, weren't anywhere near as easy to manipulate as say a very excited man? Unconscious men you could dress in women's clothing and let them wonder what they'd been up to when they came round. Conscious men could undress you and let you wonder how long it would be before you saw them coming. Jovan felt her lips curve upward regardless of circumstances. It was either cry over spilled champagne or get this man back on his feet so they could flee. She rolled him on his back, gawked against her will at the length and breadth his personal jewels held. More precious than the gems locked up at the tower, she decided. Yeah, the crowns and tiaras might gratify her momentarily, if she were to ever get a chance to wear them, but that velvety soft sword tucked just off to the right draped on his thigh would pleasure her whenever and wherever she desired him. With a loud grunt she draped the towel across him and started picking out pieces of glass in his forehead and nose. Remembering the silk thread the woman at the boutique gave her for her dress, she threaded the needle to suture him while he lay unconscious.

She'd already come to the conclusion the intruder was a scoundrel. Jovan had nothing to go on but her gut instincts and everything about André felt genuine. There wasn't one single thing he'd done to make her feel otherwise. The vile man was attempting to plant seeds of doubt when there lay no ground. Seeds. Ground. A green thumb? Was there more to her than met the eye? No time to rifle through all the problems in her head while someone else's bled out.

Twenty-one stitches later with a few extra threads here and there, André resembled Frankenstein. Clearly, a seamstress she was not. She went to the powder room, slipped on the oversized nighty and got a cold cloth and pressed the bundle across his face to help with swelling. With the blanket still covering the corpse, Jovan hoisted the feet then dragged the body into the hall, leaving a red stained trail in its wake. She then dragged André from her bed to his since hers currently resembled a crime scene. She leaned over him and with the lightest of a touch she kissed the back of his neck and mumbled, "I love you, André St. James. As odd as it sounds, I do. Even barreling me down, giving me amnesia, tying me to a bed post, introducing me to a world I didn't believe in and giving me a cigar band versus a gold one, you have me heart. Break it and I'll have yours."

****

A strange sensation drew André from his slumber. When he lifted his head from the pillow, the numbness in his face and the pain in his nose brought back flashes of a perfectly good bottle of bubbly gone to waste.

With trepidation, he ran his fingers across his face. Foreign prickly nubs protruded from his nose and cheeks. His first thought brought with it a wave of panic—bugs, leaches, adhered to him! Bloodletting, he'd seen it done countless times and knew he'd rather die by a swift arrow than have a leach, a mini vampire, suck his blood.

He jumped from the bed and made his way to the mirror and wished he hadn't. For the love of God, a blind seamstress had her way with him. He did a body check to make certain no other surprises were in store. He reached between his legs and bent at the waist. One ball had an odd color, swollen and really not liking the attention, and the other, thankfully intact. Better than nothing. Now this woman could suck on a thing or two and relieve his swelling. He chuckled. Nay, he decided, she'd have the opposite effect. He crossed the room to Jovan, who sat silent, watching him with a tear-stained face. He brushed strands of her hair from her eyes. "You're all right? What happened? Do I want to know?"

Through sniffles Jovan shook her head no. "André, what happens next? Will you leave me?"

"Oh, beauty, as strange as this sounds, these have been the best days of my life. No, I'll not leave you, ever."

123

"But the train arrives in a few hours. And the constable quite sooner, I imagine."

André rested his lips on her head. "I've purchased two tickets, and I've every intention to bring you to Paris and from there we will begin our life together. Mind filling me in on what took place?"

Jovan wiped her eyes and licked her lips. "I owe you an apology. This dead bloke—"

"What dead bloke?" André glanced around the room. Something definitely happened. Red stains dripped down the wall and the bed they started out in had quite a different look to it. And his Cherié looked distressed as well.

"The one in the hall." So, she'd held a small detail back. "He wanted a book I supposedly own except I have no idea what book he speaks of." She reached over and grabbed the wet cloth. "Hold this here for a bit or tomorrow the only thing you'll see is your nose. I think it's as broken as the bottle. I sutured you."

"And a fine tailor you are." What was one white lie? "Speaking of books—"

"You are a horrid liar. Come on charmed one. We need to run. Fast. One of the bellboys called the constable on me. He thinks I killed you and the other man." She stood and made her way back to the loo. "Really must tinkle before we bolt. Ta."

In all his days growing up surrounded by women who lacked nothing yet wanted everything, André never engaged a woman who intrigued him, made his knees weak or his sharp mind return to a state of infantile gibberish. The lady could walk up one side of him and dance on his grave and he'd allow it. Well, he reneged dancing on his grave unless he'd cheated death, and she was there by his side to celebrate. From the looks of it, they had some fancy footwork to finagle first.

Chapter Eleven

Ruckus from outside filtered into the room in the predawn hour. People in the street were belligerent, screaming outlandish accusations with regards to his Cherié.

André looked out the hotel window and couldn't believe his eyes. There, hanging from the wisteria tree, where they'd eaten their fish and chips only hours past, hung a noose with an angry mob gathering. André grabbed Jovan when she came from the bathroom and wrapped his arms tight around her. A gnawing intuition fueled his fire to protect her. He couldn't explain the depressed ideas rampaging his mind that this would be the last day he ever saw her. The harder he attempted to shake the ridiculous notion, the more his stomach ached. "I love you. Never doubt me." His arms fell away, and André turned toward the door and at the last second spun about to face her. "I won't let them harm a hair on your head. I'm going to the stables for horses. Stay put!"

"Come here, my fearless knight and kiss me proper. I know you'd give your heart for mine, regardless of what the intruder said."

André grabbed her forearm. "What did he say?"

"Now is not the time." Jovan pulled away from him.

André held tighter to her. "But it is."

"Not now!" Jovan flashed the cigar wrapper around her finger under his nose. "This is what matters, if we ever want to make this dream come true." Standing on her tippy toes because she had to, to meet him, she kissed his swollen nose. "Hurry. Also, you might want to dress first. Pants possibly?" Jovan reached behind André and slapped his naked, ripe rump.

André glanced between them. "Right! Cheers on that."

****

Impatient and not the best at staying put, Jovan skulked around the lobby trying to remain inconspicuous, ducking her head and avoiding eye contact with anyone and most likely looking more conspicuous. She heard the whispers, felt the weight of passersby's gazes. She'd seen the tree with her fate dangling at the end of a rope. What she truly needed was her lover to gallop on up with his white stallion and save this damsel before distress got the better of her. Of all the uncertainty in her life, the one thing she knew in her heart to be true was André's feelings for her. About to go to the back entrance of the hotel, two things happened at once; a man yelling from the street stole her attention, and a second man entered the lobby, hollering, "Found her!" The voice coming from outdoors however struck a raw nerve.

"Jovan!" the man in the street cried. "Jovan, please come home. It's Julian. He's ill. Dear god woman, where are you?"

Her universe shattered. Jovan staggered and clung to the doorway; her knuckles blanched. Her life whipped past her like objects inside a tornado, lost in the moment, forever changed. Entered whole. Exited fragmented.

A burly man with pockmarks scarring his face approached Jovan with caution. "Lady, come with me." He wore a blue, high collared tunic and a custodian's helmet with a golden badge in the center. She barely heard him.

Jovan! She widened her stance before she collapsed. She now knew her name. *Julian, my brother! He's ill.* Frantic, she had to find André. He could help her brother. Jovan looked past the man with a revolver aimed at her and saw a little man running blindly from one shop to the next, screaming her name. She took a deep breath and headed toward him. She tried to say his name, but instead barely managed to utter, "Nygal?"

The Bobbie blocked the doorway. "Lady, if you please? No magic either or you won't make it farther than the tree."

"My name is Jovan. Jovan Hause and clearly your intent is for me to go no further than the tree."

"Ah, but it is. Our intentions are for your earthly remains to be incinerated once your soul has departed and from there it is the will of God who receives it."

Nygal stopped in the center of the road and swiped away sweat from his upper lip. "Jovan?" He huffed, "Is that really you? Come now!"

His feet moving faster than her eyes could keep up, Nygal scurried toward her, ignored the obvious, a man with a firearm pointed at her, grabbed her arm and proceeded to drag her protesting body away… from the hotel, away from André. Away from the outraged Bobbie now chasing them both, screaming, "Stop before I shoot you both dead." He fired a warning into the air.

Nygal ignored everything, everyone and continued down the road with Jovan in tow. "Now, Jovan! It's dreadful."

"It's about to get a lot worse if you don't stop." Jovan swiped at the tears already falling. "Nygal, stop before we both wind up dead."

"I won't die unless it's silver."

"Huh? What about me? Hello?" She yelled the words with as much cynicism as she could. They came to an abrupt halt.

"There's no time, Jovan. Julian's dying."

"Dying?" The words hung out there in front of her better than a dead man swinging from the gallows. Oh, wait! Make that woman—her. She glanced at the path the wisteria tree offered. The tree definitely looked more inviting yesterday. The officer closed in on them.

Nygal yanked her hard. "Jovan, wolves ravaged him last night at the circus whilst he searched for you."

"You two, 'tis your last warning." The officer's voice bellowed, "Stop her! Them!"

People in the road circled them.

Jovan searched the crowd for her dear missing lover. Where was Prince Charming?

Nowhere! She lifted a finger to the irate cop.

"One bleedin' second is all I ask." She turned to Nygal. "How is it then you have no scratches on you?" Jovan glared at the scrawny man. Suspicion exploded in her gut. Her brother supposedly fought for his life and yet this man looked as fresh as a steaming loaf of bread? She pulled away from him. Did she really know Nygal? No. He'd always been cordial to her, but they'd never really had tea or chatted over anything other than the foul weather or her green thumb. Speaking of which, she glanced at it and began laughing. On the verge of a breakdown she didn't know how to handle this. "Do you see the predicament I face? Look, Nygal. I have a lovely rope over there with my name on it." She dropped her voice to a bare whisper, "One wrong move on your behalf and I'll turn you into dog."

"Too late," Nygal barked.

Jovan wiped her eyes again. "Explain."

"I'm a shifter. I swear I won't hurt you, and I swear I didn't harm your brother. Julian is my friend. We were ambushed last night for some book."

Her knees gave way. Jovan landed in the middle of the road and covered her eyes and wept. "Oh Goddess, no!" Finally, an answer to why all this took place. Her little book foretold the future of kings and queens. Judgment day. Armageddon. All in there. The who-done-its of the rich and flamboyant. Charms for those of a pure heart and spells for the darkened demons. Potions for love, wealth, health, and for forgetfulness— to either help with it or make it worse depending on the intentions of the caster. And death. And then there was her own little love charm she cast a few days past.

André, did he truly love her? How would she ever know? All of this was her fault. She'd placed her brother's life in jeopardy as well as her fiancé's. Not to mention the obvious. She couldn't look at the noose dangling, waiting for her delicate neck again and not shiver. And where was that blasted missing tome? Another puzzle she'd never finish. The crushing pain in her chest stymied her to the point she might welcome death. Men closed in on them, shackled Nygal from behind and a few others pounced atop of her and wrestled her into a silver garrote laced with brimstone.

With a snap of her arm she broke free of her capture's restraint and started to crawl away. On all fours one second, up in the air the next being hoisted by the scruff of her neck. "If you don't let up there will be no need for the noose. Let me go. I've had it being manhandled." She kicked with everything she had.

The ogre hoisted Jovan to eye level. "Behave woman! Your kicking me in me balls would make me wife the happiest woman alive, and I can't have that!"

Her magenta boot swung and connected one last time. "For your wife then."

Dressed in a long red robe, wearing a cowl over his head, a man strolled in and with the oddest manner gave a gentleman's bow to her before he pointed at the now ugliest Wisteria tree she'd ever seen. He asked, "Shall we? I have other things to attend to today."

And said so matter-of-factly, without any regard for life—her life, Jovan had been summoned to her final send-off. This was all happening so fast. "What in heaven name happened to due process? Innocent until proven otherwise?" Which she would be... Two minutes ago, she was the happiest woman on the planet, and in another two minutes she'd be hung out to dry. Literally. She protested, "This is all a mistake, please stop," as the giant holding her struggled to get the noose around her neck.

The man ignored her. "Ashes to ashes, dust to dust, so shall be your shell. May your soul find a swift state be it Heaven or Hell once the bell doth toll."

And the church bell sounded.

If she never heard another church bell again it would be too soon.

****

Witnessing Jovan hysterical, shackled, and with a noose snug around her neck, André halted in the middle of the walkway, his arms useless beside him. His legs barely held him in place. This was it—the feeling of doom he'd been stalked by all morning. Horrified at the sight and prospect of this happening, he screamed her name, "Cherié! No! Stop this in the name of the queen." At the same time a bony elderly gent in handcuffs yelled as well. Only the other man called her Jovan. As André shoved his way through all the death mongers to save her a woman shrouded in black slammed into him knocking his balance off. She turned and cast a malice-laced glare to him. Days past he'd seen her on the train, crying as if the sun might never shine again. Her raspy voice carried Jovan's death sentence. "If I can't have you, this hussy sure as hell won't either." She yanked the chair from beneath Jovan's feet. A loud snap and Jovan's last gasp spread over a stunned crowd. In the blink of an eye, his life, his love, his dream of happily ever after became just that, a dream. He couldn't grasp it. André lunged forward after Jovan but was held back by a few men.

The woman whispered, "How's it feel to have your heart ripped out?" She became a giant blur in the crowd of faces all melding into one ugly mask.

"Let go of me or I'll have your heads." With a twist of his arms, André broke free from the men restraining him and staggered toward Jovan's body, her feet still kicking, her face a lifeless putrid shade of blue.

André bent at the waist and vomited.

Pain consumed his heart. Never had anything hurt so badly. There had to be a rhinoceros on his chest with its horn gouging the now useless organ within. He couldn't breathe. No air in. Not one sniffle. Stars? He saw bleeding little sparkly gas bubbles circling around his head like a swarm of angry vultures. His arms tingled. His legs turned to porridge. The last vision imprinted in André's brain would be the one that replaced every nightmare he'd ever woken screaming and alone to; Jovan's blue eyes bulging from her sockets looking directly at him begging for help. Receiving none.

****

From the woman's boutique, Olivia Spencer caught a glimpse of a man fall face first into the roadway. Another toad who'd hopped off the bar stool after one too many? And so blooming early in the day, no less. Regardless, it certainly didn't look good from her standpoint. Oh, not that she worried over the welfare of the human, but more for her own.

This was one of the minor nuisances she thought she'd finally overcome. Being a do-gooder. Despised the fact she wasn't as jaded as everyone made her out to be. If only her baby girl, Serina, could see her now.

In haste she set her parcels on the counter and with a finger in the clerks face she decreed, "Anyone walks off with these, well—" One look was all it took, and Olivia realized threats might not be the best route to deal with this. The poor girl blanched. How could she keep an eye on her belongings if she went and fainted? She pat the clerk's trembling hand. "Please, just don't allow my things from your sight. Got a few things to concoct a dandy witch's brew." Olivia headed out into the road where a small crowd gathered around a man in the road and a larger crowd gathered round a woman twitching from the short end of a rope.

"Might as well call the undertaker. He's dead as well." A gent, rounder than he was tall held his beer mug to heaven. "Cheers, mate. One less in line to the throne. The Queen will be pissed." He turned and waddled back to the pub.

An eyebrow shot up on Olivia's face. "He's not dead," she countered as she moved in closer. She squatted and ran a hand over his chest. All right, so the man had indeed died, but not for long. Not if she had her way. The lady dangling in the tree was questionable. Her sight set on the tree, Olivia made a small sawing motion with her hand. "Sands of time erase the line. Hold this moment and break the twine. Free the woman from the end of the line. Spare her life. She's caused no strife." The branch Jovan swung from broke and down she crumpled into one heap. The crowd, as if on cue, all took a few steps back, yet no one approached her.

Olivia brushed the man's thick, black curls from his face and gasped. Reeled backwards. Lost her balance and landed in the muck beside him.

Chapter Twelve

"Of all the men on the bleeding island to have to save it had to be this royal pain." Olivia asked those mulling around, "Give me some space. I'm a midwife." Olivia got back to her knees and knelt at André's side. She placed one hand under his head and the over his heart.

"Well, well, look what the cat dragged in. Never thought I'd see you again, Lord St. James. You've grown into a fine-looking chap. Last time I saw you, your identical twin, and your twin sister, you all had a face full of pustules and dirty knees. Well, I won't allow you to die. Not after going to such lengths to keep you healthy all your years. And dear lord, who stitched your face? What's one more thing to fix?" It behooved her why witches longed for her powers. Some days they were a blessing. Today? She had better things to do than play Florence Nightingale and yet...

Eyes closed, Olivia drew upon her inner strengths and focused solely on the man before her.

The lovesick bloke died of a broken heart. She felt it. She'd understood it more than anyone would ever understand. Broken dreams lead to broken hearts.

Olivia bent close to André's face, tilted his head back, inhaled then she placed her lips over his newly fixed nose and mouth and breathed life into the man.

Fingers over his heart, she tapped three times. "One is for life. Two is for laughter. Three is for love. Find this André. For both of us. Do not make me regret this. I have more than my fair share as it is now." She waited for her miracle to take place. And waited. Counted to ten once again and then an unwelcome twinge of panic prickled her. Olivia pat his chest again and sent one last jolt through him. Blackened her nails in the process.

He jerked, his eyes now wide and startled. "Who— what are you? Do I know you?"

"That got your attention, didn't it? Here to save the day, Milord." She winked a mischievous green eye at him with one salacious grin giving away her soul. Hearing a rustle of fabric and heels plodding over the cobbles Olivia raised her head to witness a speeding, disheveled, woman in a black mourning gown charging them. "Hold on!" The grin vanished.

"Bitch, get away from him, you dead hag."

Couldn't quite hear what the woman yelled, but she was able to pick up on the finer points of the spiel. Bitch. Dead. Hag.

Nothing new there. Unable to get out of the path in time, Olivia shoved André in front of her as a buffer.

A thump followed. The three came to an abrupt standstill with Olivia flat on her back, André sandwiched between them and once again out cold. Her hands in Olivia's auburn locks, the woman pinned Olivia down and shoved André away. Then she straddled Olivia claiming, "He's my lover."

Olivia snarled, "It would be in your best interest if you get off me before you snuff out me soul."

"You, you have no soul."

"Who left you to be judge and jury? I'm not the

one who just kicked the chair from beneath a living being to ensure her death. That is soulless. I've never ended one's life purposefully."

"But there is an accidental trail of corpses in your wake Olivia Spencer, isn't there?"

"How in hades do you know me?" Olivia latched onto the veil and yanked it from the woman's face. "Well I'll be a brimstone bitch. This island keeps getting smaller and smaller."

Fingers tucked under her thumb the hussy made a fist and walloped Olivia with everything she had.

Olivia shrugged it off. "You done? This nonsense is trying my patience. I don't fancy women on me. Best get off before I do it for you."

"He's mine, mine, mine."

"Why are all women so filled with Shakespearean drama? You sound more like my daughter than she does. For the last time, get off me, Tess. Now!" A curious crowd huddled in. People so loved a good catfight.

More than a little fed up and her sense of humor teetering on the abstract, Olivia pointed to each person and counted, "One, two, look at the person next to you. Three, four, remember me no more. Five, six, this so gives me such kicks. Seven, eight, I'm about to wipe clean this slate. Nine, ten, all of you eves-dropping run in circles and cluck like hens." Tess jumped to her feet and flapped her arms and squawked like a yard bird.

"I told you to get off me or I'd do it for you." Tears filled Olivia's eyes as she witnessed ten or more people, some on hands and knees pecking at the ground and coming up covered in horse manure while others scattered in different directions bumping into anything or anyone in their path. "Any one of you could have stopped this atrocity and none of you did. May Hades find you all a warm cozy spot. Fear and ignorance are the deadliest combination alive."

With the slightest flick of her wrist, Olivia mumbled, "Pause!" All movement halted. Hand on her chin, finger tapping her lips she needed a moment. She'd heard someone in the crowd refer to the woman that had been hung as Jovan. Fate had quite the sense of humor as well. She could kill a few birds herself this time or save them as the case may be and possibly reap a slice of redemption, if there were such a thing. Olivia stood, brushed her gown off and floated to Jovan's body. She removed the noose and slid her fingers around Jovan's delicate broken neck. "Restore her health. Do this with stealth. She is a kindred spirit, this I claim, so moat it be. She is one with earth, allow her rebirth."

Jovan sucked in her first gulp of air and then another and another. Her hands instinctively went to her throat and massaged the muscles. She fingered the cross André had bestowed her with still clung to her neck. After she caught her breath she looked closely at Olivia and she had the exact same reaction André had, astonishment. Jovan pushed up to get away from the woman, her feet getting caught up in her clothing. "You! You are the most cynical mage in the world. You were the last person to see my mother alive. Did you kill her?"

"You're welcome." Olivia rolled her eyes. She leaned closer to Jovan and whispered, "It was a tragic accident. Let's leave it at that." Olivia narrowed her eyes and focused on Jovan's mental pathway.

"Did you save me? Your eyes. Don't look at me like that. How do you do this? You are enchanting me, I can feel it." Jovan admitted, "You are a beautiful elusion. This is a trap. You can't take my memory from me. Stop. Please? Why save me yet kill my mother?" Jovan rubbed the tears from under her eyes. "What did I ever do to you? Where's André?"

"You, young woman, will someday think differently of me. You may hate me your entire life, which shall be long, but there are more important matters at hand. Your lover will be fine. There will be a few snafus in your sojourn with the prince. For starters, he believes you are dead after seeing you," Olivia made a slicing motion with her hand to her throat "but you have more pressing concerns if I read your mind correctly—the life of your brother is at stake? If you give me but a few minutes of freedom from this menagerie and hang around—forgive my insensitivity, I mean stay put, I'll go care for him. Possibly we can save the priest a visit, although I do need to have a word with him. Prince charming will live. No applause needed. You're welcome again." Olivia stood and curtsied. "Now, each of you humans close your eyes and count as high as you can until I return. Jovan, sorry to do this to you. Nap time." With a sweep of her hand over Jovan's face, her eyelids fell shut. "Sweet dreams, little girl." With the snap of her fingers Olivia evanesced.

Chapter Thirteen

With Julian put back together again and a sleeping spell set until the next full moon ravaged him, Olivia gave herself a little pat on the shoulder before she hit the main fairway running. A little dust storm kicked up with her landing. She deemed this her calling card. Time travel held repercussions. Displacing one's humanly form to mere molecules unseen by the naked eye and traveling faster than the speed of sound rocked her little piece of the universe and others where she wound up.

Jovan remained seated on the ground wearing a puss on her face that actually frightened Olivia. Possibly she'd gone too far immobilizing the poor girl. But the bottom line was it had been entertaining. Olivia shrugged her shoulders and grinned unable to recall the last time she'd had this much fun. "Run wild and free, Jovan. Live and love and above all, make sure someone's there to break your fall." With a wiggle of her nose, Olivia removed the spell.

Trapped in some sort of time continuum, life as Jovan knew it had never been more surreal or perhaps one giant void simultaneously. A world she stood alone in without André. She searched the crowd for him but saw only strangers.

On a scale of one to ten, today beginning as the

best day of her life, with no warning it ended up under all the shite in the outhouse. There was a reason she forgot that portal to Hell. Nygal fled to her side, tears of blood staining his cheeks.

"I saw you hang, Jovan. Hang. You should be dead right now."

Jovan slowly focused on Nygal. "The last thing I recall was a woman pulling the chair from under me."

"Me too," Nygal agreed as he offered to help her stand.

"Who in bleedin' hell was she?"

Nygal shrugged his shoulders. They both looked around and saw the tree branch shattered. Jovan pointed to the splintered limb. "It must have saved me?"

Nygal nodded. "God works miracles every day, Blossom. I need to get you to Julian. He's dying."

"I need to find André first."

"There's no time. We might already be too late."

"No! I can't leave without him."

"Jovan, what in heavens is wrong with you? Your brother's dying! He needs you. This is not a time for lust."

"But…" Her voice fell flat. She couldn't think straight. She had to choose between the two loves of her life after she miraculously got hers back? Go with Nygal to see Julian possibly die, and risk André getting on the train without her, or go find André and risk never speaking to Julian again? How could life be so cruel? She understood it wasn't fair, but this twist of fate had demon shite smeared all over it. "Please forgive me, but I can't allow that man to leave without a reason. He can help us."

"Jovan, if he sees Julian he'll kill him. If Julian

isn't all ready dead."

Dammit, if Nygal didn't have a point. After spending the past days killing off strange creatures, André wouldn't think twice about putting a silver bullet into her brother or anyone once else if they posed a threat. Her heart ached like never before. Choice made, Jovan wiped the last tear from her cheek.

"Take me to Julian." Nygal's arm around her waist steadied her wobbly footing. For once she was thankful to have him nearby.

****

Awake, André didn't dare move. Had an uncomfortable sensation eyes were upon him, not including the woman holding his head in her lap. Awkward didn't begin to describe this predicament. He took a peek side to side nonchalantly. Yup! Right once again. People gawked. Actually, they appeared frozen in some macabre chess game. Mannequins in the most abstract form. Everyday people out doing their errands were now statuettes scattered and positioned in various forms. Someone's sense of humor had more of a twist to it than his aunt's and that was saying a lot. A few men stood with their arms spread wide, their faces uplifted toward the sky. One with his leg positioned up in front of him. A captain's stance perhaps. All he needed was the bottle of rum and a parrot perched upon his shoulder.

His eyes finally descended on the stranger breathing on him. "I'm going to be sick." He started to sit up, but Olivia waved her hand over his stomach.

"Quicker than a comet, you'll lose the urge to vomit. The after effects of greeting the gatekeeper, Milord. You'll be fine."

André's stomach settled. "Did you say gatekeeper? Explain to me my predicament? And who are you and how did I end up here?"

Olivia placed her palm on André's chest. "You know what happened in your heart."

"My Cherié!" Tears filled his eyes. With a stern hand he brushed those that escaped away. She was gone. He couldn't keep his thoughts from her. Her sultry smile. Her heated gaze, literally an inferno. Her gentle touch. Her brilliant, unadulterated ability to speak her mind. He saw her hanging from a dead man's knot. He choked back anger and fear.

"She lives, André. See for yourself." Olivia pointed to Jovan and Nygal on the edge of the town walking away.

His jaw dropped. She left him without so much as a, "It was fun while it lasted or kiss my royal arse good-bye." The emaciated skeleton had his arm around her waist, and she had her head on his shoulder and together they sashayed off with his heart.

Pain once more pierced his chest. A poisoned arrow perhaps? Cupid, the little fairy fart bastard of a quack. Where was he when someone needed him? Death encroached. There had to be a butcher in close proximity attempting to gouge out the remaining shred of the useless organ.

Bloody hell! They could have it! He no longer needed the defiled muscle. In the distant background the train's whistle echoed. They both turned toward the sound. A large black cloud rolled over the treetops as the locomotive drew near.

"You were headed somewhere, André. Home to Paris perhaps? My dues to you will never be repaid, but this is a start."

"What dues? Who are you?"

"Lord St. James, may love and peace find you. Blessed be if it is truly meant to be." Olivia placed her hand under André's chin, looked into his questioning gaze and bid, "Adieu." Before he could open his mouth, an intense white light poured through her orbs and clobbered him. Encompassed by déjà vu he couldn't shake, he sat there.

"Oh how I loathe being a sap." Olivia stood, brushed off her gown and asked everyone in the vicinity to gather close. Once all the squawking ceased and everyone assembled in a semi-circle she raised her arms, palms to the heavens, and released her power. The energies escaped from her fingertips in one long stream of blue, yellow, orange and red electricity. People fell to their knees one after another, inconsolable. "My apologies to each of you. I didn't mean to pass on my pain, with the one exception, Tess. You'll need a new dress, yours is a mess. Don't look back and for the next twenty-four hours I want you to continue to quack. For today forget André. You shall meet again on fairer ground, yet I doubt your luck will turn around. Scurry now to that rock you crawled from under before I bring down my lightning and thunder." Tess did as was told. She picked up the hem to her dress and fled down the road quacking without once looking back.

Olivia didn't give André a second glance. She ventured inside the boutique, asked the woman for her packages and slipped out the back door, headed to the church. It was confession time. There was a stout little priest that had some explaining to do.

****

Alone with Julian, memories flooded Jovan. Her life with him played out before her eyes. Their childhood. Happier days when Jonah still lived. Jules, always there for her, even when she didn't want him around. Her constant. Her knight in armor. The one man all others would have to match for her to give them a second glance.

Well, she'd found that man, and she'd abandoned him. André. Left him alone thinking the absolute worst of her. She prayed for forgiveness even when she believed he owed her none. Jovan babbled to keep her mind clear while she worked at patching up the minor injuries to her brother. Seriously, she thought he'd look worse. All the things she sutured didn't look life threatening unless she was missing something. But then why wouldn't he wake?

She could always ask André to try out his *true love's kiss* on Julian and with that thought Jovan burst into a mixture of tears, laughter, and hysterics.

Her entire world had flipped upside down.

She put her head on her brother's chest. She could hear Julian's heart beating strong, a bit fast. See his chest rising and falling. Nygal made it sound so much worse. And yet he slept like the dead. Why?

She recalled mending André's face and what a bleeding mess she'd made of him. The man would hate her forever. He'd remember her every time he glanced in a mirror. Looking at her handy work so would Julian. She told her brother what a kind and gentle man she'd met and fallen in love with. Even saying it out loud didn't sound frivolous or quirky, but sincere. And each time she paused, she waited for Julian to add some wise crack.

None came.

After she cleansed Julian's body Jovan rummaged her room for his leggings. They were after all his, whether he remembered them or not. Maybe if he realized she was trying to give him a final send off in these fat pants he'd awaken and protest his way out of them. With some finagling she got him into them. He looked ridiculous. He'd clearly outgrown them. When no such argument came, she placed one last kiss on his cheek and told him, "I'm going for a walk, Julian. I love you. Don't go anywhere. Please be awake when I return." Jovan left the bedroom. Descended the creaky stairs. Walked out the front door and didn't look back. She'd done all she could, and she'd come up short. Something she'd have to live with all the days of her life. Now came the time to seal her fate. One weary foot in front of the other she made her trek back to town.

Chapter Fourteen

The whistle of the train acted more like a punch to her gut. *Been here and done this once. I must be a glutton for punishment.* She picked up her gown and charged down the brick road. As she hit the town's centre she fled past a group of villagers huddled in one giant circle consoling one another. "Now what?" She slowed her stride as she approached the hotel. Mister turncoat bellhop stood in wait for new customers as they came from the train. Completely out of breath she tossed one hand on each of his shoulders. The look he gave her, eyes wide-his body rigid beneath her hands, made her feel a little evil, and empowered.

"Tell me he's still here." She knew it was a shot in the dark.

"How do you still breathe? You are a witch. I saw you swinging."

"God had a hand in this, moron. He saved me from the likes of you. Where is he?"

"Gone. Can't say I blame him. It's not right, if you ask me." The bellhop shoved a crucifix in her face. "Back away from me."

Jovan ripped the cross from his grasp and shoved him against the wall. "I'm not a bleeding vampire, but right now I almost wish I were. Things aren't always black and white. Which way did he go?"

"Only one way out."

Train station in sight, a line of people waited to board. Piled high waiting to be loaded were packages, suitcases, trunks, livestock and crates. A glimmer of hope arose. If André made it this far, Jovan would find him. She slipped in behind a rather wide man and followed on his heels to board the carriage.

"Hold up there, Miss." The conductor singled her out.

"Me?" She feigned confusion glancing over both her shoulders hoping to find another woman behind her who appeared more unkempt than she.

"Need to see the ticket, Miss. No one boards without one." He leaned in closer. "No one."

"But—"

"Go back to the window and purchase a ticket."

"My fiancé has it. He's on the train. I'm running late. Please?" She pleaded as she tried to nudge her way past the obtuse man. And if that didn't work, she knew what would.

Before Jovan realized what happened a strange arm snaked around her waist and plucked her feet from right out from under her whisking her from the platform.

"We'll have no stowaways on this vessel, Lass." A second conductor added, his tone stern. "There's no gent waiting for the likes of you on this coach or any other."

Blood thrumming and temper spiking, Jovan yawped, "My fiancé is on that train, and I have a ticket. Go look for yourself. André St. James is his name."

"Oh woman, you've an imagination." The fool hollered to the first conductor who denied her passage. "Says the Queen's nephew awaits her company." Both men laughed at her expense. "And I've got the queen's niece back in me cabin waiting on a jolly roll in the hay as well. Go home girl and for God's sake, change your bloody clothes."

Hand over her mouth Jovan looked down at the dress. Indeed, it was saturated in blood. Anyone in close range parted and let her through. "I can explain."

"Leave now before you're carted away." The man pointed back toward the village. He set her down and continued on as if she weren't standing in front of him hysterical. "All aboard!"

She grabbed his lapels. "No! Walk with me down the isle. If we don't find him, you can toss me arse off this vehicle. I'm certain once he sees me, he'll confirm my story." Jovan dropped to her knees, hands cupped together. "I beg of thee."

"Madam, the last time a woman sat this close to me groin I wore no pants."

Humiliated, she stood but didn't make eye contact with the rude man. Her worst fear realized, André likely sat on the train in a nice comfy seat surrounded by gorgeous, wanton women. Women that wouldn't throw away true love. She would not allow him passage to Paris without an explanation.

"One minute," the conductor yelled.

"Just hand him this then?" Sobbing, Jovan shoved a slip of paper into the conductor's hand. Feet shuffled. Bags were tossed into compartments, doors slid shut, and the steps leading into the train lifted and tucked away.

Alone outside the train, an outsider truly looking in, as she had been her entire life, she peered in every window as the train began its slow departure. "André, please don't leave me." Jovan ran along the side of the train even as the speed increased. She banged on windows and screamed, "André," over and over. Clouded in black rolling smoke, and unable to take one last step, she plunked down on the rocky path beside the tracks. The train gained momentum and pulled away leaving her alone, sullen and overcome with despair. Why didn't God take her an hour ago when he had his chance?

So, this was how it ended.

Poorly. No one to go home with or to. It sank in she had no one. How would she get on in life? She shook her head. Forget life. How would she get through the next twenty-four hours? Twenty-four minutes? Twenty-four seconds? Twenty-four anything?

Jovan flung her body backward on the ground and watched as the clouds floated away, wishing she were on one.

****

"Would ya have a gander at that daft women?" A lady tapped on the train's window, pointing outside. André had no intentions of ever looking at another woman. Ever! Rest did not come on this ride. Heartache hogged the vacant seat beside him. Over and over again, his mind played out every stinking scenario they shared over the past days. How did it end like this? Why? When the conductor announced Dover, André gathered his belongings and waited. Teeth grit, eyes closed he took a few breaths and vacated his dreams. What he needed was a few shots of bourbon. The trained rolled to a stop with a jerk. Halfway down the steps a tap on his shoulder stilled his motions. Would he turn around to find his Cherié waiting with a smile plastered on her lush lips? He would not get his hopes up. Couldn't afford it. Despite all the nonsense of not hoping for a miracle, he had. He swallowed his heart for the last time when an elderly woman handed him a bloodied scrap of paper.

"Sir, this fell out of your pocket when you bent to gather your belongings."

"How the hell did it get there?"

She answered, "The conductor placed it there whilst you slept."

"Thank you." His hand shook like someone who needed a drink. Now more than ever, he did. He read the note, tucked it into his jacket pocket and remembered the blank journal bound in white leather. Maybe he'd fill the pages with a love letter a day until they met again. If they met again. And with that thought he headed directly to the pub. This was how it began. Might as well end it on the same note.

Part Two: Four years later, 1896

Chapter Fifteen

Outside the church, settled in his saddle atop his black stallion, André waited, uncomfortably for his identical twin, Lucian to finish up saying his good-byes to his new bride, Serina. The entire ordeal had to be gut wrenching. Three days past they were married and then in a technical, legal twist Serina became widowed.

Sort of…

Vampires!

Bloody leaches created more loopholes, beginning within the heart. Well, as Serina put it this morning she'd told their family, "We said for better, for worse, in sickness and in health, til death do us part and on our first day together we covered the gamut." She'd nailed that.

André understood all too well what it felt like thinking Lucian was lost to her. He'd only found out this week he, Lucian and Raven were triplets, not cousins. It explained a lot of things, like the looks they got from strangers when they told people they were only cousins, or the fact they had a unique way to communicate with one another, telepathy, that most others didn't share. Found out they'd been lied to their entire lives. Again, thanks to vampires, his Aunt Chyna; whom he believed to be his mother, again another lifelong falsehood. And one greedy enchantress.

Being royal wasn't what it used to be. André let out a deep breath. In the past the only scoundrels who pined for the crown jewels were miffed uncles or aunts born one person too late who wanted to budge the sibling line. Now? Even the dead clawed their ways back into the castle.

"Lucian," André yelled to a closed church door, "Any day now. My bum's numb." Circulation to his hand had diminished. His fingers now white from holding the reins to three extra mares. "Seriously, Luce, later you can consummate your vows, again. You're on sanctified grounds for God's sake."

The church door swung open. Inside stood his brother, his sister-in-law with her lips attached to Lucian and Father Butler, a close family friend, chanting prayers and dowsing Lucian with holy water as they exited. André's first thought seeing this, he was thankful it wasn't Lucian's new dents embedded in his wife—again. If he weren't careful, he'd have her turned as well, even if she thought she was above the mutation. Even though she held divine powers of her own, André didn't hold any faith the virus would distinguish the difference between a mere mortal or an enchantress. The only thing capable of stopping it was a good old staking or a sunrise. Which brought up the bigger puzzle; how did Lucian withstand those golden rays and not crisp faster than a slab of bacon in a bon fire? Was his soul still intact? Was he truly undead?

Well, again, technically yes, yet here he stood, basking in the morning sun, with a healthy glow. "Ut-oh! Lucian, tell me you didn't. Again?"

Lucian shrugged his shoulders. "Naught more than a nibble, Ands. She'll be fine. Shall we?"

"Thought you'd never ask."

"Did you get the telegraph with their whereabouts?"

"Yes. You sure you're all right to do this? You've only been a vamp a day at most."

"Never felt more alive."

"Said the fly to the spider just before dinner was served. Who's your meal ticket when you feel drained?"

Lucian looked at André from the corner of his eye with half a grin.

"Troll turds!" André placed his hand to his neck in a protective cover.

"Don't want your neck, brother. Your wrist will do fine. I've seen it done in the same fashion."

"Well, no worrying over it now. We have much bigger appetites to quell. Let's giddy on up." With a slight, "Chic-chic," and tap to the horse's rump André and Lucian headed out on a recovery mission.

Lucian commented, "Four years later, we're still chasing the same demon that attacked Raven and myself."

"Not to bring up the obvious, but someone really wanted you dead."

The devilish twinkle Lucian usually wore in his silvery-blue eyes fizzled. André had never seen Lucian serious. Until now, and he didn't fancy it. His twin had held the most lighthearted demeanor on the planet. Possibly having been robbed of one's mortality put a damper on things?

Lucian peeled his lips back and tapped on a fang then inclined his head toward where his heart rested. "Bastard got more than he bartered for this time."

"We'll get him, Lucian. As God as my witness, he will see the sunrise."

After three hours of traveling through rough terrain both men glanced at the uneven cobbled road then one another. "We're not in London anymore," Lucian noted. "What a charming little village."

André snorted. With a severe tug at his heart he added, "You say that now."

Nestled comfortably at the base of a mountain sat what appeared to be a quaint community. Over the past week fall foliage snuck in and painted the countryside with a palate of vivid reds ready to set fire to the sky, oranges an orchard couldn't match and yellows to warm one's soul. Wildflowers dotted the path to add a dab more splendor. Even the grass shimmered a dewy morning green. A beautiful illusion.

Things were never as they seemed.

André wondered if he appeared as clammy as he felt when he realized the exact quaint town he'd trotted into again. Was his destiny about to fulminate? Or was his black cloud going to leave him drenched in misery once more? He'd been back here countless times in search of his Cherié only to come away destitute. Alone. Broken. Furious at the world. His heart kicked up its pace. A layer of sweat covered his palms and made the reins on the horse hard to manage. His mouth—bone dry. Nerves? Hope? A miracle? He realized he had better luck at having the Pope name a Saint after him than having this woman step back into his life.

Lucian kicked André's leg. "Brother, do you remember this stop on the train?"

"Nay, but then it's not on the map either. The train

will stop here every third day if people are in wait. Nothing seems to have changed since my last visit."

Lucian shifted in his saddle and leaned closer to André. "Why would you travel here? It's not really your fare. Paris? Yes. This place?" Face scrunched, Lucian looked ahead and shook his head no.

Solemnly he answered, "Four years back, right after Raven's attack. I spent a few nights in the hotel."

"Oh, I remember having strange conversations with you. Something about zombies, werewolves and, something else. Oh wait, dare I recall word of a woman?" A lopsided toothy grin spread over Lucian's mouth.

"Not just *a* woman. *The* woman."

Lucian's index finger waggled in André's face. "Do tell."

"Let us first find Duncan and the mangy wolf."

Lucian prodded, "I shan't stop badgering you until you spill the beans."

André left a huff escape as he rubbed the thick black bristles on his chin. "Remember my tale of woe I told you before your wedding last week, about my damsel in distress? This is where the little thief pinched my bleeding heart. She changed me. I've never experienced such intensity with one woman. The intimacy shared between us came as easily as the sun's rise. We both experienced the bond the moment she awoke in my arms. There was no denying it and, to this day, I haven't looked at another woman the same way. Satisfied? I lost her."

How could things go so wrong? They had two weeks to get their lives in order before he came for her. The bloodied note he'd been given on the train read:

Marry me? Come back for me in two weeks? Not everything is black or white. I'll be the one on the platform with a green thumb.

He swallowed hard and choked never lifting his gaze to meet his brother's ever inquisitive one.

"True love is never lost, misplaced perhaps, but never lost." Not a second after he said it, Lucian's brows pinched, his demeanor inimical. The veins in his neck swelled. "I seem to recall Serina's legs wrapped around your waist attempting to ride you while I tried to figure out why I wanted blood instead of wine. Not even twenty-four hours past. Doesn't quite jive with your last statement of, 'To this day I haven't looked at another woman the same way since.'"

André's cheeks flamed from shame. "Lucian—the demon that drained you, Jasper, he trapped our minds. What would you have me do to prove my loyalties? I never would have—'tis not your woman I desire. Nor she, me. You know this in your heart. You heard Serina's pleas for you, and yet you stood idle and allowed the entanglement to take place. Had Raven not been able to read our thoughts—"

In a blur Lucian sprang from his horse and took André to the ground, pinning him. André didn't flinch. Raw emotion controlled Lucian.

"I could not intervene." Spittle slapped André's cheeks. That time he flinched. "If I had you would not be of this earth now. Or possibly you would, and your fate would be the same damnation as mine."

"If you're not careful it just may be." André tapped Lucian's new ivory posts. "Do not allow Jasper to rip us apart after so long a separation. Or you me?" A lousy attempt at a smile disappeared when he saw a bloody tear form in Lucian's eye. "I'm beyond sorry, brother."

Lucian released Andre and helped him stand. "Ands, my heart is damaged. Forgive me. The image of you and my wife together is very real. I am aware you were too weak to withstand the compulsion, yet that makes it none-the-less painful."

About to argue *too weak*, André bit his tongue before his brother beat him to it. "Will we ever be square?"

Lucian gave a noncommittal shrug of his shoulders and went back to his horse.

People in the street stilled their activities as Lucian and he entered the village, their horses trailing behind them. Most people kept their distance. Studied them with prudence. "Let the games begin."

"Ands, am I covered with red ants? I'm on fire. And me damned fangs won't retract. I can't stop them."

André glanced at Lucian and didn't know whether to laugh or cry. "Try with all your might. Company. Ten o'clock."

With sure-footed strides and her appeal about as appetizing as a bowl of dog food that had been picked over, drooled on and left out for days, a woman, bold in her approach greeted the twins.

"You two are far more scrumptious than a warm scone drizzled with jam," she teased while she twirled at lock of her hair around her finger ogling from one man to the other.

André watched her waltz right up to Lucian and place a wet, sloppy kiss on his cheek. The repulsion Lucian displayed had André fighting to keep laughter at bay until she pussyfooted over to him and did the same thing to him. So taken aback by the tart, André didn't budge. He saw Lucian out of the corner of his eye pointing at him smirking. An imprint of red lips on his brother's cheek had him reeling inside until he realized he probably had the same mark.

Lucian used their psychic bond. *You have lipstick on your cheek, Ands.*

So do you, imbecile. Both men lost their composure and chuckled. The woman's flirtatious smile slid from her lipstick-smudged mouth. André was swift to offer his hand. "Miss?" He hadn't meant to be so callous or then again… What was it with the brazen women in this town?

She slapped away his truce offering. "The name is Miss Maud." She stepped backward, away from them, tripping on the hem of her skirt, now headed for a water trough.

In a blink, Lucian caught her before she sank beneath the viscous green water, but the second he had her a searing jolt pulsed through Lucian's fingers. They splayed and regardless of good intent the crone dropped into the basin. She emerged with an abundance of slanderous words.

André went to her rescue, but she yelled out, "Don't," in a voice coarse enough to sand wood. She finished, "You bleedin' touch me." More people crowded around. "What are you?" She directed the question to Lucian, avoiding his gaze like she already knew. She swung her legs over the side of the basin, pulled herself to a stance and attempted to fluff her dress. The material clung to her, a puddle claiming her feet.

"I could ask the same of you, Madame," Lucian countered.

Luce? Mind filling me in on what just happened?

Later. We need to get out of this town, Ands. It's full of witches. My skin's crawling. Those little fire ants threw on a few extra logs!

The woman wrung the excess water from her dress and once done she began to trudge away. With each step her shoes squeaked. At the last minute, she turned back. The makeup she once wore now ran in lines down her cheeks. "This clearly didn't go as I'd hoped. You are the second set of strange men to come to our friendly little village today. Don't start trouble. The men here won't stand for it, no matter what you are, they'll rip you apart. If you are searching for the shifter and his human they are headed for Doc's. And Lord St. James?" She pointed to André. "I remember you from years past. How brazen of you to return. You're too late." Her laughter echoed down the alley.

"Rip us apart? A nice friendly village? Do they even go together? Isn't that close to an oxymoron?" Lucian looked at his brother, his silvery-blue eyes wide and inquisitive.

"There is nothing friendly about this place. Miss Maud remembers me? She read our minds, Lucian. Purposefully used the word brazen. Is nothing sacred?" André rubbed his cheek to remove the imprint of the woman. The make-up tainted his fingers cherry pink. "She knew Jonah was a shifter and said human like it's a dirty word. Look, there's the telegraph office. I'll go send a quick note to the church we've arrived. Stay put." André quickened his step to the building.

"Ands, I'm not an imbecile. I know you're searching for info on your missing lover because, otherwise, you could have just sent a message through our channels. God speed."

André pointed to Miss Maud. "Our channels, brother, have been compromised."

Not fifty paces down the causeway, Jovan exited a children's boutique. Today's outfit consisted of a light rose-colored dress, her feet bare. Her hair, as usual hung in her face, but so what? It wasn't like she was going to see anyone worthy of primping for. From the corner of her eye a man caught her attention and within a split second's time her heart paused. It started. It stopped. It started. It stopped. His was next.

It couldn't be. Could it? There was no way. Was there? She was seeing things. She rubbed her tired eyes. Maybe she should have done her hair. What did the insolent clown think he was doing here? She looked directly at the man standing there with jet-black curls, dropped her packages, and with authoritative steps marched toward him.

"You!" she shouted, her tone aggressive, hostile even, her index finger aimed directly at him. She watched him glance over his shoulder. "Imbecile."

"You talking to me?" He tapped his finger to his chest. He twisted to look behind him once more. "How does she know my nickname? Someone's in a heap of trouble." Lucian turned back just in time to intercept a fist. Knocked him back a few feet. He ran his tongue over his teeth. "Blimey," came out jumbled. He leaned over and spit out a very sharp pointed tooth then produced a dumbfounded grin. "What the hell, lady?"

Jovan knew her eyes went wide. More so when a new tooth replaced the old one right in front of her.

"Craven! I hope I broke your jaw, so you'll never be able to utter another lie. What's with the dents? And who the bloody 'ell's been kissing you?" She ran a finger through the lipstick on his face and brought it to her nose and inhaled. "Miss Maud of all the women! Pig! One woman from this town wasn't enough? Now you're back sniffing about?" Her thoughts went haywire. She had no clue how to act. What to say. What to do. Blood surged through her veins in the same manner the streams ran in spring after a downpour, fast and furious. She saw red. Jovan slapped his cheek almost as hard as she'd hit him, turned and sprinted away fighting every urge in her bones to run back to him and apologize. Kiss him. Or kill him. She didn't know which would happen, so she ran.

Lucian sat on the edge of the sidewalk and caressed his jaw. In a blur, André blew past him.

Ands, you want to tell me what just happened? Who's the smashing blonde? How can you ignore me almost dying in the road?

Almost dying? You're already dead, Luce, remember? Giant pillock. Find the home Duncan and Jonah went to. I'll meet you at the pub in a bit. 'Tis down the street on your left. Order me a few pints and watch out for the wenches.

Busy giving chase to someone he never thought he'd lay eyes on again his heart raced faster than his feet to catch her. She moved as if the wind whisked her away with purpose, but André smelled her, recognized the scent, made him giddier than a pussy playing with a live mouse. It was the one and same fragrance Serina made and sold in the boutiques, Eden's Black Rose. He knew he'd never forget it, or her. He'd memorized every nuance, every nook, every cranny of the woman and locked each of his memories away for rainy days.

As of lately, there'd been torrential downpours.

She disappeared into a small pink cottage with a thatched roof. A white picket fence laced with fragrant azaleas, roses, petunias, peonies, lilacs, raspberry and blueberry bushes surrounded her yard. Everywhere, everything was purple or pink, her flowers, her shutters, her front door, even the wooden chairs on her porch. André instantly knew no self-respecting man lived here. Not amidst all this femininity. His spirits lifted.

About to enter her garden, he pulled up short. How many times had he been told love causes one of two things to take place? Either it leads you to the edge of the blackest abyss and challenges you to reevaluate everything dear to you, to make changes in your life before your dreams end up a bizarre twist of Grimm's fairytales or… it leads you down the primrose path to Eden?

André fast realized with one hundred percent certainty he would become one of the saddest fairytales ever told. He'd lost count how many times he'd been so very close to stick his tongue out and taste his desires instead only to choke on the bittersweet reality nothing would ever come to fruition for him.

Today, why would it be any different?

There he stood, across from a mammoth werewolf guarding the entrance to his sacred haven. He closed his eyes with the slimmest of hope she'd show herself, and two, the salivating creature had a full belly.

Like a good watchdog only with a lot more attitude, the wolf's growl came low and forced when André reached for the latch. He snatched his hand back. "I don't suppose if I threw you a bone, you'd go chase it and let me pass?"

"Try me. See which grave your stupidity lands you in."

André held his hands up to the skies. "Ya want to know my thoughts?"

"Not really. It's my experience that the royals have been schooled to death on telling people what they think they want to hear when, in fact, they're not telling them any such bloody thing, but usually quite the contrary with such an eloquent fashion no one has a bleeding notion of what you've said. More shite flies from your mouth then your bum."

André hated to admit the damn werewolf had a point. "You've been speaking to my aunt, haven't you? I'm assuming that since I'm still here in one piece you have orders from the little Misses not to eat me alive."

"Never assume. She wants your hide more than I. One bleeding hair closer to that gate, and we'll see what the little lady did or didn't say."

By all rights, the wolf should have intimidated the daylights out of him, but instead it/he both perplexed and intrigued him. André got a bird's eye view of a set of incisors that put Lucian's new choppers to shame. He stood on one side of the fence with the wolf on the other, waiting to see who made the first move. It turned into a chess match with stalemate the only option. André had to cross over and see her, but there he was, huge, furry, immobile, lethal.

And here he stood, completely unarmed, looking scrumptious, as described by the soggy tart. Fabulous! He truly wondered why the wolf hadn't just covered the distance and ended this game, proclaiming checkmate?

Maybe if he stood there long enough she would at least just come out to her purple haze to talk to him and call off her pet, but the longer he stood panic paced in his gut the way the wolf did the fence line. Could this gnarly beast be her husband? André pulled up a patch of grass on the opposite side of the barricade and sat down to wait it out. He had nothing to lose at this point unless the wolf decided he looked like a crunchy tidbit.

****

Well, Blossom, I see you're back to playing hide and seek. Aren't we a tad old for this? Julian asked. *Do you have any idea how utterly stupid I appear standing here on your front lawn in the midst of daylight in this altered state… doing absolutely nothing werewolf-like to frighten the blimey bastard off? This is a pathetic waste of me time. Leave now and take the back way to my home. Do not be alarmed when you enter. There are two men waiting for me. One is broken in need of medical attention. The other has a silver plug in him. You have much explaining to do when I return.*

I'm sorry. Where's my baby? I left her with you.

I dropped her with Miss Maud when I got the call about the men being hurt. This idiot seems determined to see you. Is he so daft he does not recognize imminent danger when it could bite him in the arse?

Jovan stomped to the door, grabbed the curtain and ripped it away to peer out the window. She fought the urge to go outside and throttle her brother, but what she saw left her with a smirk. He was correct. Both men looked ridiculous. *Imminent danger? You? Mister bleedin' heart? The only damage you'd do is either lick him to death or whip him with that wagging tail of yours. I'm the one he should be worried over. I just clobbered him good and still here he is…* Jovan swatted the tears from her view. She wanted to see him, even as she hid behind the curtains. She ran her fingers across her lips and tasted the salty drops. She wanted to taste him again not her own misery. Their first kiss had been Hell-fire.

Her memories were fond of their time together. Those days were a whirlwind of emotions, exploration, learning to trust another person and love. Yes, Jovan loved him. She learned the hard way time does not heal all wounds and absence does indeed make the heart fonder. And yet her feet remained planted in one spot, not running out to greet him and throw herself atop of him like a long-lost lover ecstatic to have him back in her life.

Soaking in one long lasting memory of him, she pulled herself from the window and left out the back door. *Later we will talk. Julian, don't harm one hair on his beautiful head. I mean it.*

Jovan, when you see this one again, don't make your boudoir your first stop together. Give it some space.

Julian, I won't even dignify that with an answer. And she couldn't because in earnest, the idea of bedding André had her in one flustered state of euphoria. Her moment of truth sat on the opposite side of her fence waiting for a second chance. She loved him, missed his touch, his smile, his laugh, the intimacy they'd shared, the conversations that went from the sublime to the scourge of the earth and everything in the middle the man offered.

So why not give him that second chance? The damned Bound Grimoire. The tome offered no reprieves. No lust-filled pages. No happily ever after, just the ever after. It was her cursed inheritance, the one she'd lost. Had no idea what had happened to it. Disappeared the same time she'd met this twit.

Chapter Sixteen

With her daughter's little hand in hers, they skipped down the path singing. Jovan watched with loving pride her little fireball of energy and light take in every wonder life offered her. Savanah's jet-black curls bounced wildly as she went along without a care. Her rosy cheeks complimented her red, heart-shaped lips. Her deep blue, almost black eyes were a beautiful contrast to the fairness of her skin. Jovan knew her eyes were the gateway to her heart. Once, she held that very heart, her father's, a strong, caring man in her hands.

Bloody pity he ran off with it.

Inside the wrought iron gate of Julian's garden, Savanah bent down and began to pluck small red flowers from the earth. A bouquet of them wound up bunched in her tiny hands. Jovan went to stop her, but Savanah's smile gave her pause.

The little girl gently tucked one of the red flowers behind her mother's ear and whispered, "I love you, Mummy. The rest are Uncle's." She grabbed the hem of her mother's dress and proceeded to drag her into the house.

****

After an hour of being stuck in the same position, pins and needles plagued André from his butt to his toes. Neither he nor the wolf had moved. It seemed

171

today would not be the day to see his Cherié again.

Mister Werewolf posed no real threat—yet! There! André found his optimism, until he truly absorbed the creature before him.

Reddish-brown fur masked ironclad muscles. The simplest flex of his limb or turn of his large angular head revealed the brute strength the animal wielded. Eyes glued on the beast he wondered just what in the hell he did with his brain today, because clearly, he wasn't using it as he sat in a faceoff with someone that could remove his face in one timely chomp. "You win this round. Tell her I'll be back before nightfall now that I know where she lives. She can't hide all day. I'll give her some time to think. I will not lose her a second time."

Like venom from a cobra's fangs, saliva dripped from the corners of the wolf's mouth. "You can't lose something you never had."

"Never doubt my love for her." André stood, stretched his legs, and bent over to relieve the kinks from his back. He glanced back to the wolf. He'd never changed his position as he sat on his haunches with his front legs bent out sideways, waiting to pounce if André gave one inch in the wrong direction.

"She won't be here," the beast snarled. "Go home. Go back to your palace, your servants, your mistresses, your wenches; forget this woman."

"'Tis impossible to pretend she doesn't exist when my heart knows otherwise. I will return."

"You speak of things you have no knowledge of. If true love did exist between the two of you, why did you board the train?"

"She left with another man. I didn't receive the

note she'd written until it was too late. The note told me to return in a fortnight, which I did."

"Go home, tiny prince. She is happy without you."

Tiny me? Is he blind? The absurdity almost made him laugh but being of quick mind he decided now might not be the best time to argue over size, because if push came to shove his fight would be futile. Braun over beauty always triumphed. "Allow me the chance to speak to her. Give her the opportunity to see me. To tell me to my face her heart no longer beats with mine."

The wolf hacked up a hairball. He pawed it. Picked it up with his teeth and tossed it in the air and watched it land. "You did not just say that. What man says such rubbish? I'll give you a head start. One-two-three-go!" He shooed his paw, which looked ludicrous.

André placed his hand on the fence, ready to move beyond this idiocy. Before he realized it, the wolf had him in a chokehold, ready to snap his neck, one arm bent backward behind him, feet a good three feet off the ground.

"Bleeding royals think the bloody world owes them. She wishes not to see you. If you set foot on this property again, I'll finish this." The wolf hurled him to the other side of the street so easily it was as if he tossed a cricket ball instead of a human.

Stunned and air absent from his lungs, André tried to inhale. Nothing. He thumped his chest and in a rush his lungs expanded. Possibly exploded it hurt so damned much. He squatted a minute trying to find his composure before he scraped his ego up, straightened his pants, brushed off the dust from his shirt and took a few slow steps toward the wolf. "You and I shall dance again wolf, on fairer terms. Then we'll see who walks away."

The werewolf barked, "Wolves really don't dance. Be thankful you're walking on your on accord now."

I am. André turned and limped away. *Where are you, Luce? I'm on my way.*

André, any luck with your lady friend?

I believe I've the luck of the Irish.

I'll have a shot of bourbon waiting for you then. There's a side alley off the main road that has a cottage with an iron gate. Looks to be where this lad's taking me.

Who?

The town crier, I believe. The kid 's got the gift of gab. Did you know this town has werewolves too?

No! Really? André rubbed at the stabbing pain between his brows, then his buttocks.

****

Savanah burst into the cottage in search of her uncle Julian only to find two strange men at the kitchen table.

"Mummy!" Savanah quickly backtracked to the safety of her mother's arms. Jovan walked into the kitchen prepared to introduce herself and her child to two strangers, but whom she saw left her speechless, and she almost dropped her daughter. Tears rushed her cheeks, which scared Savanah. "Oh, for the love of God."

Jonah Hause cracked a smile. "Hello, Blossom."

Jovan rushed to the man's side, her blue eyes wide with astonishment. "Blessed be."

Jonah jumped to his feet, stretched his legs and arms then turned to help Duncan up. One arm on Duncan moved. The other dangled oddly, broken just before they were tossed from a moving train.

Jovan resettled Savanah on her hip, her tears out of control now.

"Mummy?" Savanah burst into tears as well because her mother did.

Jonah moved to Jovan and tossed his arms around his sister. Savanah's gaze intensified tenfold on the stranger. Jovan was beyond certain if the child could have crawled back into the safety of her womb, she would have.

"It's all right, baby," Jovan cajoled, "Mummy's just a little overwhelmed. Well, a lot overwhelmed." Jovan pulled Jonah to the opposite side she had her daughter tucked in and held him just as tight.

"Jovan, you're more beautiful than I remember."

"I thought we lost you, Jonah," came between Jovan's sobs. "Five years. What happened?"

"I'm sorry I stayed away. Please find it in your heart to forgive me." Jonah squeezed tighter. A stream of silent tears slipped across Savanah's rosy cheeks. She played in Jovan's curls, with one leg propped up against Jonah's abdomen as she tried to push him away, grunting, "No," as she did.

With each little protest Savanah gave, Jonah flinched. "Ouch! Like mother like daughter, Jovan. She's young, but her powers are strong. She's zapping me."

"I should zap you for saying such things in front of a stranger." Jovan crooked her head toward Duncan.

Jonah began his tale of woe, "He's our—"

Jovan leaned in close to Jonah's face and interrupted, "Promise you'll never leave me, us again. Promise me, Jonah. And damn Julian all the way to purgatory. He knew and never prepared me. Later, I'll deal with his sorry little excuses. What fate is it that brought you here? Who's he?" Jovan pointed to Duncan who stood quiet as a church mouse. Jovan held Savanah out just a bit and etched out a smile. "Savanah, this is your uncle, too. His name is Jonah. He's my older brother. He's Julian's older brother. He's just old. I thought he was dead the past five years and clearly this wasn't the case." She set the weight of her gaze on Jonah. "You owe me an explanation. Make it good." She puckered her lips and blew him a kiss.

Savanah shyly looked out from under thick, long, black lashes and wiped away her tears. "'Ello, Monsieur."

Jonah started to speak. Instead he ended up coughing.

"Uncle Julian is a doctor. He can fix your tickle and mummy says if he can't fix you, he can bury you because he's a vicar too." Savanah touched Jonah's cheek and rubbed her fingers over the brown whiskers on his jaw. "Your fur is soft."

Jonah wrapped his large hand around her little one. "French and fur? She's so small and intelligent."

Jovan shrugged her shoulders. "She is well accustomed to having the finer things in life." Her head cocked, she gave him half a grin, and continued, "We've traveled abroad a few times searching for Mr. Right only to find out how wrong this world is."

"Did you ever find him? Aren't you worried for her safety?"

"No and no. Everyone in this town treats Savanah like a little princess. Everyone watches over her."

Duncan held his good arm out to shake Jovan's

hand. At the sight of his mangled limb she stepped back.

"Since it seems your brother has forgotten his manners, I am Duncan, your cousin."

Jonah explained, "I just tried to introduce you, but I was cut off." Jonah nodded toward his sister. "We had an accident on a train just before dawn. This is fate that we found you after all this time." Jonah gave her a yank and reeled her in closer.

Jovan snuggled into her brother's embrace, never taking her eyes off her cousin. "I'm sorry, please forgive my manners, Duncan. How is it we are related?"

"Our mothers were sisters. We grew up in different areas of England. You in Brahmall, me, London. Your daughter is beautiful. She is the spitting image of you."

Jovan gushed. "Thank you, but Savanah has my attitude, naught more. Truly the spitting image of her father. I do see the resemblance between you and Julian. I pray not you have the same attitude."

From the front entryway a deep husky voice echoed, "I heard that, Blossom. Where's my princess? I've some empty spots where my flowers were!"

Savanah squirmed her way free from her mother and took flight directly into Julian's outstretched arms. He picked her up and whisked her into his keep. No more reddish-brown fur, just a strong, masculine, well-kept body.

Savanah shoved the all-but wilted flowers under Julian's nose. "'Ello, Uncle. Mummy says you've an old brother. Do you like him?" Savanah trapped Julian's cheeks in her grasp, his lips squashed together. Tiny bits of flowers smeared across his mouth. Julian pushed his nose firmly up against hers and then kissed the tip of it.

"Yes, my baby. He is my older brother. I don't like him. I love him. So will you."

"He made mummy cry." Tears flooded the child's eyes.

Each tear was replaced by a kiss. Julian asked, "Savanah, don't cry. Mummy is just happy to see Uncle Jonah, so she cried. She's fine. Women cry all the time for no apparent reason. You'll see soon enough."

Savanah sniffled. "Promise?"

"I will never lie to you." Julian buried his face into the crook of Savanah's neck and hugged her.

"He's funny eyes, Uncle. They are yellow."

"Savanah, my eyes are different colors and you like mine."

Duncan piped in, "As are mine."

"You take after our grandmother then, Duncan," Julian told him, "One brown eye and one green. Uncle Jonah's eyes are the color of the sun, which is warm and beautiful, right?"

The little girl nodded as she gave one last swipe at a tear and then wiped her soggy hand across her uncle's shirt to dry it.

"Do your eyes hurt, Uncle Jonah, having the sun in them?"

Jonah answered, "Never when I look at you, Savanah."

Julian choked out a burble. "What is with men today and sappy lines?" Jovan and Jonah gave Julian a confounded look to which he laughed more.

In the kitchen Julian rested his niece on the countertop so she could see everyone at eye level, as opposed to cranking her neck up, making her feel even smaller and at a disadvantage.

A knock at the front door had Jovan moving. "Sorry. I'll go see who it is." Jovan flitted down the hallway on cloud nine; after all, she had her brother back. He was quite alive, handsome and sitting in her other brother's kitchen. This day couldn't get any better. That fluffy little cloud evaporated when she flung open the door. On the opposite side of the heavy oak door stood a pair of silvery-blue eyes in a body of someone she thought she'd never see again. But something wasn't quite right.

His eyes: Wrong color.

And then there were the red welts across his jaw, not to mention the fangs.

"You again." Both Lucian and Jovan said pointing at one another.

Lucian stepped back and away from the strike zone and held out his hand trying to be cordial. "Please don't hit me again?"

Jovan back-pedaled only to trip over her own feet. Air rushed from her lungs as she called out, "Julian?" from the floor. Before she finished, Julian stood beside her, his hand extended to help her up. One little tug and she swayed, but stood, her eyes fixated on the man.

"Is this the house where Duncan and Jonah are? My name is Lucian St. James."

"Oh Goddess!" Jovan mumbled and landed on the floor again.

Julian nonchalantly crooked his head toward Lucian. *Jovan? He looks different. I didn't touch him, I swear. I only helped him across the street. Those welts aren't from me. And I certainly didn't kiss the man.*

Could you please get up?

Jovan shook her head no as her imagination went into double time. *Oh lord! The heir and the spare.*

"I'm sorry," Lucian apologized, "I must be at the wrong home." He turned to leave when Jovan spoke up. She waggled her fingers frantic at her brother. Julian accommodated her and hoisted her from the floor a second time.

"Mr. St. John, I'm so sorry for walloping you. Thought you were someone else. Isn't that funny?" She feigned laughter. Both Lucian and Julian held an awkward moment's silence.

"St. James, my lady." Lucian took a second step back just in case.

Jovan snorted and covered her mouth. "Could've bloody well sworn you were some other bloke. Guess 'tis true that everyone has a double. You most certainly do." Without even realizing what she was doing she'd fluffed her hair, smoothed out her dress and wet her lips.

"Aye, Madame, that I do, my identical twin, André."

Her stomach rolled, and her eye began its nervous dance. Somewhat strained and rubbing the eyelid she added, "Funny, he never mentioned that."

"We only just found out ourselves. The story is a long twisted one." Lucian waited.

"This day has been filled with surprises of all sorts." Julian aimed that comment directly at Jovan. "Your friend is in the kitchen, down the hall, Lucian."

Lucian took a step into their home and before he knew what hit him Jovan and Julian watched his body take one tumultuous jerk backward. The man was catapulted across the yard on the opposite side of the wrought iron fence.

"Wow!" Hands out to his sides Julian swore, "Wasn't me!" Julian shoved Jovan back into the entryway, slammed the door in her face and crossed the yard to Lucian.

"Not polite, Jules," Jovan yelled after she opened the door again and stood in the entryway watching.

"Hmmm… It appears the mysteries of life and death affect even the royals. How long have you been not quite dead?"

"Three days," Lucian answered as he brushed off his pants and shirt.

"Seems I forgot to invite you in the most formal of manners." Julian held his hand to Lucian. "For the record, theory has it those able to withstand the sun after a life-altering event are still pure of heart. Only the depraved are doomed thru darkness. You are welcome in my home until you are no longer welcome there. Just keep the ivory posts out of sight around my niece." Once inside Julian showed Lucian to the kitchen. "Be right back."

Julian latched onto Jovan's arm and dragged her into the library then shoved her on the leather settee. "Blossom, time to fess up and let the cat out of the bag once and for all. And get the idea of the two of them out of your noggin. This one is trouble enough."

Jovan kicked Julian in the shin. "'Ave I no thoughts of me own? I don't want to lose him again, but I can't let them, I mean him back into my life." Jovan gave Julian a toothy evil grin and continued, "Kidding. Jules, you've read the book. You know how this ends. I loved him." Jovan stood regardless that her legs still shook.

"You mean love, Blossom. You've never stopped. It's an old book full of rubbish. No one sees into the future seven hundred years ahead…"

"Julian, I do. Not that far ahead but…."

"I know you felt something for the other one. We've Savanah to prove that. I get no ill feelings from this man, or the imbecile who waited at your gate. Trust him, or me. I'll protect you and the baby. Haven't I always?"

"It's you I worry for. The last day I spent beside him he said he would kill every monster."

"But I am no monster."

Jovan leaned into Julian and went pliant in his arms. Confused droplets of her soul rolled one by one from her cheeks splattering upon the floor. She hadn't entertained the idea in many moons that this man would have a hand in raising Savanah. The book said things. For seven hundred years her family kept watch over the god-forsaken tome, and it was never—bloody—wrong. And then there was that little charm she cast, something to do with true love… It was days like this if she could have kicked her own arse she would have. But how Jovan wanted to believe her brother, to give him, Savanah's father, a chance, but to risk her daughter's life? Never.

"Blossom, if you hadn't noticed, I'm still standing here. His brother is a bleeding day walker. Things have changed over the years. People lighten up or tighten up depending on circumstance. He's been introduced to a new world this week, just as we were four years ago. Go take Savanah for a walk while I set Duncan's arm. Catch your wits."

Jovan began her trek back to the kitchen. "What happened to them?"

"Tossed from a moving train by some sentinel as they carted a royal vamp back to the castle for safe keeping, well execution actually."

"Well, of course they were. Silly of me to ask." Jovan rolled her eyes. "They're going to kill a royal vampire and you think I'm foolish about worrying over you?" Jovan stomped off headed to the kitchen where her daughter entertained a room full of men. With prudence Jovan watched Lucian.

Lucian waved to Jovan. "Thank you for allowing me in." He winked.

Damn the man, he and his twin had perfected charm.

To his best mate Duncan, Lucian declared, "You, old man, look dreadful. Jonah, you smell dreadful. I see you're no longer turning your stomach inside out. It's a miracle you both survived the fall from the train." Lucian sauntered over and rested his butt closer to the little girl. He winked at her. Savanah tried to wink back, but instead pushed her eyelid down and grinned. Jovan wondered if her real father would be as smitten.

Jonah answered Lucian. "Julian's certain I have a silver plug in me—a poppet some call it."

"One by one another fairytale rings true," Duncan added.

Jonah tossed in, "Sad isn't it, Duncan? Anyway, someone around here made some pills that stopped the pain and nausea until I find the poppet and destroy it."

Savanah whispered into Jonah's ear, "Madame Maud."

"Madame Maud made the pills." Jonah bowed to

Savanah.

"I've met your Madame Maud. Quite the character," Lucian added.

Jonah turned to Lucian. "What do you think of my niece? Isn't she beautiful?"

Lucian's jaw dropped. "You're related to these people?"

"No one told you? Jovan and Julian are my siblings. Julian is the vet and a Vicar. Said he's going to cast Duncan's arm. And this peanut is my niece, Savanah." Jonah ruffled Savanah's curls.

Lucian held his arms out to her. Savanah looked up to her new Uncle Jonah who she already trusted for approval. Jonah nodded, and Savanah went to Lucian and without further ado, began playing with Lucian's jet-black curls as if she'd picked up one of her dolls and decided they needed a new style. Jovan stepped in closer.

"You have my hair," Savanah told Lucian as she twisted a chunk of his curls into a knot.

"Yours is prettier than mine," he said as he tickled her tummy.

Savanah tugged on his shirt collar. "What's your name, Monsieur?"

"Lucian, my little lady." Lucian turned his attention to Duncan. "So, I hear Julian is going to set your arm before we leave? Is there anywhere to get a good bottle of scotch in this town?"

"What the hell is it with the scotch? Julian made reference to it earlier on as well." A deadpan glare replaced Duncan's glassy-eyed look.

"It's for me, old man. Can't bear to hear you cry."

"Compassionate as your aunt." Duncan mumbled

as he poked at the bandages on his arm.

"Ah, Duncan, my aunt loves to hear grown men cry," he paused, "for their lives that is."

André, you anywhere in this town? Lucian didn't want to put the fear of God into his brother, but he knew with certainty his niece sat beside him.

On my way through the gate as we speak. Everyone present and accounted for?

Lucian glanced around, first to Julian, then Jonah, Jovan, Duncan and finally Savanah.

And then some.

Aware she appeared pale, Jovan fought the nervousness in her stomach and at the same time she rejoiced André lived. But for how long, once she finished with him would be the real question. "Savanah, come. You and I need to walk home and get a few things for supper. Jonah, we'll be back. You're going to stay with us now, right?" It wasn't a question. Jovan approached Lucian and held her arms out. Lucian lifted Savanah to his eyelevel and said, "Pleasure, my little lady," and set her down. Savanah ran back to Jovan's side.

"Blossom, I really must return to London for business. Savanah, will you come visit me?"

"Mummy and I will." Savanah tugged hard at Jonah's sleeve. He dropped to his knees in front of her. On tippy toes she tossed her arms around his neck, hugged him as hard as she could and said, "Ta," then turned grabbed her mother's hand. With a quick swing, Jovan pulled the little beauty into her arms and headed out the back door.

André go round to the back. We're all in the garden. Lucian found no harm in one little white lie.

This woman's intentions were to literally skip out the back undetected. Not on his watch.

Chapter Seventeen

Rounding the outside corner of the house, Jovan's heart thumped louder and faster than pistons on a steam engine going full speed. What would happen if she actually saw André with no fence or big brother between them? She'd landed flat on her bum at the sight of his twin. Once again falling at men's feet. She could see André so clearly hugging his sides in stitches if he knew nothing had changed in their time apart.

Would her feelings for him remain the same? Would she still find him desirable? Irresistible? If he looked anything like the man in her kitchen up close, hell yes. She'd run and fling herself right into his arms!

And there it was, that infamous saying: Be careful what you wish for.

When she slammed directly into Prince Charming coming from the opposite direction the steam engine and all those busy little pistons ceased. Or was that her heart? All the hot air she was usually so full of blew out in one gusty, "Holy shite!" Left her in worse shape than a fish on the dock sunbathing with a giant hook threw its bottom lip. That whole running and flinging herself into his arms? There she stood, frozen, mirroring a statue from Madam Tussaud's wax museum, about to become one dripping hot mess.

"Mummy, how did Lucian get out here so fast?"

Gibberish toppled from her tongue with as much eloquence as a person trying to spit a bug from their mouth. "Ah—I—ah—don't—dear Goddess—" Her legs went weak a third time. She widened her stance.

Savanah pressed her nose to her mothers. "Mummy?"

Jovan held her child with the grip of death.

There they stood, mere inches from each other, closer possibly as her claustrophobia reared its ugly head, yet the true distance might as well have been a world apart. And that wasn't far enough. Air! There one second. Now?

The only thing separating her from him.

Lightheaded. For God's sake she felt dizzy. Stars? Was she truly seeing the gaseous little annoyances and were they dive bombing her like a mob of angry birds?

She thought she'd never see him again. Convinced herself of it.

After months of searching for him, she'd resigned to the fact he'd simply fallen off the face of the earth, and she thought she'd wanted it that way, but now?

Love at first sight, she never really believed in it until she'd met this buffoon. They were so young when they first met. She had her life in front of her... now her life rested on her hip, all two stone of her. She'd been so naïve. When she met André every sane thought, desire and dream revolved around him. Three days in his company and her life changed forever and now the winds of change were about to kick up another mistral.

He made her crazy and being this close to him after so long didn't help. In fact, it did the exact opposite. She wanted to back up, turn and run, but her feet suddenly sprouted roots. She glanced down, petrified to find any ivy coiling around her legs. It happened more than she cared to admit. Those earthly powers kept her grounded. Literally.

She wanted to fling her body on his, hold him, kiss him, make love to him, and apologize for hating him. When she'd first found out she carried his child, she'd sent letter after letter to him ecstatic, positive he would bound through the universe on a white stallion to swoop her and her growing belly off her Ogre-sized feet.

André never called. Never came for her or her daughter, their daughter. Jovan's darkest fears haunted her, that the scoundrel who'd killed himself in the hotel room their last morning together told the truth: Jovan had merely been a pawn in a game she would never win. André missed Savanah's birth, but Julian didn't. He missed her first words, why and what. Missed her first birthday and the next two thereafter. Julian didn't. He'd made up for her father's absence, and Jovan couldn't have loved her brother more. As far as André's welfare, Jovan's heart turned to ash. Or so she'd thought. It wasn't as easy to lie to oneself as it was to someone else.

Mister Hot-to-trot never returned her correspondences. All the letters she'd sent, words torn from her heart, tears that had fallen and soaked into the pages as she wrote them went unanswered. Her dreams turned into an abyss of ghoulish nightmares. And now the nightmare stood a short distance away looking more like a wet dream she wanted to dive into. He may have been Lucian's identical twin, yet this man held a beauty no man could ever claim. His eyes could enthrall her without any mystical powers. His smile could have her undressing and his laughter could fill her lonely nights for eternity.

Damn him, he'd grown more handsome than the day they met, dashing, stronger, sinew…matured. She felt old and unsightly, with no time for her own needs because of the demands of motherhood. To be seen by him this way embarrassed her. She wanted to ask him to hold Savanah for a bit, dash home, freshen up and come back to him looking positively sultry. A wanton Goddess. A sheepish curl spread across her lips.

Dreams and desires battled her conscience and the warlord stood less than a foot from her staring, his lips slightly parted. He could take on the treacherous little villains with one or two swift diving plunges into her deep dark cavern and satisfy them both, caring for each and every desire and fantasy with his own little well equipped army. And then Savanah will have someone to play with… *Hold that thought, Jovan!*

For a split second she thought she recognized something she'd seen in his eyes before. Love. Desire. Honesty. A tear trailing down his cheek as he stared at his daughter? His gaze provoked unease. Could it be possible? Could he never really have known he had a daughter? The idea he never received her letters, never crossed her mind. For the past forlorn years Jovan lay in bed comforted only by the little child on her hip who asked her only for love and she got it. Jovan made up for his absence every day. She loved her twice as much. After relinquishing her dreams of their life together bitterness replaced bliss. She no longer needed him, but Savanah might. Nothing short of the Queen's pardon would exonerate his behavior. Well now—that wasn't going to work. He had a direct pathway up the royal patootie.

With a bewildered gaze plastered on his face, Jovan got the feeling he looked through her, searched her soul, while his deep blue eyes, identical to Savanah's, caressed her with dreams of what could be. Made her hope. His voice made her so hot her body became moist and wet trying to dowse the flames. Her mouth went dry. The great drought, the potato famine, she now knew what it felt like to be bone dry.

From the neck up.

Under her skirt... Some things never changed.

The nervous twitch her left eye occasionally plagued her with now screamed for attention. She thought him polite for not staring, pointing or rolling on the ground drowning with laughter. Her voice vanished, she couldn't feel her feet, she couldn't spit in his face as she'd thought about doing regardless of its vulgarity, but she could stand there and admire the beautiful statue before her. She glanced at him from head to toe. Every square inch of him was the same man she'd fallen in love. "Goddess help me," she said one notch above saying nothing at all.

****

Lucian?

Ands?

I may kill you later. A heads-up would've been appreciated.

Where is the fun in that?

Amazed he hadn't collapsed at the sight of her beautiful big feet, André realized the only thing keeping him vertical was ice solidifying his veins, his muscles, his brain... What was left of it anyway. He went for a nonchalant glance to see if actual crystals formed on his flesh. She watched with caution. One step closer and iceberg would be no more. She could melt him to the very core. Certain death encroached; his heart constricted. The satisfying pain he welcomed. When he went to speak his mouth resembled a crematorium, gritty, bone dry. His brain, now as full of thoughts as a virgin sheet of paper.

Him speechless? How many years had André waited to speak to her and now his eloquent tongue devoured his words.

Her beauty blindsided him. Over the years her features had filled out a little. Her face softened, the curve of her lips became fuller, more kissable... if possible. He intended to find out. Right this second all he was able to do was stand erect.

In more ways than one.

He found his lips were still able to produce a smile, even if the rest of his body went on holiday. He'd rehearsed every possible scenario in his head a million times of what he'd say to her, to win her love, her trust, to get her back in his life, back by his side and back in his bed. André would have sworn on his mother's grave, her feelings were sincere. Now he could only swear. He'd misjudged her. Standing this close, memories crashed into and out the other side of his chest leaving a giant hole where his heart once rested.

One of these days he'd get it back from the little pickpocket.

To look at her and not be able to touch her physically pained him. There she stood, a mere foot from him, stunning, beautiful, tall, trim, graceful, poised. The twitch he noticed in her eye, he would not make comment of.

There seemed to be an ounce of intelligence

working for him.

He noticed the three beauty marks that formed a triangle high on her cheek. The evening he'd kissed each one she'd granted him one wish. He'd asked her for her eternal love, and she'd told him he had her heart. He'd asked her for a large family, and she said, they'd start out slow and hey, practice makes perfect. He'd asked her to be his bride and she'd answered, "Let me sleep on it."

By now she should be well-rested.

He searched her face. Somewhere buried beneath all that beauty there had to be a telltale sign she still cared for him. For a brief second a glimpse, be it hope, love, or, "Oh, André, I'm so happy to see you… I've missed you so. I can't live without you," waltzed over her face and continued right on by.

The look faded to one he recognized well, contempt.

Jovan held something, no someone, in her arms. André shifted his gaze to his right and saw a pair of deep blue eyes intent on his every move. Her giant, glistening saucers held beauty, honesty, and innocence. Jet-black curly hair surrounded her cherub face. He wanted to see if it was as soft as the silk it resembled. He wasn't sure he could twitch a finger, let alone lift his arm. Certain rigor mortis crept in he tried to wiggle his fingers. They tingled yet worked.

Whew! He attempted to hoist his arm to the child's hair. The limb took on its own free will and floated into the strands of baby-soft locks.

The child reached to meet his hand. She explored, played with his fingers. Displayed no fear. Maybe, she instinctively knew he'd never hurt her, never do anything other than love her. Love at first sight is real. Both the women in front of him were a living testament to it.

"Hello, Cherié."

****

He remembered my name, one point for him. She gave her best grin, one she'd practiced for just this occasion. Snarl worked if she were to be honest.

His voice wasted no time. It went straight between her legs. No foreplay, no sweet tender kisses, all business. Nothing had changed. She clamped her thighs together. *He is making up for lost time, another point. Smug bastard. That's it. No more points, Jovan.*

"What are you doing here?"

"Do you want the whole story and nothing but the truth or my version?" He gave her his best, *yes I'm still the horse's arse*, grin he could offer.

"The truth might be entertaining."

****

"You say that now." André winked at her, trying to elicit some sort of smile. She was in a mood. Well, after four years he might be too, but he was so exultant to see her nothing could mar this moment. "All right, here goes. My identical twin and his wife had some very bad things happen to them while on their honeymoon and they wound up in dire need of help. A vampire bit Lucian, killed him, kidnapped his wife…yada, yada, yada… We, Duncan, Payton, he's our chef and quite smitten with my sister, and a werewolf, and myself came to their rescue, then on the train coming home early this morning this mammoth sentinel protecting a vamp, my not-so-dear lying, conniving, vampiric aunt, tossed the wolf and Duncan from the train. Then we,

Lucian and myself caught the vamp, my not-so-dear lying conniving vampiric aunt and sent her to the castle this morning for the queen to handle. Then we came here to find Duncan and the wolf and found you, as well, and I'm the happiest man alive." There, he'd spilled his guts and didn't even come up for air. He decided the tale really didn't sound so far fetched aloud until he looked at Jovan's astounded glare, her brows pinched, her lips pursed.

Think quick, Ands. "You are more beautiful than my memories."

"So you weren't searching for me. This wasn't fate?"

"I've never stopped. This is most definitely fate, Cherié. Cross my heart and hope to die." He moved his hand to touch her hair, sweeping a stray strand behind her ear. His fingers lingered on her shoulder, playing with a curl.

Jovan read his mind and knew he spoke the truth or some distorted version of it. *What's one more point. He'll never get to five. Jovan, what if that happens? What happens if he gets to five? A girl's allowed to raise her standards.* The nervous twitch in her eye seemed to be taking on the life of a really bad wink. Now she'd just look like some poor wench who'd had a set of falsie eyelashes threatening to blind her.

"Jovan, I'm at a loss as where to begin. It seems you began without me."

"Well, that would be because you left without me!" Fist curled up she continued to rub the twitch.

"I do not wish to fight with you, but for the record, you left me, with another man glued to your side." He looked at Savanah, still his other hand in her hair. "She is beautiful, and you are blessed."

Four points now, oh my giddy arse. Remember the book, Jovan. It hasn't lied in seven hundred years. But you will, now! "Don't touch her, André. She is not yours."

André snatched his hands back and jammed them deep into his pockets. The hurt look on his face stole her breath. *What the hell did I just do?* Jovan's stomach knotted.

"Jovan, you never once returned one of my letters. Why? We were to wed. I received one letter from you then nothing. You simply vanished. I looked all over Europe for you. I've returned to this village so many times I've lost count."

More bloody points. Damn. "I could ask the same of you. One letter? I sent you a letter every day for almost four months and then I gave up when I realized you wanted nothing to do with me. I stood at the train station for days. Julian, my brother, had to peel me away. It's as if we were cursed from the beginning."

"You couldn't have been more wrong. I came. I went to the hotel. I asked everyone. Not a person had seen you. Now it seems as if we are blessed."

André looked back to the child and smiled. "What is your name, young lady?"

Shyly, in her tiniest voice she whispered, "saVanah."

"Vanah is a beautiful name."

"Non, Monsieur," the little girl waved an impatient hand in his face. André recognized the trait as the same one her mother had. "Savanah." This time she emphasized the "Sa" part of her name.

"I apologize, Savanah. Your name is as beautiful as

you are."

Jovan set Savanah down and whispered, "Go zap your Uncle Julian for me? Now?" She pat the child on her bum lightly with a little, "Scoot." Savanah gave her mother a confused look over her shoulder as she left.

André placed a hand on Jovan's shoulder. "Jovan, I swear, I tried to find you. I had a messenger personally try to deliver letters and a few packages as well, but he always returned carrying the very things I sent you. You disappeared into thin air."

"For everyone's sake now, let's pretend I did." Why was she trying to push this man away when she wanted nothing more than to welcome him back into her life, into her heart, her bed and into Savanah's life. She would not be led astray a second time. She'd be damned before she would pay the piper again. The cost the first time included her sanity and soul.

She'd heard tales of him, the Piper. Not the Pied Piper. No, that child thieving bloke belonged in the bellows with rats clung to him chewing threw his carcass. This piper claimed relation to the Ferryman. She'd heard tell he was so unabashedly beautiful that one single glance his way could sway a person, man or woman into following him into Hell and dancing through hot coals barefoot to get there. Then she looked closer at André and lost her breath. She'd be needing new shoes soon.

André stepped closer. "I must ask. How do you know she is not mine? Jovan, I would not have thought you the casual type."

She gasped. "How dare you? You only knew me for three days, André. You may have been the first man in my bed—but you were not the last." Defiant, she lifted her head and looked him straight in his collarbone. Couldn't be accused of lying to his face that way. "And I'll have you know…"

"That you lie?" André grabbed her, pulled her body close even though she struggled to break free. "Don't do this to me, to us, to our daughter. For God sake's Jovan, she's the spitting image of me. Her eyes, they're mine. Her hair—look at this mop—" André shook his head in her face, "—mine again. Dimple—" André puffed out his cheek and pointed. "The nose and attitude are all you though. Jovan, look at me, please?"

Tears spilled down her rosy cheeks. "Let go of me. You're hurting me." Not physically. She knew he'd never hurt her. Mentally—pretty certain her head resembled a coconut after being cracked wide open.

"Please, André?" Anguish saturated her words. One second—defiant, standing her ground, the next slumped into his arms, clung to him better than his skin. Despite her words, her actions painted a poignant picture.

Doing the jig crossed his mind. André crushed Jovan to him. The trembles he could've done without. The thrill of having her in his arms took over every cell in his body. He ached from both excitement and torment. He'd wanted her for years and now she was back in his arms, holding him as if she'd never let him go…

Lying through her perfectly white teeth.

At that very second, she'd convinced him women made no sense. Ever. "Prove to me she is not mine. Does she hold the mark I have?"

A raging fire grew in her eyes. She shouted, "What mark? Men have silly little marks and scars all over their bodies that they can pinpoint and go into great nauseating detail about each and every one—how they acquired it, what it cost them—who they'd slay in the process. What makes you believe I'd remember one tiny, yes tiny little splat on you?" Jovan's foot tapped an impatient tune raising dust.

"Allow me to refresh your memory. Left hip, where you laid your pretty little head when you were fully engaged in learning intimate carnal knowledge of this." With the sweep of his hand he included everything from his head to his toes. "Ring a bell?"

The trembling came to a staunch halt. "I was a concussed woman. Remember? Didn't even know me bleedin' name."

He pressed farther. "No, you don't remember my mark, or no, she's not got my mark?"

"Neither. That damn thing was branded on you, your cousins and siblings or whatever they are to you now. No one has the same birthmark. Branded like cows you were." Jovan snapped down on her arms hard and shuffled backward from him. His hands fell to his sides.

So what if he pushed her too far with that last comment, he needed the truth. "Jovan, just tell me." He took a step towards her.

"Stop, André!" Jovan slugged him in the arm. "She's not yours. Not now, not ever. Damn you. I don't need you." And currently infuriated to the point she didn't want him. Jovan turned with haste and stomped back into the house only to find her little angel stark naked in the kitchen.

There stood Julian with a wide toothy grin spinning Savanah's drawers in the air on his index finger.

"You!" Jovan trudged to her brother and ripped the clothing from his grasp. She spun in search of her daughter. "Savanah Caitlyn Hause! Where are the rest of your clothes?" Jovan dashed about the kitchen picking up the child's belongings chasing her with them. "Get your little bum back here."

Savanah skedaddled behind Julian for protection and peeked out from his side, laughing. "I got hot, Mummy. Uncle said I could."

Jovan shot a glance at Julian that by all rights should have had him planted in the back yard. And once his ashes turned to fertilizer, he'd bring bleeding heart plants to life with regrowth. Seemed befitting. Her brother had one-upped her.

Lucian pointed to the mark on Savanah's hip then pointed to his own hip. She heard him whisper in Duncan's ear, "She's our girl! Each one of royals has the exact same birthmark." It certainly wasn't said for Duncan's account because Jovan would bet all the Queen's men Duncan had heard, and or seen the mark a million times or more. Especially if he were anything like André.

André shoved the screen door open so hard it bounced off the wall and slammed back in his face. If Jovan wasn't in such a mood she'd have laughed, but his appearance gave her pause. He appeared just as upset.

"Great entrance, Ands," Lucian added as he opened the door and held it for his brother.

****

André jabbed Lucian's shoulder. "You! You could have given me a head's up. Why don't you go play outside, you royal pain in my neck." He pushed past everyone and caught up to Jovan. No one else in the home mattered. He refused to entertain the thought of losing her again. He'd stood at the edge of sanity one too many times and would not lose it today. Not when his heart and soul stood a kiss away from him.

Or bite. She seemed to have more venom than Lucian. He wasn't expecting to see all of Savanah, but he did, birthmark and all. "Still sticking with the branded analogy?"

Her face puckered and ready for a fight, Jovan air jabbed her index finger toward him. André's momentum halted.

He stifled his first reaction, to pick Savanah up and tell her he was her father and that he would love her until the end of time because he didn't want to scare her or Jovan, who now looked positively worse than Duncan.

Once Jovan had Savanah dressed, she walked past her brothers, past Lucian, past André with no eye contact and made her way to the counter, palms down, her glare enough to form an iceberg. "Well, I certainly didn't see this coming. I hope you're all happy."

André watched Jovan reach for the bottle of scotch, hoist it to her lips, tilt her head back and chug. André reached for the liquor. "What? Stop it!"

She jerked the bottle and twisted away from him. "Paws off, pretty boy!"

Before he was able to wrangle the bottle from her grasp she got about four good-sized gulps in. She leaned over the counter, eyes glassy, and waved her hand in front of her mouth.

"Oh Cherié."

"Oh, Cherié nothing!" she mouthed back, sarcasm

thicker than the whiff of the scotch that hit him in the face.

André looked at the only man he didn't recognize watching from afar with a standoffish facade to his presence. "Let me guess, wolf boy?"

"Wolf man to you."

André gingerly extended his hand to the man. "Does she do this often?"

Julian crossed his arms over his chest. Taking the man in, André realized his foot was busy tapping out an impatient tune.

This guy and his intimidation tactics were getting old. Did he really need to boost the biceps?

"Never seen her touch the stuff. Guess you bring out the beast in her. She mentioned something like this when you two met." His head cocked toward his sister Julian asked, "Why, Blossom?"

"Don't you Blossom me either. Why, Julian, is a better question? Why go behind my back? Why would people willingly drink this sludge?" Each word fell off her lips. Her footing staggered—one step, two she clung to the end of the countertop.

André crossed to Jonah, pat the man on the back and told him, "Happy to see you made it back from the trenches. 'Twas a question in our hearts as to whether or not you and Duncan would kill one another."

"Can't kill family, André unless you have a royal scepter shoved up…" Jonah stopped and looked at his niece and smiled. "Duncan and I are related. And here's one for you—Jovan is my sister."

André's head snapped in her direction. "Please tell me she won't turn into a wolf as well. Is this a family trait?"

"No, but I could bloody well turn you into one." Julian sneered showing off all his teeth.

Discouragement clear in his voice, André sighed, "Ah, we're back to that are we?"

Jovan mumbled, "A neutered one."

"As you wish, Blossom." Julian stepped toward André.

Jovan slapped her palm into Julian's chest. "You're both in the same doghouse."

"Look," André walked to Julian. "I am Savanah's—"

Julian took a step towards André and stopped his advance. "I know who you are."

"Perfect, then would you mind watching Savanah while her mother and I go have a nice little chat somewhere private?" And with that, André wasted no time and threw Jovan over his shoulder twirled around and headed out the same door he'd only entered a moment ago.

Julian began to follow them when Lucian grabbed his shoulder. "Allow them time. Please?"

Chapter Eighteen

Thankful the drink had calmed her untamable spirit, André carried her free of any more bodily harm. The woman kicked, squirmed, and muttered nonstop rubbish over a book hundreds of years old, repeating verbatim lines of doom and gloom and what she could do to him if he didn't set her down immediately. What a handful! She did however pique his interest after telling him it was the same tome they were almost killed for in the hotel when they'd first met. Oh, did he have something to show her.

Up the pathway they went, through the purple haze of flowers that led to her home. Inside, André could've mistaken her home for a museum. Paintings decorated every wall in every room, not with hanging pictures, but the walls themselves. The Thames River as the sun rose over Big Ben took up a wall in her dining room. She'd placed a round, gold cuckoo clock in the top of the tower. André had to admit the clock brought the painting to life, especially when it chimed and startled him. Her living area held a painting of a steamboat floating along the Seine River in the evening with the Eiffel Tower lit up in the background. One of his most beloved places to go sit and reflect on life and people watch. He loved watching people interact. Had he missed her sitting there one day? Was she searching for him as well?

As if the other paintings weren't enough to stop him in his tracks, André almost dropped Jovan when he reached her bedchamber.

There it was, a painting of him plastered across her bedroom wall so life-like he thought he'd looked in the mirror. She'd painted him coming up out of the lake in front of the St. James's Manor at twilight. As far as he knew she'd never seen it, just been told about it by him. The way she had the dark lavender sky melding into the shimmering silver waves held true genius creativity. He'd never seen anything more lifelike. A brilliant blue moon bobbed in the water in the far distance with lily pads cushioning it. She had him in only the suit he'd entered the world in. Droplets of water cascaded down his chest and abdomen then trailed off. Each bead glistened like the canopy of stars on the ceiling. And that little birthmark she claimed no knowledge of? He'd remember to point that out to her once those glassy-eyed baby blues opened up.

A slight grimace gnawed its way to his face. She could have added a tad bit more paint to his manhood. *If she could lie in this room each and every night and look at me then why in God's name wouldn't she want me to know Savanah?*

One loud burble from his drunken damsel produced an aftermath of pungent liquid being expelled over his shoulder. Seemed some things never changed. After plunking her on the bed he undressed her then stripped his belongings off he found his way to the kitchen. After the clothes were rinsed and he'd had a quick sponge bath, he returned with a glass of lemon water for her. Waiting until the effects of the scotch wore off his head began to toy with him. What if she truly didn't want him? He browsed the room and on the top of her vanity he found his answer.

There, sitting on atop a small swatch of purple velvet rest a crunched cigar band. She'd kept it all these years. He hopped on the bed and lay beside her and waited for fate to once again finish the chess game. This time the king would proclaim checkmate, and he would protect his queen with his life.

Her eyelids danced. Her pink lips held a kissable smile. Her breasts were just as he remembered, firm, full, nipples taut, and as much as he'd like to have had credit for them standing at attention, he knew the cooler air played its part. His turn was coming up.

Her trim stomach showed no signs that she'd ever given birth with the exception of a few subtle light purple stretch marks. And why wouldn't they be purple? Everything else in her home was. He ran his hands over her slender hips and wondered how a baby ever passed through there.

The shape she held now left him in total awe. He wondered what she looked like carrying his child. Radiant, of course. It saddened him he wasn't a part of her pregnancy. Oh, what he'd have given to see his child growing inside the woman he loved. Maybe they could have a second child. The notion warmed him. He had a family, sort of. He just needed to convince Jovan the sky wouldn't fall from their joining. Like that was going to be easy. It would probably be easier to drive a railroad tie into his eye and enjoy doing so.

He brushed back a long unruly tendril from her face and kissed her cheek, waiting happy as a clam for her to open her eyes.

****

The moment Jovan showed signs of life, André prattled, "Afternoon, ma beauté lush. How are we fairing?"

Jovan swallowed the urge to incinerate him on the spot. She could do that at any point. He wanted to play, then play she would.

Right after the room stopped spinning.

She held onto the bed and dubbed herself a true idiot. Then she realized besides her dignity she'd lost a little more. There she lay, completely stripped of all clothing in broad daylight, although he was kind enough to drape her with a light blanket. His saving grace. She didn't remember how she got here, or why André lay next to her, also in his birthday suit, but answer to her he would, especially since it was no one's birthdays. She reached over and grabbed the glass of water and without coming up for air chugged half of it. "Did we?"

"Not yet." He poured on a half smirk while his eyebrows waggled.

She wasn't certain she was offended nothing happened or happy it didn't because she didn't want to miss out on a thing.

He stuck his face so close, so kissably close to hers and told her, "I would never take advantage of an inebriated witch," just before he bopped his nose into hers.

Jovan inched back a bit. He was too close. She might just kiss him. God help them both. "For the record, I am no longer inebriated."

"Aye, my love, then what are we waiting for?" André asked slapping her thigh playfully.

Even without bows and ribbons and pretty paper he made one fine gift. Her brain, it mutinied her every chance it got. Wasn't she ready to throttle him a second past? Would she ever be able to stay upset with all this muscle and sinew not to mention those mysterious blackish blue orbs watching her closer than a cat stalking a mouse? Not from this vantage. She could take her frustrations out on him or would that be ministrations? Without speaking Jovan looked around her bedroom for her clothing.

Nowhere.

Where the hell were her brothers? Again, same answer.

Jovan finished the rest of the water. What a joy her morning had been! She'd soon be selling the London Bridge to someone if they believed that.

"André, where are my clothes?"

"Hanging outside. We had an incident. Or more to the point, you did."

"I don't miss that word. So?" Her hands waved over their present condition of nakedness. "What happened?"

"Nothing to write home about. You covered us in whatever you ate for breakfast laced with a damn fine waste of good scotch. Jovan—I," André rested his arm across her stomach. Nervous fingers tapped away. Tympanic hollow notes resonated from within her.

This felt like history repeating itself all over again.

Testing the waters, he was. She realized he thought if she didn't want him near her, his hand would be the first thing to go. It stayed. She could tease him a little. Jaw clenched tight, she bit back a smirk.

"—You know I would never take advantage of

you."

Jovan laughed, not a kind laugh that meant, gee, I'm so happy we're both here naked together after all these years, but a laugh that died more suddenly than a person getting nicked in two by a guillotine. She'd practiced that very laugh as well. A few years of imaginary conversations and fights prepares one for almost anything. Except reality.

André's fingers sped up. Tap, tap, tap. Jovan snatched his hand. The tapping ceased. Without thinking her fingers entwined with his.

She rolled on her side to face him no longer worried she lost her clothes. So did he. Time to tango.

"Jovan, I swear on our daughter's life, I tried to find you."

"So you've said and don't you ever swear on her life again. How could it be, André, if we sought each other, we never found one another?" The anger in her voice dissolved; only sorrow for lost memories together remained. Jovan studied André. She remembered the softness of his hair on his chest and how far down it went on his body before it turned into a springy patch surrounding one solid sword. She strained to look lower without gawking. She'd wanted him beside her for so long, so badly it hurt and now with him this painfully close... All she had to do was close the distance. She knew he wanted to. Some things were most obvious. The rise in the sheet being a telltale sign.

He moved his leg closer to hers, inch by inch. He didn't think she noticed.

How could she not? She noticed everything about him. When his toes tapped her toes, a chill prickled her spine. Goosebumps sprung to life, her nipples surged forward and in between her thighs the levy broke. She became warm and wet and in need of some serious attention. For a second, she wondered if she had a split personality. The good girl screamed at her to get the hell out of the bed and run for her life, but the naughty girl had a much better idea—wrap her legs around him and let him back into her life.

And the winner is?

"Jovan, we will probably never know what happened or why, but what matters is now, what lies here, between you and I."

She knew what lay between them, an erection that simply stole her breath away… or would once she had her lips on him. Something out of the corner of her eye caught her attention—her leg, as it slid over his thigh totally betraying her.

She noticed André's hand on her hip, which also had slid closer. Cheeky sod!

"I want you… to talk to me. Please? Tell me about Savanah, everything. She is so beautiful."

She feathered fingers over his arm. The need to touch him revolved around her basic need for survival. Fact being it would be a moot point without him. The same ripple effect of goose bumps broke out along his skin. "She has your eyes, André. They are big and the deepest blue and hold the wealth of beauty and innocence. She's loving, inquisitive, loyal to a fault, and she has two pairs of pants she wears rather well— smarty pants and sassy pants. This is where the resemblance between the two of you is undeniable." Jovan babbled on so proud of their daughter, "and yes, as you've seen she's the same silly brand as you."

"I recall you liked my birth mark." His thumb shot

over his shoulder aimed toward the painting.

"That?" She snickered, "No big deal."

"I beg to differ." He bent and kissed the tip of her nose. The corners of her lips turned upward. She gave him a slight tug toward her. André obliged and suddenly the solid firmness of his erection pressed into the inside of her thigh. They both hesitated looking into one another's eyes waiting. One swift position change and the gap would be plugged.

The good girl in Jovan crossed the finish line. She pulled back from him as if she'd been scalded by boiling water. She rolled away to the opposite wall ashamed while emotions leaked from her eyes.

André didn't move. He didn't attempt to force himself on her and for that alone he won her heart all over. His patience and gentleman's scholar were two of his finer qualities she'd fallen in love with. She had to figure this one out on her own. Then she watched his hand skim her thigh and hip. In one swift shift, he sat up and peeked under the cover.

"You all right?" He whispered. "I promise I'll never hurt you." Before she realized it, his lips found her bottom.

Startled at first, it didn't take long until she relaxed to his seduction. With every nip and kiss he gave her heart picked up an extra beat or two. Sweet sensations coiled in her gut and stretched out to reach every corner of her body. His lips made a trail up the length of her body and then rested behind her ear. Again, he whispered, "Jovan, I love you. I loved you the first day we met. I never stopped. There hasn't been a woman since that I've ever dreamt of."

Jovan loved his lips. Loved the softness, the pout.

She could spend the entire night letting his mouth make love to her.

Jovan turned and looked at him once more. She wanted him. She needed him. Not for money or material possessions, but to love. Her paintings kept her very wealthy. But Savanah? Could she deny him the relationship he genuinely wanted? She could have him now, this once and see if the roof caved in. With trepidation she peeked upward, checking for signs of distress or cracks or plaster being hurled down upon them.

He loved her. She knew he did. But that damned book she'd lost. How could a book written in the dark ages plague her with nightmares yet to come? Was it only she the book cursed? Seemed so at the moment.

She didn't know of anyone else currently in bed with the most handsome man alive or only man she had ever loved, would ever love, unable to make love to him even after he professed his undying love. Jovan turned away again, chagrinned. André curled around her, snuggled in tighter. And there it was, his manhood, knocking at her back door, patient, waiting for an invite. Without hesitating she wiggled into the thickened mass and pinned his nob between her cheeks.

Her lips curled into the smallest of smiles. Within the bat of her long blonde eyelashes the tables had turned.

"What the—" André sprung out of bed. Fully dressed he stammered "—How the—" He gasped as he backed himself into a corner and stared at her, now sitting on the edge of the bed still topless, bottomless and he breathless.

"I believe introductions are in order, St. John—"

"St. James, Cherié, remember?" he asked as he touched random parts of clothing to see if it was indeed real.

"Just testing your memory. There's a few things you need to know before we take this any further. When we met I didn't remember who I was. What I am. I've had four years to conquer my demons and align my angels. I've some powers you need to be aware of." Jovan stood, closed her eyes for a moment and ran an imaginary flowing line down the sides of her body with her fingers. When she opened her eyes a lavender silk slip covered her.

****

From his vantage not only did the slip accent every curve on her, but it intensified his every desire. Disheveled beauty was his only thought. More now than ever he wanted her. Needed her. Would not leave this place of free will without her. Everything on him ached, throbbed, screamed at him and that was just the head on his shoulders. Other body parts were at a critical mass. But, since she was playing hard to get...

He yawned. "So, point proven, you're a witch. Cherié, after the past few days I've had there really isn't much that can surprise me. Trust me. What else can you do?" He tried to sound blasé.

Jovan shook her head. "You are flat out the worst theatre major I've ever met."

His head cocked to one side he shrugged a shoulder, he tossed back, "You think you are better?"

Jovan scrunched her nose and giggled. "My powers revolve around nature mostly. I bring things to light. To life."

The confined swell of his cock proved her point:

Although if left in this state of despair much longer it would be the death of him. He glanced down at his fingers trying still for nonchalant, asking, "What else?"

"I have the ability to see into the future, but I won't. Things aren't the same after you peek."

His eyes met hers with sheer curiosity. "Why?"

A grin covered Jovan's lips. "Savanah's most favorite word. Guess she gets it from you. Well, the last time I scryed—"

André cut her off, "What is scrying? Show me?"

Lips scrunched to one side, she shook her head no. "I don't think so."

"Please? I'm interested. I want to learn everything about you."

"You say that now." Jovan stood and crossed the room to her armoire. With a slight tug the heavy oak door squeaked open. She rummaged through the top left shelf tossing things over her shoulder onto the floor and out of her way. Under all her stockings lay a black velvet satchel with gold toggles tied in a bow. She crossed back to the bed and sat down. She patted the space beside her. "Come."

"Promise not to do anything to me?" He asked half jesting, half serious.

"Well, what's the worst I could do? It's not like I undressed you when you were inebriated and tried to take advantage of you! Oh, wait—that was what you did to me. The first time I awoke I was in your arms with your lips trying to swallow me whole."

"I only tried to rouse you. You were unconscious. Read it in a book that you could wake someone with a kiss."

"You aren't Prince Charming, you are a giant

nutter. And it only works for true love." Not a moment later Jovan's eyes went wide.

"Touché." André winked. "That little peck woke you up. Maybe I've got some magic of my own. And I didn't take advantage of you then and you know it," he argued. "Our first encounter you'd expelled body fluids all over everything and to top it off, you were covered in bloody demon bits. Remember that? And this is different. You're in your bed this time. No demon bits this round though. Just a little devil!" He smiled. She did not. "Cherié, I have not misbehaved. Yet." André crossed the room and sat beside her. "Go on then, work your magic on me."

"That statement leaves a vast amount of willpower on my behalf." Jovan winked at him this time. "I'll show you the tools, but will not look forward. As I was saying, the last time I scryed my vision was my mother, dead. And I owe you an explanation for everything you felt from the moment we crashed into one another." Jovan took in a huge breath. *Here goes nothing.* She had to let him know the absolute truth.

André reached for her. "You all right? You've gone pale."

Jovan took his chin in her hand and looked into his serene blue eyes, possibly for the last time. "Sometimes the truth, even as awful or innocent as it is sets you free. The morning we met I'd recited a charm from the book everyone wanted. It was a love spell. Meant to find my soul mate. So now you know."

"That explains all those men following you, bending over backward to catch your attention."

Her voice shaky, she mustered the strength to tell him the truth. "André, you were one of those men. I charmed you into loving me. None of it was real."

"Yes, you did, Cherié, but now I must tell you one thing. I am immune to hexes, charms, and spells... whatever you want to call them. Do you remember the oil I used on you the night I had you tied up?"

"Yes, but—"

André placed his finger to her lips. "I splash the oil on my body every day. It's an antidote, sort of. It, the vetivert oil wards off all magic of all sorts. My love for you was not conjured from a charm. It grew in my heart." Hands out, palms up, sincere, André asked, "About the note I found in my pocket our last day together? You'd written to meet me at the train station in 2 weeks. I didn't read it until it until I arrived in Dover. I'd had never left you. I thought you were married to some skeleton."

"Everything went wrong that day. Everything. My brother almost died. I actually believed he had, but somehow, he pulled through. He'd slept for nearly a full month. The man I was with is a family friend. Naught more. Then I lost you. Thought I died."

"Jovan, I saw you hanging from the end of a rope, dead. Then you were alive and leaving me. I thought I died both times. You and I have a beautiful daughter, and we have a second chance to fulfill our destiny. Most people don't get this opportunity."

"You are the optimist of us. You see the world as your playground. I see my garden. André all you have to do is snap your fingers."

"As do you, Cherié. I'm right in front of you." He waited for her to smile, to acknowledge his joke. And... he waited. With a slight heave of his chest he added, "Your lucky star shall always shine in one spot in the night's sky. The path which you choose to view it can always change. We are not bound to this life by structure or class."

"Spoken like someone who's never been told no a single day in their life."

"Never allow another to place restraints on you, unless, of course, they are silk and I'm the one tying you up."

The smile returned to her face. "Believe we've been there and done that. I recall giving you the boot trying to get your dead weight off of me after that bloke slammed you with a champagne bottle."

"So that's what happened? My poor jewel was discolored for a month." Both laughed recalling the incident like it was yesterday. "And for the record, what I have at my fingertips is you. You are my heart's desire. My path led me here. To your side. My heart will remain here forever."

Jovan blushed. "You're well versed. I'll concede to that." Slender fingers untied the gold threads of the pouch. She reached in and withdrew a circular, flat, shiny black stone, about the size of a pancake. "If you peer into it and concentrate on nothing at all, visions play themselves out on the surface. Sometimes it's the entire story. Others it's bits and pieces you puzzle together."

"Can I see it?"

Jovan handed the stone to him. André tilted it to see a perfect reflection of the two of them sitting together. "It's a mirror. That's all."

"Is that all you see?"

"What else should I see?" She'd piqued his interest now.

Jovan turned away from the object, her eyes clamped shut. He pressed her further, "What is it?"

"I didn't look long enough. I won't look again. The thing is a curse not a gift." A tremor ran the length of her leg.

The last thing André wanted was her mood to deteriorate. If she saw something, she could tell him when and if she was ready to. "Well, when I look into it, I see you and I together. As we should be."

"Again, the optimist speaks."

"Cherié, today I have much to be thankful for. I have the hope that you and Savanah will be a permanent part of my life. It is a gift. You are my gift, to which I'd be most appreciative of if I could unwrap you, play with you and keep you forever."

Jovan bit her bottom lip. Yes or no. She gazed into the infinite hope his eyes promised and felt herself drowning. With a smile on her face. The love of her life said the one thing she'd all but given up on ever hearing—he wanted Savanah and her in his life. Right here at this moment she understood his optimism. Felt his love. If undressed once more could feel other things…

"Birthday suits!" Dressed one second. Stripped naked the next.

André sprang to his feet. "Fair warning the next time please?"

"I said birthday suits." Jovan giggled.

His birthday suit had been tailored for him. Jovan watched with enthusiasm the muscles in his buttock work as he spun in search of the clothes. The man had one solid behind she needed to explore. His legs were shear muscle with just the right amount of hair. Nothing

Sasquatch about him. His back held chorded muscles. The simplest shift of his arms rippled strength. His abdomen, one could bounce a pence or two off. Da Vinci should have had him for a model. "The look on your face is a keepsake. I'll have fun with this."

Laughing at him one second, buried underneath him the next as he pounced on her. "Who's going to have more fun now?" He gave her a wide toothy grin before kissing her nose.

This beautiful man was well on his way to stealing her heart again. He wanted to give her time to straighten out her head and heart or to run. She didn't want to run unless it was straight into his arms.

****

"This little blinkety-blink thing you do…" André bat his eyelashes in an exaggerated fashion, "…can come in handy. Can you fashion us things other than clothing? Time travel perhaps?"

"Time travel happens only in dire events. Even then, the balance of nature can be skewered for eternity."

"I know someone I'd like to skewer." Hands on her shoulders, he rolled the both of them to their side and snuggled in close. He inhaled, his eyes closed. "You smell of lilacs in the spring."

"It's the oil from the flowers. They're my favorite."

"Of course, they are." He chortled. "They're purple."

With enthusiasm she added, "That's my favorite color."

"Cherié." André nudged the tip of his nob closer to her sheath. "I know something else that's a nasty shade of purple. I need you truly certain of your feelings or I will go. I want no regrets." *Although I know I'll regret saying this later.* "No doubts. I want you to come freely to me, to my bed—ah—make that your bed."

Holding her drove him to the brink of insanity. His hands wandered lower on her body weaving in and out of her cresson of curls. She never tried to still his movements, instead she shifted her hips to meet his touch. He found her skin smoother than satin. He heard something, a moan, but didn't know whether it came from her or him. "Jovan *puis-je vous embrasser?*" He puckered up.

She turned to face him. "Look at us, André."

He did. Her genuine smile, and the ever-present twinkle in her eye he recognized from days past.

"I would think most people in this position would have started out kissing each other. I've wanted you to kiss me since I saw you."

His eyebrows arched. "Could have fooled me." Regardless André did as he was asked and rolled Jovan onto her back. "Comfy?" She nodded yes. He blanketed her with his body, her hips pinned beneath his. The obvious state of his arousal wound up firmly between the delicate folds of her skin, so close to Eden both sinners and saints would rejoice. With a subtle nudge of her thighs he could take her, bury his cock deep inside and wait for her sheath to constrict around him. The want and desire to do just that maddened him. The restraint to not go the distance would be his demise.

He had to think of something else. Anything else until she consented. He bent his head to her and found her lips were just as he remembered. Soft. Warm. Delicious. He slid his tongue between her lips and probed. *One body part at a time. Focus André.* Her tongue met his head on. A duel to the finish. God he wanted that tongue of hers doing more intimate motions. All right, so this line of thinking wasn't going to help the situation, but it sure as hell wasn't going to hinder it either. He pulled back and kissed her cheeks, nose, forehead, eyelids...

Her eyes were closed, trusting him never to hurt her again. He'd die first and if this didn't play out the way he intended, it was pretty much a given. He slid his tongue into her mouth once more to find fever-pitched passion. Warmth flooded his heart with hope and something more—intimate trust. This wasn't about him by any means, but about them, together: Mending two souls. Hopefully melding them as well.

By the by, André's hips had their own agenda. There were thinkers and doers in a relationship. His top noggin thought way too much. His little head—he reneged that dreadful misleading image—his not so little head—was doing what he had too—grinding a pathway.

A guttural groan of, "Bebé?" squeaked out.

Jovan sounded no better. "André?"

"Do you want this, because if you do not wish me inside you to love, then what?"

"That sounded awfully whiney." She laughed.

"I drink wine, Cherié, not make girlish grunts."

"So say you." Her laughter turned into a snort and, for a brief moment, André tightened his hold on her and allowed her laughter to fill him.

Looking more demure than his heart could take she asked, "Can we just do this? What will happen?"

"We will end up changing the sheets of your

bedding." He smirked as he covered her lips once more in one hard-pressed kiss.

She broke away with a sweep of her tongue over her lips. "André, don't stop what you're doing. If this feels good to you then please don't stop."

"Oui."

"Limey's don't speak French. André, but how do you say harder in French? I'm about to explode."

"*Plus fort.*" He added some oomph behind his thrusts to embellish the phrase.

Jovan panted, "*Plus fort! Plus fort!*"

With rhythmic circular motions, he pressed hard circles over her Venus then rocked his hips as she'd asked for, harder and faster through her thighs, his cock slippery from her arousal. Didn't take long at all for the pressure between her legs and stomach to erupt. He felt her body climax and he hung on tight.

Jovan sucked in a gulp of air and mumbled, "Rapturous ecstasy. I've muscles I've forgotten I own dancing with delight. They should dance with yours."

Music to his ears. André pressed his lips against hers as her body quivered beneath him. That little turn of events did it. One head to toe shudder was the only warning they got before his seed covered the front of them.

"Check mate." Arms to each side of her in a push-up position, André ground his pelvis and tummy against her to the left then right before he moved from atop her. In a playful manner he'd slathered the sticky mess between them like icing on a cake. One long stretch later he lay on his side propped by his elbow beside her wearing a smile fit for a king, and rightfully so.

Bird's eye view; he had one. Her smile, he would

cherish the very look of utter contentment and beauty until the day he died. Her unabashed nude body glistened with a mixture of both their sex. He'd never seen anything more enticing. Yet.

The night was young.

Amusement clearer than her reflection in a mirror, Jovan shifted and said, "Oh blimey! You weren't kidding."

With his left middle finger, he drew a heart design on her belly. "Such a waste of beautiful children."

"André!" Jovan scrunched her nose.

"I'll get some clean clothes for us. *Ou` sont les toilettes?*" He worked his way from the bed to the floor.

She pointed behind her. "The bath is off to the right."

"Will you come back to London with me? Jovan, I want to be part of your lives, yours and Savanah's." He kissed her head in passing.

"André, the bath is back here."

He backed up and gave a slow spin and tightened his buttock muscles, so Jovan would get an eyeful, and winked. "I knew that." The portrait of him on the wall was almost better than him in person. Almost. She couldn't have done what they just did with that portrait. "How did you remember me so well? You painted my eyes and nose with perfection. You were selfish with the paint elsewhere. A hefty brush loaded with more paint lower would be more true to life." He pointed to parts of his body further south.

"Yes dear, you do have big feet," she jested.

His mouth made a scrunched circle and he squinted. "No, that would be you." A pillow went careening past him. "How long did it take you?" He ran his hands over the wall inspecting her work. "You are a genius, Jovan. Your home is beautiful."

"Merci." Jovan nodded. "Took two years. I live with a perfect little image of you. I see you every time I look into her eyes. I'll be honest, I painted over you more than once, depending on my mood."

"You won't erase me from your life again. Come, sit by me while the tub fills." André pat the settee next to him and gave Jovan his best come hither look.

****

It was a sinful look, but, first things first. Jovan walked into the bathroom and came out with a wet towel. "Stand up a second."

Careful not to give him a rug burn, she ran the wet cloth over his stomach, his penis and lower between his legs, fondling him as she cleansed him. Her fingers gripped his sticky shaft, while he stood above her eager—amused. Even as she wiped away the evidence of their tryst, Jovan never noticed he no longer laid flat in the palm of her hand, until he came close to poking out her eye. She looked up at him and huffed a curl from her vision. "I'm sorry. I didn't mean…" Her voice trailed off looking at the man's erection.

"There are some things a man can't help when he's in a position such as this with the woman of his dreams."

Her heart fluttered. That grin of his got her every time. "Aren't you a feisty one?" Arousing him again hadn't crossed her mind. She wanted him clean. She had pet peeves, one that he would come to know soon enough. Cleanliness had nothing to do with Godliness and everything to do with keeping her from traumatizing others who didn't see things her way. Skin liked soap and water. Her velvet settee did not. How to tell him that without hurting his ego? Nothing came to mind. She tried to avoid his intent gaze, but it was either his sensuous face, or the growing fondness in her grasp.

He tugged her hair for attention. "Jovan!" came out breathy. André yanked her up into his arms and pressed one fully engorged ready-to-spill-over-erection into her tummy. He kissed her firmly, his tongue deep in her throat. She loved his reactions. His loss of control empowered her. To be able to bring this prince to the edge of the abyss gave her confidence in her abilities as a woman.

"Please, Cherié?" He moved her hair from her neck and angled his head in. His tongue trailed lazy circles over her pulse before he latched on and sucked and left deep red marks behind. "I need you." His lips traveled to her chin. "*Je t'aime.*"

He'd told her he loved her again. Could she, would she, should she, deny him her body the way she wanted it to be between them? The way their bodies were meant to be together? What if they had another child?

That one thought gave her pause. She placed her hands on his chest, and she stepped back.

André stepped with her, as if he'd read her mind. He never relinquished his hold. His words carried gently over her. "If you are worried about another child, I would welcome one. Savanah should have brothers and sisters. I won't leave you, Jovan. Allow me to love you."

Jovan's bottom lip quivered. Making her dreams become reality seemed so simple. All she had to utter were three tiny letters, *y-e-s* that carried the weight of the world with them.

"André," She hesitated, clamped her eyes shut to ward off the tears. Absolute waste of time. Probably would have been easier to stop the sun from rising.

"Why is it I feel a *but* coming?" He moved to kiss her again. Maybe, he thought, if he continued to kiss her she'd forget her woes, but her teeth chattered so hard they threatened to bite through him.

"What if the book is right?" She sniffled.

He massaged her shoulders, down her back and worked his way down the soft curves of her bottom. He snuggled in, and pulled her to feel the still ever-present nagging, begging for resolution mass between them. Then it hit him—he would always have this sexual desire for her. He needed her as much as he needed air. More.

"Cherié, I don't know what mendacities are trapped between the pages which stops you from coming to me, but it's blasphemy. Who would write such a book and more importantly," André held Jovan out in front of him and hesitated a moment. "This book you speak of, I should tell you I have a journal of yours. I found it the first day we met and placed it in my trunk for safekeeping. It's blank, all the pages, yet they are worn as though they've been read repeatedly. Corners bent, pages folded in half and red stains across some."

Jovan's hand covered her mouth. She stepped back with a ghastly mask over her face. "Oh dear lord."

"What is written? I need to know what I stand against other than the doom and gloom of course?"

"The book holds secrets only true sorcerers would die for or kill for. The book's claim to fame isn't a happily ever-after, just life in the ever-after."

"And again, I ask you why it is you covet the book?"

"I no longer do." She shrugged her shoulders. "I lost it the first day we were together. You now have it."

"I what? It's a wordless diary."

"To you maybe. To those with special talents and a drop or two of blood, reading takes you where fantasy cannot. Is it with you now?"

André nodded yes.

"Have attempts on your life increased over the past few years?"

Again, he bobbed his head. "My brother and sister as well."

"Has anyone besides you handled it?"

"No. I clung to it because it was the only memento I had left of you."

"The last day we were together, the man who attempted to get the book said you were after it, that your mum put you up to it. That you could never love someone like me."

"Lies. The woman who claimed to be my mother had been missing eight years before she turned up yesterday. She was my aunt and I had been lied to most of my early life." André tilted her chin to look him in the eye. "I'll die loving you."

"Truly didn't sound as eloquent as you thought it." Jovan ducked her head and ran her hands over her face. "I feel horrid. I thought the worst of you for so long. Forgive me?"

"Never tell me you're sorry. You had no evidence to prove the thief wrong."

She patted her chest, right over her heart. "I had this. It was easier to believe you left me for the book instead of leaving me because I wasn't the correct pedigree."

André bent to her and kissed her. "There is no other, only you."

"You need to know death is splattered across the pages. Even our current queen and her daughters have termination dates coming up if the book tells the truth."

"My aunt? The queen?"

Jovan nodded. "André, I don't want Savanah or you mere history on one of those pages. The book tells of one of the royals going dark, killing her family."

"Chyna."

Jovan paled hearing her name. André asked, "What is it? You don't look well."

"What or who is Chyna to you?"

"My aunt. She's the one who lied and told everyone she was my mother, but it was all a preposterous hoax so she could get to the throne. She had a woman with special powers coming to the home weekly giving us potions to make certain we sat with our heads up our," André cranked his neck and signaled to his derriere then gave Jovan a noncommittal shrug. "We were clueless while she aligned her demons."

"That bony little woman told me she'd help find you. She clung to me better than me bleedin' shadow only darker and spookier. André, *je suis desole`*."

"Cherié, do not to apologize to me."

"When I saw you earlier, I was scared. Of you. Of me. Of this." Jovan spread her arms wide trying to encompass things that weren't even fathomable.

"A messy bed? Get used to it." The eyebrows lifted and the smile hogged his face before getting serious. "I should have known I had a child who needed me."

André cradled her next to his heart. "We will be fine wherever we are, as long as we're together."

"André, unless you had a crystal ball how could you see the future?"

"That's why I've got you." He puckered up those lips and blew her a kiss. "Love at first sight, Cherié. I knew before I even knew your name. Bet that's not written in your book! So—" Time to take a leap of faith. "—My previous offer of marital bliss still stands. Marry me?"

"You are a hopeless romantic."

With a slight tap on her nose he answered, "Hopeful. One of us has to be."

"Today has been a gift from the Goddess. Just give me a little time?"

His playful tone vanished, and anger rose faster than mercury in the desert on a cloudless day. He backed up. "How much time? Another four years?"

"That's not fair and not what I meant."

"What then, dear? I have known you were my destiny from the moment I saw you. You on the other hand keep placing me in the toy chest only to play with me when it suits your needs."

"André! I saw our paths go separate ways. I wanted to believe in you."

"But you didn't." His tone wounded André added, "What did you see a little while past when you were showing me your glass?"

From the corner of her eye she cast one unfriendly glimpse at him. "It's not good. Can we leave it at that?"

"Tell me, so I am prepared."

"André, this unholy tome tells me I lose everything no matter what path I choose. I will not lose Savanah."

"Just me."

Chapter Nineteen

André, Lucian? You two anywhere near home?

André shook his head taking in the absurdity of the situation. His lady held the ability to see into the future and he, well he had the ability to psychically talk to his siblings. And with that realization, he knew then life as he knew it would never be the same. André answered Raven, *On the morrow, Beauty.*

Telepathy or not, Raven screamed, "No!"

Lucian popped into the mix. *Raven? What is it? What's wrong?*

With a slight hesitation Raven answered, *Serina sprung some new dents.*

No! Both André and Lucian gasped.

She is not immune to the virus. One nibble too many Lucian. How soon can you be home? Father Butler just gave her his homemade wine mixed with a splash of heroine for pain. She passed out. Please hurry home.

Lucian told André, *I don't want to throw a wrench into your reunion, but I must leave.*

Not to worry. Jovan is rather proficient at wrench tossing.

What happened? Both Raven and Lucian asked.

See you soon. André cut his ties to his siblings. "Cherié, I have been called home. It sounds urgent."

231

The twinkle in her eye turned to a crystallized tear. Tight-lipped, she asked, "Is all okay?"

"Truly you have to ask? No." André's hands were angry knots by his side. "Once again you side stepped my proposal. You want more time? Take it. Take all you need. Forever if you like." André pointed to his naked body. "Just get me dressed today!"

Jovan wiggled her fingers then snapped them once and André was fully clothed and headed out the door, she one corset behind him.

Headed to Julian's through the woods gave them their last bit of privacy before getting asked every question under the stars when they arrived and time to figure out how to answer them without André falling apart doing it. They walked apart, both lost in thought, disconnected not only to the earth, stars and moon, but one another.

Maybe that damned book works against me after all. Tremendous! Now she has me paranoid about a book written by some loon that's older than the crust in Lucian's drawers.

You're not funny.

Lucian, it was too. Stop eavesdropping in my head. "Jovan, I am sorry you do not have faith in me. In us. I love you with all my heart, and I would give it up in an instant to protect you and Savanah."

"That's it in a nutshell. You shouldn't have to lose your heart."

"Apparently I will either way. I shan't press you further, with the exception of Savanah. I want her to know me. Her heritage. That she is loved. That she has a father and that I want to be a very visible presence in her life. I will come for her after matters at home have been dealt with."

"So, you are to leave me again after you just swore to me otherwise?"

His arms out to his side, his fists white, he yelled, "You turned down my proposal, woman! What do you want?"

Jovan glared at him, her eyebrow arched and armed. He didn't appreciate the look.

Her sarcasm on point she raised her voice. "Are you serious? I want it all, but I don't want to be looking over me shoulder for monsters in alley ways or vampires slinking across the ceiling waiting to drop in on me the rest of me life either."

André ran his hands through his hair. "Jovan, life comes with no guarantees other than death. Once you find the person to share your life with you do exactly that. Together. Regardless of the outcome. I jump—you jump."

"That might possibly be the stupidest thing I've ever heard. I die—you die—Savanah winds up an orphan."

His entire body pulsing with anger, he finished, "I'm leaving. I'll be back in a week for Savanah."

"Heard that before. So, it's just like old times. We have this fantastic frolic for a few minutes, and you run off into the night. Splendid. Really. Leave! I lived through the loss once."

"Damn you woman!" André groaned feeling the hard splat of a raindrop followed by another. Rain battered them sideways and left them both soaked to the bone by the time they reached Julian's. "Bloody splendid!"

"The plastered man is up. Come?" Savanah

grabbed both Jovan and Andre's hands as they entered the front door and dragged them into the kitchen. Jonah greeted each of them with a towel. "Ta," André said as he rubbed his face and hands dry before bending over and getting all his hair blotted dry. Savanah crawled between his legs, looked up and gave him a smile.

Trying to keep his spirits and appearance up for everyone, André whispered to her, "Call him the old man, Savanah. Not the plastered man."

"Why?" Savanah asked as she took the towel from him and wrung his hair out in the towel herself, helping him.

At that moment he'd have told her every one of the Queen's secrets and how to get the Crown jewels if she'd asked. "Just because, Princess. Thank you for your assistance." Relieved to see Duncan up and looking less pickled, André teased, "I see the effects of the scotch finally wore off, old man."

"Suppose after today I've earned that title. What did I miss besides the obvious?" Duncan struggled to hold his arm up. "Feels more like cement. You fools had best not plastered anything else on me body that looked limp or broken." Duncan yanked at the waistband on his trousers and peeked inside. Glancing out from under his brows he gave an elfish grin.

Lucian jest, "You'll need more than plaster to get that thing up and running again."

Savanah nudged André. "You have the same paint on you that mummy painted on me. True?" Savanah held out her arms to André.

His daughter in his arms for the first time, emotions swaddled him. Tears formed behind his eyes as he gazed into her innocent face.

"Savanah? Mummy painted yours on you after she saw mine. She thought you might like to have the same mark as me."

"Why?"

Lucian burst into laughter. "André, you've no clue what can of worms you just opened."

"Why?" Savanah asked again. Looking back at Lucian, the little girl pouted.

"Because mummy liked me. And she loves you. And she thought it might be nice if we had something we could share." With a slight hesitancy André glanced at Jovan. There she stood. Soaked to the bone. Red-nosed. Gorgeous.

Savanah smiled at André. "I like you too." She turned to Lucian and stuck out her tongue. "Would you come to my room for tea?" Both of her arms went around his neck and she hugged him. Just like that. She liked him, too, because her mother did.

Or used too.

"Savanah, André does not have the time for a tea party. He has to leave for a bit."

"Why?" Savanah tightened her hold on her father.

André looked at Jovan. He couldn't hide the hurt in his eyes. "I have to make a pretty room for you and your mum to stay in when you come visit me."

"Pink?"

The little girl's cherub face found the key and unlocked his heart.

"Yes, Savanah. Pink." No matter how stinking rotten he felt with regards to Jovan he had a daughter and saying no to her he decided, might never happen.

André turned fast and kissed Savanah on her cheek. "There, I got you!"

"Kiss mummy."

He met her glare. Jovan's wide, husky blue eyes still glistened with unshed tears. He took one step toward her and she backed up. He went one further until she hit a wall. "I will not walk away from you allowing you to believe I do not love or need you more than the air I breathe. This is not over, Cherié. Stay safe until my return." André kissed her trembling lips, turned and walked out with Savanah still on his hip. He glanced to Lucian, his face blank. *Didn't quite go as planned.*

Lucian asked, *You all right?*

Was I ever?

"André?" His heart stopped. Perhaps she had a change of heart? He turned back, and she greeted him by the gate.

"Here! It's a good luck charm, sort of. If you get into a sticky spot or fear for anyone's safety rub this." She tucked a gold velvet pouch into his grasp.

He swallowed his disappointment. "What is this? Rabbit's foot?"

"Ewh! No." She shrieked. "Why would you think to carry around a dead rodent's foot? How vile. It's a talisman. Little amulets. Nothing bad will happen to you as long as you have possession of it. Keep it close. Talk with me as you rub it, and I can aid you in anything."

André set Savanah down got down on his knee and hugged his daughter tightly. "God, Savanah you're beautiful."

One last ditch attempt to sway his fair maiden, he stood and loomed over her, looked directly into her saddened eyes and told her, "When you look at your painting tonight know that it is I watching over you as you sleep." He pulled her back into his arms. "My feet refuse to walk. My heart beats with purpose now. It's been so long since I've felt alive." He pressed his forehead to hers. "I don't want to lose this. You!"

With her hand on his cheek, she ran her fingers across his mouth. "You already have. You need to go." Jovan grabbed Savanah, turned and walked back towards the house.

On his stallion, André made a "chick-chick" sound and rode down the cobbled road lost by the clickety-clank of the horse's hooves as the sound replaced the awkward silence between him, Lucian, Duncan, and Jonah.

Julian walked behind Jovan and tossed his arm over her shoulder. He stood stiller than a wolf, eyes glaring through her.

"You want to tell me what happened? Should I kill the bastard?"

"No. Will you and the others see to their safety? Go with them. There is trouble coming." She wrapped her arms around his neck and gave him a kiss on his cheek.

"One of these days, Blossom, I'll learn how to say no to you."

"Doubt it," Jovan whispered while she snuggled into the crook of her brother's shoulder.

Julian tightened his grip. "You made a grave error this time, Blossom. You did the one thing you swore you'd never do. You turned into our mother." Julian kissed her cheek then headed for the stables.

Chapter Twenty

Adrift in a churning cesspool of self-pity, a series of sneezes pulled André from his doldrums. He offered, "Duncan, bless you."

Duncan replied, "Weren't me."

"Who then?" André asked looking back to his brother and Jonah.

Lucian replied, "You're hearing things."

A louder honking came deep from the woods. "Tell me you didn't hear that."

Jonah rested his head on the neck of his horse, his fingers tangling in the horse's mane. "I heard it. I smelled them about one kilometer ago. It's my brother and a few others."

"I was trying to be polite earlier, but I thought your brother had an odor to him as well," André countered.

In the blink of an eye two wolves and one hyena approached on horseback wearing packs around their waists, armed with crossbows and axes.

Disbelieving the images before him, André rubbed his eyes. "I can say with one hundred percent certainty seeing animals riding animals is the strangest thing I've ever encountered."

Duncan groaned, "What in blooming tarnation was in the whiskey you gave me today? I'm seeing things."

The shape shifters ranged in size and color. The

largest wolf had a jet-black pelt with enormous brown eyes. Lucian bent down over the side of his horse and whispered, "Lenny?"

"Sire." The wolf sneezed then smiled. Gum lines receded, crooked, yellowed canines held an aged look. The breath? Whisky. Lenny had the powerful legs and feet of a wolf, hands of a human and a bushy, wagging tail. Grey tufts sprouted from his ears.

André asked, "Luce, how do you know this animal?"

"Met him at the pub this afternoon. He is the proprietor of the establishment you sent me to."

The hyena stuck out better than a cobra in a petting zoo. "Lenny?" Lucian pointed to the exotic animal.

Lenny nodded toward the hyena. "Meet Nygal. He bites. No, seriously. There are two things Nygal hates, Lucian, and you, you lucky bastard, happen to foot the bill for them both. A vampire and a royal. It's called being a royal pain in the neck." Lenny and Duncan both laughed.

The hyena captivated André. His ebony eyes had fluid gold rings surrounding the irises like a wedding band on black velvet. His tan fur had darker brown spots. Little rounded ears reminded him of a field mouse. André found him quaint. Almost cuddly. Until Nygal caught André staring, then the lips peeled back to show off a mouth full of razor sharp teeth and a cackle that made the hair on his arms raise.

"Nygal? Pleasure to meet your acquaintance. I'm André and this is my brother, Lucian St. James."

Lucian cut André off. "Can I ask how it is you ended up a hyena? So unique."

"Lucian!" André sniped. "None of our business."

"Lucian didn't budge. "Tell me you expected to see a hyena on horseback and I'll be quiet."

Nygal barked, "Bugger off! I'm not here for you. I'm here to see my family return safely. You're no concern of mine. You'll not see me asking you how it is you turned into a bloodsucking demon. Nosey dingle berry."

André elbowed Lucian. "Good going, dingle berry. He called you a piece of—"

Lucian cut his twin off a second time. "I know the definition. A vamp named Jasper did this to me, Nygal."

André asked, "What brings you out here?"

Lenny answered, "We have orders to make certain you get back to London intact. We're your bodyguards."

The werewolf André encountered earlier at Jovan's home dismounted his horse. One finger up, he crouched low to the ground. Veins popped in his neck, his eyes bulged and became streaked with red vessels as bones reshaped themselves and his fur shed to the ground in one sloppy pile. Long brownish-red hair replaced his pelt. When Julian finished his change back to man, he stood erect, nude, completely at ease with his body in front of the others. Nonchalantly he finished with, "We will escort you to the outskirts of London. From there you should be safe."

"Will Jovan and Savanah be safe tonight?" André asked as he tried very hard to not look at his possible future brother-in-law's personal assets, which he found harder not to do thinking about it.

"Do you honestly believe I would leave my sister and my niece unattended?" Julian's anger flared. He pulled trousers from a pack on his horse and donned them.

His grasp firm on the pouch Jovan gave him, André got a bird's eye view of Julian's thoughts and wished he hadn't. Julian knew deep down André would be his brother-in-law, but did he have to like it? No. Did he have a reason to dislike him? Well, other than the fact that if Jovan had never gone searching for her future four years ago and found André, Julian would never have ended up a werewolf searching for her when she didn't come home. Guilt encased André. To find out he had been the cause of another man's suffering crushed him. Julian knew the two women in his life deserved the world on a silver platter and with that thought came an even more morose thought. Maybe he could chop up André and serve him to his sister on a shiny metal tray. Then they'd both get what they wanted, more or less.

André dangled the pouch in Julian's sight to which Julian muttered a few distinguished words under his breath when he realized André knew his ideas.

"Julian, I will do my best for Jovan and my daughter if she allows me. I will provide a safe, loving home, one in which you are most welcome."

Julian turned his head. "She cast you away."

"Yet she sent you as our bodyguards? Actions speak louder than words."

"Time will tell."

Crouched in the same position Julian had, Nygal changed from a hyena to a man. Once done, a very all-too-naked Nygal plopped on the ground and hugged his legs to his chest with his scrotum left behind in the dirt looking more like squashed grapes.

Nygal offered, "Lord St. James, it appears I owe you an apology. If you have had the same misfortune I have with Jasper, then with all I've left in this world, I will help you. That beast destroyed my life. And, so it seems, yours as well."

"Nygal, call me Lucian. You owe me no apology. Your business is not mine." He smiled at the skinny, nude man and continued, "'Tis I, who owe you. You risk your life this night for family and friends. You are a true gentleman." Lucian gave a half court bow toward the man.

"You're nothing like your uncle, the king consort, Lucian." Nygal's smile looked more pain-filled than pleasant, yet sincere.

"That, Sir, is the greatest compliment you could ever give me. Do you know the king personally?"

"Aye, indeed. We're not mates mind you. Shall we leave at that?"

Lucian nodded. "Jasper is able to savage my wife's thoughts. He wreaks havoc with our lives. My sister, Raven, shows no signs of changing, yet he's bitten her twice. Raven and I were attacked early June. Then on my honeymoon Serina and I were ambushed. It was the second time I was left for dead." He glanced at Jonah. "And Jonah! Jasper has Jonah in his clutches as well. Damn devil makes people into someone they can't live with."

Jonah gave a fast, sideways glance to Julian then hid his face.

"How do you know Jasper?" Julian demanded of Jonah.

"Julian, I will tell you what has happened when we are safely away from here. Until then you must know

Jasper does hold me to his calling. Or at least he did until I met Serina. Now it seems all bets are off. I am the epitome of a lost puppy." Jonah cracked a pitiful smile.

Julian walked over to his brother and hugged him. "I am sorry you've gone so long, alone. I wish you'd have come home to us."

Jonah averted his gaze. "I'd been certain you would've condemned me for my past. In fact, you've done the exact opposite, shown compassion when I deserve none."

Duncan asked, "Why did all of you shift?"

Nygal explained, "Weren't certain what we were in for. Jovan said to expect trouble. We can shift on a pence if needed." He turned away from the twins as he hopped about and redressed himself. "Jasper killed my sister and nephews after I refused to do business with him and this other leech, Chyna. No offense meant, Lucian. He approached me because I had a beef with the royals."

"What did he want?" André asked.

Dressed, Nygal jumped back on his horse. "I believe the Queen and her princesses dead."

André asked, "How long ago did they come to you?" André reached over and placed his arm on Lucian's. "Jovan said the Queen might be in trouble if a book she owns is true."

"She lost that book," Julian added.

"No. I found it when we first met. Shite! I forgot to give it back to her. We should turn back."

About to answer André, Jovan sent Julian a message. *Julian, are you out there?*

Are you all right, Jovan?

Yes.

Are you still safely tucked in with Walter?

Jovan hesitated.

Blossom? No!

We left just after you. Walter is with us. Not too far behind.

"Jovan!" Julian screamed.

Julian, we're fine. Savanah is sound asleep.

Jovan. Keep contact with me. Julian looked André squarely on. "You won't have to turn back. Someone's on her way."

"Alone?" At this exact moment all the insanity and fear he'd experienced over his lifespan did not compare to the terror knowing his two ladies were out gallivanting over the river and through the woods to get to him. The woman would be the very death of him.

Julian nodded. "She has a companion of mine with her."

André tossed his arms wide. "Why?"

Julian answered, "She's always been stubborn, but not usually daft."

"I must go to her. Lucian, can you get to the church safely?"

"Yes. Go find your lady. Make things right. Be swift and safe, brother."

"You as well. If you need blood?"

"He's got me," Jonah answered.

Julian said, "I'm coming too, André. Lenny, Nygal stay with Duncan, Jonah and Lucian. Please?"

"You needn't ask," Lenny said.

Wildlife, deer, rabbits and wolves, both manmade and natural scurried into the thicket with their approach. Julian looked nothing like the first encounter André witnessed with him outside Jovan's gate earlier. Then he was a lamb. Tonight, that cute, furry little animal would be dowsed with mint sauce and served rare.

Jovan? Where are you? Even though he felt rather foolish he rubbed the pouch Jovan gave him until her voiced popped into his head.

Walter and I seem to be coming into a small village. The fog in the moors is denser than Julian's head.

I don't know about that. André laughed. Julian did not. André rolled his eyes. Privacy—a thing of the past. *Where you are?*

We've past the White Church Tavern.

"Then we need to ride. Can you keep up with me?" Julian asked.

"The only thing I cannot do in comparison to you is wear a fur coat."

"That can be arranged," Julian laughed, but it lacked both warmth and sincerity.

Stop it! Jovan scolded them both. Walter, Jovan's companion, nudged her side. She tried to ignore the older man, but if nothing else, he was persistent. He poked harder.

"Jovie!" Walter tugged at her pigtail.

"What?" Jovan turned around to look at him, but he wasn't alone. *André, we've got company. Don't panic.*

I won't.

I wasn't talking to you. I was talking to myself. Jules?

I'm here. Do nothing rash. We aren't far from you. Jovan, what does the person look like?

Ugly. Hideous. André, he's got a knife at Walter's

throat.

Blossom, a little more description would be helpful. One red eye, one black, ashen skin, foul breath like Nygal's. Obviously not smart enough to lie down and die.

Don't do a thing to upset him, Cherié. Be cordial. Be sweet. Be charming.

You're an arse, André, but I love you. Truly, I do.

There. She'd said it aloud. Sort of. Sounded rather nice. Felt warm and gooey all over saying the words, and she was not a warm gooey kind of anything. She'd dealt the cards out for him. Now it was time to see how he played his hand. Would he fold or shuffle her away?

Change of heart, my lady? We'll talk once this threat is eradicated. Remain calm.

Don't worry I'll be everything he wants me to be for the time being. Hurry up. Jovan swallowed her heart with one big gulp and faced the man while she carefully covered Savanah's body with the blanket to hide her.

"If you're looking for a ride in town, we'll gladly give you one without the use of a weapon."

"I smell two very distinct odors on your person. Your stench caught me."

"My stench? Did you truly imply I stink?"

What happened to sweet and charming, Blossom?

Shush, Jules. The vampire hissed showing off some rather decayed dents. "Ooh! So scary," came out drenched in sarcasm.

"No jokes, woman." Xavier Sinclair grabbed her hair and with one hurtful tug yanked her head backward leaving her neck exposed.

Both her breathing and pulse sped up. The body's chemistry for all its good intentions went up in smoke when threatened by vampires. These creatures thrived on fear. Jovan had witnessed it first hand and right now she wasn't too pleased with her reaction. Less so when he poked the knife into Walter's throat so the tip of it just nicked his skin starting a thin trail of blood down his neck.

"Don't look away, tart. Move, wolf, and it'll be her last breath. You, trollop, reek of mange and a St. James. How is this so? Do you have two lovers, whore?"

"I'll bet you don't have a single friend in Hell, do you? It would be in your best interest to take your filthy fingers off me and remove the weapon from my friend."

Jovan, really, what happened to sweet and charming? André asked.

Did you hear what he just called me? Scared and mad were not her best combination on any given day.

Ignore him, Blossom. Julian knew how quickly things could escalate, literally if she felt cornered. *You know vampires feed off fear.*

Jovan snorted. *He's about to get his last supper.*

Breathe, Cherié. How's Savanah?

Hasn't seemed to notice her, thank the gods.

"So, strumpet—"

Before the vampire finished, Jovan twisted through the biting pain of hair getting yanked from her scalp, and she ripped off the cross André had given her years ago. She raised her voice, "Sit tight and do not fight. Allow me to brand you right so you will forever be in God's sight." She slammed the cross into his throat and held it there while the monster sat in shock that he'd been hexed. When Jovan pulled the crucifix away there was a perfect imprint of the cross across the vampire's Adam's apple. His one eye reminded her of an evil goat when he squinted. No more sweet and charming. It wasn't Jovan, especially with a homicidal vampire in the back of her coach threatening her family. Jovan's smile mimicked his evil intentions. Still not satisfied she envisioned the blade the vamp grasped the color iron turns when a blacksmith tenders it in the flames. Xavier wailed better than a starving newborn. He dropped the knife in Walter's lap. Walter picked up the blade and plunged it through the vampire's chest until the tip protruded out of his back. Disbelief covered Xavier's face when Walter ripped the blade through his chest. All done with good intentions, except Walter had the knife on the right side of his chest, completely missing his heart even though he did a great job at ripping open the vamp's lung and enraging him.

Pity—Jovan had none for the beast.

"This can't be. I am superior to you. To everything. You will pay, whore." Before Jovan could move he was on her, his teeth embedded beneath her skin.

"Burn from the inside out you odious leech." Jovan twisted and bit him back. Two could play this game.

He pulled away simpering. "You lack the right equipment to satisfy me, tart."

Jovan reached between the vamp's legs to latch onto his testicles and rip them off him but came away empty of hand. "Apparently so do you."

"Swing to the side, Jovie," Walt yelled before he took a second stab at the vamp catching his left upper shoulder. Xavier pulled away from Jovan and began to cough and choke. Some projectile clump of god knew what expelled from his mouth. "You're just like your mother, whore. What did you do to me?"

"That's it, Jovan bellowed with her fist clenched

and shaking. "Name calling hurts more than sticks and stones." Jovan yanked the knife from Walter slashing the weapon wildly through the air hitting nothing. "Where the bleeding hell did he go?"

Walter snatched the blade back. "Tend to your wound."

Jovan pressed her hand to her throat to inspect the damage. He'd only nicked her. Walter pulled a rag from his jacket pocket and went to hand it to her, but because his hands were shaking so badly he dropped it. In that instant their eyes followed the hankie and both had something new to focus on—a finger, a pearl and ruby ring still attached. It lay at Jovan's feet. Jovan pulled her feet up on the seat. "Ewh! Walter, where is he? Did he hurt you? Can you get that—that thing out of the carriage?" She pointed to the severed, somewhat digested finger.

"Gone, Jovie, he's gone!" Walter added a bit breathless. "I'm mostly fine. I've never seen anything so hideous." Walter bent over and grabbed the hankie and gingerly picked up the digit with it. He asked, "You want the ring?"

Repulsed, Jovan jerked her head back and hugged herself. "No!"

"You certain? It's pretty." Just before Walter tossed the finger in the grass he asked, "For Savanah maybe?"

Jovan's eyes bugged. "Ick! No! Stop. He just disappeared. Did we do that or did he?"

"He did that. Are you certain you're all right? Jovie, you were bitten." Walter hopped out of the carriage to survey the area.

"I'm fine. Flesh wound, that's all." Jovan tucked

Savanah's feet in the blanket. Still reeling in astonishment, she never saw her two men approach.

"It seems you don't need me."

Hearing that sensuous, husky voice, Jovan spun around and bolted for André. She barely gave him time to hop off his horse and catch her when she jumped into his arms. "You couldn't be more wrong, André. You and Julian kept me calm."

"Calm?" André chuckled. "I don't ever want to see you upset."

"You won't." She slathered kisses over his face and neck. "I'm so sorry. I'm an arse. Please forgive me, but I'm scared. And I think I have the right to be."

"She was bitten, Julian," Walter added.

Before Jovan could protest another, "I'm fine," Julian grabbed a flask of holy water from his satchel, grabbed her pigtail, tilted her head sideways, and poured the liquid over her wound. "Jovan, what were you thinking coming out in the middle of the night? With Savanah? I cannot, will not lose you both." Upset, Julian turned away.

André watched Julian walk to Walter, take Savanah from him and basically hold the child as tightly as he held her mother. He watched Julian bury his face into Savanah's curls, and whisper things André couldn't hear. Savanah's little hand went to her uncle's face and wiped away tears. At that moment, André realized exactly what his coming into Savanah's life cost Julian.

Julian had been a father to her in every sense. The man had raised the child as his own, loved her, cared for her, provided for her. André now understood where the aggression Julian harbored grew from. The man truly loved his niece. André stumbled to Julian, Jovan wrapped around his waist.

"Want to switch?" he asked with a giant smile. "This one's slightly mouthier."

"Give this one time." Julian kissed Savanah's head.

"Jovan," André whispered a hair's distance from a kiss, "did you really tell me you loved me?"

"I love you." Her lips met his in a soft kiss.

"Never do anything so insane again. Please, Cherié? You are my heart. Without you, life would be a forlorn abyss where I would exist, stuck with your brother." André pressed his forehead against hers, raised his eyebrows, and again, asked her without words to be more careful. He pressed his lips over hers and felt it. "You're still laughing when I kiss you!"

"Sorry. I'm trying to picture you and Julian together without a buffer."

He kissed her once more because he well realized, his sanity, orbited around their connection.

"I want one of those." Julian displayed a giant moue. Walter jokingly puckered up in front of him. "Wally, you mangy hound." Julian grabbed the older man and hugged him. "Good to know you still know how to skin a bat."

Walter pointed at Jovan. "Weren't I. Best not to get her dander up."

Jovan slipped away from André's grasp and walked to her brother. Once André had Savanah, she rested her head on his shoulder, closed her eyes, and drifted to sleep. His heart simply melted.

Chapter Twenty-One

Once home, with Julian and Walter squared away, and Savanah safely tucked into his bed, André gave Jovan a tour of the manor's grounds. By the water's edge, André admired the way the waxing moonbeams appeared to waltz with the lake's ripples while soft hums of nightingales summoned slumber. Jovan held her arms out with her palms to the sky and stood in silence as she basked in the moonlight as others would the sun. André watched. "What is it you do?"

"We are given energy from the Goddess Diana as the moon's phases change. The larger she grows, the more power you feel. You could say I'm stockpiling my energy for a rainy day."

"Or I could say you are simply beautiful."

"That remark had an ulterior motive all over it."

André walked to her, slid his arms around her waist from behind and brought her to him. Nothing more. Nothing less. He needed her close, to know she was indeed real. At his home. In his arms. His. "Pinch my cheeks. This is too good to be true."

Opportunity to sink her fingers into something solid, Jovan pinched his bum and laughed. "Better?"

"That was indeed cheeky."

She rested her head on his shoulder and when she turned, he kissed her neck, just where the demon bat bit her. "Feel better?"

She nodded yes. His lips made a path to hers and gave her a soft kiss. "You are stunning in this light."

"You mean the dark where you can't see me so well."

"Those are your words, not mine," he teased. It was all he said before he turned her in his arms and started to kiss every available spot on her body. In one smooth move he scooped her from her feet and carried her down the dock to the rowboat. With some minor tweaking he managed to get the two of them in without the boat capsizing. Once he had her afloat, he asked, "No rocking the boat just yet. Just stand there."

Jovan did as asked. With his legs at a slightly wider stance, he crossed his arms to his sides and lifted his shirt over his head.

"I knew there was more to this."

Her grin went past her glistening blue eyes. They twinkled in the night's backdrop better than the stars. "Hold that thought." Next André undid his belt, then the buttons on his pants. They dropped to his feet, and he stepped out of them, cautiously.

Her voice almost lyrical she asked, "Boating in your birthday suit. Do this often?"

"There's a first time for everything. I think we'll like this."

"We?" Jovan's eyes grew wide. "Don't get me wrong, lover, there's nothing on this earth more magical than you with nothing on, all hard for me, but even without my scrying mirror, I'm seeing the two of us soaked to the bone at some point swimming for shore."

"Definitely soaked." André sat on the bench, his

erection stuck straight up. "Your turn."

In the same slow-motion André had undressed, so did Jovan. One button at a time on her sweater came undone. She neatly laid it on the bench. Next came her camisole. She untied the lace, loosened the material and pulled it over her head. Her long blonde curls ended up tussled. Her breasts reacted to the cooler air before André's hungry eyes.

"Speed it up a bit there, Princess."

Laughter filled the night air. "Aren't you the one who told me patience is a virtue, my lord?"

"Screw virtue, my love." André stroked his shaft. "Any more blood rushes to this monster and we're in for a blood bath."

"In a moment or two I'll relieve some of the pressure."

Fist to the air, he answered, "That's my girl. Take it up a notch or two." Jovan never picked up the pace, which added both excitement and madness to his already anxious body. Impatient, he watched as she undid the side buttons on her skirt and it too became a victim of gravity. Then her petticoat fell and last, but not least, her drawers disappeared into the pile. With sure footing she turned and flashed him a view of her rump.

By the end of the night that seat of hers would be sat on his face. "Moonlight eves and you are harmonious. Come sit on me lap. Right here." His index finger pointed to his solid penis.

"You're drooling, boyfriend."

"Fiancé," he corrected.

Jovan reached over and massaged a pearl sized drop of his juices over his nob. Then she bent a little further over and licked his shaft. André's body shivered with her touch.

"Cold?" she asked, her tone playful.

"Quite the contrary. Sit on my lap. Please? Before you finish me off and there's naught to prod you with other than my tongue."

From under her lids Jovan glanced up to his eager face. "I fancy a good tongue lashing."

"Oh god, woman, your words are gifted." Again, he pointed and then grabbed her and pulled her on top of him. Her body accepted his rod with one smooth plunge… and a hiccup. Seems he wasn't the only one all set to rock the boat. He handed her the oars.

"Surely you jest?" She laughed.

"You row and I'll be the cock's man."

"I believe the term is coxswain, my lord." After one hip thrust into her overtly aroused core, she changed her tune to, "Or cock's man works."

André grabbed a handful of her hair and wrapped it around his hand tight. With a slight tug and authority controlling his speech, he announced, "You, woman, are my stowaway. I am the Commander. Do as I say, or I shall plant you over my knee and paddle you." Jovan turned and opened her mouth, but he cut her off. "Row." He winked at her with a mischievous tone. With his other hand he cupped her breast and tweaked her nipple. The bud solidified in his grasp. With a little hip thrust he got her to move. The forward lean shifted his cock right over her erotic patch.

A low growl of contentment purred from her throat. "I can't move. This is so outrageous."

"Please? I need you to move for the same bloody reasons." Each stroke of the oar proved not only to move the boat forward but to also accelerate her climactic voyage. She picked up the pace.

This time André groaned.

Her body shuddered against him. She wiggled her ass backwards to get even closer, more friction. Each stroke gave way to tummy tingling sensations that spread through her like lightening. When his teeth latched onto her neck a blaze of white energy streaked across the sky horizontally. Her second orgasm she saw shooting stars.

"Make a wish." André whispered.

"You saw that?"

Jovan reached between her thighs and made a fist around his heavy sac. "I thought I was seeing things."

"You are, Cherié. A vision of what our life will be. Now ease up on the grip a bit or we won't have one."

With caution she turned and twisted her way free him and shoved him on the bench they first began on. "Allow me to kiss you better, boyfriend."

On cue, he pointed to his shaft. "Fiancé to you, my lady. Right here."

Jovan squat in front of him and licked her way up his cock and just to be thorough swirled her tongue in circles over his head. His legs began to shake. Two deep thrusts down her throat and one loud grunt, it was over. She pulled away, wiped her mouth with the back of her hand and said, "Once more, Savanah gets no siblings."

André bent over and kissed the top of her head. "We can try again in a little while." Dressed and drifting around the lake until the sun rose with Jovan asleep in his arms, André somehow managed to get them back to the dock and out of the boat without a mishap. He carried her to the manor.

Eyelids droopy she murmured, "I can walk," feeling foolish.

"My feet have not touched this earth since I laid eyes on your angelic face. My wish is to have you feel the same. This is your home, Jovan. Make everything within these walls yours, ours. Please? Paint it, add your touch, your fragrance, your laughter, you inside these walls, this heart."

"André, my you are poetic this morning. We only arrived last night—please lover, let me have a few days. I have loved you for so very long, but this is so fast. In the past twenty-four hours, my heart has healed. I'm not saying no, just asking for a small amount of time? Let Savanah get to know you, us together. Come. We need to be in our room when Savanah wakes. She will wake frightened if we aren't there." Inside the main entrance André set Jovan down.

"Our room sounds divine, but," André hesitated, "what if she's scared of me?"

"Savanah fear you? Never. Trust me when she wakes to you, she will smile like I have."

"Now who's poetic?" André kissed her nose.

"There's poetic, André, and there's mushy. That was shameless mush."

"I like mushy." André slipped his hand into Jovan's sweater and tweaked her nipples to firm peaks. He bent forward, pressed his lips to her breast and kissed through her sweater. Her nipples pressed back through the material. Rather pleased with the outcome he smiled.

Arms out to her sides, Jovan grinned. "André, what are you like on Christmas? You act as if I'm the biggest present you've ever been given, and you want to share me with your family."

"You are, Jovan. The best present I've ever been given, but sharing you is not an option." André led her up the main staircase, down the hallway and into their room. "Freshen up. The loo is off the bedchamber. I don't believe anyone is here so you should have the place to yourselves." André pressed his lips against Jovan's with a renewed passion for life. "I'm going to run a few errands. Be back a bit later. I've never seen anything more precious in my life than the sight of you and our daughter in my home. Thank you for coming home." He blew her one more kiss as he walked out, because if he actually met her sensuous mouth one more time he'd never leave.

Chapter Twenty-Two

Not a happy face in the crowd to be found as André, Julian, Lenny and Nygal approached the moat to the castle. If it were possible André felt worse than Nygal looked, both acting like someone died. After this meeting, the possibility existed. Bitterness replaced what should have been sweet memories of a loving and loyal family. Years of denial, deceit, and debauchery, coupled with so many unanswered questions lay the foundation of the family's castle. The walls between the queen, André and his siblings were higher and more solid than the castle she coveted.

André pondered the scenario; did he just storm the castle demanding to see the Queen about a book written hundreds of years ago that proclaimed death and misfortune? Her majesty's? Or his if she didn't like the ending to the book? Should he relay the message that one of her nephews, Lucian, now lived as a vampire and, oh by the way, accidentally destroyed an orphanage this morning when he and his little enchanted wife, Serina, also afflicted with the toothy disease, melded their powers? Earth shattering sex held a new meaning. André closed his eyes and rubbed his throbbing temples. They needed money to rebuild. He needed to rethink how to word that one.

And, last but not least, he wanted answers. Why his

siblings and he weren't told they were triplets until they stumbled upon it this past week. Thinking back to all the times someone had told Lucian and he they were identical, and he would laugh it off with the same answer, "Aye indeed: As identical as a unicorn and a rhinoceros. It would take more than magic to make us identical." And people would nod in agreement. Indeed, it took magic to make them believe they weren't identical. André decided they must have been the laughingstock of the country.

So, did he risk seeing a birds-eye view of the dungeon over the ordeal? Or, option number three, his favorite by far, did he spill the beans and hope the Queen believed he wasn't certifiable, which even he thought to be a distinct possibility as he rubbed his magical pouch that lent him super powers. André never smiled, barely even looked at anyone. Only a fine tremble in his hand gave away his dilemma.

Julian startled André when he put his arm around his shoulder, whether to comfort him or throttle him remained to be seen.

Gesticulating, André pointed ahead. "'Tis not just that bridge that separates our lives. Our past is as murky as the stagnant water beneath it."

Lenny added, "Think of it as a new beginning, my Lord. You've a second chance at life. Not many are so fortunate. Many of us are fed a steady diet of lies and half-truths our entire lives, and we never find out until it's too late." Julian's other arm went around the big man. Lenny turned his head slowly and cracked a splinter of a smile. "Apologies on my tales of woe."

Nygal, full of vim and vinegar piped in, "I say we storm the castle, drag Chyna's black box out into the noon sun and have us a little roast, then go up to the sanitarium, pop in on Lenny's ex, tie her to a tree on the next full moon and let her fend for herself. And lastly, let me have the King for lunch. Who's with me?" Hands clasped in front of him, Nygal dropped to his knees. A roguish smirk, with more teeth than a bear trap glistened in the early morning's sun.

André's flesh prickled. "Who invited Nygal?"

"Relax, tiny prince," Nygal said from his knee-high position to the giant wall of muscle. "I was only half joking. But some day"—Nygal closed his gold and black eyes and licked his lips as if he were savoring a fine delicacy—"I'd enjoy finding out if the king's ass is as sweet as his wife has made it out to be."

"Nygal, I must ask. What beef do you have with my uncle?"

"I used to take people on safaris. To look. No hunting. Took your uncle and some of his cronies this past year. They left me in the Serengeti to die. He slit me open waiting for the hyenas because he fancied them the most exotic animal and he wanted to capture one. I woke up to animals tearing into my flesh. One must have carried the shifter virus. Satisfied? A witch doctor named Sabine saved me. Someday I plan on showing the king consort exactly what a wild hyena is." The pain in his voice carried the weight of his words.

"I'm—"

Nygal cut André off. "Your apology isn't warranted. It weren't you. You and I, we are comrades."

From the castle wall, the yeomen stood tall, statuesque, all lined up like sitting ducks, looking more identical than Lucian and André, donned in bright red and yellow uniforms with starched white shirts and stiff, uncomfortable, scratchy white collars. For a brief second André found concentrating near impossible.

The men looked as if they'd been in a war between ketchup and mustard. The battle of the condiments.

There they stood, muskets aimed.

As if on some unspoken cue, all the men with André took one step back from him leaving all the guns aimed at he alone. He did one of those slow turns back and gave each of his companions a cocky smile. "Cowards," he cursed. He took a long deep breath and handed the reins of his horse to Julian. "Good day, gents," he shouted, "I've come to see my Aunt, your Queen as it were."

"Your name, Mister?" The biggest, most obtrusive guard shouted.

"André St. James. My apologies for coming unannounced, but this matter is most urgent to the Queen. Could you please knock her up?"

"Funny, you don't look like the Queen." The obtuse man yelled snickering among his fellow puppeteers.

"Your name, peasant? I do not resemble her because I'm about two feet taller, male, and don't wear my jewels open for public viewing! Today please."

"Me name's Henry. Named after the eighth king, I am, I am!"

"Don't let it go to your head." Nygal hollered up to the dolt, while he jabbed Lenny in the ribs laughing. "The king had a thing for collecting them. On pikes."

An hour passed before the rusted iron drawbridge lowered to connect the two worlds. Two guards marched across the planks, their steps synchronized, their affect flatter than a squashed bug. They unlocked the gate and removed the large wooden barrier. The earth shimmied up Andre's leg when they dropped it.

"How long can you stand in that position? What happens if your balls itch? What happens if you have to piss? What's it like wearing those furry top hats all day? Have any of you ever had the Queen? Plum pudding at its best I bet." Nygal sucked his thumb as they passed the two men.

"Nygal, shut the trap before you find your bony carcass in one," Lenny muttered under his breath.

Slick condensation and black slime lined the castle's walls. The aromas that escaped the lower chambers of the dungeons were not the fragrance of fine blossoms, fine wines or even fine cooking. The scents were born from someone who died making them.

"Tell me again why we came here?" Lenny asked, as he turned sideways to get through the crimped hall, his belly pressed firm against the slimy blocks.

"To warn the Queen of impending doom and gloom. Of course," Nygal yelled back to the men as he skipped down the corridor.

"I believe we are too late." Julian's words hung in the air.

"Oh, Henry?" André rubbed his jaw. Out of the blue he craved chocolate and peanuts, a treat he'd been given multitudes of times as a young lad. He hadn't had one in years or even thought of one until dear sweet Henry emerged. "Would you hold up a second please? Where is it exactly we're headed?"

Henry replied, "To see your Aunt as requested, my Lord. Her Majesty is conducting business down below today. So if you don't mind, watch your step gents, there's sixty-six stairs. Count them so you'll know when you've hit bottom. Every step with a number three in it is off margins. I'd hate to see you break a nail or something else—your neck." Henry laughed alone. The men didn't budge. Henry stopped and yelled, "At least it's not the Tower I'm escorting you to. Remember the last set of princes to turn up missing?"

Dagger to André's heart, yes, the bastard hit a sour note.

At the bottom of the stairs, an iron door caked in rust creaked open. His eyes played a cruel hoax on him. Before André lay a man staked by tarnished silver spikes driven through his ankles and wrists onto a large wooden table. Above him towered a little slip of a woman with thick, long, dead-straight silver hair. She stood on two wooden boxes, and wore a deep red velvet gown, the long silk train behind it, saturated in only God knew what. A black leather apron attempted to cover the front of the dress. She grasped an instrument that resembled a crochet hook so tight her hands were bone-white. She drew the weapon close, inspected it, then with determination, drove the hook diabolically back into the man's nose. Unfortunately or fortunately, the man didn't make a peep.

André however grimaced. The Queen turned with precision. André had seen that move before; it was one of those turns that ended up in his nightmares when the monsters found him.

The Queen focused her attention on André. "Don't mind me, nephew. I'm just trying to get to the heart of the matter." Her piercing laughter crowded the chamber.

"Nice family, André," Julian whispered. "Now I

understand the reluctance to cross the moat."

A whisper of a whisper came from one of them. "Let's run. Now." Didn't matter which man said it, they all thought it.

"So, nephew, which one are you? André or Lucian?" As she extracted the hook again a scraping noise followed. She flicked the hook toward the floor. Grey matter spewed across the stained blocks. "I never could tell the two of you apart."

André didn't want her to be able to tell them apart. Ever.

She gave him a sideways glance. "So what brings you by? Did you tell me your name yet?"

All André could think was letting someone take her head seemed to be the best idea all around. "I am André, Auntie..."

The hook got pointed at his nose. "It would be in your best interest if you addressed me by my given title. So, André, is it? Come closer. Let me have a good look. It has been eons."

André didn't budge. Closer, it seemed, was not an option. Running. Now that had possibilities. Julian shoved him forward. André mumbled, "Prick," to Julian catching his balance.

Julian countered, "Poltroon."

"You seem busy, Majesty. We can always come back." He glanced over his shoulder to Julian and teased, "I'm telling your sister."

"Are you the one with the silvery-blue eyes or the deep blue-almost black eyes?"

"Just blue, Majesty."

Her blood drenched hook in one hand and her other pointed at him, she barked, "Why come now?" Her anger piqued and then just like that, she flipped her demeanor once more. "Oh yes, André, now I remember. That black box you and your twin sent to me is two levels lower. I had some of my men open it to see what you gifted me. Is it a crude joke? I wasn't impressed. Best not have had my name intended for it!"

Behind André, bones popped and cracked. Every hair on his neck stiffened. They would all end up in the stocks if the queen noticed what André's quorum consisted of. Preoccupied with the spread before her, the men got a break.

André shifted his stance so he could see behind him. There sat Nygal, now a sloppy hyena, cowered in the corner. André mouthed the words to Julian, "Get him away, now."

Julian didn't have to be asked twice. He grabbed the hyena's tail and bolted with the speed of the wolf because one blink after Nygal shifted, Julian did.

"Auntie…"

She raised her gaze toward him. Her frigid, ice blue eyes held the propensity to dispel frostbite. A warm, bubbly personality, she lacked. "Never address me as Auntie."

"Majesty, the first is to ask your help."

"Can't you see I'm busy, Lucian?"

"It's André."

She slapped the hook on the table and reached for a small metal scooper.

His imagination working just fine he turned away from her.

"Why should I help you? Did I not just tell you I wasn't happy with the black box? It is empty."

With one quick flick of her wrist an eye popped out

from the body on the table and came to a rolling stop at his foot like a stray marble.

"Jesus, Lenny, Chyna's out." Defeat conquered his tone. "Now what?"

The memories of this night were going to be engrained in his brain better than the nail scratches were in the table. "May I inquire as to when you inspected the box and found it empty?"

"Why?"

"Because, Majesty..." Apprehensive to say the least, how did he tell her he gave her, her sister, a demented, tormented vampire, wrapped up nicely, of course, in a black gift box with silver chains and crosses? "Aunt Chyna was in the box."

The Queen never flinched. Ah, she wore a great poker face, but then she probably had years to practice a face that gave nothing away.

"What happened to her? We thought she died years ago. Where did you find her and who killed her?"

"Well actually," André caught his breath and attempted to come up with logic that made sense, like that would ever happen. "She's not quite dead." The Queen did look then. André wished she hadn't. It was not her best face to put forward. "She's a vampire." He waited for her to say something, call the guards, or toss him in a birdcage, anything...

Eyebrow arched in dismay, she tapped an impatient finger on the lifeless body before her.

"She tried to kill us night before last. Lucian trapped her and sent her to you for safekeeping. We knew you'd have the finest guardsmen, and you would want the last word on her fate."

The other eyebrow lifted. "You did, did you?"

"Yes, Majesty. And we thought it best to keep it a private matter."

"Maybe you are wiser than your appearance tells." She rubbed bloody fingers over her jaw, remnants of the poor bugger beneath her smeared over her nearly translucent skin. "André, do you really expect me to believe my sister is indeed now one of the living dead?"

Certain words would fail him he nodded. Her cherry-glazed finger inched toward him. He cringed. Her index finger tapped his nose twice and left a drop of the dead man's blood behind. He swatted the liquid away as if it were a bee.

The Queen's laugh was soft as she wiped the drop from him. "You'll need more backbone, boy, if you intend to stay around me. Countries aren't run by poofters, well maybe in some, but not this one. Well then, we need to find her before she does anything else she'll live to regret. I'll have the castle searched. When we find her, Chyna will see the next sunrise. What else did you need?"

That went so much better than he'd imagined. "Your Majesty, we need food and a small amount of money for a local orphanage that received some structural damages today from a storm." Mostly true. He could live with it.

"André, I'm amazed you take an interest in orphans. I thought your interests ran only as far as the courtesans. Are any of them yours?"

"No, ma'am. From what Lucian told me there will be two children staying permanently. Lucian and Serina adopted them earlier. I've changed much over the years, Majesty, as have you."

"Been told beauty comes with age. Do suppose

I've finally achieved it." She aimed the scooper in his direction and gave up the grin that had always made his skin crawl. Grey teeth, or nubs, some jagged sneered at him.

Was she trying to make a joke? Or was she dead serious? André had no idea how to read her. The truth was definitely out. She wasn't a pretty woman by any means. Insulting insane people never goes well. He couldn't go telling her that people don't raise kids and countries during the day and mutilate them come nightfall. Do they? "I never knew how involved you were in dealing with the everyday problems of the castle. I thought you delegated others to deal with the dungeon." He took a deep breath and calmly said, "And your hair has a lovely new shade."

"Eight years does that, nephew." She plucked the other eye from the socket while still carrying on what would be a semi-normal conversation. "So you want money. Did your parent's inheritances get spent foolishly?"

He shook his head a firm no.

"Done. Are your brother and sister well?"

A loaded question to be sure. "That would be my next question. 'Tis answers we seek." With a shrug of his shoulders, André looked back at Lenny. This really wasn't so bad if he pretended not to notice the carnage dripping onto the floor, rolling under the table, inching its way toward his feet.

"You want to know why Chyna raised you instead of Lorelei. And who came first, second and third. Are you prepared for the answer?"

"Yes." And no.

"Chyna used black magic on Lorelei and Christian

from the day you three were born. She hired some witch. Her name begets me."

"You must remember her name."

"André, most days I can't remember my own daughters' names and you expect me to remember someone twenty-four years prior? It began with an O. Ozzie? Nope. Ollie, Olive, no wait, I've got it, Olivia, I think." The Queen scratched her head. Strands of her hair ended up tainted red. "Yes, Olivia. She married one of the officers in the Sorcerer's Squad. We had the Squad checking into her multiple times. Always came away spotless."

Possibly because she's a witch and can manipulate any given situation? André remained quiet. The witch in question, Serina's mother, Olivia. What a time bomb! One that would explode sooner or later. With all that was taking place, later worked.

Seemingly oblivious the Queen continued, "Once Chyna was dead, we thought the spell would be broken and you three would snap out of your delirium. But I suppose if she's really hanging around that's why the spell's continued to work."

His voice echoed the room. "You knew and stood idly by?"

"Pick one now; your tone or your tongue, André. We tried telling your parents the truth multitudes of times, even snuck them antidotes to the potions we thought Chyna used yet nothing worked. We even went as far as procuring a white witch from Brahmall to reverse the spell.

André's mind went into overtime. A witch from Brahmall? Possibly Jovan's or even Duncan's mother? The forces of nature had a sense of humor. A twisted one.

"After some time, it almost seemed cruel to tell you the truth. And in all honesty, we thought the three of you would have looked in the bleeding mirror and had a scant of common sense. By God boy, look at you and André. You're identical."

"I'm André!"

"See what I mean? I am teasing you." She nodded with a smirk that made André's toe-curl.

Exasperated he asked, "Would you please tell me who was born first and last?"

"Your sister was born directly in between you and Lucian. If anything ever does happen to them, you will be king after my daughters of course. Satisfied? That's why Chyna wanted you. She wanted a direct pathway to the throne. She always loathed my being born first."

Right then and there a feather could have tipped André over.

"Henry?" The Queen shouted. "Where is that insolent guard when I need him?"

"What is it your Majesty needs?"

"This," she waved her hand over the tortured, mangled mess of a man, "gone."

"Queen…" André placed his hand on her shoulder, "there is a book written possibly you've heard spoken of, the Bound Grimoire?"

"Gibberish!"

"There are pages within the tome that resemble you and your daughters. You should take safeguards to protect your family. That is all."

Her tenor dropped a few bars. One side of her lip snarled, and she bit out, "How sweet, André, after all these years you come looking for me to warn me of my safety, ask for a dole and to see who's next in line for the throne? And then inform me that you've dropped off my semi-dead, vampire sister to hand-cockle." Her eyebrows were as high as they could go and not get lost beneath her hair. Her pursed lips left her looking like she'd sucked all the venom from a Black Widow spider.

Call it a hunch but André didn't like the way the conversation turned, her face, being a dead give-a-way. No more playing poker. The cards were face down on the table; André held a pair of two's where the Queen had a royal flush, as it were.

"Aunt Mattie…" The Queen glared. He no longer cared. "I have come in good faith. And trust me, my Queen…" This time she smiled. God, he wondered, did vanity rule her? "I wish never to be seated on the throne. You do a splendid job ruling your people. You care for them well." A quick glance at the mauled man… André wasn't about drop back to the level of nitpickers. "You are a true protector of the people." He gave the Queen a half court bow and remained kneeling at her feet.

"André, if I find out you've lied to me in anyway, I'll have your sister's head on the fence by the Tower's entrance. Do we have an accord?"

André's blood roiled. *Control, Ands. Gain control.* "Best you understand, if you ever touch my family, it'll be your head your people shall toss rotted veggies at on the fence. No one harms my family!" He stood, straightened his trousers, smoothed out his shirt, turned and walked out of the room tugging at Lenny to get up and get moving. His intent? To never look back.

The Queen slapped her hands together and out of nowhere guards blocked the doorway, both holding spears crossed over one another for no escape.

Lenny and André came to an abrupt standstill. "A little overkill, Auntie."

"Look around André. I do everything in exaggeration. The wolf stays."

"Like bloody hell he does."

"He stays with me until Chyna is found. If it is true what you say, then I will need someone with stronger powers than my guards. No harm shall befall him."

"I will not leave him here with you."

"Then we have no deal for the rebuilding of your orphanage."

"Lenny is my comrade, not a vigilante."

Lenny put both hands on André's shoulders, looked down at him and nodded. "I'll be fine. My Queen, it would be an honor to serve you." Lenny walked to her and bowed.

What just transpired? One second Lenny is scrunched down trying to look like part of the wallpaper and the next he's about to shout, "God save the tiny tyrant?"

"Lenny, have you lost your marbles? We still have to hunt Jasper." They once more had the Queen's complete attention.

"Who is Jasper, nephew?"

"Another vampire trying to kill Lucian and Raven." The words fell from his mouth. He was too tired to play parliamentary bullish games with her. He really didn't like her, her ruling capabilities or her daughters. For a second, he wondered if it would have been better for everyone if he hadn't interfered and let the Bound Grimoire play itself out. "I, we, need Lenny to help us."

"Do you put your own safety above your Queen?"

André didn't quite know how to answer that. Either it was a trick question, a rhetorical question, or a serious question. How to answer her and keep his head, he found to be the real question.

"My Queen, your safety is utmost in the forefront of my thoughts and prayers. 'Tis why we came here today to inform you of a possible threat."

"If you ever decide your future is in politics come see me. But the wolf stays."

Lenny turned to André. "I am a big boy, my Lord." In a most inappropriate fashion, he bent and plucked one of the stray eyeballs from the floor and held it in front of him. With a wolfish grin of his own, he said, "I'll be your eyes and ears here tonight. If we find Chyna, we'll secure her. Go now to Lucian. Take Julian and leave me Nygal."

André shook his head a quick no. "Do you think leaving Nygal here is a good idea or a really bad idea?" He cocked his head toward the queen. "You know he just loves the King to bits and pieces."

"Right. You take Nygal, and I'll keep Julian."

"How do we contact you?" André asked.

"Three way—Julian to Jovan to you. Don't lose the satchel."

"Enough! You speak in more riddles than this lost soul did and look what happened to him." The queen's hand waved over the dead man. "The pair of you is enough to drive a person crazy."

André had no doubt someone beat them to the quick.

"I will seek protection from my guards. Go now before I change my mind."

Maybe it wasn't so horrible having a Queen and aunt with a split personality. She could be deranged on cue for her country, and loyal and generous for her family.

One level up they found Julian and Nygal, both men again, donning some interesting new clothing.

"Would either of you care to explain?" André pointed to the battle of the condiments outfits each man donned.

"We met up with a bit of resistance on our way out. Found we couldn't resist these outfits." Julian's wide smile held mischief as he thudded his new coat like a giant ape would his chest. Who knew the man actually had a sense of humor?

"Anyone notice anything odd, other than Lenny, the werewolf, and you two dressed for Samhain?" The men glanced around, but no one said the obvious. "There are no guards. Where are they all?"

"Tea? It weren't me." Nygal half-heartedly suggested.

"We have to go back down. She's alone."

"No, we don't, André." Nygal huffed. "She's more than proven she can care for her little body."

Halfway out the door André added, "She's in trouble. I can feel it."

"What bloody gives?" Julian's sense of humor disappeared quicker than the guards. "The royals really do have a love-hate relationship, don't they?" Julian grabbed Lenny and crooking his finger, motioned for Nygal to follow. "Come on, Nygal."

Chapter Twenty-Three

Once again at the bottom of the musty stairwell, André realized he carried no weaponry. Just went to show how high in the clouds his head was when he left Jovan earlier. When he entered a room with an arsenal of weapons, torture devices, spikes, leatherwear for the not-so-faint-of-heart and anything he didn't want touching his body—ever his prayers were answered. Displayed next to the door, in the corner, stood a casket with long blood-encrusted spikes. A crown of thorns dangled from a chain with a ring of dried blood caked on the floor beneath it. Directly beneath the thorny headpiece a rusted large steel spear (a lateral shish kabob) came up through the floor. Dracula had left his mark on mankind. In the center of the room, a chipped pendulum loomed over a stained reddish-brown table, ready to divide and conquer. Fingernails protruded from the wood. On the far wall hung swords of steel in every shape and size sharpened fine enough to shave a mouse's balls or mans'. The opposite wall held crossbows, silver-tipped arrows, machetes, axes and a bola ball attached to a short chain.

André crossed the room with a new enthusiasm, grabbed two swords, one crossbow and a handful of arrows. The bola ball he tossed to Julian yelling, "Think quick."

The ball soared past Julian and sunk into the brick wall. "Try something like that again and you won't be telling my sister anything."

With a half smirk André added, "At least you were smart enough to try not to catch it. You thought quick."

Nygal popped his awkward-shaped hyena head into the room growling, "Now is not the time to be greedy, tiny prince."

"You shifted again?"

Nygal shot back, "Simply genius, you are."

The scream lasted what seemed an eternity. The men dispersed in different directions. André found a room full of guards with neck and chest wounds. Most had taken their last breath. The Queen lay strapped to a table, two holes in the side of her neck, her dress torn away to reveal more than André cared to see. Nygal and Lenny crouched over a man draped in a crimson-color velvet robe. Gold embroidered ropes along the lapels were ripped and tied around his throat. From the neck up his face matched the color of his robe.

"Is he alive?" André asked begrudgingly.

Lenny growled, "For now. Tend to your aunt. This one tried to kill her. So much for *God Save the Queen*."

André grabbed a jacket from the floor and covered his aunt's chest then untied the heavy leather straps that locked her to the table. He wrapped her neck in a cloth, not as tightly as others might have liked, but he stopped the bleeding. He looked at the queen, her eyes somewhere in the back of her head. "What do you wish his fate to be, Majesty?" He asked, not really expecting an answer.

The frailest of a voice whispered, "Call me Auntie. He once followed in the Lord's grace, André. Seems he inspected my gift you sent me. He knows where Chyna is. Find out where before you kill him. Be swift. Kill him kindly." The queen's jaw dropped, her mouth filled with blood. André rolled her to her side so she would not choke.

Kill him kindly? His Queen showed mercy. Wasn't she just full of surprises? "Nygal, Lenny, don't kill him until he tells us where Chyna is. Queen's orders, not mine. Where's Julian?"

"Chasing another one dressed in a black cloak and hood, the one responsible for killing most of the guards. Even our Henry. Pity." Nygal's hyena cackle seemed to fit right in this place.

"Where is Chyna?" Lenny poked the Cardinal in the chest. "Every impulse to shred you and eat you and not necessarily in that order is a test of my wills and I'm about to fail. Is she still within the confines of these walls?"

"What are you?" the Cardinal asked as he gasped for air.

"Your worst nightmare. You think Chyna is scary?" Lenny bared a full set of canines, snarling as some of his saliva sprayed onto the man's face.

Nygal stood and skipped to the table. He picked up and waggled an instrument for all to see. "Pliers!" After skipping back to Lenny and helping to secure the man he asked, "Give us a grin, Cardinal. Let's see what you've got hidden in there. I found your little crimson zucchetto over in one of the dead guard's fingers. Mine now."

Lenny watched as Nygal pried the man's mouth open. Low and behold, four fangs sat slightly recessed in his gums with venom trickling out.

Nygal clamped the pliers on one of the fangs. The more the man struggled the more the fang creaked and wiggled from the socket. Nygal didn't have to pull the fang. The Cardinal ripped his own tooth out with his struggles.

Lenny grinned. "Let's pull the other three then he's defenseless." They went to work, the novice dentists they were.

With his aunt slumped in his arms, André headed for the door. "I'm taking her to the rectory. We need holy water."

"You'll need more than that, my lord," Lenny bellowed.

The marble fountain of Mary, her arms spread wide, took up the entrance to the Chapel. André placed the Queen's pale body at the base of the fountain and using his hands, scooped the water onto her, drenching her wounds. The holes in her neck started to fester.

A little sluggish, the queen blinked. With her once commanding voice now sounding defeated, she asked, "Help me up." The fingers snapped. André pulled her to a sitting position and filled her in on what just happened. Most of her yeomen were dead, and soon her cardinal would be. Chyna was out and about and another vampire stalked her as well. How much worse could it get?

"Take my girls back to your manor, André. I want them safe at all times."

The cannon ball didn't just drop; it rolled to his feet and exploded.

"Majesty, our home will not be the safe haven you desire. Much has happened in the past weeks."

"André, I killed that man in the dungeon for

reasons that had everything to do with what happened here today. He spoke of one vampire so powerful that he'd have my throne in a matter of weeks. He refused me details. Then you and your shifty friends, and yes, I mean shape shifters, come in here carrying on about the Bound Grimoire. Nice timing."

Pale and bitten up, the Queen didn't miss a beat. André's level of respect rose yet another notch.

"I don't know the one here tonight, but I do know my friends risked their lives for you."

"André, they were not here for me, but for you—to see to your safety. That is the sign of a great ruler. When a person is willing to risk his or her life for you."

"Not necessarily. It just means that you have earned their trust and friendship. And that they know you would do the same for them in the blink of an eye. Auntie, I have no safe haven to keep my cousins. This vamp has taken a personal interest in us. Chyna, Jasper and this other one want the throne. That's basically what the Grimoire states."

"How is it that you know of this book?"

"A dear friend of mine."

"And does she have a name? Your dear friend?"

André felt the burn of his cheeks and the rush of warmth fill his heart just thinking of her. "Yes. Jovan. If we live to see the morrow I shall introduce you to her."

"It's about bloody time." The Queen listened closely as he finished explaining.

Lenny and Nygal entered the rectory immersed in laughter, each trying to trip the other one up by biting at their front legs, tails wagging. Lenny wore the crimson zucchetto that once belonged to the Cardinal.

"Guess who I am?" Lenny snickered.

"Red riding hood's big bad wolf." Nygal boasted. "How funny is that?"

The Queen spoke up, "Not very." The laughter stopped.

"Killjoy," Nygal mumbled.

Lenny yanked Nygal's tail making him yelp.

"We need to find these animals." The Queen gestured her hands to the were-animals. "No offense gentlemen."

"None taken," Lenny answered.

Julian stormed into the rectory with one arm limp to his side, covered in blood and fur. "Can I borrow some holy water? The vamp got me." He didn't wait for an answer; instead he walked to the fountain and submerged his arm. A few clumps of fur floated to the top of the basin and the water titrated to a light black hue. Then Julian walked to a wall and with one gut-wrenching shriek, he slammed his shoulder into the stone, forcing his arm back in its socket. "Dislocated my shoulder. Vamp with the red eye that attacked Jovan was here. Got away again."

"Nice pants, Jules," Lenny said as he crawled over and jammed his snout on his leg.

"Back off, Red." Julian shot back.

"See, André, he knew who I was."

"Did you learn anything from the Cardinal before—" The Queen coughed, "—you killed him?"

"Your Majesty," Lenny got serious, "The Cardinal's last words were, 'Go to Hell—' Oh hold on, those I believe were directed at me, not you. My apologies. His words for you were, 'Your head's too puny for the crown and she's coming for it. Laugh,

laugh, laugh.' I myself found no humor. Oh, and one last thing. Chyna told the Cardinal she'd see you on Mabon."

"How many days out are we?" André asked.

"Just over two weeks," Nygal answered.

"André, take my girls with you. See no harm bequeaths them. That gentlemen, and I use that word with an added note of disparage, is an imperial order. If I have offended anyone it is only because my faith in humanity and humankind has all but been lost. Help me regain this. Please?"

André needed to forewarn Lucian of yet one more snag in the day. Three cousins they hadn't seen in eight years were now under their charge. Tremendous!

Luce, what's going on at home? Have you seen Jovan or Savanah?

Cleaning up and tucking in my wife, my kids and any other stray that ends up here. No, come to think of it. Nor Raven.

Get one or two more rooms ready if we have them. How are the children?

Avery and Sydney are settling in. Can't wait for you to meet them. So, who else is coming?

Our cousins.

Have you lost your mind? My God, man! What the hell happened? Jesus, Mary, and Joseph. Ah, speaking of Joseph, where the hell is he? He should have been back here hours ago.

Joseph—don't you mean Jonah? André asked perplexed.

Just make sure that for the next day or two you call Jonah—Joe. We're trying to break Raven into him slowly, so she doesn't do something to him. You know, kill him with kindness or something to that nature? She is truly miffed over the ordeal on the mountain with him trying to kill us and harming Payton. Had he not been compelled by Jasper none of this would have happened. Calling him Joe is Serina's idea.

Right. By the by, Chyna's on the prowl once again. Julian got into a scruff with a red-eyed vamp who flew the coup, literally, all the Queen's Yeomen are dead, and I don't think I missed a thing, minus of course, all the gory details. See you soon.

Chapter Twenty-four

Inside his bedchamber, André eyed Savanah spread across the bed with pillows tossed on the floor, and Jovan glued to the edge of the bed.

"Bonjour tiny bed bug." André wiggled Savanah's toes. With one glance he'd turned into a love-struck fool. He couldn't get over the fact he had a daughter and that she was indeed asleep in his bed. She stirred slightly and reached up to touch his hand.

"Bonjour, Monsieur."

"Savanah, call me Papa please."

"Oui. Are you mine? My papa?"

"Yes." He barely managed to say it without choking.

Savanah looked at André with a giant grin on her face. "I always wanted a papa. Mummy?" The little girl held her arms to her mother. Jovan wrapped her up in her arms and kissed her nose. André jumped on the other side of them, Savanah sandwiched between them. Savanah looked at André and began to giggle.

"Great, this one laughs at me as well."

"Mummy, what's Papa doing?"

"Is it all right if he wakes up with us from now on?"

André felt his entire skeletal system go brittle. His fate now rested in the hands of a three-year-old. What if she said no?

Still with giggles, Savanah nodded hard and sent her hair over her head into her face. She gave a big huff of air from her lungs into the mop of curls and sent the jet-black tendrils into the air and back into her face. She laughed more. So did her mother.

"You're a big help now aren't you, Mum?" André pat Jovan on her delicate little tush. Savanah laughed to the point she gave herself hiccups.

"You"—hic—"spanked"—cup—"Mummy," came out in spits and sputters.

André hugged them as he never had before, part of a family. His family. "Anyone want to meet my sister and some other nice people running about this old house? Savanah? Come with me?" André hopped off the bed, his arms open to her.

"Back up," she stated as only a three-year-old could, all too cute and bold. André looked at Jovan for direction.

"Just do it. Keep your arms up and cross your legs. Protect thy royal jewels, my love." Jovan winked then counted out, "Ready, set, go." Savanah leapt off the bed landing in André's arms.

"Again." Savanah wiggled her way out of her father's grip and climbed back onto the bed. Again, she flung her tiny body back into his arms still in hysterics and still with the hiccups. Savanah wrapped her legs around his waist and let go with her arms doing a back dive. Once more André swallowed some internal body part hell bent on expelling itself. Both his women were daredevils. He caught her mid-air and reeled her back up to him and held on tight.

"Let's go meet Raven. You—little lady," André

tapped Savanah's nose, "look an awful lot like my sister."

"Come, Mummy?" Savanah reached for Jovan's hand, entwining her fingers with her mother's once they met. Down the hallway the three of them tiptoed.

André slid the door to Raven's bedroom open, nudged his nose in and peeked. Raven appeared resting. Not for long. He carried Savanah to the bed and set her down and told her to wake Raven. The child followed orders. André hid while Savanah crawled on top of Raven's pillow and plinked Raven's nose.

Raven barely had time to blink before Savanah yelled, "Boo!"

"Good morning, little one. Who might you be?" Raven looked around for the child's parents, seeing no one. Her first thought, she'd missed this little girl at the orphanage, but Raven knew it was impossible. Angels aren't overlooked unless they're already in heaven.

"Savanah."

"Well, Savanah, my name is Raven. Who are you here with today?"

"Mummy."

"Sweetheart, Mummy could be anyone. Is she nearby?"

Savanah shook her head yes and once more her curls flew into her face. A deep belly laugh roared through Raven's bedroom. The melodic sound left Raven smiling.

Savanah got nose to nose with Raven and whispered one octave lower than a full-blown shout, "Hiding behind the door."

Raven rubbed her ears. After the ringing subsided, she managed to say, "Let's go get her." She swung the child on her hip and grabbed the handle to the door.

One hard unexpected tug on the door and André lost his footing and did the perfect nosedive skidding to a stop. He rolled onto his back, propped his body up on his elbows, stretched out his long legs and smiled like he owned the world. "Good morning, Beauty."

Raven looked between her brother and Savanah.

Ray, whatever you're about to say, keep it between us.

Raven walked the child over to the looking glass. "Savanah, let's do your curls in a pretty twist for your Mum when she comes in from the hallway." Raven put a little oomph into her voice to reach outside the room. She stood Savanah up on the dresser then turned back to André giving him the half-up-eyebrow shot that demanded answers.

"Mummy?" Savanah found that last octave and used it to the best of her ability. "Come here."

Someone snuck in and glued Jovan's feet to the floor. Her legs went weak just like they did after being on the boat in some precarious positions. Her palms became slick and her pulse picked up. Never being shy a day in her life, she decided the timing couldn't be worse. *Oh for Goddess's sake, Jovan, she's a woman. It's not like she's the Queen. Just related. All right, that really wasn't a comfort. You're not going to sit here talking to yourself all day, are you? Possibly. Why? Why not?*

"André, did you come alone?" Raven asked.

André pointed out the door with his toes and a nod.

Raven looked down at André once more. *Please confirm what I feel.* She continued pinning Savanah's curls in place. *She looks exactly like you.*

"Ah, Ray," he answered through a giant yawn, "Beauty, meet my little beauty."

"Me, Papa?" Savanah asked as she smiled and made faces to her reflection in the looking glass.

Raven hugged Savanah. *Such a blessing.*

"Her mother must have ice running through her veins. Jovan? You still with us?"

Jovan's voice cracked. "Coming." About to take that step, a vexatious tremor rattled her eyelid. She rubbed the offensive twitch until it finally stopped its assault and was probably red. Red on any given day, she knew, is better than a twitch. If someone were to notice the obnoxious little muscle misbehaving, it would be all they'd focus on. So much for trying to look respectable! She straightened out her peach linen skirt, and gasped when she noticed her sweater still undone from André's affections earlier. No need to worry about the twitch, especially after she waltzed in baring breasts. As the annoying little eye spasm screamed for attention, Jovan seriously thought about leaving the sweater unbuttoned.

Once Jovan entered the room, Raven's smile took on the décor of a glimmering jewelry store until Jovan stumbled with each step. Raven shot a glance to her brother. *Heine-Medin disease?* She set Savanah on the floor next to André. André wasted no time and hoisted his daughter into the air to pretend she was a bird.

Does she have a sickness that prohibits her to walk correctly?

André laughed so hard he almost dropped Savanah. Jovan turned to him, no amusement noted.

"Nerves, Ray." He said out loud. "Jovan, meet my sister, Raven. Raven," André pointed backward, "meet the love of my life, Jovan. You've both met Savanah."

Savanah smiled at her mother from an upside down position. "Mummy knows me, Papa. Mummy look at me."

"You can fly." Jovan said excited for her daughter's happiness. She set her wild eyes on André with a hungry grin and added, "Drop her and I'll turn you into a goose and have you for Christmas supper."

André scrunched his nose to her and set Savanah down. "Savanah, jump on my back. Hold tight." André crawled out toward the door on all fours with Savanah riding him. "Duck, duck—goose, Cherié!" André nipped her bum as he crawled past. "Ladies, get to know each other. We'll be in the kitchen making a mess."

After spending close to two hours in Raven's room talking and telling each other their best-kept secrets Raven led Jovan down the corridor. "Time to meet Serina."

"Spencer? Serina Spencer?"

"St. James now."

The closer Jovan came to Serina's room the more spine-tingling jolts of energy assaulted her. Welts formed on her neck, chest, and forearms, and oh how they itched. Nausea curdled her stomach, and oh how it burned.

"Raven, excuse—" Jovan sprinted towards the powder room praying to get there before anything more embarrassing happened. As if hobbling into her room earlier wasn't bad enough now she looked like she'd rolled about in poison ivy.

Once on the other side of the door Jovan clung to the toilette, positive some incubus attempted to suck the life from her. The room suddenly became a merry-go-round, except there was nothing merry about it. Hand on the sink, she pulled her body to it, twisted the knob and splashed cold water on her face. Relief was brief. Something was wrong.

Jovan stepped out into the hall determined to know who wanted her dead.

A woman with fury blazing in green eyes staggered from her bedchamber in an oversized blue silk shirt. Jovan's and the woman's eyes locked onto one another, ready for battle. Neither woman moved.

"Serina?" Silence. Raven looked at Jovan and then back to Serina and screamed, "Help!"

Lucian tumbled into the hall still thick with sleep. "What? Who?" He asked confounded.

André met the women with Savanah tucked under his arm like a gunnysack of flour. Serina sank to the floor and melted into a proverbial puddle. Jovan lost her footing and hit the floor with a thump. The two men respectively ran to their women.

Avery, the young lad adopted earlier by Serina and Lucian, peeked out the door and once he saw Serina, he picked up his little sister, Sydney, and headed away from everyone. "I'm going to Poppy."

"Avery, I'll be down soon," Lucian hollered after him. Avery never stopped or turned back as he struggled not to drop Sydney.

"Luce, I'll go to him. Take care of Serrie." Raven crept by both women and picked up Savanah. "Come on, baby," Raven whispered, "let's let Papa get Mummy feeling better. Then she can meet us shortly."

Jovan cried, "Don't you dare take her from me." Raven stopped.

"Would someone please tell me what just happened?" Lucian picked Serina up, draped her in his arms and turned, the bathroom his destination.

Serina licked her lips and explained, "Seems our powers met each other before we did. Can I have a drink? Me mouth's bone dry."

"Me too?" Jovan asked. "Serina, how are you?"

Serina tapped her husband's hand. "Lucian, turn back." She stared at Jovan. "Have we met?"

Jovan shook her head no. "I know of you through André, your husband and your mother."

Serina's lips thinned. "Tremendous! Here we go again with me mum!"

Jovan returned Serina's hostile glare. Jovan honestly didn't know what to make of the other woman knowing her mother practiced the *Black Death*. André and his family loved Serina, but this power struggle came unprovoked.

A moment of awkward silence hung between the two women until a roaring slap of thunder shook the estate. The air around them became a living entity. Blue and red sparks sizzled before withering to tiny tendrils of smoke.

Lucian muttered, "Not again," seeing Serina's eyes turn incandescent green. "Her eyes turn when she believes there is a threat. It happened on our honeymoon. And oh how sadly that day ended. Please ladies, take a moment. All day if needed."

Jovan uttered, "So much for merry meet and merry thy greet. Think I am in the hot seat."

"Sweet Jesus, close your eyes. Both of you. Before you kill each other," Julian yelled from the far end of the hallway, making haste toward them. "You're like opposing forces of nature right now. It's like introducing a virgin into a brothel full of prisoners." Julian grabbed Jovan's arms and yanked her to a standing position. "Blossom, why did you endanger yourself?"

Side-by-side Jonah and Payton slid to a stop when they turned the corner in the hall.

Jovan hid her face. "I wanted to make a great impression. I forgot our powers might clash."

"You're a witch, too?" Raven scathed. The hurt in her voice could not be mistaken.

Jovan shrugged her shoulders. "I guess somewhere in the back of my mind I felt at odds over Serina, her mother and Jonah."

Raven accused, "Jonah! That's that scoundrel from the mountain that tried to kill Serina, Lucian and who sliced Payton wide open and probably infected him too. What's he got to do with this?"

"He's my brother." Jovan pointed to Jonah.

Raven shook her head no as she stepped back. "That's Joe. We met yesterday under the direst of circumstances. Serina saved him. He then saved Serina. The vampire Jasper had his way with them yesterday, tried to kill them both. By the end of the day Joe and I found a spark of hope to build a fire upon. He is not the murdering lackey, sidekick of a deadbeat vampire. He is not Jonah. Right? Somebody deny this wicked lie." Raven eyed everyone in the hallway waiting for answer. "Someone please tell me my Joe is not Jonah." The vexatious glare Raven wore made Jonah step back. With that realization, Raven spewed, "My heart has been kicked around like a child's toy once too many times. Everything between us yesterday, everything you'd said… lies!"

Payton mouthed the words, "My Joe," but was ignored by all.

Serina tapped Lucian's arm and butt in, "I can explain, Raven." Lucian set her down.

"Do explain, Serina," Jovan jumped in. "Why would you lie about my brother? And, Raven, what the hell are you talking about Jonah killing anyone?"

Raven added, "You lied too, Jovan."

Jovan tapped her hand to her chest. "Me?"

André touched Raven's shoulder. "Raven, you don't want to do this."

Attempts to reach Raven through their mental pathway proved futile. Raven's anger consumed her better than an irate bull punctured by the Matador's banderillas. She'd shut everyone out. It's what Raven did. Her safe zone had walls thicker than the castle and damned anyone who tried to breach them.

"You knew, Serrie. You knew I'd hate him for trying to kill you and Luce, and hurting Payton yet you still protect him, why? I don't understand."

"Because I knew you would act exactly as you are now. Upset, angry, protective…."

"And you!" Raven closed the distance to them and shoved Jonah so hard he slammed into the wall. "You vile coward, you led me down a dark path!" She straightened her stance.

Jovan screamed, "Raven, what shite are you spewing about my brother trying to kill Serina and Lucian? And who's this Payton gent? Jonah wouldn't hurt a flea."

Payton stuck his hand up and waved. Even went as far as yanking up his tunic to show off the lovely scar he'd endured at the paws of Jonah when he went on a mission to save Lucian and Serina and almost ended up gutted.

Again, ignored.

Jovan didn't give him a second glance. She turned to her brother. "You see, Julian? She's like her mother, black charms and black lies. Jonah would never hurt anyone." She turned to face Serina.

Serina tried to explain, "I didn't accuse Jonah of trying to kill anyone, even though—"

"Shut up!" Jovan shouted. She stomped over to Serina.

Serina backed up. Jovan followed. Serina put her hand in between them to stop, but Jovan pressed into her.

"Jovan," Serina bit out, "I am fighting for every ounce of control I can grasp and if you know nothing of me, my control lacks. One of the two of us has to be an adult so you, shut up and listen. You too, Raven. I told Raven Jonah was Joe for two reasons."

"This should be good," Jovan slathered on the sarcasm. "Come on then, out with it," she said as she snapped her fingers in Serina's face.

"Right, then. Let's start this conversation over. I'm not a black witch." Serina jabbed her fingers into Jovan's forehead and added a little zinger of energy and at the same time slid her foot behind Jovan.

Jovan hit the floor. "What the hell?"

Serina leaned over her. "I'm not known for lying unless someone's health is at risk, and yesterday, Blondie, your brother's life clung in the balances. A very unfriendly vamp tried to kill him for helping me. And yes again, after he attempted to kill us on the mountain on my bleedin' honeymoon, thank you. He'd been compelled to do things he had no control over. Oh, and Payton. He's the handsome gent stood beside Jonah you keep ignoring. Jovan, your brother, Jonah was under the vamp's compulsions. That's why I protected him. We went through the monster's compulsion as well. I couldn't leave him. He'd never hurt anyone willingly. Ask Lucian." Serina pointed her fingers at both Raven and Jovan. They both ducked for cover.

Serina went on, "Raven, I did a quick scan and found you and Jonah well suited to each other, but I feared you would hate him without ever giving him a chance to get to know him if you knew his past, hence the new identity, Joe. I'm indeed sorry Payton you are hearing of this now, this way, but all is not lost. Trust me."

Going for a truce, Serina held her hand to Jovan to help her up. Jovan shooed her off and stood on her own. "Jonah didn't want you to find out his past like this. He was going to tell you in due time. He is loyal, trustworthy and caring. He's capable of great love, Raven."

Jaw dropped wide, Payton held his arms out and asked, "What is this nonsense?"

"Now is not a good time." Raven replied with indifference, her focus on the floor.

Red-faced, Payton shouted, "Well when would be? Damn, Ray, I thought you and I had something. You know, like a future together." Raven turned her back on both Serina and Payton, tears pooling in her eyes.

Serina went on, "Jovan—Jonah stayed away from you and your brother to keep you both safe from Jasper. He knew Jasper would do anything to keep him as a pawn. If Jasper knew of you two? Jonah could not live with anything ever happening to you."

Jovan looked at her brother. Anger spilled from her. "Five years later you remain a pawn? How'd that play out? Being on your own? Maybe we could have helped, Jonah."

Serina answered, "Jasper takes no prisoners, Jovan. His pleasure is derived from other's pain. It is by the grace of the goddess we are here today."

Serina told the truth. Jovan knew it in her heart. She also knew Serina wasn't capable of black charms, but some serious, gnash your teeth together magic, definitely. Serina's powers outdid hers. God help them all should they ever end up in the wrong hands again.

Raven glared at Jovan. "You also lied. You are as guilty."

Jovan looked Raven in the eye. "Of what? I just thought everyone called him Joe. It is short for Jonah. For whatever reasons this has turned into quite the debacle." Jovan turned to Jonah. "Please tell me none of this is true. Please tell me you had no part in Lucian's change or that guy." Jovan pointed to Payton, as she looked to her big brother and prayed he could still make everything all right even though logic told her otherwise.

Jonah stepped toward Raven, but she backed away with a quick hand to his face. "Don't. Not one step."

Jonah mumbled, "Serina, I wish you'd have let me die on the mountain or in the church yard yesterday. This is exactly why I stayed away. I hurt everyone I come in contact with. People I love die or have bad things happen. I am the black death."

Serina took a step to Jonah, but Lucian grabbed her

hand. "Jonah, trust me? This will work out. Your family needs you and loves you."

"I did trust you, Doc. You're killing everyone with kindness and don't even realize it."

Payton walked on eggshells past everyone in the hallway to get to Raven. About two feet out he held his hand to her. Raven looked between Payton's hand, then to Serina and then Jonah. She passed Savanah to André and left.

"Raven, I'm sorry." Serina raised her voice to deaf ears.

Raven never acknowledged her. She grabbed Payton's offering and kept walking.

"André?" Jovan collapsed into his arms. "Please tell me you knew nothing of my brother trying to kill Lucian and her." Jovan pointed to Serina.

André realized either way he answered her he was in trouble. If he told her the truth, she would accuse him of holding out. If he lied, he'd be in the doghouse with Serina. Trying to think of something really fast and intelligent wasn't coming to mind. Go for the truth. At least it wouldn't come back and bite him in the tush, even if Jovan did. A smile poured onto his face. That idea held possibilities.

"Jovan, I met your brother after the fact. I saw him protect Serina and put his life on the line for Duncan. Payton happened to be in the wrong place at the wrong time and ended up a casualty. It was not my place to interfere with your relationship with Jonah. If I'd said anything to you at all it may have held bias. Serina is right. Jonah is a good man when Jasper doesn't have his fangs in him."

Jovan turned to her brothers. "We need to talk.

There better be no other surprises."

"Lucian, will you see to Sydney and Avery? I need a few minutes." Serina turned to Jovan and André, Savanah in his arms. "She is a gift to you, André. A beautiful gift." Serina left without a word to Jovan.

"What a hellish morning. Come on, Luce. Let's go get Avery and Sydney and make sure they're all right."

Lucian put his hand on Jovan's shoulder. "I understand you are nervous and don't know us, but please don't judge Serina by her mother. I only met her mum once, a little bit of a domineering despot, but I know Serina. She loves your brother enough to cause such chaos. We've made peace with him. You need to."

"Does it bother you, Lucian, that she does love my brother? He had a hand in your change. Is there no animosity or jealousy?" Jovan had to know.

"Not in the least. Serina has a heart big enough to supply all of London if need be. And I top her list. It is my bed she lays in, my love that keeps her warm and safe. She and your brother survived Jasper because of each other when I was busy dying-changing." Lucian shrugged his shoulders. "Look at it this way; if Jonah wasn't on that mountain for all the wrong reasons, Serina and I never would have met him. And Jonah and Duncan would never have met, when Duncan, Payton and André came searching for us. And if Jonah and Duncan hadn't gotten tossed off a moving train they wouldn't have found you and Julian, do you see where I'm going with this?"

This time Lucian's smile was the mirror image of André's, and Jovan couldn't help but return it.

"And then André and I wouldn't have come looking for Jonah and Duncan, or found you!" Lucian bent and kissed her cheek. "Yesterday you were given back your brother and your lover and much more. Your true future." He ran his hands over Savanah's hair, turning it on her, to tickle her nose.

"Lucian, you are right. André, please forgive me. I have ruined this for you in so many ways. You may want to reconsider your offer to have me stay with you here or any other place."

"Jovan, find your way to the atrium and I'll bring tea. No, this isn't how I envisioned our first day together, but we move forward. And now, Savanah's going to teach me how to make waffles with thick gooey batter. Aren't you, my little lady?"

Savanah nodded. "Can I lick the bowl?"

"It's all yours. Give your mum a kiss and tell her you'll see her later."

Savanah grabbed Jovan's face and pressed her cheek hard against her mother's. "Mummy?" Savanah reached for her mother.

"I'm fine, princess. Go with Papa." Jovan produced a weary grin as she watched her daughter and lover disappear. Regardless of how badly this went, she had everyone she loved under one roof. A giant roof, she decided, not knowing where she stood in this mini palace.

****

Didn't matter how slow the stable door opened, it let out a pitiful creak when Jovan inched it open. The four horses in the barn all made their way to the front of the their stalls, nostrils flaring and curious large eyes roaming to see who entered.

Serina popped her head out too, then quickly turned back to one horse, a bottle of wine in one hand

and a brush in the other. A loud belch rolled through the barn. The horse beside her cocked his head and looked at her. She pushed at the horse's broad chest. "Don't give me those big brown eyes."

Jovan walked inside the stable. "You and I need to chat." She tapped at the bottle. "Interesting start to the day."

Serina wiped her eyes, sniffled, put the bottle to her lips and chugged. After a few gulps she quipped, "Trying to end it, thanks." She wiped her mouth on Lucian's blue silk shirtsleeve. Jovan remained silent.

Irked, Serina asked, "What? I've never been in a situation as this before. I've never had so many people upset with me all at the same time. It's unnerving. I'm an only child. I've never fought with anyone other than me mum and ya see blasted well how that turned out."

"You handled yourself better than I did." Jovan snatched the bottle from Serina and took a hefty swig as well.

Hand out in front of her, Serina wiggled her fingers for her wine bottle. One more gulp disappeared. Her face hidden, she prattled, "I'm sorry about this. I'm sorry I lied to Raven. I'm sorry about everything. My intentions were earnest."

Jovan searched for a rag to hand her because the runny nose Serina had going on overpowered the sniffles. She found an old shirt wadded up in a ball atop a dusty leather storage trunk. She shrugged her shoulders and handed it to Serina. "It's better than your sleeve."

"I must look dreadful. This isn't what it looks to be. I've afflictions to dust, straw, women screaming at me... I've not been standing out here feeling sorry for myself at all." Serina gave Jovan a sideways glance. "All right, maybe I am, but I never meant to hurt anyone." Tears continued to run races down her cheeks.

"I know. This meeting didn't go well for anyone. None of us are perfect."

"Speak for yourself." Serina tried to smile but her lips remained stiff, awkward.

Jovan offered her hand to Serina. Sparks between the women discharged.

"Is this how it's to be between you two all the time?" Raven startled both women when she entered. Their hands dropped and both women spun forty-five fast degrees to witness Raven with a disgusted look on her face.

Raven snapped, "Serina, you look pitiful."

"Ta."

Eyes squinted, Raven told both women, "I will not stand idle by and watch either of you break up my family or home. If this began with Jonah, then finish it with him." Raven pointed to Jovan. "He's your brother, so you feel protective of him. I most certainly do mine. Hopefully, you spent some time with him talking." Raven turned to Serina, her voice laden with accusations. "I know you have feelings for Jonah. Just how deep they run concerns me. That you would lie to protect him worries me. You want truth? I hope it's just friendship and nothing more because I'd hate to be you if you hurt my brother."

Serina snapped, "How dare you suggest anything other than friendship? You're worried about competition. I love Lucian. You want truth? You're burning the candle from both ends, lady! And Payton's getting the short wick."

Raven gasped. Jovan stepped back. Serina leaned in. "You walked away with Payton today when deep in your heart you have real feelings for Jonah. You just hurt both men. Jonah thinks he'll never get a second chance, and Payton thinks he just got his."

Raven admitted, "Out in the open, everything sounds so dreadful. Somehow, I need to fix what's between Payton and I, but Jonah can get skinned alive with a dull, rusty blade for all I care."

"That's my brother you speak of. Be careful," Jovan warned as she took a step closer to Raven.

Raven held her hand in front of her. "Hold on, Jovan. You weren't there! Compelled or not, he tried to kill Lucian and you, Serina. And what's worse, he is a coward." Before Raven realized what she was saying she opened a new can of worms. "Serrie, what about you and André?"

Interest more than piqued, Jovan's head twisted in Serina's direction. "Do I want to know?" Her wrinkled forehead and pouty face said she didn't.

"What about André and I?" Serina shrugged her shoulders.

"Yes, what about André and Serina?" Jovan waited.

"Your honeymoon?" Raven pressed, "Me playing monkey in the middle?"

"Oh goddess, Raven," Serina mumbled shaking her head. "How could you?"

Jovan looked at Serina with fire in her eyes. "Oh goddess Raven, what? Explain you and André on your honeymoon. Please?"

"Raven, you're spiteful beyond compare. There's no truth to that, and you know it." Another mouthful of wine slid down Serina's throat.

Jovan raised her voice. "Truth to what?"

Raven answered, "She and your fiancé came very close to fornicating on the mountain, and they would have if I'd not stopped them through our telepathy."

Hands over her ears and her eyes clamped shut Jovan muttered, "I knew I didn't want to hear this."

Serina's pitch intensified. "Thank you, Raven. I'm one-step away from brewing up some itchy lotion and bathing you in it. Jovan, open your eyes."

Jovan glanced between the two women wondering how much worse this day could get.

"Before you say or do anything that you will regret, or I'll pay for with my life, hear me out. I realize this sounds appalling and it was. Jasper left Jonah for dead. Jasper killed Lucian in front of me, bit me, took over what mind I had left then he used me to get compulsion over André. Neither of us had a clue until Raven stopped us. He was playing a sinful game hoping to get us to do things we would forever regret. Yes, I think your future husband is beautiful, but how can I not? And Jasper used that to his sadistic vantage. Yes, my mind wandered to what it might be like to be with the two of them at the same time, but can you honestly tell me the thought never crossed your mind when you saw Lucian? They're identical for Goddess's sake. Nothing happened other than blue balls and rug burn! I swear."

"No more wine for you and family secrets." Jovan nodded and reached for Serina's arm. "I believe you, Serina. Relax. And as for your little confession?" Jovan raised her hand. "So guilty! The boys are beautiful." The tiniest smile painted her lips. Just maybe the family dynamics here could work between them. Jovan turned to her future sister in law. "Raven, why you would bring this up knowing the tragic events that took place? That's pounding salt in the wound."

Raven looked at Serina, then Jovan. Big teardrops slid down her face. She hugged herself.

Serina stuffed the wine bottle in Raven's hand. "You might need this more than I do."

"Ta." Raven took a few sips before confessing, "I feel so alone. Both my brothers are happy and in love and now with children." Raven sniffled, grabbed the balled-up shirt from the trunk, and wiped her cheeks. "Serrie, please forgive me. So much has happened. First Luce and I are attacked outside your home that fate filled night we met you. Then Lucian, André and I find out we're triplets the night before Lucian's wedding to which I still can't believe someone pulled the wool over our eyes for twenty-four years. Then you and he are married. Then you and Luce are attacked on your honeymoon. Then we find out Chyna's alive and kicking... more or less. More kick—less alive! Then André comes home with a beautiful woman, who's also a witch and has a beautiful daughter, who's probably one, too?" Raven looked up to Jovan for confirmation.

Jovan nodded yes. "She'll grow into her powers. You've been forewarned."

Serina laughed and tapped Jovan's shoulder. "We should compare all our mishaps growing up. For the record, I still have them."

"So I've heard." Jovan teased.

Raven blew her nose and took up space in a hay pile sitting down. Serina plunked down beside her. "And then you and Luce adopt Sydney and Avery. You can stop me anytime now… because I'm out of, *and then*."

"No, you covered everything." Serina threw her arm around Raven and hugged her. "We don't waste time, do we?"

Raven leaned on Serina's shoulder giving her a big fake pout.

"There's that reason the boys call you Beauty." Serina kissed her cheek.

Jovan watched the two women go from fighting one second to laughing the very next. When she and Julian fought, it took days to recover from, not minutes, and usually required all the contents in their emergency box.

"Jovan, come sit with us." Raven extended her hand to her. "We're sorry if we scared you. This is our first tiff. Life is full of compromise. We don't bite."

"Speak for yourself, Raven." Serina groaned.

"Are you telling me you're a vampire? You and Lucian?"

"We weren't kidding when we said a lot's happened around here lately." Raven answered for Serina.

"And then…" Serina winked to Raven, "my husband got carried away and turned me. Father says as long as we don't go on a killing spree, we won't turn mad or evil and may remain on the brighter side of the sun. Hopefully, he has a clue as to what he says."

"Who's Father?" Jovan asked.

"My best friend. He ran the orphanage Lucian and I destroyed yesterday."

Jovan mulled it over. "Must be nice—to have a dad that is. Never met mine. My brothers and I have three different fathers. Hmmm! I've never told a living soul that. Must be the wine." Jovan held her hand out for the bottle. "Our mum drove men away. Hated her powers— herself more. What happened in the orphanage?" Jovan sat on the cool musty ground with them.

"You'll love Father Butler. He's the kindest, gentlest man. He isn't my dad, just always been there for me. Yesterday, Lucian's powers and mine mingled. It was explosive to say the least. The home literally crumbled."

"Serina, have you heard of the Bound Grimoire? Can I ask something?"

"Ask away."

"What happened between you and your mum?"

"She started hurting innocent people. People I took an oath to help."

"Let's get the book out and do some planning on how to get rid of that vamp, Jasper." Jovan started to get off the floor but then turned around and dropped her bottom back down, "Oh, I should tell you there is another vampire that has his sights on this family." Excitement bubbled from Jovan as she told them about her encounter with the red-eyed vamp. "Walter and I had a run in with him. We got the best of that ugly goon, but not before he got me." Jovan pulled her hair back and showed the ladies the nick she'd received.

"There's more than one nibble mark, Raven whispered."

Jovan felt heat spreading upward to her face, ultimately flushing her nose a brilliant red with embarrassment. "Your brother will pay for this. The lower one with holes." Jovan went on as she felt the damage done to her skin, "He had only one eye, and what looked like a red marble in the other eye. Odd thing he said though," Jovan scratched her nose, "he said he smelled St. James on me. How would he recognize that scent if you don't know him? Is Jasper the only vamp you've had the displeasure of meeting, besides Chyna? She's a sweetheart." Both Raven and Jovan looked at each other and chuckled. "I am kidding! And then... Julian almost killed him at the Queen's castle, but he flew away."

"Flew away? Red eye?" Raven asked.

"Yes and yes."

"Xavier."

Serina touched Raven's arm. "He wasn't a vamp, Raven. What makes you think he could be the one?"

"Call it instinct, Serrie. And I did gouge out one eye when he assaulted me. I have to go." Raven left the stables without looking back.

"That thing is a vamp. Trust me."

"The man that tried to kill Raven four years ago could have been in the process of turning. Come on, we'll go see that she's all right."

"I hope it was him. I know what he looks like. I'm sorry for this tiff." Jovan held her hand out to Serina. She poured on a devilish grin. "I promise, no sparks."

Serina took her hand. "I promise not to bite. What else can you do? Can you do the flash light?"

Jovan glowed. "Yes. You?"

Serina shook her head no. "I guess it's a family trait. I wish I could."

Jovan placed her hand atop of Serina's. "I wish I could heal others as you do. So, we each have our strong points. We'll work well together. Can you evanesce, Serina?"

"Jovan, you jest? We can't really do that."

"Your Mum could—"

"Not!" Serina interrupted.

"Too!" Jovan didn't miss a beat, "At least that's what I heard. Some say she is the most powerful witch of all time."

"This is true, powers or not." Both women laughed.

Jovan added, "And then there's the time flashback."

"Now I know you're pulling me leg. She can't go through time. Can she?"

Jovan nodded yes.

"The more I hear about me mum the less I realize I know. Let's go after Raven."

Chapter Twenty-Five

Mabon

Over the past two weeks, plans went in one window and flew out the next as how to find and dispose of the menacing triad of vamps, Jasper, Chyna and Xavier. With every lead came a dead end. Rather appropriate, Jovan decided. Mabon, the harvest moon, was about to come down on them like a whore who'd been given a month's worth of monies for five minutes of work and they had nothing to show for it.

If the Bound Grimoire held souls, then all Hell would soon become a winter wonderland. Jovan prayed the book was full of manure, that Julian was right. And she'd even admit to it willingly. Maybe. If her arms were twisted behind her back. All right, she had no intentions of admitting to being wrong. Especially to her brother.

Waiting for the proverbial pendulum to rip her world in half, Jovan sat uncomfortably at the kitchen table with Jonah and attempted to play poker. She was anxious to hear word from André, if they'd found Jasper or the other two, Chyna, and Xavier. The boys had been hunting all day. In the meantime, Jovan watched and waited for another life prepare to cross into the shadows.

Capricious, Payton paced the kitchen, seemingly

unable to focus on his duties of preparing supper. His attention span mirrored a squirrel's. He'd start one thing and seconds later scamper onto another project. Tonight, if he finished anything, they would eat like, well, royalty. Father Butler paced beside him, picked up knives Payton had strewn across the counters, and hid them as he followed on his heels. The two men reminded Jovan of a poorly orchestrated Vaudeville act.

Father Butler stopped short in Payton's path and said, "It's only a really bad case of nerves, not the fact that you might turn into a werewolf at any given second. Relax son."

Jovan gasp. "You did not just say that."

Payton shrugged it off. "It's fine. We were all thinking it." The young man turned on Father Butler, his usual cheery smile absent. He tucked a clump of his sun-drenched blond curls behind his ear. His amber eyes looked more reddish tonight, stressed, Jovan decided.

"You'd make a lousy pick-pocket, Padre." Payton chuckled as the cutlery behind Father's back clanked with his every step.

Father asked, "What? Who? Me? These?" Father gave up a cheeky grin.

With only a grimace for a warning, Payton grabbed his stomach and bolted for the bathroom. Jonah stood pointing to the hallway. "Father, Blossom, get out now. Make sure everyone stays upstairs together until sunrise." Jonah nudged Father Butler down the hallway faster than his short little legs could carry him. "Have Serina set safe boundaries."

Father Butler hobbled up the steps, answering, "Of course."

Jonah turned to face Jovan.

Jovan stepped back and put her palms out in front of her, stopping her brother. "I can help."

Jonah grabbed Jovan's shoulders. "If I lose him do whatever you must to save the family. Promise me." He stuffed a pistol loaded with silver bullets in her shaking hand. "Aim, point—"

"This isn't my first rodeo, Jonah," Jovan cut him off.

"Oh, so now you are a marksman proficient in shooting? When was the last time you took aim at anything?"

"When you taught me." Jovan inspected the weapon avoiding her brother's glare.

"Jovie, that had to have been close to fifteen years ago."

"Not nice to bring a ladies age into it, and besides it is like riding a bike."

"That's just it Jovie, one you aren't a lady and two, you've never ridden a bike."

Jovan straightened her posture and held the gun to her side. "Harshness does not become you brother."

"Neither do bullet holes. Just be careful."

Like a sentinel, Jonah leaned against the wall outside the bathroom as agonizing yelps leaked out from under the door followed by hair-curling cries. Jovan covered her ears. Then an eerie silence made her hands shake because she knew whatever lay on the opposite side of the door broke all the barriers of nature. Jovan watched Jonah's hand.

It didn't just shake. It could have been the catalyst for the next earthquake. He opened the door a crack, and Jovan jut her neck out to get a view. There lay

Payton, panting for his former life, from a pink spotted muzzle, covered in slimy, blood tinged, blond fur. Amber eyes illuminated the room. His canines were picturesque. Sharp. Pointed. Lethal. Ready to be broken in.

Soft yet stern, Jonah cautioned, "Payton, don't move."

His voice high pitched and clearly petrified, Payton replied, "Couldn't even if I wanted to. Oh my God— I'm talking like a human, and I look like an overfed hound. Christ, Jonah! I'm talking, not barking. Oh, this is not God's plan!"

"We clearly have no idea of God's plan or we would not be here." Jonah approached him. "You and I are going out the back door. I'll teach you everything you need to know to survive."

"Don't want to survive." Payton's words came strained, "I—want—to—die!"

Mesmerized by the transformation before her, Jovan couldn't move a muscle, the exact opposite of Payton. Payton's body resembled someone hooked up to the electric chair. His paws twitched, his head jerked, bones snapped in his back, and his facial muscles contorted into unnatural lengths. Thick black talons clawed their way free through the tips of what used to be his fingers. Imagining the pain, Jovan's gut clenched.

In one stressed, long drawn-out breath Payton pleaded, "Jonah, kill me now. Before I beat you to the quick for doing this to me. This is not right. How is it I can think and talk as a man yet live in the form of a wolf? I want to tear something or someone apart. Might I suggest you back the hell up! Jovan, get the hell out of here." Payton's terror strangled each syllable as he spoke. He rolled his gaze up the length of Jonah and focused on his face. "Kill me now as you intended on the mountain." His voice came off gruff where before he had always been soft spoken. "I don't want this life. Jonah, get me the hell out of here. I smell Raven and I want her." Bloody tears pooled in his eyes and left him to look more like an abused animal instead of something people feared.

"Sex or food, Payton?" Jovan asked.

"Does it matter? Both! Get her the hell away from me or kill me. Jesus, don't make me beg."

****

After biting her nails down to bloody stubs, Raven babbled to the universe, "Here I come. Ready or not. Truly, how bad can it be? My unhealthy curiosity over Payton might be my Achilles heel. I've still never seen a werewolf before these past few weeks. None of the men have shifted around me. The people I've met thus far all seem to lead normal lifestyles. They all joke, eat dinner with a fork and knife… no slurping from a bowl off the floor. No one other than Lucian begging for table scraps.

I heard that Beauty. Not funny.

Lucian, it was too.

I thought it was, Raven. André threw his two pence in. *Raven, we are a distance from the manor and cannot save you from yourself if there is need. Please remain in your room.*

Too late.

Dammit, Ray! Lucian and André said simultaneously.

Jovan watched Payton's reaction to his reflection in

313

the length-long looking glass. His expressions alone spoke volumes without a single word uttered. In no uncertain terms he'd been to Hell and died along the journey back. Probably wishing he had stayed there wouldn't help his cause. With awkward ambulation, he rose from the floor, ready to try out the new limbs. His back arched, his front legs out in front of him, his claws connected on the marble floor as he claimed balance and… he slid back down, all four legs out to his sides. Attempt number two had him up, his legs shaking, his tail tucked between his legs.

When his huge odd-shaped head undulated in Jovan's direction, Jonah took one step in reverse taking his sister with him "Go!"

"Where is everyone?" Raven's voice made its way to the kitchen.

"Blossom, get Raven to safety."

Understanding the urgency in Jonah's decree she moved like lightning.

Raven never had the chance. A whirlwind of speed, fur and brute force blew past Jovan and slammed Raven to the ground. "Wholly mother."

Her voice barely above a whisper, fear her new shadow, Jovan implored, "Don't move, Raven. Your life depends on this. Jonah shifted. He's got you."

Raven tried to lift her hand to her head, but she'd been pinned down. "Please," she pleaded, "fear I have never wanted to relive once more festers. I beg you, release me. Do not restrain me."

"Jonah, get off her. Get Payton. I'll get her out of here." Jonah snarled at his sister.

Raven whimpered, "I now have a pristine view of the bottom of a black hole where monsters really exist.

I barely survived the brutality of Xavier's ravaging. I am not strong enough to suffer another. Please. Let me go."

Jovan glanced to the opposite end of the hallway to see how far Payton had moved. Way too close for anyone's safety. With only seconds to act Jovan threw herself on Jonah's back, wrapped her arms around his neck and tugged. "Get off her."

"Blossom, get out of here. I'm not the problem. I'm the solution." With one arm he reached behind him and latched on Jovan's blouse and in an abrupt jerk, tossed her aside. "Go to Savanah." With a quick snap of his head he turned his attention back to Raven. With a soft yet stern tone he growled, "Don't move and stop biting me. You're not helping matters."

"Me? Well neither are you."

"God, woman, I'm so sorry for not telling you the truth."

"This now?" With her last ounce of strength Raven squirmed to break free, her sapphire blue eyes overflowing with tears.

"No tears. Hold still. It doesn't matter you're petrified of me, I mean to protect you. Payton still has to get past me and that will never happen."

"Jonah! Get off her," Jovan stammered to her feet and closed the distance ready to blast her brother with her flash of light to stun him and if that didn't work? She'd zap the fur off him.

The scratching nails across the floor made Jonah jump up and push Raven behind him. "Jovan, get Raven away... from Payton."

"And you!" she added curtly. "You dodged a bullet brother."

A split second later Lucian and André bound into the hallway.

"Payton, Jonah? What the hell's—ouch—happening?" Lucian sputtered, his hands headed to his lips. His finger came away dripping in blood. "Damn dents. This is beyond bogus."

Payton's gaze did a methodical pinpoint turn, scenting fresh blood. His lips peeled back, an unnerving growl echoed through the home.

"No!" André blurted never losing focus of where Jovan stood in this mix.

An elbow to his brother's side, Lucian asked, "What are you worried about? It's not you he drools over! For once someone can tell us apart. Who doesn't love the scent of fresh blood?" Lucian waved his finger in André's face.

"You are both imbeciles." Payton spun back and began to close the distance to Raven. Before he knew what hit him, his face had been squashed against the floor, Jonah on him. Payton pushed up with a fast twist and kneed Jonah's balls to get out from under him. With his new speed and talons, he planted his back leg in Jonah's chest and pushed, ribs snapping easier than ribbon candy.

Jonah ignored the pain and chomped through Payton's front leg hitting an artery. Blood spurt in a rhythmic fashion coating the floor, wall, and the two wolves. Payton stumbled and went down, resting on his haunches, tongue out and breathing heavy.

Jovan dragged Raven kicking and belligerent by the hair to the stairway when Payton pushed his body up and came after them again. "Shoot his arse, André." Jovan yelled as she blocked the werewolf's advances.

"You can't kill him, André." Jonah pleaded, as he stumbled after him.

"Yes you can, Ands," Raven yelled. "Bloody let go of me, Jovan."

"Payton, back away from my sister now." Lucian aimed his gun at the new werewolf, his finger firm on the trigger.

"Don't shoot him, Lucian," Jonah again pleaded.

"You are only feeling guilty because if he dies the loss will be on your head, Jonah."

"I'm trying to save him, not pump him full of silver. He won't kill her. I'll protect her with my life." Jonah got between the twins and Payton and stood awkwardly on his hind legs.

"That could very well happen. And you know what, Jonah, that's my sister. Get the hell out of my way before you're next!" Lucian pulled the trigger back on the gun and aimed.

"Move, Luce." Patience gone, André shoved Lucian over and fired his crossbow. One arrow impaled Jonah as the fool jumped in front of the new wolf. The arrow tore open his leg. André mumbled, "Jesus, Jonah, you're a masochist."

"Possibly—you're correct." Jonah toppled over. "Bleedin' silver tipped arrows? Really?"

Before the wolf knew what bit him Lucian had his dents embedded in Payton's neck.

"Look at that." André pointed to Payton's leg. "Isn't it funny how a double loss of blood will knock a person out...permanently...Lucian!" He tapped on his brother's shoulder. "Luce? Let up." André dug his fingers into Lucian's shoulder.

When he jerked back Lucian's eyes had gone

obsidian. His breath came in spurts and sputters while he fought to regain his composure. Covered in a mist and blood splatter, he admitted, "That was close, Ands. I could've done it. Drained him."

"You didn't, brother. Remember that. You didn't kill him. Now stop Payton's bleeding."

Lucian bent over and dribbled saliva into Payton's wound to seal it. There was no struggle, no howling, nothing other than Payton scratching his belly with his hind leg, his tail thumping on the floor.

André muttered, "That whole swapping spit when we were children? You never grew out of it?"

"My saliva has a coagulative property to it. It comes directly from the vampire bat. Who knew?"

Skeptical, André asked, "And you know this how?"

"Read it in a vampire courtesan book, *La Morte Amoreuse*." Lucian shrugged his shoulders. "A salacious tale."

"Lucian, the book is fiction."

"André, so was I until a month past."

"The lot of us are doomed." André buried his face in his hands.

"Jonah, your turn. Sit." Lucian spit into his hands and rubbed them together.

"I'd rather die." Jonah paled. Whether the blood loss caused it or the idea of Lucian's saliva entering his body, one will never know but he passed out. He came to a few minutes later, wounds healed.

"You're welcome. It seemed the least I could do since you were so generous to me yesterday." Lucian pat Jonah's shoulder and went to greet his wife coming down the staircase.

Serina approached everyone gathered at the base of

the stairwell. "Do I want to know?"

A collective of heads shaking left to right ensued.

Jovan asked, "How are you, Raven?"

"This tends to shed a different light on things. I can't do this." Raven pointed between the two wolves. "Whatever this is. I want no part of this. Call me selfish, or old-fashioned, I want a nice gentleman who doesn't bark at the moon or needs blood nightly to survive. One day I have two incredibly handsome suitors chasing me, the next day I have two werewolves… ready to hump me like I'm the only bitch in town."

Lucian stepped toward Raven. "Sister, you crushed my heart with your bare hands."

Raven reached for her brother, but he brushed past her and headed up the stairs. "Luce, I didn't mean it like that. Please?" All out of fresh callus remarks to throw in Lucian's face, and noting the aloofness the two said werewolves cast her way Raven bolted out the front entryway door.

Chapter Twenty-Six

The front doorknob twisted, stopped, jiggled and twisted again. Lucian stood at the base of the stairs before anyone noticed him. "Jasper's outside, and he's not alone." In one swift move he had Serina behind him. "He has Raven. Let the bastard in, Ands." Lucian pointed to the front parlor. "Jonah, Payton, in there. We'll surprise them."

"What can I do?" Jovan asked André as his face went from controlled fear to an all-out state of panic.

"You can turn around and get upstairs to be with our daughter. That's what you can do."

"André, truly you jest?" She stopped one step above him.

André pointed back up the stairs. "Jovan, I mean it—out!" Past the point of hysterics André went to toss her over his shoulder.

Jovan reeled him in and kissed his quivering lips. "We're in this together, my little lover—"

André leaned in and whispered, "Remember past conversations? Not little."

"Twit," she murmured, and she hugged him. "The children are safe. Father Butler is with them. Serina created an impenetrable prism and oh, I love you." Jovan kissed the side of his neck before she turned to Serina. "Ready?"

"I'm on it," Serina answered.

Raven, don't touch the doorknob. When you enter, duck. What happened?

Serrie, tell Lucian I'm sorry for being an insensitive wench.

Lucian commented, *You're not a wench, Raven.*

Just insensitive. Funny!

Do as Serina asked. Can you break free?

No. Jasper has me. Xavier had me and Chyna wants me. Chyna killed our guards. That conniving fiend didn't even say hello to me. We haven't seen her in how many years, and she can't even be cordial for five seconds before killing everyone?

Raven, are you all right?

Was I ever? No answers required. Let's see, two of our cousins are missing their heads and one is just missing. If we survive tonight the Queen will kill us come morning! Xavier plotted this entire charade. The demon thinks he's in love with me and for the record, he is the one-eyed vamp. That miscreant bit me and flew off. He left this miserable excuse of an imp to do his dirty work.

Jasper burbled, "Keep prattling, my beautiful informant."

Raven turned on Jasper. "Drop dead, fish breath!"

"You first!" With the snap of his fingers, Jasper produced an eight-inch silver dagger and pressed the tip into Raven's neck until blood appeared, then he attached his mouth to her throat.

Done, Jasper dropped Raven to the ground. With his nose pressed flat against the thick glass door, he muttered, "Can't make out a single person inside. Damn I hate the whole vampires need to be invited in ritual or else they're stuck out in the rain."

"Lucian?" In front of Serina one second, the next he'd vanished.

"Lucian?" André yelled to no one visible, "Really? Now is not the time for childish games of hide and seek. How did you do that?"

"Do I look like I know?" Lucian answered.

Somewhat frustrated André replied, "I don't know. Do you? We can't see you Luce."

While André and Serina felt their way around searching for Lucian, Jovan decided to let the demon on the flip side of the door know he would not be welcomed in. She chanted, "Make the knob molten hot. Tug as you might, you'll lose this fight. Once in your grasp let me hear your gasp! A finger here, a finger there, it is not I that cares." Being an earth witch Jovan controlled metals, gases, pretty much everything except her temper.

Jasper whined like a baby with his hand adhered the handle. He dropped the steel blade to work at his trapped hand. The intense heat of the metal adhered his flesh to it. After one all or nothing yank three fingers and his thumb dangled from the door. The front door swung in, and Jasper took up the entryway. Having stolen blood from both Lucian and Serina from past encounters, Jasper tapped into Serina's mind. *Ducky, I see you're no longer held up on consecrated ground. Lucky me. Why not help me out here? Lend us a hand.*

Serina gave him a blank stare. He returned the look attempting to give her big puppy eyes.

Dear Goddess, you are serious.

Together we could rule England.

England's already got a queen. Jasper, I've a

lovely stake with your name on it.

Inviting me to dine with you, are you? Lucian will be jealous.

Trust me, Jasper, he'll join us.

A three-some sounds devilish. This entire play is coming together quite nice. Oh Ducky...

"Oh, Ducky nothing," were the last words uttered before gunshots rang out. Jasper hiccupped once.

"Who is Ducky?" Jovan asked.

Serina pointed a finger to her head. "I told him to stop calling me that."

Jasper bent forward, opened his mouth to a flood of pink saliva pouring from his lips. He straightened his posture and with garbled words said, "Ducky, your little housewarming gift almost took my breath away. Your aim is about as good as your magic."

With a hint of sarcasm André added, "You do realize she still has a gun aimed at you, don't you?" He nudged Jovan's side. "What a berk."

"André you're being to kind," Serina added. "Jasper, I'd like you to meet my brother-in-law and his betrothed, André and Jovan."

"Ah, the identical mutant you spread your thighs for, Serina. Too bad he wasn't man enough to finish the task."

With her fingers outstretched in front of her Jovan aimed the gun she swiped from André's holster and fired. "I don't have time for this nonsense. My aim is better. Sorry Serina."

André bent down and looked Jovan in the eye. "You swiped me gun? You little pickpocket." André snatched the gun back. "I'll have to keep a closer eye on you."

"I'll hold you to this." Jovan winked at him but then turned a wild eye back to Jasper. "Later, after the demons have been dealt with."

Jasper spit a broken fang out. "Two for the price of one." The vampire eyed Jovan from head to toe, a grimace working his bloodied lips. "So this is the woman Jonah kept hidden from me. Shame I don't fancy women."

"Feelin' is most assuredly mutual." Jovan straightened and crossed her arms under her breasts.

"Have we met? You look an awful lot like a strumpet at Cheapside." He scratched his nose with the only finger he had left, his middle finger looking directly at her.

Her anger in control, Jovan took a step toward him. "I've bloody had it with names. How are you still rambling on or breathing? Is it just me or does it stink like a bad barbeque?" Jovan pointed to Jasper's hand.

"Cherié, you are an instigator." André reached around her waist and dragged her back to his side.

Serina aimed her gun again in Jasper's smug face and pinched the trigger. "One of these has to hit his brain."

"You assume he has one." Jovan grinned but her smile lacked all sincerity.

Grey particles speckled the wall and floor.

André's shoulders slumped. "Troll turds, it's the dungeon all over again."

André?

Raven, where are you?

The other side of the door trying to become as invisible as our brother seems to be. Ands, I don't feel so fantastic.

Ray, don't move. I'm coming.

Couldn't if I wanted to.

Jasper simpered as Lucian appeared then disappeared in front of him. "All this proves, Lucian, is that you are indeed one of us. Purely a matter of time before you realize there is more light in the darkness than meets the eye."

Lucian poked Jasper making him turn and spin trying to find him, as he nudged the ghoul back into the front sitting room, away from everyone. "Where is that spineless, necrophile, Xavier?" He prodded Jasper backward another step.

Jovan's eyes went wide when she saw the occipital portion of Jasper's shattered skull. "There's a nightmare in the making. Not that he isn't one now. Good shot Serina, not that it did any good." She leaned on the doorframe to keep her balance because honestly, how often did this level of madness present itself? Only one other time she could recall. The hotel in her sweet little hometown of Lore Cove. Was it she that brought about this chaos? Was it André? The two of them together? Were they just innocent casualties of others delusions or were they the catalysts that fed the fire?

"Jovie," Jonah yelled, startling her. "Think with your head and heart." He pointed to the fireplace. "What does it take to rid the world of a vampire?"

So lost in turmoil, she almost forgot the colossal cluster of confusion happening all around her. "Head and heart," Jovan mumbled and with the snap of her fingers the unlit logs in the fireplace roared to life. Sparks of tiny red woodchips went askew.

"Show yourself, Lucian," Jasper demanded.

From thin air, Lucian ripped open Jasper's shirt.

Just beneath his parchment-like skin a black tiny malformation beat out of sync with the universe. Lucian appeared like an apparition in front of the hideous remnants of a vampire and whispered, "Last chance."

Jonah nudged Payton. "Go get him, Fido."

"I despise you, Jonah." Regardless, Payton army-crawled over and drove his canines deep into Jasper's lower leg.

Jasper's arrogance ended as he hit the floor in hysterics squealing.

Lucian squat down to Jasper's level and looked him in the eyes. "This is for ruining my honeymoon, hurting my wife, brother and sister and lastly for trying to make me like you. It'll never happen."

"Already has, Lucian if you're trying to take a life."

"You're already dead, Jasper. Doesn't count." Lucian wrapped his hand around Jasper's throat and yanked him up, Payton still clamped onto Jasper's leg, gnawing away. Before Jasper could protest Lucian's fist plunged through Jasper's ribs, crushing bone until his fingers wrapped firmly around Jasper's departed heart. After a hefty tug Lucian held the sluggish organ out in front of him. "Can I go on record and say this is so much worse than they made it out in the books? I might be sick."

Reeling in heartless shock, Jasper's vacant eyes grew wider when André came in and flashed the dagger Jasper used on his sister. "No!"

"Yes!" André nodded between him and Lucian. "Angle him away from you brother. Don't want to get you accidentally."

"How thoughtful." Lucian shot a deadpan glare to

his brother.

After André gave two hard whacks, Lucian stood there holding Jasper's head in one hand and his heart in the opposite. "Definitely going to be sick. Jonah, is this what you meant by head and heart, because honestly that wasn't my take when you said it to Jovan." He crossed to the fireplace and chucked the head and heart in the fire pit.

André tossed an arm around Lucian's shoulder. "You all right?"

Lucian gave solemn nod before he leaned over the fire and retched.

Serina tapped on the wall gathering everyone's attention. "One down. Julian dowsed Raven with the holy water hoping to quell any advancement of the virus, but she needs blood. I will supply her. I can't believe she is still with us. Three different monsters got her tonight. I have a feeling, not a good one mind you, she will turn as well." Serina nodded and left.

After an hour of Jovan's chants and Julian's prayers Lucian cradled his sister in his arms, André sat beside them, and they waited for Raven to come around, all camped out in the entryway of their home.

Her equilibrium regained after donating a large amount of blood, Serina stood. "Lucian, I have to go free the children. Somewhere it may be considered vituperative to lock them up, even if it is for their own good." Hand on the banister and one foot on the stairs, the front door rattled again. Serina stopped and turned back. "Dear lord, please tell me it's not those fingers twitching on the handle. Someone took care of them, right?"

Payton waggled what appeared to be the remnants

of what was once a meaty bone. "I may have consumed the evidence."

"I'm sorry I asked."

"O—open up!" A deep, husky voice bellowed from outside.

Serina walked to the door, pressed her nose against the thick glass and looked out. She spun to her family. "It's worse than the fingers. Lucian, it's that rude woman you introduced me to the night of our engagement, Contessa Van Holstein."

"Tess?" Both André and Lucian asked.

"There are at least five others with her. What does she want?" Serina stumbled. Lucian placed Raven's limp body in Jonah's lap and crossed to her.

He steadied her. "You, no longer at my side. Slow down or she'll get what she wants."

"Her voice," Jovan spoke up, "I recall that grizzly accent seconds before my ground and life gave way. She killed me."

Everyone looked at Jovan. Serina asked, "What do you speak of?"

"Our last day together, four years ago, when André and I met, I was executed for being a witch." The banging on the door intensified. Jovan shoved her palm out, daring anyone to open the door. "She said, 'If I can't have him, you sure as hell can't,' along with some rather rude acronyms before she sent me swinging."

Lucian stated the obvious, "Jovan, I don't need to point out you're very much alive. How?"

"The tree branch snapped, and I fell. I suppose those who wanted me gone took it as a sign I was meant to be salvaged."

Each of them watched the would-be murderer

through the glass. Contessa pointed her red-leather opera-gloved arm to the door. "O—open it," she demanded.

André added, "She fled past me and asked me how it felt to have my heart ripped out. I thought you'd died until I saw you waltz off with Nygal, and dammit if I didn't die again. All this was my fault. If I'd married her when her father drew up the arrangement—"

"You'd in all likelihood be dead," Lucian answered. "She said the same thing to Serina and I at our engagement ball this summer. She wanted one of us and clearly it didn't matter which one."

Before anyone had a chance, the door swung inward. Everyone inside who could speak, said nothing. Serina, Lucian, Jovan, André, Julian, Payton, and Jonah stared.

Gawked, actually.

Contessa crossed the threshold looking like she'd just stepped out of a peep show, donned in what had to be a painted-on black leather dress held together by sheer luck, and a few strategically placed silver buckles. Jovan fought a smile.

The five men accompanying her looked no better in their black-velvet hooded robes. Built-in mesh facial protectors like the type fencers wore, glared when the light reflected on them. Their white-linen trousers held pink protective cups attached to the front of the groin. Lucian and André exchanged an identical glance.

"Ser-Serina, so nice to see you again. For being so little you've turned into a giant nuisance!" Contessa turned her attention to Lucian and André. She lifted her breasts toward the men and traced circles over her nipples. "Oh, boys! These could have been yours, instead of those eyesores on your whores."

Jovan lunged. Guns were practically shoved up her nose.

She stopped. Miffed—yes. Stupid—no.

Contessa shook her finger in Jovan's face. "You!" The woman's brown eyes practically bulged from their sockets. "Thought I killed you a few years ago. You must have the lives of a cat. Well, 'tis naught you we seek. Tonight anyway. Your powers are too weak. You are meek, yet if you move a muscle your blood shall leak."

Jovan shot a look to André. He gave a slight shake of his head, asking her without words to curtail her temper this once. "Are you serious?"

Both André and Contessa answered, "Yes."

Arm stretched, fingers pointed at Serina, Contessa hollered, "Little witch. Soon you'll be naught more than charred flesh in the bottom of a ditch."

"Tess, you can't be serious?" Lucian asked.

"Did you miss the last question, Luce?" André asked dead serious. "Contessa, there's just never enough time between visits. Really." He got up and crossed to Jovan, pulled her to him, his arm draped across the front of her collarbone.

Contessa's lip twitched. "André, pleasure as always. I see you and the spare are still identical morons." Her laugh burbled out as a baby spitting up milk would.

"Silver is an earth metal. Mine," Jovan whispered. She directed her anger toward the buckles on the trollop's dress. The clasps melted faster than a snowball on a hot, sunny beach. The woman's, if Jovan were to call her one and she wasn't, breasts exploded from the material. Contessa spun and stripped one of the guard's robes from him to cover her body. Her five marionettes gathered close to protect her, but she hastily shoved them away as one does a stray dog moving in for a quick sniff.

Somewhat decent again, Contessa gave Jovan a vexatious glare before returning her attention to Serina. "Why so quiet, Ducky?"

"Ducky? That better be a coincidence."

"Serina, there are no such things."

Absent of any humor, André asked, "Tess, what brings you and the fair maidens by?"

"Where is my gre-gre-gre-great-grandfather?"

André scratched his head. "Did you mean grandfather or what you said? Because that is a lot of gre-gre-greats." André studied the woman as if he'd never known her. "Jasper's at least three hundred. Just how old are you?"

Contessa cocked her head to one side and ran her fingers over her cheek. The movement drew her hair so tight her eyelid pulled back into her hairline. "A lady never tells her age. I am breathtaking, don't you agree?"

Jovan jumped on that one. "Enough so to suck the very life from a person."

André tossed in, "I find no beauty in a woman who presents herself in the manner to which you display your assets, and might I emphasize the ass part?"

Lucian whispered in Serina's ear, "M'lady, please refrain from any derogatory comments we both know you desperately want to make. André and Jovan seem to have that avenue covered. Do not tell of Jasper's demise."

Two of Contessa's henchmen marched to where Julian, Jonah and Raven sat on the floor, and pressed the tips of their bayonets to her throat and waited. If Raven sneezed, it would be her last. André said a silent prayer Raven hadn't come to yet. This would be the icing on the cake for her. And she wasn't a frosting person.

"We've been after you for many moons, Serina. You might want to say farewell to Lucian now and everyone else here. You will burn tonight in the town square, high on a cross. Can't say it'll be a great loss."

"Lucian?" Serina turned to her husband, despair evident.

Lucian brought her against him. "You'll have to get through me first, Contessa. I'll have you swinging in the gallows by sunrise with the Queen's blessings."

"Oh, Lucian, all of you, you're are so far removed from reality or royalty. This time tomorrow we'll be having ourselves a new queen."

André demanded, "Remove the blades from my sister's neck. She has done nothing to you and is not well."

Lips thinned Tess gave an indignant snort. "Lucian, do I really look as if I care about her?"

"I'm André!"

"Ti-ti-ti-tit for tat."

Jovan screamed at the woman, "Who the hell are you besides the worst murdering rhymer I've ever had to listen to?"

Serina answered, "It's a phonological disorder. She can't help it." For a brief moment each and every person looked at Serina like she had some disorder. Her tone clearly aggravated, she barked, "What? Forget I am a physician? I know things."

Jovan added with a tiny half smirk aimed at Serina, "And when she drinks, she tells of them."

Contessa shouted at Jovan, "All I ever wanted was him." Contessa pointed to André, then she pointed to Lucian. "Or him."

Jovan gave the guards her complete attention and settled on the largest man. She forced her way in his head to redirect his thoughts. The guard lifted the gun from Raven and pointed it toward his comrade and rammed the bayonet through his gut.

One down.

Jovan finished, "My promise to you; I will be the last person your ugly mug will see before you fall flat on your overzealous sense of self. I'm the fat lady singing at your departure." Jovan closed her eyes and chanted, "Light keeper find the souls of those dark. Be gone to Hades' park. You're not the only one who can rhyme."

The crystal chandelier hung in the center hall's entrance and currently above Contessa swayed like branches in a torrential windstorm back and forth cracking the molding. Clumps of plaster resembled huge, hefty snowflakes as they crashed to the floor.

André looked up. "Awe, Jovan, not the chandelier. It's been in our family for two centuries. Napoleon's family gave it to us for allowing him safe passage."

Jovan shrugged her shoulders. "You might want to back up."

The chandelier's last bolt clinked on the marble. Glass bullets peppered the room when the giant bauble exploded on impact. When the dust settled a second guard lay dead next to Contessa's foot. She kicked his limp body out of her way and headed toward Raven, shards of glass tacked in her chest and face. Jonah cradled Raven as he backed away.

Contessa stopped in front of them. "I have an army of men outside. Your guards are dead. Serina comes with me tonight or all your children die." The wench clapped her hands. "Come on then, out the door we go."

Serina looked at her family. "How do we get out of this? The children must be safe at all cost."

André asked Jovan, "Can you flash them?"

"Now is not the time, brother," Lucian answered.

André shook his head. "I didn't mean in the biblical sense, imbecile."

Jovan answered, "Believe it or not, the masks block the light. Whoever designed these uniforms—color blind or not knew what they were doing. I'm so sorry."

Because of the blood bond Lucian shared with Jonah, Lucian sent Jonah a message. *Get the guard.*

Gingerly Jonah set Raven down and moved. With a quick swipe of his razor-sharp claws, Jonah ripped out the guard's jugular.

Julian followed suit and raked through the last guard inside the manor. André grabbed Contessa by the hood on the robe. Heels kicking, he dragged her to the sitting room. "It is time to see your gre-gre-great granddaddy." This rage brewing in him had the storm of the century looking like a mild summer breeze. It was one thing to even think of threatening their children, let alone their women. André jammed Contessa's face close to the scorching flames. There sat Jasper's head, blackened, smoldering, stinking up the room.

Contessa screamed, not for her guards, but for, "William!" one of the children displaced after the orphanage collapsed.

Jovan glanced at Serina. "The older urchin? He wasn't upstairs when you set the phylacteries."

"He didn't have to be. One of the children most likely invited him inside," Serina answered. "He is very close to Avery and Sydney."

William, a long, lanky lad sauntered down the stairs holding Savanah and Sydney's hands, Avery one step behind them. Serina mouthed, "Oh dear God!"

"God has naught to do with this, Doc. Trust me," William answered. The young warlock's wispy white hair resembled a dandelion gone to seed. His frosty blue eyes chilled the room of onlookers. Overnight he'd grown from an innocent lad; one Serina and Father Butler had mentored from a tender age, now to a true scoundrel.

From the corner of his eye André noticed Raven coming around. *Raven, be still. After William passes, find Nygal, Lenny and Walter. Go to the Queen. Grab a gun from one of these things on the floor and don't turn back. The Sorcerer's Squad intends to crucify Serina. There are others out there. Godspeed.*

"Listen up. If we do not proceed to the square for your roasting, your children shan't grow old. Probably won't regardless." William's immature voice tweaked odd notes.

"William, what happened to you?" Serina pressed, "I've cared for you since you were a baby. How could you turn on us?"

"I was offered a home. One where I can practice my charms and people appreciate them instead of quell them like you and Father."

"Where is he? Father Butler? If you've hurt him…" Serina shouted.

"Upstairs snoozing." William gestured by knocking his fist to his head.

André moved close to the children, but more robed men burst through the windows and door, their guns aimed toward Serina and Jovan.

Her hands clasped, the tremors quite noticeable, Serina stepped forward. "I will go with these heathens. See our children and family to safety. And then you damned well better come and rescue me or I'll haunt you through another death!"

"Once was enough, my bride." Lucian attempted to cross to Serina, but two men lifted their crossbows to Savanah and Sydney. "Contessa, order the weapons away from the children. They are innocent."

On her feet again, Contessa said, "Lucian, don't even think about disappearing. The second you vanish your children perish. Serina—no magic. Same rules apply to the dead witch."

"Bloody hell," Jovan bit out. "You'll die. You'll regret this."

"Serina—" Lucian stretched his hand out to meet hers, but the guard jerked her away.

"Lucian, I have cherished our time together. You will make a divine father. They love you all ready. Death cannot separate us, my love. Only time and circumstance."

His eyes filled with rage, Lucian yelled, "Serina, you did not just say good-bye to me. Over my already dead body!"

"Papa, no! Mummy!" Savanah screamed and

tugged to get away from William. She even tried zapping him, but he laughed with each attempt.

"We'll have fun with this one," William affirmed wearing a smirk full of cruel intents as he headed out with his hostages.

André choked as the guards held the guns close to his baby's head. They stole her away from him. From her mother. Jovan came up on his other side in no better shape than Lucian.

His voice hoarse, Lucian barely managed to yell, "William, this is your last night on this earth as you know it. Serina, there is no good-bye between us, M'lady. We've done this dance once and I refuse to do it again. I'll rot in Hell before that happens."

"You'll be in good company, Lucian." Contessa tightened the robe and limped out the door. William and the children followed with muskets aimed directly at their heads.

"No!" Jovan screamed, and she didn't stop. "André, no! They can't—" her voice shattered "—take the children, not my baby. Savanah!" Jovan dropped to her knees, cried, choked, as André held her and tried to tell her anything to stop her crying. She kicked him, dug her nails in him and drew blood in lines down his arms and cheeks as she fought him. What could he do? One wrong move and one if not all of the children would perish.

"They can't have her, André, they can't. She's ours." Jovan screamed, unwilling to give up. Untamed emotion saturated her voice. "André, do something. Please?" She choked on tears and rage. "You promised me nothing bad would ever happen to us. I believed you, André. Damn you, I believed you." She punched him hard in his gut. "You bastard, you lied to me and I bought the whole line."

André caught his breath, reeling in pain from her shot. How he managed to catch Jovan when she collapsed in hysterics he didn't know. "Cherié, listen please," André wiped the tears from her face as well as his own, "we'll get her back. I swear this on my life. I will allow no harm to her or Lucian's children."

"How? Your cousins are dead. Did you protect them as well?" Her lips trembled, her big blue eyes drowning in sorrow.

"We will get our daughter back, Jovan. We will get Serina back with her children. William is a dead man as is Contessa and any other bloody turncoat in our way." André kissed her forehead. "Trust me, Cherié. I won't let you down."

"I did trust you, André, and look what happened. I believed you." She turned away from him, her body tense with tremors.

André looked at his brother, broken and outraged.

Lucian hugged Jovan hard, and cupped her reddened face in his hands. "We'll get them back, Jovan. Meet me at the town square."

"Bloody hell they'll take my baby..." Jovan reached and grabbed a gun from a dead guard and bolted out the front door after the children. André gave chase, Lucian one step behind.

Shots rang out, and André stopped dead in his tracks when he saw Jovan stagger, turn, her shocked eyes set on him and collapse.

"No!" His cry stole the night. "No, Jovan, no!" André fled to her, picked her up and ran for the home. "Help me!" Angry disbelieving tears burned his eyes.

"Lucian? Please?" His voice cracked. He cradled her lifeless body against him and began rocking, smoothing the bloodied hair from her face and kissed her again and again. "Oh god, Cherié, what have I done?"

"You did not do this, André." Lucian squat beside his brother and with a fast swipe, wiped his own eyes. "She's gone, André. Let her go. We have to get the children and Serina."

"What have I done? Lucian—"

Lucian reached in and lifted Jovan's body from André and headed for the stairs. "Come brother. Let us lay her down and then go kill every last one of them."

"Jovan?" Julian and Jonah fled to Lucian and André's side. "Who did this?" Jonah threw his furry arm over his brother's shoulder and held him.

"Contessa," André barely managed to get her name out.

"She's dead, Contessa." Julian turned to Jonah. "You with me? I have to get Savanah. Hurry André."

"I'm here." Father Butler crept down the stairs slowly, his hand tight on the banister, blood caked on one side of his face. "Set her down in the parlor and I'll stay with her till your return. I'll take care of her, André. Go get your children and my girl. Say nothing of Jovan's circumstance. They have enough to deal with. God speed."

Once Jovan was laid out in the parlor, André made one last stop and walked over to the fireplace. He reached inside his jacket and pulled out the white journal. "Good riddance." He tossed the book into the fire and left.

Chapter Twenty-Seven

Thick dark clouds pulsed above the gathering crowd with as much lethality as a black lung that consumed its host. Leaves hurled through the air, branches snapped from trees, and yet people crawled out from under every rock to see a woman—a true witch, burn at the stake, regardless of its illegal, immoral nature.

Stuck in the coach with Tess, Serina spoke her piece. "I finally understand. People fear these rogues who defy the laws. That would indeed be you and your fair maidens I speak of just in case you can't keep up with me. You are a conjugated collective of nincompoops who take into account your own prejudices as righteous and holy, never knowing or understanding right from wrong. People never challenged the Squad—again you, for fear of their own lives, and rightfully so because to challenge, in your small feeble minds, means they must be a witch too, or just bloody ignorant. But sadly, those who watch the killings are drawn in, hooked with an exigency and persuaded to join in the rituals of death. And they do. Goddess help the insufferable lot of them, they do. Going to a stoning or crucifixion, or both is the same as going to church on Sunday, in a manner of speaking. In church one person chants or sings and begins a chorus of people swaying in each other's arms, just as at a stoning one person screams, picks up a rock or any object available and hurls it towards the defenseless person tied to the cross—tonight that would be me, while other hordes of mindless matter follow suit. There is safety in numbers. If one person does something, others follow. Right or wrong. Holy or evil. Both supposedly in the name of God." Serina rested her head on the window of the coach and gazed out. "I have a bird's eye view of Hell. I am surrounded by utter morons, a mountain of wood, barrels of petrol, and a large wooden cross lying on the ground, waiting to end a life. Mine."

Amazing how fast word got out! She rolled her eyes.

"You done whining?" Tess didn't wait for an answer and stepped out of the carriage and headed toward a group of men piling on the logs.

Lucian choked on his words. "If Serina uses her magic to save herself, it is a doubled-edged sword. People will know she is what they accuse her of and kill her anyway. If she does naught, she dies. She loses her life and I, my heart. I won't live without her, Ands. I can't." Lucian stilled and then blurted, "Oh, blimey brother, I am beyond callous. I'm so sorry. I am babbling on over Serina and you just lost Jovan. I am beyond a callous imbecile."

"Shut up, brother. My grasp on reality has but one purpose." André stopped and started again, "Two. Get my daughter and send Contessa to her ancestors."

In the center square, André glanced around, amazed at the three-ring circus the place had become. Vendors pushed their carts selling turkey legs, mead, fireworks, rotted veggies, manure balls, hot potatoes that doubled as hand warmers on cool nights—until launched and, of course, polished stones. As they closed in on the carriages, a hair-raising hum vibrated the ground all the way up his legs.

"Where's Contessa?"

Lucian shrugged his shoulders. "Xavier is here. I can smell his decay. I should've bloody known when we were at university he was changing. The man reeked then."

Absent of any humor, André added, "Luce, most days so do you." André pointed to the carriage the children were in. "There. I'm going to get the children."

"Let me check first. It could be a trap." Lucian evanesced then seeped inside the carriage. Avery and Sydney weren't crying, but Savanah more than made up for their silence. The little girl sat in hysterics clung to Avery.

Lucian's eyes grew wide. There sat William cocooned in thick vines, thorns piercing his flesh. His mouth had a pink flower growing from it. He immediately looked at Savanah. "Nice work, peanut."

"Mummy says if you've nothing nice to say then grow flowers. He wasn't being nice."

Tears laden with turmoil streamed down Lucian's cheeks. "You are an angel. I need to do something to him as well, so he behaves. All three of you close your eyes and sing 'I love you a bushel and a peck, oh ya bet your pretty neck I do,' till I tell you to open them." The children did as asked, no questions.

When a merchant strolled by offering, "Witch's brew," Lucian sunk his teeth into William's neck and took enough blood to have a blood bond with him. With the swipe of a talon he slit his wrist, popped the flower out from William's mouth and jammed his bleeding wrist inside William's mouth and compelled him to drink just before he sent him to sleep. This ensured Lucian could control the boy. Once the flower had been set back in, Lucian whispered, "André is right outside coming to take you home. Don't look out the window of the carriage no matter what you hear or see. Promise me. And don't wake Will. He needs sleep."

Lucian jumped from the carriage and snuck up on André. "The children are safe for the time being. Your daughter is amazing. You needn't worry over her."

He had to see for himself. André stuck his head inside the coach when he heard his brother saying, "Get them far away so they don't see Serina being taken away."

Lucian? Did I hear you right? You don't intend to let them stake her to that cross? We've already lost Jovan.

Only for the amount of time it takes for the others to show themselves. Then we get her down and slaughter the lambs. The tides have turned, brother. In our favor.

"Luce," André yelled to no one, "this isn't in our favor. This is the devil dancing on our bloody graves." André reached in and grabbed Savanah and hugged her to him, heart-broken beyond words. He couldn't hold back the tears. Then he saw William and didn't know whether to laugh or cry or do both, so he did both.

"Papa, who made you cry? Where's mummy?"

How do you tell your child their mother was murdered when those innocent eyes are looking at you with all the trust the world has to offer? He physically couldn't bring himself to say the words. If he said it aloud then it was true. She would be forever gone.

"Papa!" Savanah squashed his cheeks together.

"Oh little angel, you have your mother's patience. Come on, let's get you to Uncle Julian."

André squat to Avery and Sydney's height and shifted Savanah around on his knee. With a free hand he wiped Sydney's face of tears. "You're safe sweetheart. All of you are. Julian's waiting for you."

Avery asked, "Where is Poppy?"

"Father Butler's fine. He's going to get Serina right now," Julian said as he approached everyone. Julian held his arms out to Savanah. "Come to me my little nut."

Savanah hugged André harder, and cried, "I want Papa!"

Julian turned his head. André mouthed, "I'm sorry," to Julian and he meant it. "Go with your uncle, baby. I will see you soon. I promise." André kissed his daughter's cheek and didn't look back. If he looked back, he would have seen his baby reaching for him, and Julian fighting the tears André never knew the man owned.

Chapter Twenty-Eight

"I am here, Serina."

"Yes, and here I am, hanging around. Literally hanging. Lucian, I realize you feel you are stating the obvious in a comforting way, but the reality is that it is obvious you are invisible to all and as I stand here talking to no one, people will indeed assume I have demons either beside me or trapped within me. What little self-control I held was lost when everything decayed on the planet was slung at me. Now, about getting burnt and blistered?" Her sarcasm thick she finished, "And here I went to such lengths to keep my complexion with a healthy glow. I shall remain chipper…" Her words were cut short when some brute tossed his lit fag into the woodpile. Petrol plus fire… Poof! Flames began catch the underlying tinder. "It's getting toasty in here, Lucian."

Still invisible, Lucian watched while the rogue picked up the sledgehammer and a huge spike and attempted the unthinkable, placing it through his beloved bride. The nail took a dramatic turn. Lucian drove the nail through the bloke's Adam's apple. The man turned blue and dropped into the dirt, feet kicking, eyes bulging, grasping his throat. "Let William Tell top that." Lucian gave a gentleman's bow over the man's body and then kicked him in the head.

"Lucian, wherever you are, I know you're trying to protect me in some arse-backward way, but this crowd really wants me dead now. They probably think I did that. And I think my shoe is melting. No, I'm pretty certain it is. Well Mister now I see you, now I don't, at least I am drenched in fear. This is good. It will take an entire minute longer to crisp me while the dress dries out. Who needs feet?"

"Optimism, M'lady," Lucian jest, "You nailed it."

"And now I completely understand why Raven and André call you imbecile."

"I'll have you out of here soon, my love. I promise."

Serina chanted, "Lady of Light show those of ill-repute. Make them mute. Raise the nefarious, malevolent and impure of heart and anything else dead out there scouring the land. Dangle them in the air as I do from this stand."

Stood at the base of the cross as he worked through the fire and ropes that bound Serina, the ground shifted beneath Lucian. He glanced past a maraud of people, to the cemetery at the end of the road. Any day of the week, its peaceful, serenity coveted so many unearthed secrets.

That time had ended. The ground turned. Corpses climbed through dirt, rock and debris. Eyes wide, Lucian pointed. "Serina—bodies. Bodies in the crowd are starting to levitate. Don't believe me? Look." He pointed at another one. "Almost eyelevel to you. What spell did you cast this time, M'lady? This is macabre. There must be hundreds of entities all wanting retribution for past wrongdoings. Serina—you might want to tweak the spell. Seems a bit vague." Lucian noted the obvious, him now clung to the cross upside down, screaming, "M'lady! Get me down. Where in hell is my brother?"

Those the spell encased yelled and groped tree branches to go no higher. Skeletons danced on air, their clanking bones mimicking broken wind chimes. Those with their feet firmly planted on the soil, scattered.

Serina yelled, "Lucian, is that?"

"Xavier, the raping, cannibalistic, scourge of the earth, one red-eyed vamp, and my lying, conniving, deadbeat vampiric aunt, Chyna? Unfortunately for all of us it is. Them moreso."

Serina again chanted, "Drop the dead back into their earthly beds."

The deadbeat, lying, conniving vampiric aunt and raping, cannibalistic scourge of the earth, one red-eyed vamp, spiraled to the ground, and scrambled to hide amongst the rats.

From the corner of his eye, André caught sight of one of the most horrific atrocities to forever be etched into the pages of history. Eden didn't have dark sins like this, did it? Was the promise of the forbidden fruit transposed into the glory of being crowned majestic? Was life worth nothing more than a jewel sat upon your head? Was this all because his aunt wanted to sit at the top of the proverbial totem pole? Could this night get any worse? Seriously, his fiancé, the mother of his child was dead. No, it couldn't.

When Olivia Spencer appeared before him, André broke out in a balmy sweat. Green eyes glaring, she grabbed his chin. "Do nothing rash. I've something you need." She rooted through the pocket of her cape and pulled out a vile of silver dust mixed with red flakes.

She slipped the container in the front pocket of his pants. "Use this to slow him down. 'Tis your only chance. Give it to Lucian. This is snake venom and heroine with a wee pinch of blackness. Lucian will know what to do and can handle the contents without ill consequence. I cannot get close enough. They know me."

Overwrought with emotions, André embraced her. "Lady Olivia, is it true you can turn back time? My fiancé—"

"Get my daughter off that cross or it'll be the last night your family lives. Not a threat from me, but a promise from those who dwell in the cesspool. Now, let me go."

"But—" André held her shoulders tight, not wanting to lose his last hope of getting Jovan back.

Olivia pulled away. "If Xavier sees—"

Julian saw and charged. "André she is the woman who had a direct hand in my mother's death. Step away. Don't you dare hurt him, Olivia." Julian descended upon the two and without thought he plunged a steel blade into her back, in one forceful moment he would forever regret. Blood soaked the back of her frock. Only the whites of Olivia's eyes remained wide. Her final words were, "Big mistake, Bucko!"

It all happened so fast. André didn't have time to react. "What did you do, Julian? She meant no harm. She came to help her daughter. I was going to ask her to save Jovan. Damn you." André hugged the woman's listless body with one arm as he fished around in his pocket. "I have no hope of ever getting her back. Give this to Lucian. It's to be used on Xavier. Where are the children?"

"With Jonah. André…"

"Go." André set Olivia down, and knelt beside her. He held pressure over the wound in her back and looked around hoping to find help. Two women dressed in white sheaths approached him and without so much as a word lay their hands atop of Olivia and evanesced, leaving André alone in a puddle of blood. Shaken, and heartbroken he stood and headed toward the woods to find his daughter.

****

Lenny and Walter escorted Father Butler through what was left of the crowd to the town center, stepping over bones, rotted vegetables, piles of manure and decayed body parts.

The priest gasped and landed hard on his knees when they approached Serina staked to a cross. He struggled to say, "My child, forgive me. I failed you. I've let you down all these years."

"Father, hush. You've been the one man I've loved all my life. Let me down? Never! Help me down? I'd truly appreciate the help since Lucian is having issues. Now, get up you daft old man."

Father Butler ignored her. "You and your sister will never forgive me."

Brain and lungs clogged with thick black smoke, Serina still managed to shout, "What? My what? Who?"

"Me." Jovan walked up and placed her hand on Father Butler's shoulder. "Seems we have some catching up to do. I don't know anymore than you do at this point."

****

With the blaring of horns informing the arrival of

the Queen, a hush befell the remaining hordes as her mahogany gold embellished coach rolled to a stop. The Queen extended her hand to her coachman and stepped down. Raven followed behind her. Before she spoke, she took in her surroundings, squared her shoulders, and roared, "This barbaric ritual is the last time this will ever occur. I'm the only one allowed to pass judgment." Her gloved hand rose, and people knelt. She pointed to the cross, engulfed in smoke and a fire ring growing dangerously close to the woman screaming obscenities on it. Her majesty raised her voice. "Remove my niece from this cross immediately. Get this fire extinguished and shoot anything left hanging in the night air."

The crowd went to a low chatter of, "She can't be a royal witch."

With a snicker the Queen answered, "Clearly you've never been introduced formally to me then. Get her down now!" Her guards ran toward the hydrants.

Better than a spider creeping about, Contessa leaned behind a barrel of petrol and gave one hefty shove. "This is for my great, great, great, grandfather!" The reactant spilled onto the wood, leaves and surrounding ground. One spark led to another that began a fire and the conflagration grew in frenzied need. Flames danced freely in the cool night while they reached for the moon.

Father Butler stood. He roared, "NO!" as he waved his arms frantic in a crisscrossed jumbled pattern toward the heavens.

Battling the heat, flames and his wife's constant fidgeting, Lucian asked, "Can you do some sort of incantation to make people freeze so I can get you down without people seeing you float on air?"

"I can't but Jovan can." Serina's nose twitched. "Lucian do you smell that? That's my hair sizzling! Hurry up."

Lucian grumbled, "No, actually it's mine, what's left of it. Serina, about Jovan…"

"I know, she's my sister."

"What? That's not what I was going to say. She had an accident tonight."

"I know. She told me."

"But she didn't survive."

"Again Lucian, I know. Jovan told me whilst you were busy."

"Then how did she tell you if she didn't survive?"

Completely aggravated she yelled, "Have you not been paying attention to anything here? There, over there on the opposite side of this bonfire. I'd point if I had a free finger."

"Serina, bit busy here. I've been trying to undo these damned restraints. The bloke spelled them or something, so they won't come undone."

"Lucian they're here. Look up for a second."

"Don't have one to spare."

"Jovan? Can you dazzle the crowd?"

The incessant jeers of, "Kill the witch," continued regardless of the Queen's decree. What bloody fools these people were. Jovan chanted, "Be still thy beating hearts, before I rip them apart. Pity if you were to choke, then you'd be the brunt of the joke!" Suddenly it got quieter. Not silent, but less hecklers as one or two of the more boisterous gagged on turkey legs and popped corn. Jovan jumped up and down when the vendors selling sparklers stood by helpless as his profits light up the night without being purchased. "You wanted a fire, you got one."

"Have I witnessed a miracle?" Julian walked up to her and threw his arms around her neck and hugged her until she could barely breathe herself. "Oh, Blossom, I knew you weren't dead."

"But I was, Jules. We need to get Serina down. The ropes are spelled. I've used a spell similar to get out of a tight situation." Jovan thought back to the night she and André were in the hotel and he'd restrained her to the headboard. Oh how things had changed since that night. "Jules, help clear the area? Where's André and my baby? I can't find them."

"She's with Jonah. Does André know?"

Jovan shook her head no. "He doesn't have his pouch. I can't reach him."

"How are you here?" Julian kissed her forehead and hugged her again.

"I don't know. I woke in Father Butler's arms. Let me set Serina free before you take me to André and Savanah?"

Serina, on my count of three tell Lucian to move swiftly. Jovan gave the crowd all she had. That eerie calm before the storm didn't exactly settle in over those straggles stupid enough to defy their own common sense to get the hell away from death's door. No, this time the flash had the intensity of staring into the sun without blinking on a hot sunny day until the aqueous humor in the orbits turned to dust. *One, two, three…*

Then she sent the unbinding spell out to the universe and prayed. "Goddess release the restraints which bind my sister here, so I may help mend someone I just learned to me is dear. We are bound by blood, sisterhood; we are family through love, which trumps all of the above. The longer she hangs the more I fear, my sister will be taken far from here. We have a life to share. This cross she does bare, it is unholy. It is unfair. Set her free. I beg of thee, so mote it be."

A stream of searing red energy struck every person in her path. It leeched from one person to the next in a steady mind-altering pulse. Every person in the town's center, the Queen included, stood wide-eyed, jaws forming an O. Jovan giggled.

Julian uttered one word. "Enough."

She shot back, "I knew I always liked Jonah better than you."

"Smart arse." Julian hugged her again.

André glanced over his shoulder to the mob. His heart stopped. There was only one person he knew that could do this. But she was gone. Couldn't get his hopes up. Savanah was too young, or at least he hoped she was. God help him. He was about to raise his daughter, a little enchantress, on his own without the vaguest idea of Wiccan or their beliefs or powers. Not only did his heart stop, pain consumed him. Across the park he heard Savanah's giggle. It brought him back from the abyss he nearly leapt into. She would be his saving grace. His reason to live. He decided Jovan must have taught Serina how to do the flash. He glanced at the queen. If she recalled this, she would be one to reckon with.

André headed to his daughter and Jonah. Once he had Savanah in his arms, he buried his face into the little crook of her neck and practiced breathing. Savanah's hands tangled in his hair.

"Papa, there's mummy." She waved.

"It's impossible, baby." He gathered his will to tell

her the worst news she would ever receive.

"Hi, Mummy."

André whipped his head around. With strides a leopard couldn't match he crossed the distance. He stopped within an inch of her, terrified if he reached out, she would be naught more than an apparition. "Please tell me I'm not seeing the most glorious vision alive. Jovan, don't do this to me if I can't have you." Tears streamed down his cheeks.

"I'm not leaving you, lover. And yes, I believe I am a gorgeous apparition. We have unfinished business, boyfriend."

"Fiancé!"

The next minute of his life wound up a complete blur. All he remembered doing was drawing Jovan's body to his and sandwiching Savanah between them and dancing with his two ladies. Rejoicing in life. "How? I held you—"

Jovan pressed her fingers to his mouth, which he kissed. "I don't know." Jovan leaned in and kissed his trembling lips. Then she kissed her daughter's nose. "Hi, my beauty." She turned to her brother. "Jonah hold onto Savanah?" She passed her daughter to her bother, grabbed André's hand and headed for her sister.

Both feet finally on the ground, burnt, blistered, clothes one thread away from igniting Serina said, "Brilliant. Simply brilliant plan, Lucian."

"What?" Lucian asked. "You're still standing." And then she wasn't. Serina crumbled to the ground too exhausted to do anything other than lay in one giant smoldering heap.

In a moment's time black funnel clouds descended in a vortex. The sky became a whirlpool, dynamic, changing its appearance every second. Hefty drops of water plummeted to the ground only to become a painful reminder how miserable the night had begun. And just as swiftly as the rain began, it stopped when the last flicker of fire fizzled. And the crowd awoke.

Lucian shot Serina the look. "Did you do that?" Serina shook her head no just as puzzled. "Jovan, then?"

Jovan shrugged her shoulders. "Not this time."

Lucian met his brother and Jovan and hugged her. "You are a walking miracle."

"You say that now." She answered in a smothering embrace. Out of the corner of her eye, Jovan saw Serina point to Father Butler. "Oh dear Goddess, you did this?"

"Guilty. Confessions are in order. You might want to stay seated a minute, Serina. I have something rather delicate to say so I'll just blurt it out. I am your father, both of you. You have my powers as well."

"What?" Both Jovan and Serina yelled simultaneously. Jovan reached for Serina's hand and clung to it.

Serina asked, "Jovan, did he say what I think he said?"

Jovan nodded.

"It is so, ladies."

Father held his hands to both, but Serina shooed at him. "Don't you dare!" Serina's voice cracked raw with turmoil.

"There is more."

"I'll bet. This is nonsense, Father." Jovan's words were harsh.

"Serina, think my child."

"I am not your child. Stop calling me that," Serina tried to raise her voice but she came across gritty.

Father dropped back down to his knees. Jovan bent to Serina and lightly placed a kiss on her blistered cheek before she crossed to him and got in his face. "Serina, allow me to speak until you are healed. You practice living. Father Butler, for twenty-four years you'd kept this tiny fact from me, from us. For twenty-four years, you could have picked a day, any day and told me—us the truth. That day never came. Do you know how many nights I'd dreamt those very words? 'Jovan, I am your father.' How hard would that have been to spit out? I've wanted a father my entire life and never had one. I had a sister? Again, I, we, were robbed of the opportunity to share a life together. And—"

Serina cut her off, "How many times did we say, 'No secrets between us?' Liar! God, you are a hypocrite. You're worse than me mum."

Jovan accused Father Butler, "What you did to Serina is far worse. She lived right under your bleedin' nose and you never told her the truth. You make me so angry." So mad Jovan forgot all the times she'd have given her powers up to know her father.

Jovan's heart filled with fear that she would hate him for never coming clean, hate him for not being a proper father. But she did love him. He'd grown on her over the past weeks. He had been such a humble, caring, gentleman it was impossible not to love the man. Everything was just so different now.

"Jovan, I met your mother one stormy eve. She came to me in search of help. She didn't understand her powers. She wanted me to revoke them. I helped her and, in that time, grew to love your mother, but she cast me away. Never told me about you. Until four years ago, I didn't know you existed."

"Thanks, really, for letting us know all this now. You can do that? Revoke one's powers? What are you?" Jovan asked.

Father Butler inhaled sharply and pat his chest. "We'll go into detail when we are home of what I can or cannot do. Serina, I loved your mother before I became a priest. Someone contacted the Sorcerer's Squad days before our wedding. Oliver, the man you believed to be your dad, knocked down Olivia's door with intent to kill her and her unborn child—you. Olivia did the only thing she could to save you. She charmed the murdering bastard into marrying her. At the time he was betrothed to Contessa's mother, who was with child. Oliver lived a loveless marriage—existence. His family shunned him. Hated even more from the Van Holstein's side. Please forgive me, ladies. I did my best."

Both Jovan and Serina reached for Father's hands just as a forceful boreal gust whipped through.

Father barely brushed their fingers.

Chapter Twenty-Nine

The pounding of horse's hooves impaled the cobblestone hard and fast.Through the smoke a glint of silver slashed through the crowd followed by a warm spray. Jovan, André, Serina and Lucian's faces all resembled a canvas of red splatter.

"Checkmate." Xavier's voice hit exposed nerves. He disappeared faster than Jovan's dreams did.

Time sped up in increments just as Jovan's heart did then abruptly halted. Father's hand thumped to the ground, fingers in spasms. In less time than it takes to blink Father Butler's head lay at the base of Lucian's feet, his convulsing body a good two feet away.

Jovan wiped a warm sticky fluid from her face and then turned to Serina. Serina had known the priest her entire life. Had a clad-iron relationship with him and now this. Copper's stagnant scent clogged her nostrils. She opened her mouth to yell or scream or cry denial except silence consumed her. In one svelte slice of the blade dreams had been severed. Jovan's heart went to her sister. Serina said nothing. Her mouth covered by her burnt hand, she sat in motionless shock rocking.

Chyna sauntered to the Queen, her own dull, dirt encrusted tiara lopsided on her head, held on only by the prongs stuck through her flesh. "'Ello, Queenie. Miss me? I've waited two lifetimes for this night." The skeletal remains of the vampire hissed and gave a little flash of her stained fangs. She curtsied before her older sister, some habits apparently dying hard before Chyna yanked her stupefied Majesty's leg out and knocked her on her royal rump. "You should 'ave done away with the likes of me when you 'ad your chance." Chyna stretched her mouth wide then attached herself to the Queen's throat in rapacious glory. When done, she discarded the Queen and skipped away from death and destruction twirling the Queen's staff as it were a baton. "Mine," she declared. "About bloody time."

"Oh, this can't be happening," Lucian whispered, clung to Serina.

André rushed to his aunt. He ripped his shirt off and jammed the material into the hole in his aunt's neck a second time. "Lucian, I know timing is everything and this couldn't get any worse or at least I hope it can't but get Serina over here. The Queen's not dead. Serina can save her. Please?"

Lucian gave André a look that questioned his brother's sanity. "Serina, I know this is inconceivable, but can you save my aunt. God, please don't hate me for asking this of you now."

"Lucian," Duncan nudged him. "Set your wife down and come with us now."

"Old man, I cannot leave her. She and Jovan just lost their father. Raven, where the hell is she?" Lucian yelled.

"Xavier has her. Come now." Julian answered. "He stole her just after he," Julian pointed to Father Butler, "and while Chyna distracted our queen."

Lucian tried to focus, but... Father Butler's head sat at his feet looking up to him with his giant blue eyes unaware he was even dead. His aunt lay a few feet farther gurgling.

Julian approached Lucian and exchanged Serina for the vile André had given him. "Blow it in his eyes," he instructed, "Then kill the bastard. I'll stay with the women and children."

Lucian kissed Serina's face before he limped away, the soles of his shoes missing.

Jovan stared at her father's expressionless eyes, her face quite the same. There Father Butler was, pouring his heart out to her and Serina one second and the next, his blood. Her heart imploded. She cast a longing glance to her sister. Her sister and she'd never felt more alone. Serina hung in Julian's arms sobbing in silence. Jovan read her mind and felt every ounce of her pain as if it were her own. How could she not? For the past weeks Jovan had a family, she had a father, a sister, her two brothers, the loves of her life, Savanah and André all under one roof. Now?

No more smiles, no deep belly laughter, or late-night chitchats over a cup of tea or a bottle of wine with her father. No more warm embraces. The man truly loved to hug people. No more silly cheers, clinking glasses every time they were together. No more anything. And she never even told him she loved him or that she was the happiest person alive just to have known him, even for the briefest of time, let alone be her father. Jovan hugged Serina and pulled Julian in tighter. "You have me. Always." She turned and headed for Savanah.

Her gaze caustic to Julian, Serina promised, "Set me beside the queen, Julian. And then run as if your life depends upon it, because it does. You tried to kill my mother."

"I thought she was trying to hurt André."

"Your depraved mind thought more than that! Get the hell out of my sight. You think this is bad?" She pointed to Father's remains. "You'll wish I beheaded you!"

André, Lucian, bring me the heart of the man that stole my father. Bring Raven home to us.

Jonah exited from the woods carrying masses of weapons of destruction, armed to the hilt with crossbows, spear shooters, and his favorite, the semi-automatic Borchardt gun, only recently invented.

André tapped Jonah's shoulder. "Van Helsing would've been green with envy."

Jonah handed André a crossbow. "Let's see who else we turn green."

Duncan, Lenny, and Walter took their places beside the twins. The sound of six sets of heels echoed off the buildings they passed giving chase to Chyna, Xavier and Raven.

Heavy breathing and coughing followed from behind. Lucian and André turned. Contessa moved in with a pistol, the weapon swaying between her two targets.

"Your turn, Cupid and Eros. This ends now. If I can't have you, Jovan and Serina sure as hell won't."

About to put a silver slug into her, Lucian noticed Jovan coming toward them. He couldn't take the chance of hitting Jovan.

André muttered, "Women."

Jovan screamed, "She's mine, I mean it. Touch her and I'll turn you into a toad and dine on succulent frog legs tonight and suck them bone dry."

André placed a hand on his brother's shoulder. "Trust me—she can do that! Suck someone bone dry." Lucian's face contorted. He shook his head and wisely said naught. Contessa spun with the gun pointed in Jovan's face. One bullet went whizzing by Jovan.

That's when Jovan walloped her with her white light. This time the children were safe. Her sister was safe.

Her father was dead.

She added a second blast just because. Jovan would unleash her vengeance without worry of retribution. Contessa stumbled backward. Jovan followed. "Contessa, in case you're wondering—let me break this down for you—this is a not-so-subliminal message. You've aimed your gun the wrong way. Turn it around."

Truculent, Contessa tried to understand why she now held the colt revolver pointed at her own head even as she fought the compulsion.

It would be one puzzle unsolved.

"You can kill me once or even twice but the third time's a charm. I told you my face would be the last thing you ever saw." Jovan brushed her hands of her.

With the sound of the gunshot, Chyna stopped. Xavier continued to drag Raven behind him toward the cemetery. Chyna faced her nephews, her orange cloak swirling around her malnourished shell the way ribbons wrapped around a Maypole. "Ah, me boys, give us a hug. JoJo, I see you're still chasing André around. You stupid little strumpet!"

"That's it!" Jovan snatched a crossbow from Jonah and drew the bowstring back.

"Blossom!" Jonah went to retrieve the weapon, but

Jovan whisked it away.

"Don't even," she barked, twisting away from her brother's advances. She struggled to keep the arrow aligned on the miserable vampire. "Bows and arrows," she groaned, "this is harder than it looks. Damn werewolves make everything look effortless." She pulled back on the tickler and fired. Arrows went askew through everything except her nimble target. Windows broke, and water troughs now leaked.

"You can't kill me," Chyna boasted.

"Chyna, I, unlike my lady, have never missed a target." André greeted his aunt with two wooden tipped arrows, one through her Adam's apple, the other her heart. He grabbed Jovan's hand, turned and walked away without an ounce of remorse.

Stunned, Chyna stood in the middle of the road trying to yank the arrows out of her.

Lucian walked to within a foot of her. "I never believed I could kill someone, let alone family." A sardonic giggle erupted. "I also never thought I'd say this—I was actually wrong!" Lucian unloaded his bow. The brute force of the arrows sent her withered body through the air and left her tacked up against the wall of a taxidermy building. "May the sun scorch you a hundred ways to Hell." He walked over and pried her fingers from the gold staff. "This is the queen's."

"Damn you, Lucian," she gurgled.

Jonah approached her, ripped the tiara from her head and shoved it in his pocket. "Ta!"

Chyna cleared her throat. "Give me that back. It's mine."

"Come and get it." Jonah taunted.

"What are you doing?" Lenny asked.

"Giving my niece a present after I clean it up."

Lenny's lips puckered. "Her father owns the crown jewels, mate. Put that jaded thing back."

Jonah ignored both of them and continued toward Raven and Xavier.

"Jovan, please go back to the children." André pleaded.

"You certain you don't need me to help?"

Oh, how he wanted to crush the woman against him and love her to death that very moment. "Savanah needs you. I need you alive!" André brought her hand to his mouth and kissed her.

Scraps of twilight squeezed through edging the nightshade back into a lonely abyss. Xavier turned around and cowered behind Raven's violet velvet cloak.

Raven, keep your eyes closed and hold your breath as long as possible. Lucian dug into his pocket and produced the vile given to him from Olivia, opened it and blew some of the poison at Xavier reciting, "Seek the cankered heart. Vanquish him from his insides out. Tear him apart. Judgment day has arrived." The air sparkled when the sun's rays caught the powdery tendrils drifting toward their intended target. A pinch later the sparkles formed an angry swarm of bees and slammed into Xavier's astonished face the way a boxer would connecting with his best right hook. Xavier fell trying to protect his eye—his eye that now resembled lard in a skillet thanks to the poisonous glitter. Xavier landed in a water trough, wailing something about melting. Raven lay crouched on the ground next to him, her hair entwined in his grasp.

"Get him off me."

Lucian and André approached. Lucian dowsed

Xavier with the remaining potion.

André nudged Lucian in the side. "A sparkling vampire. Who'd have thought?"

Lucian added, "He looks ridiculous."

Raven added her two pence, "He did even before this. Could you get him off me?"

With Xavier's incessant cries, the substance coated the inside of his mouth and lips much like a powdery confection on a cake.

Xavier tried to pull himself up using Raven as a crutch but he tripped. His legs were now paralyzed stubs.

Yelping, Raven went down with him a second time. "Just let me go."

"Raven—everything I've done, it's been for you. This empire could be ours. I love you. Help me." He groveled at her feet.

"I may not know what love is, Xavier, but I certainly know what it is not." Completely drained she added, "Dear God, just die all ready. You're worse than a villain in a scary novel that has naught the sense to remain dead but continues to get back up."

André took aim with the Borchardt. Five silver bullets formed a perfect cross on his forehead.

"Seems we all have our cross to bear, Xavier. Somehow you've been ours." André set down his weapon.

Xavier gasped and turned his focus to Lucian. "Lucian, you and I are not so far gone from Jesus you know. We, too, have been resurrected."

Raven's eyes went wide as she back-pedaled from him. "Do you bloody see what I mean?"

"That's blasphemy, Xavier. You are not a god, but

the devil's pawn. Tell me, do you not fear God?"

"No. Want to know why?"

"Not really," Raven added tossing her hands in the air.

"Because I've met the antichrist. It is he I fear. Your God is kind and forgiving, where mine is anything other than the Devil himself."

Unable to take another second, André latched onto Raven and dragged her behind him. Before Xavier realized it, André pulled the sword from his holster. In one hefty stroke he turned and swung the steel with lethal accuracy. When done, Xavier's head rolled unevenly down the hilled road.

Raven toppled over hysterical with laughter. "If it talks back I'll rip its bleeding tongue from its mouth." Then an odd expression crossed her face, and she rose. Raven pinched the knife in Lucian's belt and followed the rolling head until it stopped. "On second thought. I'm pretty certain I'm getting the last word this time, Xavier." All squeamishness aside she opened the mouth, jammed the blade in, and sawed off the appendage. Held up between her index finger and thumb she dangled the leathery clump for her brothers to see, then with an awkward indifference she flipped the little clump of muscle over her shoulder and skedaddled back to the safety of her brothers.

Lucian did as asked of his wife. Fist through the headless vampire's chest wall, Lucian extracted the stilled, ebony heart, wrapped a hankie around it and tucked it in his pocket for a rainy day.

Andre pulled out a pouch of salt and dowsed the corpse. Just in case.

****

Plagued by nightmares, others in the manor shuffling up and down the hallway past her bedchamber attempting to whisper and doing poorly, Jovan gave up the notion of sleep. This was too much work, tossing, turning, thinking! She glanced at her two angels, both oblivious to the conscious world. After the worst night of her life, Jovan needed some positive motivation. Everyone in the house did. Eyes closed she envisioned candles lit, rose petals across the floor, the bed, and a vase of lilacs to freshen up the room. Vines of roses climbed the canopy of the bed. With a quick blink she changed her nightdress, which was originally Julian's shirt, to a scrumptious lacy negligee. She quickly braided her hair, slurped down a glass of lemon water to freshen her breath and reached over Savanah, then brushed the curls from André's face, to wake him. It was only fair. If she couldn't sleep, why should he?

He squinted and rubbed his eyes. "What time is it?"

She shrugged her shoulders. "You've been out an hour."

He sat up and stretched. He took in the room's ambiance. "Nice touch." He winked at her. "What's up?"

Tears filled her eyes. "André, after tonight it didn't take much of a wakeup call to realize life is short, or to cherish those you love. Marry me?"

"Now?"

Jovan nodded. "Tonight, while the moon glows brightly. I don't want or need a large gathering. I want a small intimate ceremony. Julian can preside over us."

"Cherié, I want nothing more than to say yes, but you and Serina just lost your father."

"We can't change the past, André, but we can our future. I won't lose you again."

André met Jovan halfway and placed his lips over hers in a warm, soft kiss. "Tonight, it is. You just gave me back my heart, Cherié. Twofold."

****

In the sun-filled atrium Jovan fingered the rim of her teacup oblivious to the high-pitched noise it made or the attention it drew. All eyes lifted from their plates, some mouths stuffed with kippers, sausages, some covered in syrup waiting for her to say something. Awkward silence loomed.

"Sorry." She attempted a smile as she reached for the fork in her left hand and stabbed at the egg yolk on her plate, popping it. She pierced a slab of bacon, swooshed it back and forth in the yellow slush and daintily jammed the food in her mouth. She set the fork down and wiped under her eyes then dabbed the napkin at her nose. She cleared her throat yet remained silent, searching for the right words. She set the napkin on her lap and smoothed the edges to cover her dress then aimed for her teacup once again. Nerves didn't give her away until the cup started to rattle in the saucer. She finally broke the uncomfortable silence. "I knew you and I were two peas in a pod, Serina. I knew. Father Butler's attentiveness and curiosity over the past weeks since I'd met him confounded me. If he wasn't questioning me about my past he was trying to get acquainted with Savanah."

Serina reached over and placed a hand on top of Jovan's. "Jovan, he pulled the wool over both our heads. You all need to listen for a minute. I have news. Don't become exasperated. Me mum dropped in last night and gave me a walloping headache. Probably not as bad as the stabbing pain in her back she survived no thanks to you, Julian, but she's still with us. Seems she has friends in high places. She tells me Father Butler lives yet has no memory. She proved your point, Jovan. She went back in time and attempted the impossible. She'd have been able to do so if someone—" Serina glared towards Julian "—hadn't tried to kill her."

Julian slammed his utensils down and tossed his arms in the air. "How many times must I apologize?"

"Stop raising your voice to my mum," Avery scolded Julian. "That didn't sound sincere. Where is he, where's Poppy," Avery asked.

"I'm not sure, Avery. Me mum has him and is trying to help him get better. She said it could take quite a bit of time."

Savanah scooted her bottom from her chair. Her bare feet hit the floor with a thump. "May I go outside, Mummy?"

"Yeah, us too?" Avery asked looking at Lucian.

Lucian grabbed Sydney and swung her to the floor. "Stay with her. No lake. No pond. No chasing the geese."

"What else is left out there?" André asked. "You just took all the fun out of being a kid."

Savanah started to say, "I want to show my new friends—"

"Cousins," Jovan interrupted. "No magic either, Savanah."

"But I just want to show them how to make flowers grow." The little girl's pout grew.

Julian pushed his chair from the table and stood. "I'll take them. I need air anyway. Come on, Peanut.

Show us."

André waited until the children were outside on the veranda before he asked, "What's the rest? There's always more."

Serina finished, "So, as for the Queen's girls, they're home safely in one piece. Me mum was out here last night trying to undo all the terror raining down on us. And the last thing she said is our father is a white lighter. He lost his wings when he became intimate with me mum. Black witch, white knight. The Gods, they reprimanded him. Told him the only way to get back in the graces was to serve God by serving the powerless. So Jovan, you and I will acquire more powers over time. Our grandfather was the healer, the archangel Raphael. Jovan, he saved you last night. It was Father Butler, our father. You really were dead, again. You have seven lives left. Be careful, please?"

Jovan laughed and didn't stop. After she wiped her eyes she asked, "Does it get any more bizarre? I hope not. Lucian, Serina," Jovan walked to stand beside André, "I have a request. We're saying our vows tonight at midnight. Julian is going to preside over the ceremony. It would be our honor if you were to stand beside us."

Serina limped over to her sister and tossed her arms around Jovan's neck in a warm embrace. "Blessed be."

Raven closed in too and hugged her. "Come with me. You'll get most of what you need upstairs. Something old, borrowed and blue. The new part is on you, André. Might want to head over to the tower." She grinned and waggled her left hand under his nose. "The cigar band won't do this time."

"Oh!" André blushed. "You told her about that,

Cherié?"

"Well of course I did. You placing that band on my finger, I'll cherish forever."

"As will I."

****

At midnight under the glowing blue moon, a canopy of diamonds twinkled in the sky. The nightline's beauty didn't compare to Jovan as she walked down a path lined by carved pumpkins, with candles illuminating the night. Pink and purple rose-petals covered the path to the water's edge. An arbor at the end of the dock had been decorated with lilacs, ivy and bluebells. Savanah held Jovan's hand and tried to skip beside her. Jovan wore a light blue silk and satin dress, lace gracing every square inch. The sleeves were capped, and the neckline cut just under the collarbone. In the back, the dress plunged halfway down, and buttons trailed down to the train. It was Raven's mother's wedding gown and fit Jovan as if it were made for her.

The soft melody of a harp and violin warmed the cooler night air. Walter, all cleaned up, looked well-groomed as he plucked each string of the harp. Nygal stood there with tears in his eyes moving the bow across the strings of the violin. Jovan blew him a kiss. Lenny even shaved his beard. Jovan looked twice at him before looking forward to her family in front of her. She scratched her chin and mouthed the word, "Dapper," to him.

With Jonah on one side of Raven, Payton on the other, both with their arms looped through hers, and Raven with a giant grin on her lips, Jovan briefly wondered who would be having more fun tonight, the three of them or she and André? All bets were off. Love was in the air. Duncan and his lady Molly waved sparklers, hooted, and giggled as Jovan and Savannah passed by. Serina and Lucian waited with Sydney on Lucian's shoulders and Avery tucked under his arm. Julian stood at the trellis beside André. Her best friend and her lover.

He had to be the most handsome, beautiful man on the planet and in a few minutes André would be hers! She still couldn't believe it. Tonight, his curls were tied behind him. Later on, her fingers would be tangled in them or they'd be skimming across her bare flesh. He wore a dark double-breasted waistcoat with a crisp white shirt and a black bow tie. His pants too were dark, showing off the trim waist, and long legs. In a little while they would be lost in a heap in the corner of their room—if they made it that far.

Jovan had a plan. Her eyebrow danced, not twitched. Out of all the misery they'd encountered, she'd been doubly blessed by so many miracles. She found the love of her life after four lonely years. She found her brother after five years of believing he'd died. She'd survived death because her father was a healer and white lighter. Her daughter would spend the rest of her days as much in love with her father as Jovan, and she got a sister, a quirky, inconsistent enchantress whom she adored. She got a sister in law, Raven, a woman who wore her heart on her sleeve and shared it every chance given. Jovan knew she'd been blessed to have Raven in her life. Each and every person she made eye contact with she loved.

Only one thing missing if her dream she'd had four years ago was to come true.

"Birthday suits."

"Oh, Cherié," André laughed as he pointed behind her. "Look who else came to celebrate with us."

Jovan turned to see the queen stood in all her glory hysterical with mirth. "Love the crown, Majesty. It matches your eyes."

The queen raised her gold scepter to Jovan and André. "Cheers to a lifetime of love, laughter and nights like this."

Jovan couldn't contain the smile on her lips. Nor could she wait to place them on her soon to be husband's. Tonight, under the beautiful moon's glow the beginning of this little tart's fairytale began a new chapter.

A word about the author...

Jaclyn Tracey's life began in merry old England with a divine view of the North Sea. At a very tender age she moved to the US where she grew up in Saratoga Springs, NY. She married her best friend and together they have two children and four grandees (grandchildren). Best part of life ever!

Unconditional love knocked down Jaclyn's door when a Pit Bull rescued her twelve years ago. Lonny, the not-so-little lass moved in on St.Patrick's Day, took over the castle causing shenanigans and merriment every day of her beautiful life. She passed a year ago. This month we welcomed our second angel Eden, another Pit Bull, into our clan. Who doesn't love dog fur as an accessory?

Jaclyn is a Registered Nurse patching up hearts by day and shredding them by nightfall ~ job security at its best.

Besides her paranormal works she has published a few children's books too.

Thank you for purchasing
this publication of The Wild Rose Press, Inc.

For questions or more information
contact us at
info@thewildrosepress.com.

The Wild Rose Press, Inc.
www.thewildrosepress.com

www.ingramcontent.com/pod-product-compliance
Lightning Source LLC
Chambersburg PA
CBHW070807030726
47504CB00003B/732